You Again

By the Same Author

Suburbs of the Arctic Circle
Shinny's Girls and Other Stories
Centre/Center
The Private Eye: Observing Snow Geese
Flashing Yellow
Shinny's Girls, the Trilogy

You Again

by

Mary Burns

Copyright© Mary Burns, 2013
www.maryburns.ca

Published by burningBooks, Grantham's Landing, British Columbia

ISBN 978-0-9920026-2-6

Cover art by Stephen Harlow
Design by Kathryn Para

This book is dedicated to
Oola Roo and Harris Finn Dixson

2009

I

January

The way he looked? When she saw him through the peephole? Shinny didn't know it was him. The lens ballooned his forehead and stretched his mouth, shortened his body. He knocked again, waited, stepped back from the door, glanced from left to right along the hallway, over his shoulder to the elevator, then squinted directly at the peephole as his front teeth settled on his bottom lip. That gesture is what impelled her to call out, "Yes?" And when the lips turned up and he said, "Grandma?" that's when she knew it was Matthew, Mattie. Knew, as if the experience had a direct relationship to the word. I knew it was you. Because, while the young man who has been sleeping on the blow-up bed in her storage closet is surely her grandson, he is not the same Mattie she has known since she held him in her arms hours after his birth. Why would he be? He's grown up. He does things, associates with people that will remain a mystery. Unless he tells her. Which he is not doing. Never a spiller, but more a child who has had to be drawn out, he is expecting extraordinary compliance from his grandmother as she waits for his next step. She hasn't said this, but he must suspect. He has asked her not to tell his parents that he is back in Vancouver; he has arranged his hours so that when Shinny is out, he is in, which works for space management in an apartment of six hundred square feet, but eliminates opportunities to talk. When she leaves for her job at the postal outlet, Mattie is sleeping. When she returns, he is gone; a note on the back of an envelope—a ribbon of newspaper margin, a square of paper towel—says he's not sure when he'll return and not to worry about supper. The same words for several nights; he might as well give up searching for something to write on and use the same note. The image of matryoshka dolls surfaces in Shinny's mind. But the Russian dolls contain exact, if smaller and smaller, versions of themselves. Masks? Maybe, except that masks display, even exaggerate, character, whereas the face Mattie has been wearing since arriving at her door is as featureless as hockey goalie masks used to be.

Her customary dinner companion, Kevin Newman, is off tonight, but his replacement at the anchor desk begins the newscast with the usual litany of tragedy. A violation of the ceasefire in Gaza, the death of another Canadian soldier, Brian Good, 42, in Afghanistan; fifty-thousand more layoffs in the United States and some, fewer, in Canada. Vancouver has made it into the national newscast via another targeted shooting, the phrase police use when one gang member goes after another. That, and, the victim was known to police. Such euphemism. Further decline in stock values, in house prices across North America. The personal good news is that Shinny sold Glen's farm before prices fell. The personal bad news is that the value of her share of the proceeds has shrunk like all investments, and not because of a single fast-talker like Carter Biggs, who once lured her into believing he could spin gold out of straw. No, this time it's a whole raft of Biggs-like moneymen who thought they were magicians. This time the entire continent has been under a spell. Which is why she is still working, though part-time, but the good news about her job is that she has a reason to go out the door some days, and this not only boosts her general morale, the sense that she is still herself, but also, now, the feasibility of living with her grandson.

Optimism has seldom been hard for Shinny to muster, which makes her a lightweight in the opinion of her son-in-law Brendan. He didn't say as much, and good thing, too, it having been Christmas when family gatherings are as crystal that can shatter at the drop of a careless word. Shinny had raised her glass and called for a great year ahead for everyone. The best year yet, is how she put it.

"I don't know how that can be," said Brendan. "We don't know where the credit crisis is going to land us, the mess in the Middle East isn't getting any better. There are wars in Iraq, Afghanistan …"

"Things can change, though, Brendan. That's what I'm hoping for."

"Yeah, okay. I can drink to change."

She saw forbearance controlling condescension. Then Mariah, her granddaughter, asked him if he knew some movie producer she used to know, who now works in New York, where Brendan and Elfie have been living since they returned from Europe. Shinny studied the crisp point of the unclaimed turkey wing on the platter and sipped her wine, reminded herself that the apparent surliness in Brendan could be inseparable from his genius as a composer. Look at Beethoven. Of course, Beethoven was deaf. Brendan just insensitive.

And hasn't she turned out to be right about change? There's now a black president of the U.S., with an extended family that looks like the illustrations in old Sunday school readers, the multicoloured family of man. Not only that, but his election is a private triumph for Shinny because Barack Obama is the son of a single mother, who conceived her second child, Barack's sister, with another man. Obama's ascendance has validated Shinny's life; she was ahead of her time. When she called Elfie the day of the inauguration, after gloating about successful children of single parents, Shinny was tempted to reveal Mattie's sudden appearance; considering the continent between her and the rest of the family, Elfie should be able to keep the news to herself until Matt went public. Should be able to, Shinny thought, and yet with everyone emailing everyone else so easily, or posting notices on each other's walls, or texting or calling on cell phones, how could the news stay private for long? She resisted temptation and instead let Elfie go on about the mood in the city, the party she would be attending. The commission awarded to Brendan not only in the spirit of diversity, Brendan being of Indian heritage, but because he is a composer to follow, according to a review of his "Ligurian Suite" that Elfie cut out and mailed, the conventional way, to her family in Vancouver.

"It's going to be much better to visit now, Mom. When can you come?"

At the time, Shinny didn't say. Tonight she sees a trip to New York as potential escape, yet if Matt is in trouble, he might need her. He has not said that he's in trouble, but he has been evasive. And his reputation as a storyteller? The time he invented an entire family history for a school project? She can only sift a long breath in through her teeth, shake her head, glance again at the digital time display on the DVD player, let the breath out in a whoosh.

Local news has segued into weather. Temperatures still near freezing; the uncharacteristic snow on the shore of False Creek will not be melting tomorrow. Then sports, which she watches for news of her team, though the boys have been testing her loyalty.

Matt could come in at anytime. She has given him a key to both the outside and inside doors, and to anyone questioning his presence in this over-fifty-five building, he says he is visiting his grandmother. That no one has questioned him makes her wonder about security, not that Mattie is a dangerous looking fellow. Taller than both his parents, baby fat now definitely gone, his brown hair cut close to his white scalp, like most of the young men in the city, but unlike those who like to keep their faces scruffy with three-day-old beards, Matt is clean shaven and his jug-handle ears glow pink when the sun backlights them. He wears the ubiquitous jeans and t-shirts, but with no labels that identify him as part of a tribe, or a fan of some rock group or political group or any group. Except for a slight overbite Lawreen always meant to get corrected, teeth that rest on his lips when he does not consciously remember to keep his mouth closed, he could be mistaken for anyone.

Now a commercial and the usual volume increase so that she has to mute the sound when the phone rings. Since Mattie has made her promise to keep his presence here a secret, it's strange that the call is for him, some-one asking for him by his full name, Matthew Webster. A man, to whom she replies that Matthew is not here. "Can I take a message?"

"Thank you all the same, ma'am," he says. "I'll call tomorrow."

Ma'am? Who would be calling Mattie here, and also calling her ma'am?

Lying in bed, gazing through the thin slats of the open blinds at the red, green, blue and yellow Christmas lights that outline construction cranes parked at building sites around False Creek, she hears Mattie come in a few hours later, urinate, flush, twist the bathroom door handle, turn on the computer. She listens for the beeps of the phone, to determine if he has seen her note; if he is going to call someone back, but no. The fridge opens and closes, the TV bursts on, and then she inserts the earplugs she bought his second day here.

CBC BLASTS OUT BEFORE he can mute the sound. And there it is again, that commercial: Fight fear, fight chaos, fight distress.

He doesn't hear any snoring from Gran's bedroom, but he will. She's a dependable snorer. Did she say he was out for the evening, or that he wasn't here? He hopes the latter, because he doesn't want anyone, but especially Berk, to know that he's in Vancouver. When he and Berk were still in college, they drove down to the States and dropped in to visit Gran and Glen on their farm. Good she didn't recognize the voice, but it was just that once they met, for the afternoon. Gran wanted them to stay but Berk had a guy to meet in Seattle; Berk isn't the rural type, and Matt doesn't think he is either, but he liked it down there in that big house that felt like a TV show about the old days, when houses smelled like baking and people were happy to see you at the door.

Silk22@hotmail.com, the address he opened on Gran's laptop is full, mostly junk, but five messages are from Drude, Berk's attempt to present himself as a legendary dude. How does he do it? How does he guess what name Mattie might use? He knows him too well, they've talked about stuff like this too much, endlessly, over beers, and that nasty liquor Berk likes, the cloying German stuff he used to mix with Red Bull. He must be out of the hospital. Or maybe he's still in there, with his laptop, and not much else to do but try all the email addresses he can think of. Mattie has to drop the associations with Webster. Web, spider, silk. They used to like it that they thought alike; it made them good partners, but Mattie has to slide away, for self-protection, because Berk has a mean streak. That one of their clients went after Berk was not Matt's fault. Hadn't he warned Berk about that possibility? Instead of reading any of the messages, Matt clicks delete on the account menu. Are you sure, the computer asks him? He'd laugh if it weren't so stupid.

WHEN BRENDAN TWISTS OUT of bed, a draft wisping through the old window finds Elfie, who pulls the covers back up and watches his muscles tense, goose bumps pimple his caramel skin before he can dance into his sweatpants and pull a t-shirt over his head. She reaches out, but he's gone. She dozes. Half an hour later, showered, coffee-ed, dressed, Brendan returns to kiss the spot beside her nose where her freckles are densest, resists the tug of her hands, and is out the door before they can talk about dinner.

"Whatever," he calls. "You decide."

As he walks to the subway and rides uptown he will be hearing melodies, rhythms, colours he has been turning over in his mind, potential ingredients for the piece he has been commissioned to compose, the symphonic poem he hopes will win him the regular faculty position he wants, meaning his and Elfie's future in the city would be set. If he is able to develop the idea that inspired the dramatic and intriguing opening he put together on the computer, if he is able to challenge and thus satisfy Ping, who will be the principal soloist, this will be Brendan's next step forward. They won't have to stay in New York, but should be able to move anywhere a position opens. Maybe back to Canada. Maybe the West Coast.

Dawdling, reluctant to leave her warm bed, Elfie thinks of Vancouver, so sleepy compared to Manhattan. But the big universities on the West Coast have strong music programs, and of all the places they have lived, Vancouver best reflects the stew of cultures she and Brendan embody; it's where they come from, who they are. When they are ready for children, Elfie wants to be nearer to their families. Holidays should be like this past Christmas, everyone gathered in one place: Dad, who used to want them to call him Smokey, but now prefers Dad, or John, and his two kids, Aidan and Eve, and Annette and Greg flew up from California; Lawreen and Ken, Mattie and Mariah. Mom, of course. As a child, Elfie insisted on rituals, and her years in Italy expanded her sense of the possible. Music, candles, dress-up clothes, special food, words taken off a shelf and polished for the occasion. At this age, she has outlived both her childhood need for the security of repetition, and the teenage urge to toss out everything old; her love of ritual has roots that curl deep, feeding off archetypes she feels more than knows.

She and Brendan brought panettone from Bel Paese, Lawreen put striped-foil Christmas crackers at everyone's place, Mom set out her traditional shortbread. Annette heated a round of goat's milk brie. They survived the present opening with no major disappointments, at least none expressed, and lowered their heads for Ken's annual thirty seconds of thanks for their good fortune. Dad exacerbated his natural resemblance to Santa Claus by wearing a red sweater and actual trousers, instead of his usual overalls. Are you too big to sit on my lap, honey? He winked. Although he moved to California when Elfie was very young and she has seen him erratically since, he never forgets her birthday or Christmas, and at the bottom of each birthday card he prints, in small capitals, "don't be afraid to ask if you need anything, babe". There were times she has taken him up on his offer. If it hadn't been for Dad she would have had to take out a student loan to supplement her scholarships at university. And while the money he happily doled out manifested her father's success as a marijuana grower, he got out of that business years ago. He's a retired farmer is all, a phrase that conjures a dignified, slightly bent character, sitting on his porch, considering soybean futures.

The California group had not spent Christmas in Vancouver in years, but Lawreen wanted everyone together. She missed Mariah; if Mariah knew that everyone would be there, she would have to come home, want to come home. Beautiful Mari. So lovely, with her big eyes and that clear, smooth skin and her way of looking around, as if waiting for someone to say something nice to her. In anyone else, the sense of entitlement would be gag-inducing, but Mari has somehow remained genuinely sweet, if a little preoccupied. Mattie stayed in the background, as usual, but responded cheerily when noticed, or called on. He and the SUV his friend had loaned him for the trip from Alberta. Because of the uncharacteristic snow in the city, Matt did most of the driving; he even managed to get Brendan to an open Canucks practice and stayed to watch, though he isn't the hockey fan Brendan is. Greg shovelled sidewalks and helped Ken clear away a young Japanese maple that had broken under the snow load. Annette painted Mom's bathroom. At one point, all three daughters and their mother worked around each other in the kitchen, with little Eve lingering nearby. Tense, but happy, as if happiness were an elastic pulled tight, Lawreen gave orders, assigned tasks. Elfie got table setting, and took the opportunity to gather every candle she could find in the house. When Lawreen came to inspect, she didn't scold as she might have once, but, quiet for a rare instant, stood alongside her youngest sister, both transfixed by the lustrous halos of a dozen flames. Greg carried in the turkey. Mom made the gravy. When everyone was finally settled, Brendan pressed play on the remote control concealed in his pocket and the Hallelujah chorus of "The Ode to Joy" burst out of the speakers. Better, no one rolled their eyes.

Remembering all this impels Elfie to sit up, to force herself out of bed and reach for the phone to call her mother. But it's still only 10:00, meaning 7:00 in Vancouver. Mom will think something's wrong if she calls so early. Instead she drops half a bagel into the toaster and considers the coffee Brendan left.

IN THE MORNING MATT is still sleeping. Shinny boils the kettle and drops a tea bag into a large yellow mug, waits for the water to darken before adding milk, then stands at the window to sip the tea and watch the kids in the park across the street throw snowballs at each other. Wet snow, good for packing, evokes damp wool mittens, fingertips burning red. Before she finishes her first mug of the morning she turns on the computer. No email. No new matches on the dating site Lawreen signed her onto. Life's not over yet, Mom. Lots of people your age are using the web to find partners. Shinny doesn't think she wants another partner, but she has never been rock sure about anything, so she let Lawreen go ahead, and now it is something to do, look at images of the men the site has chosen for her, read their profiles. The pictures are good for a chuckle, one of a man with his shirt unbuttoned, as if he still had the muscled upper body of a twenty-five-year-old; others sincere, white-haired or bald smiling grandfathers, some with glasses that darken automatically in response to light so that they appear sight-impaired, blind, as people used to say. Strange that romance could proceed from need so raw that a man flaunts family ties at one extreme and sleazy self-delusion at the other. She hasn't posted a picture of herself because there's no choice but outright fraud to deny the ever more progressive thinning of her hair and display instead a woman with the springy platinum mane that had defined her since she first bleached it at sixteen; and a face with bones like bridge supports, no cracks, no patches of rust on the surface. The way other people see her is not how she sees herself. It's complicated, yet despite her missing photo, several men have added her to their collection of favourites. When the site notifies her, in pink lettering, that she has made someone's list, she feels an instant of pride, but what are they seeing in those words she and Lawrie typed in? Enjoys movies, the outdoors, fine dining. It's ridiculous. Something as simple as a coffee date would be awkward, false; she can't imagine herself doing it. Yet she doesn't close her account. The site is like a TV show that can fill a few minutes on a day that lags, like this morning while she waits for her grandson to wake. She checks the weather, though she saw the forecast on last night's news, reads the headlines on her personal Google page. She sees more of the world through the small windows of the TV and the computer than out the glass wall that overlooks the park and False Creek and offers vistas of Vancouver's south slopes.

Mattie emerges from the closet late morning, in a t-shirt and boxer shorts, his pale, almost hairless legs not quite bandy, but not straight. He hugs her and she smells warmth, a little sweat, but no booze, no cigarettes. He hasn't been out at the bars. No expectation, no explanation in the hug, just simple affection.

"No work today, Gran?"

"Well the thing is, I never know. It's not one of my scheduled days. What about you, Matt; everything ok?"

"Oh yeah. Hey Gran, should I make enough coffee for both of us?"

Although she drank two mugs of tea waiting for him, this could be a chance to talk. "Sure, honey, thanks."

She looks back down at the bank statements she has been organizing, as if these are more interesting than the boy standing sleepily at the kitchen sink, because her girls always hated it when she talked at them first thing in the morning—Lawreen the one who used that phrase, talk at. While the coffee is brewing Matt steps past her, to the window, and stretches. His feet are bare and there's a bruise above his left ankle, but she sees no sign of needle marks, not that she suspects that he's been using heavy drugs.

"Did you get my note about the man who called for you last night? He didn't say who he was. But he called me ma'am."

"Oh, yeah? Maybe one of those phone things."

"But Mattie, he asked for you by name, Matthew Webster. You're not in some kind of trouble, are you? It sounded official."

He carries her coffee to her, then retreats behind the counter that divides the kitchen from the living room area.

"We could sit at the table, Matt. I could make you some eggs."

"I'm good, Gran. No. I'm not in trouble. You shouldn't worry. Is it okay that I'm staying longer than I thought?"

"You could stay forever if you need to."

She says it, but doesn't mean it. How could they live in this small place, though people do, in the countries she is learning more about as curiosity impels her to follow, "the people who read this story also read" threads on various websites.

"I just want to know what you're up to."

"Sorry. Just a sec."

Will he leave her hanging again? Find some reason he has to rush out? She hears the buzz of his electric shaver. Water needling the plastic shower curtain. His coffee cools on the counter. Shinny stacks the bank statements. The bathroom door opens and he steps out in jeans and white socks and a plain black t-shirt. Tosses the cold coffee down the sink and pours himself a fresh cup. Holds the pot up towards her.

"No thanks."

"Okay, Gran. Sorry, but the thing is, and this is why I didn't want to let Mom know I'm here, I've been talking to the Forces about joining up."

"The army?"

"Well, the Forces. I guess it used to be called the army."

"Why would you want to do that? You're almost finished with university. In fact, aren't you missing a lot of classes?"

"I'm taking a break from that. I mean, why stay in school when you don't know what you want, eh? It's just a lot of money. I could get career training. Free. Actually they pay you."

"So that's who called last night. That explains the ma'am."

He shrugs. Her darling boy. The only boy she had helped to raise, until she moved to Washington to live with Glen. Would it have made any difference if she had stayed in Vancouver until Mattie grew up?

"But Mattie, there are wars going on. Another Canadian soldier was killed this week."

"I know."

"You might get career training, but they'd probably want you to fight."

"I know."

"Do you want to fight?"

"That's what I'm wondering about, Gran. But I better get back to that guy. We were gonna have another talk today. Or I could text him."

Head down, front teeth agitating his lower lip, he presses various numbers on his keypad. This operation would be impossible for Shinny because the pads of her fingers seem to have splayed and are now too broad to accurately hit the right button; she ends up with the wrong number, the wrong channel on the TV. A website she didn't mean to go to, or her search engine getting back to her with the question, did you mean …? Meeting with a recruiting officer? This sweet boy at war?

LAWREEN IS RUNNING LINES. Why don't I just pop down there? Hey, you know what I was thinking would be fun? Pacing, phone in hand. Rehearsing what she needs to say to her daughter Mariah, who has been living in California for six months now, with little to report on career advancement. Lawreen believes she could help. She has been involved in Mariah's career since finding an agent for her when she was barely six, and such a little doll. Mariah worked through her childhood, the big break a series that ran three entire seasons. Teen roles came easily after that because Mariah was a pro; people liked working with her. She showed up on time, thanks to her mother, and took direction well. Oh, she'll never be out of work, people told Lawreen. But the business has gone south in the last couple of years. Almost no Movies of the Week being made in Vancouver, certainly no new series. If she had won the big part in *Smallville*, but no; that went to a young actress from California, which is why Mariah decided to move.

"Nobody will take me really seriously if I stay here, Mom."

But there are so many beautiful girls in Hollywood, all wanting to be actresses. When they talked last night, and Mariah said that she was working on an indie to add to her reel, Lawreen immediately thought porn.

"You're not talking porn, are you Mar?"

"Oh, Mom, what's porn anymore? Everybody takes their clothes off, if that's what you mean. No, this is legit. We start shooting next week and it's going to be short. Ten shooting days max. Everything in studio."

In studio, a relationship drama. Code? Has Mariah, desperate for work, opted to go with someone who will exploit her? She needs her mother, whether she knows it or not. She might have been around the movie business for fifteen years, but only recently has Lawreen not been by her side on set. In fact—though she would cut out her tongue before saying so to Mariah or anyone else, except Ken, to whom she confessed in one of those moments when frustration obscures good sense—she sacrificed her own career for the sake of her daughter. Well into her forties, Lawreen is supervising the sort of data entry clerk she used to be herself, when she was Mariah's age. She could be managing the company by now. At least. Or have gone back to school to finish the degree she began working towards when she was working full-time, organizing the family, trussing up her daughter's career. At one time she had thought she would go for an MBA. But she stayed with All Season Insurance because her boss allowed her frequent, short-term, unpaid leaves.

Lawreen stifles her instinct to call California by returning the phone to its cradle, pouring herself a glass of wine and touring her house, which is too large for her and Ken, but with the real estate market in what is called "a correction," they will hang on for a few more years before they make their move. Besides, Mariah could change her mind about Hollywood, come home, reclaim the room with adjoining bath that Lawreen visits periodically, a pilgrim seeking a blessing from a holy one no longer present. Mattie has been away longer, over three years, and it is unlikely that he will return, but he could, and he still uses his room—they both use their rooms—when they visit.

From the white tile and stainless steel kitchen through the formal taupe-toned dining room to the edge of the living room's cream-coloured carpet, up the stairs, along the hallway where doors are closed to all but the master suite. Her heart is racing. The wine? The steps? This is ridiculous; she's in good shape. She should slow down, stop thinking so much. Everything's good. Mattie's bedroom is neat. The navy duvet on his single bed smooth, the closet doors shut, drawers closed, bookshelves tidy. Strange that a boy his age would want fake stars on his ceiling, but he asked her to leave them, and she did, though she got rid of some of Mattie's other junk after his Christmas visit, the cables he left lying around, his stack of Smart Techie magazines, which, with the continual updates in technology, have to be out of date. He is neater than his sister, so there wasn't much, whereas Mariah left a trail of panties edged in lace, flannel pajama bottoms, the odd ankle sock, a dropped mascara wand, coins, shopping bags, wrapping paper shreds, the whole walnuts Lawreen religiously dropped into

Christmas stockings, though only Ken actually cracked and ate them; tin foil wrappers from chocolate, odd receipts. Lawreen spent a morning tossing out the garbage, laundering and folding the clothes, dusting the headboard and footboard of Mariah's sleigh-style bed, snapping the sheer white curtains free of dust, vacuuming the teal, short-nap carpet. Some children enter the world with an abundance of gifts. When everyone thought Mariah smug, stuck up, she was only focused, and eventually people accepted that she was just being herself. Somehow confident from childhood, Mari knew exactly what she was supposed to be doing. Lucky her.

Opening the door to her daughter's room today, Lawreen gets an immediate whiff of the perfume rising from the pink sweater she purposely left on the bed, which deepens her sadness. She resists entering, pulls the door back towards her, and it shuts with a melancholy click. Keeping the doors closed lowers heating costs, and both she and Ken are alert to opportunities for saving money. Never profligate, always sensible, it is how they manage to own a three-bedroom house on Vancouver's expensive West Side, maintain their late-model Lexus and Ken's old Corolla, take a vacation once a year. All the middle-class niceties Lawreen envisioned when she was growing up, if not ashamed of, then impatient with the standard her mother could afford. Lawreen swore her life would be different, better, and it has been, it is. Outside, a brick and cedar patio and a locked bin for garbage the neighbourhood raccoons would dearly love to raid, but haven't been able to since Ken Fort Knox-ed it last summer. His phrase for everything he wants secure, let's Fort Knox it. If he could only do that with their daughter.

This is it. She's going to call. She picks up the phone on the nightstand, presses the button that automatically links to Mariah's number and listens while her cell phone rings, while the message plays: "Hey, this is Mariah. Sorry I missed your call. Get back to me. Or leave me your number and I'll get back to you. Ciao!"

So zippy, cheerful. Lawreen suspects that Mariah is actually "there", wherever "there" is with a cell phone, but having seen the number on call display, has decided not to pick up. Unless she's filming, or at a screening, and had to turn her phone off.

With her mind in California as she wanders back downstairs, Lawreen is startled to come to awareness in the den. Ken set up his model train set up on a piece of plywood he painted to resemble a prairie landscape. Instead of the green of coastal British Columbia, the tracks run through rectangles of blue, for flax, of yellow, for canola. He has left his engine on the tracks and Lawreen pushes the switch that starts it chugging along, its whistle blows, a miniature version of the mournful sound Ken must have heard when he was a boy in Saskatchewan. Not staying, only passing through. Not staying. Sorry.

She swallows, works her mouth from side to side, rolls her lips together. But the tears come anyway, and since Ken is not home to ask her what's wrong, she sits down and gives in. It's just so stupid. She misses Mariah, her energy, her beauty; she misses the thrill of walking onto a movie set, or into a wrap party, of dressing up, of not pretending to be but actually being someone. The star's mother, or the second-lead's mother, or the girlfriend-of-the-lead's mother. Mariah has not actually needed a chaperone for years, but no one minded Lawreen tagging along. Everyone knew her, the crew, the producers, some of the regular Vancouver actors. She went from vigilant at first, to eventually relaxed, and could sip a cup of coffee and make small talk with anyone. It isn't her life, it's Mariah's; she knows it's time to back off. But she misses it. Oh how she misses it. What will she do with herself? Now her chest is tight and she's struggling for air as if she has run a marathon. Could it be asthma?

IT MUST HAVE BEEN Berk. And what's he doing saying ma'am, coming off as some kind of recruiting officer or policeman. Scum. He probably looked up all the Shinnans in the book and found Gran's number. Smart scum. He remembered Gran's name. Smart. In stupid ways. Matt is finished with Berk and his scams.

Four AM. But it's cool. He has been sitting in Denny's for an hour, drinking coffee kept warm in the pot for too long, and he has just ordered a big breakfast. The special pictured on the laminated menu, with eggs and sausages, hash browns, pancakes. That will take awhile to eat and the girl—well she's too old to be a girl—the waitress won't chase him out because it looks better to have somebody taking up at least one of the tables in this open-twenty-four-hours restaurant. He chose a big booth with invitingly soft, plaid fabric seats, place settings for four on the table.

Without really thinking of it, he arranges the knives into two Ts, one on either side of his place mat. After breakfast and another cup of coffee he'll decide where to go, what to do.

His place in Edmonton, though; too bad about that. The pool in the basement, the workout room. Even if he didn't use them it was cool to know that he could use them, and he offered the opportunity to girls who came over. Well, the one girl who came over. His girlfriend, Laura; ex-now, because he didn't tell her he was splitting. He's sorry about Laura. They used to lie in his bed, her hair tickling his bare chest, and talk about stupid things: what mind games they used to play when they were sitting in the back seats of their parents cars; the foods they used to hate, and the tricks they developed to avoid eating them. Silly talk. Yet how was it that at those moments, he felt most completely himself? Does it start from the body? From sex, where you get so erased that every time you come out of it, it's like you are new? And who is the first person you see? Goodbye, Laura, I miss you already, he thinks.

Clothes. But he can replace them. Already has bought some underwear and t-shirts, socks, everything white, and another pair of jeans. What else? He's going to have to buy another laptop, because he smashed his old one and fried the hard drive on the stove, then threw the mangled mess in the dumpster behind the Chinese supermarket at the West Edmonton Mall. That was fun, going out and buying a sledgehammer. He didn't know what a sledgehammer actually was until he went into a Home Depot.

"Um, where do you keep your sledgehammers?"

"What size do you want?" the orange-jacketed clerk asked.

"How big do they come?"

"Got a big job, do you?"

He did. He had to destroy a whole other life. Deleting his search history, all his email accounts, quitting Facebook and MySpace and Twitter didn't mean that he couldn't be traced on that computer. He has to be careful. Which is why he also dumped the cache of disks he and Berk had assembled, with all the information they had used and could use. In that he had felt like a gangster from an old movie, putting all the stuff in a sports bag, with fifty-pound weights. Had to be two hundred pounds he slid off the bridge, into the North Saskatchewan. The panic, not knowing. How would he get to the bag if it didn't shatter the ice and sink through?

The dark blot of it on the snowy surface, him leaning against the bridge rail like a potential jumper, waiting, chewing what was left of a thumbnail on a gloveless hand. Then a branch of dark water began to rise. Finally!

Amber-ish light from the low hanging lamp falls onto the front page of the commuter newspaper he could pretend to be reading if he wanted to avoid anyone's glance. He takes a big breath and looks around. He's still the only customer, and now the waitress is smoking towards him with a big white plate in one hand and a small white plate in the other. She sets those down and he nods, and she comes back with ketchup and syrup and a coffee pot. Refills his cup. "Can I get you anything else?"

"No, this is good. Thanks."

She waits, this woman who must be close to his Gran's age, wrinkled skin on her hands but fingernails painted blue, maybe wanting to ask him what he's doing here this time in the morning, if he's on his way to work, on his way home. What could he say? He could pretend to be a musi-cian coming down from a gig. What kind of musician though? She might want to make conversation, or maybe not, maybe she doesn't care, but she stands by the table a beat longer than she needs to, until he feels she wants him to look up, and he does and she squints back at him for long enough that he feels the panic of being found out. But she's nobody!

Though it snowed again in the night, the temperature has struggled upwards and the curving paths through the whitened park gleam black with meltwater. The bars of the climbing gym are clear, the swing seats swept off by mittened hands. Shinny has been stewing over Mattie, drink-ing cup after cup of strong tea from her yellow mug. Why didn't he come back? Did she drive him away? How many times has she filled the kettle and plugged it in? Tahir's call rescues her.

"You work today? Few hours?"

"Sure. Just give me a couple of minutes."

"At two," he says. "At two until post office closing."

This is their agreement. He promises three shifts a week, and more, should he need help. He could not predict when the need would arise, and if she couldn't make it, all right. Most of the time, Shinny is not only available, but grateful for the call, and it is easier for her to duck out the back door of her building and walk the half-block across the narrow red bricks of the Roundhouse courtyard than it is for one of Tahir's relatives to take the forty-minute SkyTrain trip into Vancouver from Surrey. Three hours today, then, and while she is unlikely to face a barrage of customers—it being well past the holidays—there will be the usual trickle of people sending parcels, buying stamps, acquiring change of address forms. Sliding cash across the counter for a MoneyGram. She will be busier than she would be otherwise, and by the time she is finished, the day will have diluted her worries about Matt.

When she wants to avoid the people in her building, Shinny takes the stairway down, yet it is clear from the balled up Kleenex in a corner and the brown spots of spilled coffee on the yellow-lipped treads that somebody besides her takes the same route. Out the door into the cold with only some slight dizziness caused by the rounding down from floor to floor; seven stairs, landing, seven stairs, landing. Over the bricks to a stamped-metal strip of walkway flanked by railway ties, down two cement steps to the street and she's there, Davie News and Postal Service, the dullest name; no personality, but reflective of Tahir and his diffidence. When she returned from Washington after sorting through Glen's things and closing up the house, she had not intended to work at all. She hid out here, in the apartment Lawreen helped her find; watched too much TV, went to bed early, slept as late as she could in the noise of the city, the light that seeped through the blinds. When she did go out she sidled towards neighbourhoods further east, where she used to live, half-consciously yearning for the woman she used to be. But her old friend Tina had moved to Prince George with Rod and the boys, Annette and Elfie no longer lived in Vancouver. The hardware store had become a depot for used electronics. The woman she used to be had vanished too.

Then instinct drove her to spontaneously pitch in on an early December day when she stopped at Davie News to mail a letter and found a line up stretched nearly to the door. A frowning Tahir barely had time to lift his head as he furiously weighed, stamped, clawed coins up from the change drawer, swiped debit cards. She cleared a space on the counter for people to fill out customs slips; she organized the line so that it didn't block the cash register where other-than-postal customers wanted to pay Sima for magazines, newspapers, cigarettes. Tahir offered Shinny a job when it was finally her turn to buy stamps.

Now she is meeting the public again, as she did for years at Stone's Family Grocery, when the girls were growing up, and later at A and C Hardware. Her only non-retail experience came from Glen's Riverbend Farm, helping him to create a line of organic herbal infusions for various minor complaints. And salves. Not that she created the salve herself, but she and Nita had created the label and pasted it on each loonie-sized tin. Just the year before Glen's death. She is standing at the entrance of Davie News, automatically straightening the newspapers on the outside rack, yet her thoughts have veered back to Glen. This happens too frequently, steering towards a familiar turnoff, but one that leads to a ghost town.

Tahir shoves an arm through the sleeve of his jacket, the dark grey combination of nylon and fleece that exaggerates his taper frame, the narrowest end being his head. Behind glasses with black plastic frames, his eyes are the shape of a teardrop turned on its side. A striving mustache crosshatches the upper lip above a mouth Shinny has yet to see spread in a true smile.

"Just to deal with the Canada Post pickup, paperwork is ready there," he says, his hand flipping over in the general direction of the desk. "My father will be here soon for looking after counter."

"Sima is off today?"

"Very long story."

Tahir backs around to the door, then out, nodding. His lips part to allow his few, emotionless words through. If he relaxes and watches soccer or a movie and forgets himself and the dutiful life he has created in Canada, Shinny does not know of it and finds it hard to imagine, because he has relatives to look after as well as this store. Today she suspects a family emergency has taken him away. He is not a father nor a husband, but the main support for aging parents and a parchment-skinned grandmother, and the devoted brother of a fellow ten years older, brother-in-law to his wife, Sima, and uncle to the couple's two daughters. The brother was blinded in some battle in their home country, maybe with the Russians, maybe the Americans, maybe the Taliban, maybe the thugs who pay farmers to grow poppies. Tahir has revealed nothing about his past, or his present for that matter. It's only because Sima helps out at the store, and the father, Hassan, that Shinny has been able to piece together images of the lives they left behind in those enormous sweeps of khaki desert, those mountains pinched and bitten by the ages, where Hassan used to walk his donkey along dusty paths to what passed for a store in their village; where people seemed to disappear in clothes the same greys and browns as the landscape, and maybe that was how they had survived for centuries. In the photos Sima had showed Shinny, the brightest colours came from the rugs they wove, little children weaving, Sima herself and maybe Tahir, though he has never said so; and skies dense as if rolled with coat after coat of blue paint.

It's nearly 4:00, the grey afternoon turning as dark as the big crows that dive into the street looking for garbage, when an SUV motoring up from the underground parking lot beneath the building crashes into a van moving down the street. The store shakes, and Hassan instinctively crouches. Shinny first thinks earthquake, but earthquakes don't begin with metallic crunches. When she sees what has happened she calls 911. The driver of the SUV barrels out of his vehicle, blood streaming from one thick eyebrow down the side of his sandalwood cheek, and confronts the van driver, who is leaning against the window of the van, perhaps unconscious. A clutch of people have stopped to witness the drama. Snowflakes drift around them as if they are all part of some gone-wrong glass snowball scene. Shinny, who stands at the store's entrance with each hand clutching the upper arm opposite in an attempt to keep herself warm, thinks that the somewhat Japanese-looking, yelling, bleeding man should be lying, or at least sitting, down. Instead he wants to fight, until the police arrive and pull him back, and do sit him down.

"It's his fault! Maybe doesn't have the licence. Never fucking should drive!"

The ambulance attendant that hurried up to the scene is trying to minister to him, but the SUV driver stands again, a big man, his camel overcoat open to a shimmery maroon shirt.

"Sir, sir?"

The ambulance attendant is trying to get the man to calm down so that she and her partner can examine him. But the ambulance driver, a big man himself, has to physically restrain him by holding his arms. The reluctant patient looks to be in that general mid-range, thirties to forties, when people think the world is theirs, even more so than the young who have not yet considered whom the world belongs to, and the old, who have to admit that their time has passed. His self-importance apparently has convinced the medics, for the van driver continues groaning unattended, except by the police. The crash has jammed the door mechanism. After trying several times, one of the officers goes round to try the other door. Maybe, Shinny thinks, they will have to bring in the jaws of life. The jaws of life had to be brought in to extricate the passenger, the newscaster will say.

But they don't need it, and when the smaller man—who is wearing shorts and knee socks, as if it isn't the end of January but the end of September—when he is helped out and propped on an overturned plastic crate, Shinny steps back inside the store. It's too cold to stand out and she can see well enough through the window. Old Hassan, who never strayed from behind the counter, has gone back to watching his small TV. Already the accident has become more inconvenient than traumatic. Walkers are stepping around the emergency vehicles; drivers are finding ways of reversing until they can turn down another street. One of the medics helps the van driver into the ambulance, while the other attendant, the ponytailed girl, finishes bandaging the SUV man, who has taken his cell phone out and is yelling into it.

"Sir, sir," she says again, or so Shinny imagines. His blood pressure will have spiked, he'll want to call his lawyer; he may try to sue for damages to himself and his vehicle, but mostly for having his day upset. He'll sue for audacity.

But does anyone know what really happened? Can you assume that the bellower is likely the guilty party? Or, does his humility betray the van driver? Humble because he truly did wrong? Shinny will never know, because a customer is pushing through the door with a stack of legal-sized envelopes, and he wants them all sent registered. Occasional spurts, more than a stream, of business fill the hour before she places the closed sign on top of the counter. Hasssan waves goodbye. "Khoda hafez," she calls. Sima taught her that.

At home, no Matt and no more insight into his sudden departure, and since she doesn't trust herself to talk to Lawreen, sure she will give something away, she phones her middle daughter, Annette, who has just finished the evening milking, has her hands full, and promises to call back. That leaves Shinny hanging, unable to try her third daughter, Elfie; if she does, the line will be busy when Annette tries.

She opens her laptop, and while it hums awake, she turns on the TV, where the perky anchor of the early news reports on another apparent drug-related gang shooting. As before, the primary persons of interest, as the police say, are the Bacon brothers, high up members of the Red Scorpions, most notorious, because most ruthless, of the Lower Mainland's hundred gangs. Another of the worst calls itself the U.N. gang. Shinny imagines the gangsters as delegates from various countries, each of them with their country's emblematic patch sewn onto the hooded sweatshirts they wear. The Johals, and Dhaliwals, Toors, Wus, Lees, an Iraqi immigrant called Barzan Tili-Cholli. From what she has seen on TV and on the front page of *The Province*, they are mostly men in their twenties and thirties who favour elaborate tattoos and shaved heads; they often have some kind of facial hair design, some closely trimmed variation on a beard; they wear chains, earrings. They smuggle potent B.C. marijuana across the border, and gangsters on the U.S. side pay them in guns, thus the weapons used in the targeted shootings.

Mattie dresses in the hoodies and jeans gang members wear, his hair is cut close to his scalp if not exactly shaved, but he couldn't be a gangster, not Matt. He's thinking of joining the Canadian Forces. He left the apartment two days ago, on his way to meet the man who had called, a recruiting officer. Why didn't he come back? If he joined up on the spot, why didn't he let her know? The days he stayed here she used to hope that he would one day forget to log out of his personal sites, leaving his email open for her to peruse, his Facebook page, his search history. This did not happen. And she has no luck when she enters his email address and clicks the password space, thinking the computer will have remembered him. Of course it would be invading his privacy were she to succeed, but she's motivated by a loose, vaguely anxious sense that Matt needs help, despite what he says. She can't confess this to Annette, because Annette would be sure to speak to Lawreen, who would be furious that Shinny had not told her first. Sibling relationships indelible as birth marks: Annette envious of the relationship Shinny had with her oldest; Lawreen resentful of the youngest; Elfie feeling deprived of the concern of both older girls. Tensions scour surfaces to expose this long-standing dynamic. Sisterly love.

GREG HAS BEEN OUT all afternoon delivering milk to their customers in Sebastopol, and to Josie, the cheesemaker. He called Dad from Josie's to say he would wait for Aidan, who has basketball practice after school on Tuesdays and so misses the bus. This will save Dad a trip, but if Greg did not have a legitimate reason to be in town, he would invent one. Annette slams a pan of lasagna into the oven. Considers the blown-glass pipe lying on the windowsill. Decides no. Talking to her mother will fight the calming effects of the weed. Instead she will wait until after supper, step out to the barn, climb the ladder up to the loft and listen to the goats chew hay.

She dials the number in Vancouver and her mother picks up on the first ring.

"Hey, Mom. I had get to myself cleaned up. What's with you?"

Shinny talks about the weather, about her job, which Annette thinks she should give up. Her mother seldom calls to make small talk. Something is bothering her and Annette suspects illness, the next big thing.

"Are you feeling all right? Have you seen the doctor about that spot you found?"

"That spot on my leg? It just went away. I'm fine. Perfectly fine. How's your dad?"

"Dad's getting old. I think he should move into town, but he won't, even though Aidan and Eve would like to be closer to their friends. Aidan especially."

"He still thinks he's a rebel."

"It's not that, Mom. He really likes it here. I do too. You really should think of coming down. Quit the job."

"I need a job, Annette."

"Well ask for a vacation then."

Out the window Annette sees the flashlight beam that precedes her father down the slope between his place and hers. Most nights he comes for dinner, meaning Eve and Aidan do too, making five. Sometimes he cooks, or washes the dishes. But less and less these days. He walks more heavily, and doesn't stand until he has to, and then he leans on whatever is near to hoist himself up.

Though she just put it in the oven, she tells her mother she has to take the lasagna out and promises to call later in the week. She can't handle both parents at once, and it strikes her, a small bell at the back of her brain, that while part of her has fantasized a reunion between them, were they both to be living next door she might find it hard to breathe. Images from childhood reel through her mind, life before Elfie: Dad bursting through the door, home from what Mom called a "business trip", lifting Annette onto his shoulders and pretending to be a horse as he ran around the modest yard of whatever house Shinny was renting at the time. Lawreen staring out from beneath her honey-coloured bangs. When he set down a laughing, dizzy Annette, he would invite Lawreen to climb on, but her older sister would decline. I'm too big for that. In Annette's memory, Dad played horsey only with her. Then he would open his rucksack, which was stuffed with treats for them. All-day lollipops in bright colours. Lawreen called red before Annette had a chance and she would cry, "I wanted red," but Smokey would offer something more unique: a hummingbird's nest, the bud of a deer antler, tiny worry dolls with actual expressions inked on their woven-string faces, embroidered dresses from Mexico that were either too big or too small, or too gaudy to wear, unless for Halloween. When Annette couldn't find herself reflected in her mother's eyes, her Dad was the beacon she homed toward. Pre-Oona. Pre-Greg. But they have been in the post-Oona era for nearly ten years, and father-daughter positions have reversed. Now it's him homing towards her. Getting old. A fringe of long hair, white, around the bald pate he covers with a red John Deere cap; overalls. Boots that he doesn't bother to lace. John Lennon-style glasses that bounce from a leather thong around his neck. He uses a walking stick, but claims it's for show. Although he denies it, she thinks his knees are paining him.

"Hey, Dad. It'll be awhile. Where's Eve?"

She knows Aidan stays in town on Tuesdays, so she does too.

"Well like I've been saying …"

"Don't start, Nettie. You want me to be one of the old guys who sit on the bench outside the store? Some character from a Norman Rockwell calendar? No, thanks. I didn't settle here for town life. And I'll never be so ancient I want to spend most of my days on a bench."

"That's a movie you remember from somewhere. There is no bench. Will you check the fire?"

"Yeah, well."

He takes his boots off and pads into the main room to the large wood stove, which screeches open. The thud of logs, the screech again as he shuts the stove. Sixty-six his next birthday and his youngest kids not in high school yet.

February

When more than a week goes by and Mattie has not returned, called or emailed, Shinny phones Lawreen.

"Matt? He almost never calls, Mom. You know that. I guess he's busy with schoolwork. And he doesn't like it when we call him. He said he doesn't like me checking up on him. Why?"

Lawreen has no idea that Mattie quit school, that he visited Vancouver. He wouldn't have had to get his parents' permission to join up if that's what he did; he's over twenty-one. Shinny clicks into the Contact Us page on the Canadian Forces site and writes an email explaining that her grandson is missing, that he talked about joining up. Can they check to see if Matthew Webster of Vancouver enlisted? If he did, will he be sent to Afghanistan?

Another soldier was killed over there last week, Sean David Greenfield, only twenty-five. A sapper. His comrades described him as a funny guy, friendly, quick with a joke. His commanding officer testified that he was a professional through and through. Will any of these well meant phrases comfort the grieving people who loved him? Who watched his coffin being lowered from a huge military plane and carried at a mournful pace to the vehicle that drove it along the Highway of Heroes, as it is called, where veterans and supporters stand at attention on a highway overpass as the funeral procession motors beneath? Now NATO wants Canadian forces to get involved in targeting opium traffickers. That targeting word again. Drug wars here, drug wars there. Around Kandahar, where the Canadians are stationed. Tahir's family fled Bamyan Province, the centre of the country. Do you know Kandahar, she'll ask Sima. Because my grandson may be going there; may be there already. No, not already. Not just a week or so after he closed the closet door and disappeared. He'd be in training camp. Lawreen sounded testy when his grandmother asked about him.

He has his own life, Mom. You know, Matt. He likes to play his cards close to his chest. Shinny answered that cliché with one of her own. Well, no news is good news, I guess.

It's not the first time they have leaned on such conversational crutches, for while Mattie is a mystery, there's nothing puzzling about Lawreen, who is having hormonal problems Shinny never experienced herself. Where did it come from, that tendency? Lawreen's father? The Blake side? Is it genetic, or can you blame the chemicals in modern foods? Did cave-women suffer through these changes in their lives? Why isn't this news? Internal chemistry can transform individual lives that then affect the lives of others. Who knows what hormones are affecting the soldiers? Testosterone surely, but anything else? The aggregation of small, apparently forgettable factors influences world events. Not that news reporters credit them. "Russian President Medvedev was hungover the morning they tried to hammer out an agreement ..." Imagine how painful it would be to hammer out anything meaningful when you're hungover.

Glen got her out of sitcoms and into this nightly TV news watching. First when he came to visit her in Vancouver, in the winter, and tuned into one of the American networks to hear the latest about the U.S election. Glen had supported the man who lost, the fellow who has been going around the world talking about global warming. If he'd won, Glen believed, the terrorists would not have flown those hijacked airplanes into the twin towers in New York. Glen was about to head home that September after a long weekend in Vancouver, during which they'd talked and talked about the pros and cons of Shinny moving south to live with him on his farm in Washington. When he switched on the TV to check weather conditions, he saw instead the replay of the image of the first plane smashing into the first tower. "Come here," he called. "Look at this." Shinny sat down and watched and Glen took her hand, to comfort her, though he needed the comfort as much as she did.

Everything seemed tenuous after that. If men could crash airplanes into high-rise office buildings, without a care for their own lives, not to mention the lives of others, what else might humans be capable of? While it might have been foolish to move to the States, more of an obvious terrorist target than Canada, it was important to be with people you loved. Elfie and Brendan lived in Europe, Annette in California. Lawreen encouraged her to go. "It's not so far, Mom. We can still spend holidays together. Maybe Mattie can come down for the summer." Is she trying to get rid of me, Shinny wondered, because Lawreen had once expressed resignation about her future role as her mother's nurse. Was this an out Lawrie saw?

Glen, already sixty. After he left that September, Shinny thought, what if this is the beginning of the end of the world—as we know it? That ominous phrase every news anchor repeated in sonorous, tones. If it was the beginning of the end, she couldn't leave Glen at Riverbend, watching the nightly news by himself. The terrorists probably had no interest in rural Washington anyway.

When she announced her intention to move, Canadian Thanksgiving, 2001, everyone cheered. She felt as if she had been pushed onto a stage, unaccustomed to attention, and she made a joke of it. I see you've been wanting to get rid of me. No, Grandma, Mariah said, hugging her, we've been wanting you to be happy. Shinny was happy, for five years of sitting next to Glen on his overstuffed harvest-gold couch, watching local stories, then national. Laughing through drug company commercials for products aimed at curing high blood pressure, erectile dysfunction, osteoporosis, as if the advertisers assumed that young people, healthy people, weren't interested in the news. Shinny learned about various controversies in the State of Washington while she cooked, and the progress in the War on Terror and the wars in Iraq and Afghanistan while they ate, as they did many nights, in front of the TV. She saw the statue of Saddam Hussein fall in Baghdad, she learned to pronounce Middle Eastern names from the priests who lead the liturgy on the evening telecasts, and sometimes she repeated those names when she had trouble falling asleep: Mahmoud Ahmadinejad, Hosni Mubarak, René Moawad, Ariel Sharon, Yasser Arafat, Hamid Karzai. Shia, Hamas, Netanyahu. Musharaff, Osama bin Laden, of course.

The news was a meal in itself and she got hooked, hungry when she missed it. Which was ok, because Glen did, too. She continued the habit when she returned to Vancouver, and now it has become important again in a personal way, the news. If only Mattie hadn't disappeared so quickly, she would have had him talk to Tahir, or Sima. Then he would know better what he was getting himself into, unless he didn't join up, and if that's the case, should she check with the police? They will ask for a description, which she practices as she stands at the window. About six feet tall, or maybe not quite. Very short brown hair. Yes, just ordinary brown. Some acne around his hairline and his chin. Clean shaven. He's a quiet boy. He bites his fingernails.

Any distinguishing features, ma'am? That's what they say on the cop shows.

Well actually no, he's a plain looking boy. Brown eyes, very sweet. Longer lashes than his sister's; oh and there's a little scar in his eyebrow from where he got hit by a golf ball when he was little. Is that what you call distinguishing? His nose may be a little big for his face, a little rounded at the end, but I don't know that you'd see that if you weren't used to looking at him. And he has a slight overbite. He's the kind of boy—well, young man—you wouldn't mind talking to, to ask directions, say. Oh, and running shoes, like everyone else, and a dark blue jacket. And his ears stick out a little.

And you think he's come to some harm? He's disappeared without a trace?

Yes he has officer. About the harm, I don't know. I hope not.

If she were to really make this call, would they go looking for him? And if they did would they find him and say his grandmother was worried about him? Mattie would be mortified.

IN THE TUB, WHERE she took Shinny's call, Lawreen is first angry that her mother should be asking after HER son, then devastated. No, it's true, she hasn't talked to Mattie since Christmas, and when she gets out of the bath and hurries to the computer, still dripping beneath her robe, to check her inbox, she sees that she hasn't had an email from him in all that time either. It has always been that way, Mattie in the background. But this is very far in the background. She tries his cell phone, and a voice informs her that the cellular service has been discontinued. She tries Skype, but it says the user is not online. She emails: *Call home as soon as you see this*; and then regrets the urgency, because the only emergency is the guilt she feels for not having thought about Mattie and what he's doing since he hugged her goodbye at the door and drove back to Alberta. At least that's where he said he was going.

She cries every time she's alone in the house, and often when Ken is home. Engrossed in hockey or curling or some other sport on TV, or playing with his model railway, he seldom notices. He has become accustomed to the sound of her weeping, a realization that exacerbates the sadness.

How could it be that someone who has done everything right in her life, to the point of having a daughter who is virtually a movie star, how can it be that she feels so lost? She adds more hot water to the brimming tub and steps back in and steams her face with a cloth just short of scalding. This will stop the tears and open her pores and afterward she can rub in the new cream Mariah found in California.

Though people have always told Lawreen that she looks young for her age, people in the film business, too, who know, she has to work at it now. When she does fly down to L.A., she doesn't want her daughter to see that she has been crying for what seems like months. Although it might be pre-menopausal, as her doctor suggested, her sadness also has to do with rejection and she doesn't need Mariah to recoil at the sight of her. Yet, she hasn't taken the mild anti-depressant the doctor prescribed, nor has she accepted hormone replacement pills. Not after what she has heard about those. She feels it will go away, this feeling that life has betrayed her, that all the verve she had in her twenties, her drive, the hard work of raising the kids while she worked full-time and Ken worked full-time, the opening Mariah gave the whole family with her beauty, her talent, the promise of a future where they would be the golden people—all that was a lie. If there is a golden future, she hasn't seen it glinting just ahead. She no longer has the hope she used to have, and Ken wouldn't know what she was talking about if she tried to explain, which she has.

She steps out of the tub a second time, more carefully, grabs a fresh towel, white, fluffy; in her bathroom everything is white, or cream coloured or stowed in the cupboard. With just the towel wrapped around her, and another around her head, she returns to the desk to see if Mattie has answered. Although it has been less than an hour since she wrote, if he's anything like he was when he last lived at home, he won't be far from a computer. Her inbox is empty. She tries Facebook, which she joined because everyone was joining, sending invites to every name on their email contact lists. Wanting to be friends. When you got a message that so-and-so wanted to befriend you, how could you say no?

She asked Mariah if she could be her "friend", and thus access her page, but Mariah said, sweetly as always, that she thought it wasn't for parents, really, but for friends, like I mean, real friends, Mom. People my age. Okay, she asked, hugging her, both the same height now. But Lawreen has access to Mariah's page through a mistake Mariah made herself, of signing in and forgetting to sign herself out when she turned off her mother's computer. Since Christmas, Lawreen has been sneaking looks. And it's how she has gained what little knowledge she has of what Mariah is doing. Her new pictures, the breezy notes about her latest club night, her latest audition, the hush-hush movie she's making with a really hot indie director. The occasional conversation.

Sharon 8:49

It astounds me daily....sometimes I am amazed that the human race has lasted as long as it has with the way some people are.

Aslan 8:51 So rude. people are just so freakin' RUDE.

Sharon at 8:53 I have learned to expect to be treated like garbage by Evaryone. That's just the way of the world these days.. In no way is it right, nor should it be, but that is how people act. "SCREW OTHERS BEFORE THEY SCREW ME" - The new golden rule of the 21st Century.

Mariah at 8:55 i used to be like that. but i found that it started affecting my attitude and my personal well being when i was being negative towards Everything and Everyone. so i am just open now. i know there are good people and i know there are shitty people. and that's about it. take it all in stride, i say. and never be surprised about either side that comes your way.

Sharon at 9:00 I agree with ya. I know that some people appreciate it, and that's good enough for me.... albeit annoying...

At least Hollywood hasn't hardened Mariah the way it has hardened Sharon, whoever she is. With that sunny outlook, could Mariah really be involved in porn? A beautiful child, people always wanted to pat her head or touch her, even kiss her, when she was a baby. She expected to be loved. You can see it in the dazzling smile. Dazzling, bright as sun on the ocean.

That's what that reporter called it in the feature he wrote for *The Vancouver Sun* on upcoming stars. Mariah was just fifteen. She had made it through adolescence, when teeth tended to need straightening and pimples broke out, and once-lovely girls gained or lost weight, or their faces changed from kid-cute to average. Mariah grew taller; willowy, that reporter wrote. Time chiseled a more mature beauty. She lightened her hair so that, according to her grandmother, she looked like one of the TV weather girls. Shinny had not said this to Mariah but to Lawreen, who responded defensively to any comment on Mariah, no matter the intent.

"TV weather girl?"

"Well it's true, Lawreen. Glen and I were just saying the other night that all the TV weather girls seem to be streaking their hair."

Goose bumps have risen on Lawreen's bare shoulders; still, she sits at her computer desk in the alcove off the stair landing, waiting for something to happen, one of her children to contact her, or someone to email her or instant message her out of the blue, one of the casual friends she used to make on set, the costume designer who talked about moving to Vancouver. Hey, she could write, in the breezy way of the business, so did you make the big move? Give me a call if you're in Van. Or the camera operator she met during the TV series in which Mariah had the third lead. He loved Mariah because the camera loved her, but it was Mariah's mother he talked to at breaks. Paul somebody. She fingered in the title of the series and followed the link to the crew list. Paul Reljic. Next she typed his name, and it came up on the Internet Movie Database, and she saw that he last worked in Vancouver in 2008. Just last year. So maybe she will see him again. Maybe they will bump into each other on the street, and she will summon that extra energy she used to bring to the set. The controlled excitement, like fire in a stove, until you take the lid off, which she never had, never would.

Oh but now she's really cold, and her chest is feeling tight again. Could it be she does need hormone replacements? In her bedroom, the sight of herself in the cheval mirror—a surprise from Mariah for her 40th birthday—the pouchy eyes, her winter-pale skin, strawberried with dry patches around the nose and chin, starts the tears all over again. This isn't her!

March

Brendan has a moment of shyness, something in him thinking, unconsciously, that their lovemaking should proceed in darkness. That same timidity can accompany him onto the stage, before he sits and lifts his bow and the music unlocks him. Elfie is naked beneath an emerald velour robe, standing at the window in the kitchen, which overlooks a courtyard big enough for the three tables Francisco sets outside his restaurant in fine weather, for customers to dine al fresco. This time of year the courtyard is a square of dimpled snow, and someone has thrown what looks like a pair of boxer shorts onto it, though it could be a cleaning rag. Brendan, still damp from his shower, embraces her from the back and she feels him harden immediately. It's this exhibitionism, even though the window is complicated by a tangle of plants and prisms and strings of coloured beads that Elfie has hung to create some privacy without wholly blocking light. He takes her hand and leads her the length of the apartment, to their bed at the front, where winter sun falling through the spots on an otherwise clear front window speckles her white skin, her face, then the small breasts Brendan exposes by untying her robe, and her stomach, where he rests his head. When they lay together naked they sometimes raised their arms and twisted them around one another, a human barber pole, but in brown and white. Not now. He's kissing the dip above her hip bone and the stubble on his face is arousing rather than irritating. She tugs him up to lie atop her, and once he is settled, his lips on her throat, she slides her arm down between their bodies, finds his penis and adjusts the angle so that it slips easily inside her. She raises her knees to draw him further into herself, and contentment wrestles the agony of anticipation, before sensation stages a coup against thought, and familiar, urgent moves, a slight twisting to the side for maximum contact, bring them to mad, explosive, somehow still original, release.

Brendan begins to peel away, but slowly. When Elfie pulls him back, wanting them to curl together and sleep a little, he gives in, but then a fight erupts on the street and they wake, startled and cold, and this time Brendan does get up. It's some wrangle over parking. Ridiculous. But with snowdrifts blocking the curb, people are more territorial than ever, and they say what's on their mind. It's New York. Fuck, asshole, douchebag, cunt, bitch. Elfie hears a car door crunch shut, tenses for a gunshot. She had not heard a gunshot until she and Brendan moved to New York, to this East Village neighbourhood, which is otherwise, on the whole, safe. No gunshot this time, and she can't linger to listen to the fight play itself out because she's expecting a student at 11:00, and she needs to shower and straighten the bed. Brendan has started coffee, is peeling an orange; she steals a section on her way through to the bathroom.

"Remember that Hilda is coming over," she hollers. "Are you going to be here?"

"If Hilda is? No way."

"Well don't go to your office, ok? Just wait at the deli, and I'll meet you there after. It's supposed to be warmer today. We could take a long walk and stop at MoMA for a drink."

"Did you raise your fees? We can't afford MoMA for drinks."

They have agreed not to talk to one another from different rooms, because messages get garbled, misunderstandings irritate, but when she thinks of something to say, Elfie can't stop herself. "We can afford one drink," she shouts.

He doesn't answer, not so she can hear; he is more disciplined than she, about everything.

Unlike Brendan's position at the music school, Elfie's job is anything but prestigious, yet she likes the flexibility of teaching at home, keeping herself available for the occasional call-out as a studio musician, or fill-in violinist for a quartet. Never as ambitious as her husband, she has not sacrificed any goals for his sake. She likes her challenges on a smaller scale, even if what she is facing in Hilda's case is hardly small. Although she has attended lessons and practiced daily for over a year, dear Hilda shows little sign of advancing beyond the first few songs in Volume 1 of the Suzuki series. Brendan thinks it would be compassionate to suggest that Hilda consider another instrument, or accept that she's more a music lover than a musician. But, odd as it has been to watch a 50-year-old woman struggle with "Twinkle, Twinkle Little Star", Hilda has not only been Elfie's most reliable student, she has recommended other students, also adult, who have taken up the fiddle as a hobby and want to play it for their friends on St. Patrick's Day, at weddings, at funerals. Elfie has made them pledge to make it through Book 1 before she will teach them "Danny Boy", or "The First Noel", "I Love You Truly", or "Ave Maria". They all think she's a genius and encourage her to play for them—a quick sonata or minuet—though it's their time, paid for with their money. Before she and Brendan flew west to Vancouver for the holidays, the students presented her with chocolates, Christmas cakes, little Christmas cacti and pots of poinsettia. Brendan wonders why she encourages them, but then he has never understood people who don't take themselves as seriously as he takes himself. Including Elfie, whom he continues to send to auditions he sees posted.

He's dressed to go out, in a leather jacket and the burgundy cashmere scarf Lawreen gave him for Christmas.

"Promise you'll wait at the deli?"

He burrows into her chest, licks a bead of water off the cleft between her breasts. That, and the creak of leather, the smell of her still on him, make her regret the imminent arrival of Hilda. But there's always tonight, the rest of their lives.

"Just don't be too long."

Crumbs on the floor, and something oily. She should scrub, or at least sweep the broad floor planks once she's dressed, but a Bach partita is singing out from iTunes, the luscious James Ehnes. She goes to turn up the volume and sees an email from her mother, subject heading, Mattie. Then the buzzer sounds. Hilda, early. Elfie grabs a long wool skirt. Finds a sweater, socks. Then Hilda's at the door knocking. Her bright pink toque is pulled down to the frames of her steamed-up glasses; she's huffing from the stairs and stuffed into a child-size winter coat because she insists that women's sizes don't come small enough for her.

"Elfriede, you beauty. How wonderful to see you. I just hope you and your handsome husband didn't put a cent in that crook's fund. That Bernie Madoff, gives the Jews a bad name. Shyster. No wonder. I tell you. But he's gonna get what's coming to him. Did ya see the paper?"

She fizzes, a shaken bottle of soda, irrepressible. Elfie doesn't know what Hilda is talking about, but how could she turn her away?

ALMOST THE MIDDLE OF March, but cold enough in the morning that snow skims the soccer field beyond the playground. Flocks of robins and thrushes pick through the crust before a running dog stirs them up and, like flung seeds, they spatter the brightening sky. Shinny turns off the radio before the broadcaster can finish his story about another ramp ceremony at Kandahar base. The latest casualty, as they say, a twenty-two-year-old. Same age as Mattie. What's casual about that?

And now Annette. Her call last night, the higher breathy voice—Mo-om? —that betrayed the hurt she immediately layered with sarcasm.

"Good riddance, I say. Greg was doing fuck all anyway. Sorry, Mom. I just feel like I'm mad all the time. But I'm going down to once a day milking. I've got it figured out."

"You sure? You don't want me to come down there, just to visit?"

"Mom, you're afraid of the goats."

"I know, but I could cook. We could talk. You used to want me to come."

Hesitation. Shinny imagines Annette's thoughts knotting, too many threads to sort out before she answers. Their relationship has always been complicated. Impulses wound up in a skein of expectations, obligations, habits. It's never as good when Annette comes to Vancouver and tours the feelings that drove her from here. She wouldn't anyway; wouldn't leave her beloved goats, not so soon after the Christmas trip. Does the hesitation mean she wants her mother?

"I'm going into work today. I'll tell Tahir it's a family emergency. I'll book a plane ticket."

Waiting, waiting, years of disappointments, longing. Reality. Annette is a practical girl.

"It's not an emergency though, Mom. It's been coming. I'm okay, really. I just wanted you to know. Anyway, Dad's here."

Dad, as water poured on the kindling of Shinny's intended devotion.

"Okay, then. But call me, okay? Or I'll call you."

On the way across the wide brick and concrete lane between her building and the Roundhouse, Shinny sees the homeless man who patrols the neighbourhood for refundable bottles. His grey toque is scrunched close around his narrow face, his large, watery eyes beseeching.

"How are you today?" she says, expecting the words to stream behind and wilt. But he answers back, pausing her.

"Sorry. I'm feeling kind of sick to be alive today. Sorry. Kind of topsy-turvy."

"I'm sorry, too."

"Everything's going to turn around in a couple of days. Kind of topsy-turvy now."

"Well, good luck."

Shinny has seen him with a shopping cart before. Today he's cart-less, wandering. How will he carry the bottles, assuming he finds any? A notice recently posted in the elevator urges residents to stop their practice of placing refundables alongside the iron gate that keeps the garbage safe from dumpster divers. The poor man. No wonder he feels topsy-turvy. A big crow complains as he flaps above them towards Pacific Boulevard. The man huddles deeper inside his coat.

At Davie News and Postal Service, Tahir is caged in conversation with someone whose back is turned to her. Neither man sees her enter. They are speaking in their own language and while she has picked up simple words, *salam, khoda hafez,* the sounds rising from Tahir and his friend are stew that has been bubbling so long she can recognize only the meaty scent. The bigger man is wearing an overcoat and slacks, a snappier dresser than Tahir. When he turns, he seems familiar. The sandalwood skin, the thick eyebrows. The somewhat Japanese appearance. Friends of Tahir drop into the store now and then, but most dress like he does, in jeans and shirts or sweaters. This fellow looks prosperous. The crash! The silver SUV, the big man who was bleeding and yelling. It's him! Tahir doesn't introduce them, but, when he notices Shinny, waves the man towards the door and follows.

"I get coffee. Back in ten minutes. Should be okay, yes?"

They want privacy, though their language creates that, in Shinny's presence. Why leave? Tahir returns when he said he would, alone, carrying a Starbucks cup.

"Is your friend ok now?"

Tahir's eyebrows lift in a question. "Okay? Sure." He shrugs.

"I mean, didn't he get hurt awhile back? That accident right out front? It looks like the same man. Oh, but you weren't here that day."

It's an out for Tahir. He opens his laptop and the Microsoft song signals the end of the conversation. Then a woman pushes through the door with a parcel balanced atop her baby's stroller.

Six hours later Shinny is home and, as is her habit, she checks her phone for messages, flips open her laptop. All channels are clear but little is coming through. The last few years Elfie lived in Italy hardly a week passed that Shinny didn't get a Skype call early in the morning. At its clearest, the connection allowed her to see her daughter at home in her apartment; Elfie and Brendan even played a violin/cello version of "Happy Birthday" for her. You cannot actually touch anyone through the screen, but that may be just a matter of time. And there's no way the computer connects to a network in the afterlife, where she might talk to Glen, or her mother, or to Carlo, her old boss. But earthbound people can stay in touch easily. Annette almost never emails; her hook-up is too slow, she doesn't have the time, she says. There's nothing from Elfie tonight either, only a note from Nita, Glen's former housekeeper.

After Glen's son sold the farm, the place where Raphael and Nita had raised their three kids, Raphael and Nita moved to California to be closer to their extended Mexican family. Nita's big news is that her David has joined the Marines. David, the boy who almost got Mattie killed by daring him to hand himself across the river on a rope. Without mentioning that frightening incident, Shinny writes back to say, isn't it a coincidence that the boys who met as adolescents on the farm might reunite in some desert camp somewhere? She clicks onto the Canadian Forces website, as she has done frequently enough that she knows how to navigate immediately to news about training camp. The only response she ever received was impersonal, perhaps automated. *Thank you for your inquiry. The Canadian Forces is bound by the privacy laws of…* So she knows nothing. He could be in Quebec right now, or Ontario. Thirteen weeks of training. He's been gone for six weeks. Even Lawreen is worried. Mattie seems to have dropped off the rim of the earth. His phone has been discontinued; he doesn't answer email. Shinny is going to have to let his parents know that she saw Matt in late January, that he was fine, although he had quit school. She is going to have to tell them he was considering joining the army, too. Lawreen will have a fit when she hears that. War as a way of losing a child has never been a reality for them because Mattie is the first boy in the family. And though girls can join now, and do join, and die right alongside men, she and her girls have been the kind of people who oppose war. Smokey, whom she still thinks of as Smokey, although he wants to be called John, bears some responsibility for that attitude, him being an old hippie who lived by the slogan he adopted before Shinny met him—make love, not war. Not only him, but many people who lived through the Vietnam years and were sickened by pictures of napalmed children, mutilated women and old men lying dead in their rice paddies.

But news of more recent wars skipped right by her. There was Desert Storm; she can't remember the year of that one, but the older Bush was president and he didn't win it. Newspaper pictures of burning oil wells, rolling black smoke, orange-hearted fires. Those years, with Elfie growing up and Mattie just born, and Lawreen needing her as much as Elfie, what time had she to think about war? The next one she paid more attention to because Glen did. She knew about the potential of WMDs. She knew what the letters WMD stood for. Even Glen thought that Saddam Hussein might have some of those, and when it turned out that he didn't, Glen grew uncharacteristically angry at the president, the younger Bush, Baby Bush he called him, because he had lied to get everyone's support. Those were American wars. Canada has always been a peacekeeper. She thinks. Yet peacekeepers go to warring countries and often get killed there. In Afghanistan it's confusing; maybe it's always confusing, practicing war to make peace. What is Mattie thinking? Why doesn't he come back? Does he think they'll disown him if he joins up?

HE THREW OUT HIS cell phone and bought a new pay-as-you go model with a Vancouver number he hasn't given to anyone. He rented an apartment as Randy Phlueger. The landlord won't bother checking his ID because Matt could tell that the guy, Ali, liked what he saw, a clean-cut young man in jeans and a new polo shirt, a self-described computer software creator—his cover for spending so much time at home—three months rent up front, in cash. The cash might have been suspicious, but he explained that he'd closed his bank account in California. It's an open-ended arrangement. Matt likes the idea of open ends; he pictures frayed cords, paths that lead somewhere but you don't know where. Scary but cool.

He goes out only at night when there is no danger of running into his Gran, or his Mom and Dad, although it's unlikely he would see any of them, but particularly his parents, on this side of town. He hasn't talked to his Mom since Christmas holidays, and not to Gran since he bailed out of her closet. He wants the scam to settle before risking contact with anyone he knows, so it's a quick getaway kind of life. The apartment is basically empty. A folding table for his laptop, a blow-up bed like he slept on at Gran's. At the bargain shops on East Hastings he bought a few dishes, two towels, a set of sheets, more cheap underwear, enough so that he doesn't have to wash clothes more than once a week.

The thing is to keep yourself unconnected. Your real self unconnected. Here, he's Randy. That's the name he uses for his email account and his new Facebook account. He could get credit cards, but he's keeping it simple, everything in cash. He's creating a life that has almost nothing to do with his actual personal history. Randy, the software designer, who lives in front of the screen. Who, with his degree from Caltech, is better educated than Matt; a bit of a gimp because of a childhood illness that paralyzed his left leg. Depending on the weather, he may limp or not. Creating characters is Matt's specialty and what made the business with Berk succeed. It happened almost by accident, him finding that tax return from the former tenant of the Edmonton apartment they rented when Berk convinced him to move up there from Vancouver. The former tenant had died. Matt was going to put all the mail back in the box, for the postman to forward to wherever you forward mail for dead people, but Berk convinced him to hang on to it. With the tax return they could get the information they needed to fill out an identity, and that offered dozens of possibilities. Man, I'm not into ripping people off, Matthew told him.

Like credit card fraud? No way. No, it'd be like a public service, Matt. I know a guy, old guy, been living underground because he jumped ship in

Vancouver. Friend of my old man's. We could sell him this new guy, who bought it, so why would he care? My dad's pal would be legal, he could apply for a passport, who's to know?

The idea intrigued Matt, and their first success, the easy money it brought, encouraged him. Between classes at the U of A, he would stroll through the library, the computer labs. People who forgot to log out of their accounts were the easiest targets, something he discovered by accident, too, having sat down at a terminal to search for a book for his class in macroeconomics and finding, instead, that the previous user was still logged in, with tabs open to his Facebook page, his email account. Jordan Spychka, 20; hometown, Grand Prairie, Alberta; not currently in a relationship. It was crazy, Matt couldn't resist. Macroeconomics slid to the farthest back corners of his mind as he jotted down Jordan's information, his birth date, his parents' names, which he got from emails, from links to other Facebook pages. With the name and the birth date and his mother's maiden name, Bodyan, Matt got a birth certificate replacement, used that to dig up Jordan's SIN. Intoxicating. Way more satisfying than inventing stories where characters could function solely in an imagined world, such as in computer games. There was the obituary avenue, too, but that was riskier because clerks can cross-check requests for birth certificate copies with death certificates. That they don't routinely do so incited Matt to hunt through old newspapers for kids who died, maybe ten years ago, who would be young men now. Creepy in a way, and yet, in another way, when you think of it, he was giving the dead kid another shot at life. He liked finding pieces, putting the documents together, the outline of a person, and imagining a client stepping into it. While he seldom attended classes that first semester, he signed up for the second term. Then he just didn't bother.

Meanwhile, Berk covered the mail angle. Followed postmen on their routes, got to know which apartment building mailboxes were vulnerable. As far as he knew, Berk was not ripping off anybody's credit card accounts. Not directly. Their income came from sales. What their clients did with the identities they purchased, Matt did not know and did not want to know. Berk reminded him that gun salesmen don't ask their customers what they are going to do with the rifles they purchase; car salesmen don't need to know the driving record of the purchaser. It's business, cut and dried. When Matt had a full set of documents, Berk would peddle it to illegal immigrants; that's what he said and what Matt preferred to believe, but he knows now that Berk's clientele grew to include gangsters developing grow-ops, who needed new identities in order to purchase or rent. With every sale, the purchaser was obliged to provide a photo, so that Matt could complete the set of documents with photo IDs. Somewhere, Berk found driver's licence templates, the embossed paper for official letters, passport blanks. He got too ambitious, and when it came crashing down on him, because an alert airline security guard questioned the authenticity of one of their client's passports, Matt knew he had to destroy their materials and equipment and split.

Reclusive by nature, it is not difficult to stay in the apartment until dark, when he walks the streets of the Downtown Eastside, visiting bars where people are already drunk, going to movies near Chinatown. It's a dicey place to wander late at night because drug gangs have been using the streets to work out turf disputes. When he talks to anyone, he might be Randy, the computer nerd; sometimes Tim, who works retail; Jason, a student. The girl he picked up one night thought him Skip, an oil rig worker passing through town. She never questioned the softness of his hands on her skin; she knew he couldn't stay. She led him to an old house off Commercial Drive, an unlit entrance to the basement suite around the side, into a messy bedroom, giggling. Shh! My roommate's sleeping. Roommate? He almost left. But there she was peeling off her jeans, tossing them onto a pile that looked like the stuff his Mom dragged out of the closets for the Salvation Army. Then crossing over to where he stood, hot, despite his doubts about being there at all. Skip, the oil rig worker. Skip would definitely be there. Her fingers scrabbled at his fly. He grabbed a condom out of his pocket before the jeans were totally off. Although he left while she was still passed out, he doesn't want to do anything like that again; it's dangerous, because she might see him on the street, recognize him. But can he stop himself? No drunken girl he picks up is going to replace Laura, her straightened hair, her long, slim legs below one of his t-shirts, puttering around his place in Edmonton. Gee, Matt, you have so much equipment, she said once, referring to the printers and scanners, the light table for tracing signatures. Well, you know, it's my office as much as my house.

Laura mixing batter for pancakes, smiling with her head tilted to the side a little, as if to ask, is it okay to love you? A history major, she had a part-time job in the library, which is where he'd met her one day when he was checking out computer stations. Amazing, when he thought of it. Laura accepted that he was someone like Randy Phlueger, who worked from home for a software company; she would have bolted if she knew the truth.

Today when he wakes up his laptop, he clicks open the Canadian Forces site. They've done a good job with the graphics; if he were back in that college class where they analyzed examples of graphic art, the teacher would have pointed out the intentional choice of a cool-looking guy in shades, with lips big as Angelina Jolie's, like a movie star playing a soldier. They don't always have the same face on the home page; he has looked often and sometimes they have girls. The language is good, too, appeals to young guys like him. He knows because he has played with language a little when he posts on people's walls, or gets involved in chat; if you're going to pretend to be somebody else, you'd better be able to talk like that someone. He bites down on the nail of his left pinkie finger and tears off a crescent too close to the quick. Shit. It stings. He tries to cool the skin by sucking on it.

Afghanistan. Gran was right. His career training might begin with war. Could he do it, could he go from someone who sits at a desk to someone who dresses in combat gear and carries a rifle? Matt pushes away from the table and goes to the fridge for an orange pop. There's some lefto-ver wonton soup in there, too, which he puts into the microwave. If he signs up, it's like he's saying, okay, if I die, it's worth it. I'm dying for my country. But is he dying for his country? What's Afghanistan ever done to Canada, except to Canadians who went over there? That sick story about the guy being hit in the head with an axe. Surviving. But, shit. And the guy wasn't asking for it; he was trying to help. Trying to talk things over with warlords. So not fighting for his country, but fighting for other peo-ple's countries, which is charitable, nice, but would you want to die for someone else's problem? Grandma Webster, who lives in Saskatchewan, liked to say charity begins at home. But what if Berk finds him? Or the guy who was busted, who sent his friends after Berk? Would they kill him? Does Berk have it in him? There's a T at the top of the window, where the frame meets the slider mechanism. The bar of the T divides everything in half. Despite all the cop shows Mattie has seen on TV, he never considered the business he did with Berk, not his end of it anyway, dangerous, that he might end up murdered. How much worse could the army be?

After lunch and a shower, he returns to his MacBook. He doesn't see the equipment, but the content on the screen: the generic screensaver, the empty desktop. He clears his search history every day, not that he has been doing anything illegal. Not that he intends to. Kate forms in his mind spontaneously and he isn't sure why; he hasn't invented too many girls. He and Berk didn't have many girl customers. Kate. A popular name. You can tell by the number of variations he has to try on the name Kate when he tries to set up the account. He has to be creative, tries K8; that's not available either, unless he adds the random number Windows Live suggests. Kite. Crate. Ate-kay. That one works. Pig Latin, like Gran used to speak when they were driving somewhere and she wanted to keep him busy.

Ate-kay@hotmail.com. She's going to be a friend of his, from Alberta. A girl Matt gave his Gran's email address to because, um.

Hey, Mrs. Shinnan, Matt once gave me your email because I was telling him I wanted to grow herbs. He said you used to live on an herb farm.

His little finger stings when it hits the "a". He's going to have to pick up some Band-Aids.

April

Bunches of yellow, white, purple and red tulips flute the buckets tiered at the entrance to the market near Davie News, and more people sit at the tables outside, some smoking, others tolerating the second-hand smoke to enjoy the sun with their coffee. Shinny waves to Irene, unmistakable for her white hair, pulled tightly into a bun, and her big glasses with the round, white frames. Irene favours leopard skin, in bags and printed scarves. She wears high-heeled white boots and a nice perfume. Shinny doubts they would have much in common were she to take the initiative and join Irene at her table, yet the day they met at the postal counter, they talked and talked. Irene was mailing a small packet to her son in California, and Shinny said she had a daughter in California; children led to husbands, partners. Since no one waited behind Irene in line, Shinny let her talk. It seemed she needed to, and Shinny could understand that. Like her, Irene had not married officially, but lived with a musician for twenty years, travelling all over North America, until he died of lung cancer when they happened to be in Vancouver. Shinny liked the way Irene described him. "An absolute genius on the tenor sax," she said. "And honey, he was a genius in other ways, too."

Shinny supposed she was referring to sex, and laughed, as if she were in on some lewd private joke. Could she describe Glen as a genius in that department? She missed lying on top of him, both of them naked, the shape of her body defined by his, as if he were a kind of outer self, an outline she fit inside. Oh, but here she is thinking about Glen again. At least she doesn't cry anymore when his sweet face darts into her mind. Tall and only a little stooped, lean in the way she liked; the waggly earlobes she nibbled on when they were in bed, or when she wanted to get him there, the narrow-lipped smile.

Tahir nods a greeting and points to the big canvas bag behind the counter, which he has started to fill with packages for Canada Post. "You wait, maybe half hour, then you can finish to fill it. I be back soon."

He ducks into the backroom, where they keep parcels for pickup, then hurries out the door, sprints across the street to the bank. There's no one behind the sundries counter, but it's okay; she and Tahir can cover both, unless it gets busy, and this is a quiet time of day. Shinny studies the candy rack, picks out a roll of Mentos and pays for it with pocket change. There isn't much cash in the drawer, which explains Tahir's trip to the bank, unless there are bills beneath the cash drawer. No, only MoneyGram receipts, the one on top addressed in Tahir's familiar small, clear, upright script to someone in Bamyan. No message in the space meant for one, but a large amount, $5000. How good of him to be helping out those potato farmers and rug weavers. Yet so much money? He can't be making that much from the store.

Tahir returns and Shinny resumes her place at the postal outlet counter and for the next four hours provides stamps, weighs packages, distributes customs slips for people to fill out. In all this time, she and Tahir speak only about the store and the chores he needs done. She wants to ask him how his relatives use the money he sends. Can they buy tractors to make their work easier? Shinny and Tahir have that in common, farming, though, since childhood, her only experience was with Glen, and for fewer than five years. When she tries asking Tahir a personal question, such as how his parents are, how his brother is, as a way of edging into what she really wants to know, his brow relaxes for the second or two it takes for him to reply, fine, thank you, and then he's all business again.

AN UNFAMILIAR NAME IN her inbox that night tweaks Shinny's generally dormant suspicion. She could be exposing herself to a virus that will infect this electronic limb she has become so dependent upon. There is no spam warning, though, and curiosity trumps caution. Could it be the note she's been waiting for from the Forces?

Dear Mrs. Shinnan, I'm a friend of your grandson Matt's, who gave me your email. I hope you don't mind if I write but I'm thinking of growing some herbs in my backyard and Matt said you used to run an herb farm. That's so cool. What advice would you give for someone just getting started?

Yrs truly,

Kate Babcock

A nice sounding girl, polite. And she knows Mattie? Maybe his girl-friend?

Dear Kate. I'm glad you wrote. I haven't seen my grandson for a couple of months, but I guess you have. The thing is, what you grow with success depends on where you live, ie, the climate. And the soil. Can you tell me a little about where you live? Oh, and if you see Matt, tell him I said hi, and that I won't be mad at him for not writing for so long.

Sharon Shinnan

She reads over her note, to check for obvious anxiety. If she were a forensics expert, knowing the soil where Kate lives would give her a clue to Mattie's whereabouts. She doesn't want Kate running over to Mattie's—your grandmother is really freaked out, Matt. You should call her or something. If Mattie needs some time to himself, she can understand. Still she wishes that being alone did not mean cutting himself off from the people who love him, specifically her. She moves the cursor to the send button and off goes the email, to her new friend Kate.

Tonight also, an inspirational chain letter forward from Mariah—send this to seven women in your life; a YouTube link from Elfie that shows Brendan playing as part of a string quartet, unfamiliar music, full of notes and sounds apparently unconnected to a melody, at least as Shinny understands it. Brendan needs a haircut and he has added a mustache, which makes him look older, though it isn't much of a mustache. Why is it that some people on the far side of the world, like Saddam Hussein, can grow bushy ones, yet Tahir, and now Brendan, have to make do with versions that seem to advertise their lack of something.

She calls Lawreen as she does a couple of times a week, but she doesn't say anything about the surprise email from Mattie's friend Kate, nor does she ask if Lawreen has heard from Matt. She has avoided the question foremost on her mind since Lawreen scolded her in that withering tone—Mother, if I'd heard from Mattie I'd obviously let you know—that instantly shrunk Shinny. I know that; I was just asking. Stupid, meaning-less words. As now.

"How are things?" she begins, brightly.

"Oh you know, same old, same old."

"Just thought I'd say hi."

"Okay, then. Maybe we'll see you this weekend."

And that's that. Still light, the buildings of the West End like teeth in the gaudy mouth of the sunset. Soccer players running on the field below, scuffing mud patches in grass that has just begun to revive. Kevin Newman introduces a story about one of the four Canadian soldiers killed in the roadside bomb explosions outside Kandahar a few weeks ago. Shinny stares at the weeping pregnant girlfriend on the screen, the somber faces of the soldier's parents. They're holding on to one another, but listing, like poles in shallow holes supporting a sagging tent. Mattie has been missing since the end of January. Almost enough time to have finished basic training. He may be heading over there.

She can't play dumb anymore. She has to talk to Lawreen and Ken.

A MISSED PERIOD? IT could be late, but she has always had regular cycles. She must have missed it, which can only mean that she's pregnant. Which is good, even if they haven't been planning on having a child. Not yet. Strange. She feels as if her jacket has tightened and that the people stepping across ribbons of slush on 2nd Avenue exist in another reality, outside this white space that edges her. Could it be true? She stops at the Duane Reade for a pregnancy test kit and keeps her eyes on the counter while the clerk takes her bill and makes change. It's Thursday, which means that Brendan will be home for supper. She could wait until then to do the test, or do it now and surprise him with the news. Will he be happy? They want children; they've talked about it. Will he feel as she does, that he has boarded a space shuttle, that a slight echo accompanies sound, that the air has been piped in specially for her to breathe?

Here's the library next to their building, the blue awning over Francisco's restaurant. Home, already? If she does the test now and it's positive, she will have time to pick up champagne and balloons to go with the announcement. But maybe Brendan would feel left out? But how can she wait with the kit sitting right here and hours before he'll walk in the door?

Oh the insistence of biology, and while Bren will be surprised, he won't be shocked. But he might be stressed. Timing, okay, timing is everything. He has lost confidence in his direction; using exotic scales with instruments diverse as the violin, the sitar and the erhu, which initially excited him, now has him stumped. The beginning phrases that seemed to hold such promise have waned to near silence. He has been preoccupied, grouchy, but it's the schedule. When classes are over he will have all the time he needs. His future sparkles, and whatever happens, she can continue teaching from home. Even with a baby.

Something that will become a person growing inside her. So you're a vessel, already? Hilda would say. In the middle of the long, narrow flat, where the plank floor is reasonably level, Elfie stands with her arms stretched out, eyes closed. She's virtually certain that she's pregnant. It's crazy; she's sure, but she doesn't know how she is sure. Balance, maybe, a slightly different way of adjusting her feet. Astounding. She can't wait, and so she follows the instructions on the package, almost blasé by now, certain that the test will confirm what she suspects, and it does.

If only there were sunlight instead of the mucousy sky over the park, with its remnant snow banks soiled by city soot and leaking dog turds. A baby! Of course, it will change their lives. But there are babies everywhere in New York. People register them for school before they are born. Is that really necessary? Oh, but the stairs. Down five flights to the street, bouncing from stair to stair, one hand lightly on the rail, she thinks, how will she ever get a baby carriage up five flights? And onto the street, where her perspective has changed to that of a person who will be raising a child here. The playground at Tompkins Square. She will be one of those women chatting casually with other mothers, jiggling the stroller or the carriage, or, if they stay in the neighbourhood long, pushing her baby—will it be Johann or Johanna, because they have long planned to name their first child after J.S., whose two-part inventions they learned when they first met and were paired in a chamber music group at U.B.C. —pushing Johann or Johanna on the swings. The public library, too, will be a plus. Traffic is not too bad this side of Avenue B and there must be daycares or playschools or something in one of the community centres or schools nearby.

Here she is, thinking of childcare when she hasn't even informed her husband, and she wants to tell her mother as soon as she gets home, but

Brendan first. Mom keeps asking if they're going to have kids. She asks in a worried way, as if she will be disappointed if they don't; Mom loves kids. But you better decide to settle down, Elfie; you can't raise kids while you're traipsing around Europe. Then, when they left Europe so that Brendan could take the job here, New York is no place to raise kids. Odd that while she wants them to have children, Mom never seems to think them in the right position. It's just that New York scares her, Elfie thinks. It's a target for terrorists. Yet no one has stopped breeding because hijacked planes flew into the World Trade Center. There are children all over the place. Babies, kids, teenagers.

Reluctant to tempt fate by dashing across on a yellow, she waits for the light to change. A small bottle of champagne, a small one of sparkling apple juice, because she can't drink, which isn't a big loss—she has never been much of a drinker—and now flowers, which she cannot resist, a dozen red tulips, no two dozen. She would like to gather the whole bucket of them into her arms. But no. She has already spent all the money she earned from her last student, and she hasn't bought supper. They should go out. Yes, down to Francisco's to share the good news. Francisco gives them special treatment because they can speak Italian, and it's Francisco's nephew's rent-controlled apartment they are living in. A deal arranged by the cousin of her mother's late boss, Carlo, when Elfie and Brendan moved from Italy to New York. The nephew had been suffering from nightmares since the fall of the towers; he had to get out of the city and was happy to pass on his place to Elfie and Brendan, who didn't have his fear; they hadn't lived through the attack. Francisco is almost a relative. He must be among the first to know.

Buona sera, Francisco. Buona nuova!

WITHOUT THE USUALLY DEPENDABLE, almost daily spring rains, the upper pasture is already starting to yellow. The girls keep their noses to the ground and nip the shoots of brush that persist in returning. Only three have not borne their kids; none are first time mothers, so Annette doesn't expect any problems. If there are difficulties, she has enough experience to handle them. Or Dad can help. It's the rare morning he doesn't hobble down the slope soon after Aidan and Eve have left on the school bus.

If he doesn't hobble down, he drives around to pick up the gallon jars of milk he takes to the cheesemaker twice a week. For now there are a dozen does to be fed and milked, equipment to sterilize, kids to monitor. When Greg left, she put Billy and Bob up for sale. The bucks are more than she wants to handle and Dad is no longer strong enough to take them by the horns. When breeding time comes this fall she'll hire bucks, and that way she will introduce new DNA into the herd. In this year's crop so far, four males and six nanettes. The little boys she will neuter and either keep for company or sell for pets. She doesn't want her animals butchered, though she won't know what happens to them once they're sold. And what you don't know can't hurt you, right? As for Greg, she sensed what was going on before she knew for sure, and it hurt from the beginning.

The trunks of the fruit trees glisten black with collected dew, and the willow branches, fully green, weep over various "hot" spots she and Greg identified when they first built the house on this lower part of Dad's acreage: one on the side of the stream that shishes and trickles until early July most years; one near the barn, where Eve likes to play house; and, closer to the house itself, the third willow, alongside the rock garden she planted with visions of colour and texture she could savour year round, but which has become overgrown with scraggy lavender, volunteer dill and some kind of daisy, more weeds. When she wanted to hide out—from Greg, from Dad, from the children—she used to seek this willow and the refuge its cascades provided.

No one to hide out from today. The morning sun coaxes her eyelids down and she stands at the fence for a minute listening to the thump of the kids frolicking, the more distant mmaaaa of a girl with some small thing to complain about, the tinkling steel tubes of the wind chime Mom sent for Christmas one year.

Seeing her at the fence line, expecting food, four does hoof over and gaze at her with their sweet yellow eyes. These LaManchas are not as pretty as the floppy-eared Nubian Cleopatra, the most expensive and most beautiful of her herd, but Cleopatra is standoffish, as if she is aware of her beauty. Not so lovely tiny-eared Marie, shiny and brown as a preserved date, and spotted Loretta, with the scar at the side of her head where Billy, in a moment of enthusiastic rutting, shoved her right into a barn wall. Poor Loretta. Poor us, Greg said; we're the ones with the vet bill, though

Annette didn't call anyone. She could treat small wounds like that one. Greg never loved the goats as much as she does. The goats are her passion, and when she was Greg's passion, he was right here with her. But she can't let memories distract her. Marie is prone to foot rot. Annette should trim her hooves and check the feet of the others tomorrow morning, when she milks them. The girls protest when she attracts Marie's attention by rattling grain pellets inside a plastic bucket and harnesses her small head with a nylon strap to lead her through the gate to the barn. Marie trots over to the milk stand, and Annette pours the pellets into the plastic feeder attached to the head gate. At seven, a successful breeder, having birthed twins every season, and a reliable milker, Marie was a bargain buy. Annette cannot afford to let her hooves get infected with the crud that collects in the unusually deep grooves of her frogs, and the hind hooves have grown enough that pockets have developed between the walls and the frog. With a brush dipped into her bucket of soapy water, Annette lifts a foot and scrubs it, then puts the brush down and uses a sharp-pointed hoof pick to dig out the dirt. A funky smell rises, the goat version of toe-jam. Marie is docile, no objections. Until she feels the metal blade of the orange-handled trimmer. Annette can feel her muscles contract as they predictably do at this point in the process. Does it feel cold? Did someone once hurt her? She bought Marie as an adult, from a farmer who was reducing his herd. It could be that her previous owner cut too close and wounded a foot, or didn't trim as often as he should have, and poor Marie suffered infections. Annette rests her head against the doe's rounded side. Hey, sweetie. I'm not going to hurt you. The front feet naturally wear down on this rocky land, but Annette checks them all the same and clips a rough edge, before releasing the head gate and shooing Marie back toward the pasture. The gleaming brown doe trots as if her feet have not been touched, which satisfies Annette that she can do this. She can. And if she needs help, there's Dad, who used to run a herd much bigger than hers.

Mom calls every other day, apologizes for calling so often, but if Annette would answer email … Mom, you know how slow my connection is. I don't have time for email. Despite Annette assuring her mother that she's fine, Mom is torn. She thinks she should come down to help somehow, but she hasn't heard from Mattie in months, and neither has anyone else, and if he should show up at her apartment, looking for her, what will he think if she's away? Everyone but Annette thinks Mattie will return, get in on the round of birthday dinners, holiday dinners; that he will pick up where he left off, as Lawreen says, but with a girlfriend now; maybe even a wife. That's one of the stories they invent about Matt, that he's gone off with a girl. Annette's instincts tell her otherwise, not because she knows Matthew so well, but because she understands how it is to feel you don't belong somewhere and to take the chance that if you leave you'll find out where you do belong. That's what she did—how many years ago? Long. A lifetime. Mattie's lifetime, because Lawreen had just found out she was pregnant when Annette left Vancouver with her Dad. She has visited but never lived in her birth city again. You're a California girl now, Dad says; but that's not how she sees herself. California girls are prettier, smaller, tanned, blonde; if they're not dancing or drinking, they're at the beach.

But she does live in California, not so far from the ocean, and the conifers are big here, just as in B. C., although B.C. has no redwoods, no manzanitas, not many madrones, which they call arbutus trees there. She doesn't live in California so much as she lives in the country; she's a country girl now. She thinks Mom understands; that looking for yourself, as young people are supposed to do, means that you don't know where you will find yourself, and it might be far from the place you used to think home. Mom found charms in the country herself. It's just too bad that Glen had to die, because she and her mother had quite a bit in common for a few years. Those times they visited back and forth, Glen and Mom making the trip south, or Greg and Annette driving north. She felt like the child she had wanted to be, both parents involved in her life, approving, affectionate. Mom flew down for her birthday one year, without Glen. In the afternoon she stuffed a chicken and put it into the oven to roast, then washed Annette's hair at the kitchen sink. She had to stand on a chair to gain the most effective angle, but once she was comfortable she spent a long time massaging Annette's scalp and rinsing with warm water from a pitcher she filled and poured over, filled and poured over until she'd sluiced out all the shampoo and the hairs squeaked when she pinched part of the tangle together. Annette remembers the press of her mom's small body; the birthday gift, intimacy.

"You're sure you're all right, Nettie?"

This was last night. Mom wants to be let off the hook; she wants Annette to assure her that she isn't suicidal, that she won't do anything rash in response to Greg's desertion. It's because Shinny can't forget the depressed teenager her middle daughter used to be. The long days in her darkened room, the interminable nights behind the counter at Dairy Queen.

"I'm sure, Mom. Anyway, he didn't desert *me*; *I* kicked him out."

Which is technically true. She kicked him out, though it's also true that by taking up with the cheesemaker's sister, he was deserting her in body and in spirit. The spirit went first, and what timing. Every single doe successfully bred; kidding about to begin. The busiest, most exciting part of the goat year, when they didn't take the time for proper meals but inhaled sandwiches and fruit between trips to the barn. You live with someone so long and rhythms become automatic; Greg would boil water for tea while soaking tools in the bleach solution; Annette checked the does closest to term to see if their tails pointed up, if they had that characteristic faraway look in their eyes, were pawing at the ground to make a nest. This year Greg dutifully went through the motions, and the tears Annette customarily produced at the sight of each healthy newborn flowed more freely as he stood well back, available if she needed help, but with his heart and his thoughts in town at the cheesemaker's. He passed the antiseptic solution to her when Loretta pushed and the little hooves stayed put and Annette had to pull on one tiny leg, then the other, until the head appeared. But he got excited only when Jasmine self-sufficiently popped out three babies, one after the other, identical black triplets with fawn legs and beautiful fawn face markings. Identical triplets! How rare was that?

The triplets are leaping at each other, scurrying after their mother, literally kicking up their heels, their hooves barely touching ground. The boys are about ready to be neutered. Dad's going to hold them while Annette applies the Burdizzo to their little scrotums and crushes the spermatic cord. She hates to hear the little guys holler, but imagining that it is Greg's balls she is crushing will motivate her.

Enough dawdling for this perfect morning. She walks as far as the steps up to the deck that surrounds half her house and stops again, unable to relinquish the pleasure of absolute quiet. A robin is singing a complicated melody that may have some significance other than the pure joy of being, which it sounds like. Though she doesn't much anymore, now that Greg's gone, and she should take it easy during kidding season, because she has to have her wits about her, she reaches for the pipe on the sill inside the opened kitchen window, and the lighter next to it, and sucks in smoke from the organic marijuana strain her dad used to grow. Just a toke, which distances her view, as if she has changed lenses on a camera. The pasture rising to the right, the nannies and their dancing kids in groups that separate, join, separate again; the forest across the stream, also rising, to the road she can't see. The various shades of yellow, to blue, to dusty green, of the willows, the conifers, the apple and pear trees, the trembling aspen and scrub oak. The silver of the weathered cedar-board barn. The cloudless creamy blue sky. She hasn't felt so peaceful since March. This is a sign that she's going to feel better any time now. She already does feel better. Who needs him?

LAWREEN WANTS TO SHAKE her mother. The emotion cached beneath her perfect grooming is rising as anger. She feels it pushing up, something yeasted, fermenting, beyond the capacity of a bowl to hold it. Her heart is speeding. It all comes back, Shinny's insistence that Lawreen keep the child she and Ken conceived before they were ready to marry; the pal-sy way she took Matthew with her on trips when he was younger. Why didn't Mattie come to his parents if he wanted to join the army?

"I'm not sure he joined up. He only said he was thinking about it. And I haven't seen him again, so I'm worried. I just thought you should know."

"Oh you finally thought that? You never thought of it earlier, that I might be wondering where my own son is? I haven't been able to get him on the phone. He hasn't answered email. Ken, you've got to do something. I don't want him to join the army."

"A lot of boys want to serve, Lawreen. It's not a shameful thing."

"So you wouldn't care? You're his father and it wouldn't matter to you if he got sent to Afghanistan?"

Because she doesn't know what to do, the rage continues to climb; soon it will escape and then what? She can't stand to look at her mother, sitting there with her eyes big behind her glasses. A woman her age wearing jeans still. God! To think they had welcomed her unannounced visit with concern. She had to talk to them, Shinny said. Well sure, come in. Are you okay, Mom? Loving, supportive, thinking her mother about to admit that she has cancer. She hasn't just dropped in since the first year after Glen's death, when she didn't know what to do with herself. Panic gusted in and swept the concern away, because if it were cancer, what kind, and how fast would it go and would Annette and Elfie help her at all? With Glen gone, somebody was going to have to take care of their mother, and what if it fell only on her? Now this.

"I called the recruiting office downtown, but they said they couldn't give out personal information. Maybe if his parents called, if you said it was an emergency."

"Ken, you should call right now. What else did you find out?"

Mom is nervous, knitting her fingers together. She has already finished the wine Ken poured for her. She has said a hundred times that she's sorry, but that doesn't help; she might as well be squirting gasoline on Lawreen's anger.

I mean, gee, mother; can't we adults all be on the same side? Didn't you think I'd want to see my own son?"

Shinny shrugs, says she's sorry again. Lawreen gusts out of the living room because tears are building up right behind the anger, and tears are a sign of weakness. She feels stomach sick. She has to calm down. Take deep breaths, imagine a metronome, a steady pulse, sixty beats per minute. If she cries, her mother will come over and put her arm around her, pat her back, use that "aw, honey" voice that comes so easily. The "aw honey" can dissolve Lawreen, despite herself, so she goes to the downstairs bathroom and flushes the toilet, then runs the water in the sink, fighting to hold off the crying that attacks even when she doesn't have a good excuse for it. She gulps one glass of water, then another, inhales through her nose, wishing she had continued yoga classes, because if she has ever needed to know how to create inner calm, it's now. Matthew? Don't go away like this. Don't go over there and get yourself killed.

But she can't go back to the beginning of time when he was an embryo whose existence she didn't believe at first, to the extent that she bought a second pregnancy test kit. She decided to have him, didn't she? He knows she had a choice. Did they talk about it, or is she imagining that they did? Did he know? I was the accident, she heard him say once, jokingly, to Mariah.

Mom has put on her jacket, that Gore-Tex parka she insists on wearing, though Lawreen has advised her to change her style now that she's back in the city, living downtown.

"I'm sorry," she says again. "I'll let you know if he contacts me. Will you call if you find out anything from the recruiting office?"

Ken looks over at Lawreen. He's waiting for her, as is Mom. The easiest thing would be to say, yes, we'll let you know, but she detests Shinny right now. For all the things she has done, all the things she has been. For keeping Lawreen away from her father's family, the Blakes, who might have established a relationship with her on behalf of their late son, if they knew her, but no; Shinny wouldn't contact them. Instead she got together with a hippie pot grower and had another baby, and though Smokey—John now—treated Shinny's oldest as his own child, though Lawreen can't help but think of him as her dad, she isn't his own child in the way Annette and Elfie are, and something in the air always made that plain. Lawreen hates her mother for raising such a haphazard family, for not having been able to get better jobs, for stealing Mattie away when she and Ken were so busy with Mariah and her career. Was it her who told Mattie about his beginnings? More than anything right now, she hates her mother for looking so goofy, with her crazy hair and those turquoise frames of her glasses, and the stretched tendons in her throat that say, Oops.

If Lawreen speaks, the details of her hatred will tumble out; Ken sees this on her face.

"Sure we will," he says to his mother-in-law. "I'm glad you told us."

Neither of them accompanies her to the hallway, though Ken responds when she calls goodbye. The door closes and the tap opens.

"Can you believe she didn't tell us? Can you believe that she would conspire with him like that?"

Ken picks up the wine glasses, though Lawreen hasn't touched hers, and stands for minute.

"Don't make excuses for her. She always wanted another kid. She always felt possessive about Mattie. Oh Ken, do you think it's true? Why wouldn't he tell us?"

Now he puts the glasses down and goes to comfort her. She lets him hold her for a second, but fury stops her from caving into sympathy. It's not sympathy but blood she wants. Also, for her heart to slow; instead of one heart it feels like a herd of hearts thundering in her chest. She feels as if she is on the verge of passing out.

May

Brendan had wanted Elfie to wait until a doctor confirmed the pregnancy before telling her mother.

"Why? The kits work."

"I know, but let's keep the news to ourselves for a couple of weeks."

The shyness again. He hates sentimentalism in music, in movies and books, but there he was looking at her with eyes gone soft, his chin up. The doctor has calculated that she is eight weeks pregnant; she and Brendan have been living with the reality for three of those weeks, so Elfie is hurt by her mother's first response; not when or how do you feel, not how happy I am for you, but—are you sure?

"Sure I'm sure, Mom. I waited until I was sure to tell you."

"You've missed more than one period?"

"Yes, and the test kit came out positive, and I saw a doctor yesterday. After all this time, you're going to be a grandma again."

Even then, hesitation in Mom's voice, though she said the right words, like a student who has memorized a piece but isn't sure her fingers will find the right notes.

"Oh honey, I'm so happy for you."

What's wrong? They don't have a lot of money, but Mom never had a lot of money either. Is she worried about how the baby will look? Half and half? According to an article Elfie saw on the web, the entire population of the world is destined to look like the pop star Beyonce, that café au lait complexion, the features that are neither too broad nor too sharp. Their little Johann will be part of that dominant group. It couldn't be racial impurity motivating the hesitancy Elfie has detected; her mother has always been open-minded, friendly to everyone. She lives in a diverse city. Whatever is bothering her, she layers it with more characteristic enthusiasm.

"So the baby will be born near Christmas?"

"Early December."

She wants her mother here, or wanted her; maybe she should reconsider. She had assumed that Shinny would be here to help with the baby, wondering how they would manage three adults and a baby in this small space, but the space will be even smaller if Mom is not as supportive as Elfie expected her to be.

"Is Brendan overjoyed?"

"Yeah. You know, worried, like he gets. And he's been more distracted than ever, because he's struggling with his new piece. But we both want to be parents. We didn't plan to get pregnant right now; we were surprised, but it's a welcome surprise. Like you always said I was, a welcome surprise."

Or could it be Brendan himself? Mom hasn't trusted Brendan since he had an affair with another cellist at the music camp in Italy. Elfie doesn't like to think of that time, but it's there, a thorn that snags her if she squeezes down that path. Shamed, she tries to block the memory of her ridiculous suicide attempt. Then he called and persuaded Elfie to return to him and they married, without telling her Mom, who felt cheated because there had not been many marriage ceremonies in their family; only Lawreen, actually, who was four months pregnant at the time. Mom was sure that their hurry-up wedding was Brendan's idea, which it sort of was, though Elfie had not protested.

"The doctor says that everything is all right? You're not having morning sickness?"

This is better, motherly, more what Elfie expected. Her shoulders drop and she talks on, about their plan to stay in New York, at least until they know Brendan's future. If he is offered a permanent position, she will fly back at least twice a year because she wants the baby to know its family. Not to mention Canada, Vancouver especially.

"I bet the blossoms are out. I used to love this time of year. If they don't offer him a job, we might move back right away. We miss the West Coast. By the way, any word from Mattie?"

Mom immediately clicks into the conversation, as if the lip movements and the sounds of an out-of-synch movie have caught up with each other. "I haven't heard from him," she says, "and don't say anything to your sister when you talk to her. It's a touchy subject with her. Have you heard from them? Your sisters? Because I wanted it to come from her, Annette, but you'll find out eventually."

"What?"

"Greg left. Another woman. Poor Annette is on her own now with all that she has to do."

"Oh no."

"You know how that feels. Remember?"

"I'll call her. I was going to call her anyway."

"Sure, that would be nice, honey. And don't forget that when you talk to Lawreen, don't say anything about Mattie, and especially don't say that I asked you not to. She hasn't spoken to me since I told her about Matt's visit."

"She's still mad?" Elfie pictures her oldest sister. Was there ever a time when she wasn't stressed? But she'd call her. She wants to call everybody.

"And you're really okay? Feeling fine?"

Here it is, the deep cushion Elfie has been able to sink into whenever she needed to, all her life. It has just taken Mom awhile.

ARE YOU SURE? SHE said. What a stupid thing to say. Of course Elfie would be sure.

It was bound to come one day, this news that breaks through Shinny like a foot breaks through a surface that appears solid but is sodden, infested, rotten underneath. For it is possible that Elfie's baby will display characteristics of his grandfather, the green-eyed man his grandmother slept with once, long ago, and never saw again. Funny, I wonder where the red hair comes from, someone will say, and Shinny will make up a story about an aunt, or a great-uncle, someone so far back in their ancestry that no one will be inclined to doubt her. This has been her strategy: to respond with great vagueness to Elfie's questions about why she's different from her sisters, the isn't-it-all-a-mystery attitude that has successfully allowed her to continue the lie that began when Smokey/John agreed to assume fatherhood for a child whose conception he had nothing to do with.

"Should I call your sisters, or do you want to? Lawreen's been hanging up when she hears my voice, but I could talk to Ken."

Elfie laughed. "She's still mad? I'll call her, Mom. I want to call everybody!"

So happy. And Shinny is too, except ... She steps onto the balcony. Many of the shrubs in the park are flowering, the big creamy magnolias, the ornamental cherries. It's that pink and white time in the city, fruit trees blossoming everywhere. She should let the season buoy her, as it always has. Elfie is surely old enough to hear the story of that night when her mother was still young, well, under forty, and impulse led her to join the crowds at the beach for the Sea Festival. She wouldn't do the same now, even in the unlikely event that she saw a man she wanted, but people do have sex impulsively, maybe even more often now than in those days. On the perfectmatch.com site that she hasn't checked for weeks, with everything else on her mind, there's an option to sign up for dating only, which is a euphemism for sex without complications. The same TV networks that spout purity and anti-abortion feature prime time reality shows where young people flirt with each other in hot tubs, doing God knows what beneath the foamy water their glossy breasts and pecs bob above. And despite the pious life-is-sacred views of the commentators on those networks, if anyone in the hot tub crowd gets pregnant, she aborts the child, which Shinny could have done, which Lawreen considered doing when she learned she was pregnant with Mattie.

The Singh-Gill family will be over the moon, the turbaned grandfather, the grandmother who dresses in bright saris; the more Canadianized parents, both teachers. The parents accepted Elfie, but Shinny suspects that the grandparents have needed the birth of a child to fully sign on. With her own family so scant and scattered, Elfie may even give the child a traditional Indian name, to please her in-laws. Harbinder or something. Harbinger.

Life is a wheel that collects bits in turning, and now each revolution is bumpy, requiring more power from Shinny to move forward.

John answers on the first ring. "Hey, I've been thinkin' of you."

"I guess you've heard from the Elf?"

"Just got off the phone with that sweet girl, but what, you worried again? Why don't you just come clean? Do you want me to tell her? Or us tell her together?"

"You mean like a conference call? I'm not sure what I'm going to do, but don't say anything until I decide. She'd really be mad then."

"There's a whole raft of kids born in this world who don't know who their real parents are, their dads anyway. Could be some soldier rapist fathered them, or some drunken politician, or egotistical jock. You worry about it too much."

"Not as much as I used to. Until today. Everything okay down there?"

"Funny you should ask. Because I've been thinkin' you should pay us a visit. The daughter who is mine is awful blue, and also mad, and she works around here like she's digging a grave for herself."

"I offered. She says she's managing fine, but that she's busy. That she doesn't have much time to talk on the phone. And she never emails."

"You wouldn't either, you had our setup. That's why you ought to come down. See for yourself."

"I will, as soon as I can get away. And I'll call more often. Not that she answers. A few weeks, okay? Meantime, keep your promise, Smokey. Sorry, John."

"I always keep my promises, babe."

Babe. But she can count on him. Mattie, Annette, now Elfie. All these hands tugging at her.

Tahir is ready to leave, his grey fleece jacket zipped to his throat, though it's too warm for that jacket.

"Okay, I'm here," she calls, and he nods and walks out the door without speaking, a slight rebuke for her slight tardiness. Customers dribble in with letters for her to process, but also large envelopes and a couple of parcels addressed to places she has never heard of. Some days she copies down place names and Googles them when she's home. The most rhythmic chant in her memory like the names of world leaders and hockey players, and lately Canadian soliders who have fallen, as they say, as if they were leaves instead of people. Phnom Penh, Arghandab, Tuukka Rask, Valtteri Filppula. Sean David Greenfield, Brian Richard Good, Dany

Olivier Fortin. Just as photos can convince you that you will keep an experience forever, names fool you into thinking that you somehow know a person, or a place.

Before Tahir returns, the tall man with the thick black eyebrows bulls through the door.

"Tahir?" He pronounces the name like Tahir's father does, accenting the last syllable.

"Tahir is out, but he'll be back in an hour or so. Can I help you?"

The eyebrows lower and tighten, pushing a furrow into the flesh between them.

"You could wait if you like?"

He stuffs the envelope he's carrying into his small bag and strides out without answering. "I'll tell him you stopped in," she calls. It is possible that he doesn't speak English, but he has to have passed a driver's test. And she did hear him cursing in English the day of the accident.

That night she sees the man's face in a dream. He is sitting at a table outside the market with Irene of the white-rimmed glasses and white hair, who is spooning into a tower of white ice cream while the man watches. Shinny seldom remembers dreams, but this one stays with her, the image of the two figures, one white, one brown. Instead of hopping out of bed to set the kettle on to boil, she lingers, thinking of Elfie and Brendan, their whiteness and brownness. It seems dark would prevail in the genes; brown eyes are supposed to dominate blue or green. The internet can help her; the internet has answers for everything. But not conclusive answers, she discovers, for many genes in incalculable combinations determine skin colour, hair and eye colour. And those are just the visible characteristics; the matter of who the child turns out to be, even harder to predict. People will say, oh she has your mother's eyes, or she's good at sports, like your uncle; ask, where does that stubbornness come from, as if each trait can be linked to a distinct source. Soon there may even be a way to determine which genes you want and which you don't want. Already, ultrasound informs prospective parents of their child's gender. In cultures where boys are still prized over girls, women who discover they're carrying girls actually abort them.

But here's another new name, in bold, in her inbox. *Dear ma'am,* it says. *I'm a friend of a girl you know? Kate Babcock? She said you were*

worried about your grandson going to Afghanistan, well, ma'am, she forward-
ed me your letter because she thought I could tell you how it is. Like Kate said,
she don't know if your grandson is over here. I never met anyone named Mat-
thew Webster but there's a lot of us here, you know- Like 2800. Not as many as
the Yanks or the Brits but we work the tough parts of the country. We're doing
are best and if your grandson does come over here he'll be doin the right thing.
But I see why you worry. My name is Kev and I've been stationed here in the
ghan for about two months from Edmonton. I got a girl there and when this is
done we're going to get married. All of us over here like to get news from home
ma'am and any letters are welcome. I can't tell you everything but I'll keep an
eye out for a guy called Matthew Webster and if I run into him I'll tell him his
family's worried about him, he ought to write.

Yours, Kev

She's a wonder, that Kate; so sweet, understanding Shinny's anxiety, wanting to help without being too obvious. Support our troops. Well now she has a personal connection. She'll send him cookies or something, if that's allowed. If Mattie knows that while she is worried she isn't mad at him, maybe he will feel freer to write. And maybe being over there is the right thing. Because the morning news shows a clip of distraught parents at a hospital in Charikar, at the bedsides of their white-veiled daughters who are being treated for the effects of poison gas fed into the school by the Taliban. Last year girls had acid thrown in their faces. Shocking that someone who calls himself a human being could do something like that. This is a degree of evil hard to comprehend; worse than the drug gangs in Vancouver, who mostly kill one another; worse than war, because in war, once it starts, anything can happen and people more or less accept it as a necessary consequence of the overall goal. Collateral damage. That odd term. Shinny thinks of collateral as what you offer to the bank as proof that you have assets to cover your loan. Those poor girls, collateral? What kind of lives will they face, the acid-scarred, the gassed, the raped?

Shinny could mention this if Elfie turns on her. It's not so bad, Elfie. I may have lied to you about your father, but at least you were able to get a good education, live with your boyfriend, travel freely. At least you were not gassed, or raped; no one threw acid in your face.

Yet, can you count yourself lucky if your life is not as horrible as it is for people elsewhere? Here women start from a higher platform; they don't expect their lives to be horrible. Here girls have the freedom to do anything they want, including getting themselves blown up in the same country where girls can't do anything they want. Killed, like the beautiful twenty-one-year-old trooper from Quebec, just last week. Karine.

Dear Kev. I was really surprised to get your letter and really happy to be in touch with someone over there. It feels so far away. You know I work for a guy from Afghanistan. I know from him how bad things can be ...

What else can she say? Will anything be censored? Maybe she should keep a lid on her opinions and tell him about spring in Vancouver instead. People rollerblading, winter-bleached feet in flip-flops for the first time. The white masts of sailboats turning a cantaloupe colour as they catch the rising sun.

JUST THE FACTS, PLEASE, we don't need the story of your life. Lawreen is trying to contain herself but she realizes there is a story of her life; she realized it last night when she was practicing what to say to the recruiting officer. Ken offered to make the trip, but because her office is downtown, it's easier for her. Besides, she doesn't trust Ken to press the case. If the officer or the receptionist or whomever it is you encounter when you drop into a recruiting office—if that person were to tell Ken that he is not free to give out such information, as the person on the phone told Lawreen, Ken might just accept that answer. Lawreen won't. It's her son. Even if he is twenty-two she has a right to know where he is, and it was hard enough to wait until the Monday after her mother's visit to call, only to be put off. She doesn't intend to wait any longer.

She's walking down Georgia Street, a brisk, sunny afternoon, daffodils and hyacinths blooming from concrete planters set into the recesses of forty-storey cement and steel, tinted-glass office buildings. Businessmen and women, but also young people on skateboards, and shoppers stream, roll or amble past her, but in her mind she is explaining herself to the recruiting officer and she can't help but start by mentioning her own father, Larry Blake, the teenage football sensation from Meadowvale? You're probably too young to remember him, officer. Or should she call him officer? His parents ran a big horse operation out in the valley? The reason I'm worried about my son is because my father fell to his death when he was just a teenager. Though Lawreen was more an embryo than even a fetus at that point, the trauma has narrated her existence. Her life story has been governed by the image of that handsome falling teenager; she thought her mother's was too. Or certainly had been. Now her mother must think of her life as a trilogy, each section connected with a man— Larry, Smokey, Glen.

If the recruiting officer understands Lawreen's traumatic beginnings, he will be more likely to help her track down her son. A good boy, but he dropped out of university. He was troubled, you must know the kind. Still waters running deep, and the last the family heard of him he was thinking of joining the Forces. All she wants to know is if he has joined up, and where he is. He always admired the Canadian Forces, she will say, because that will surely also help her case, although Lawreen doesn't know this to be true. Maybe Mattie admired the Forces, maybe not. She doesn't know. The guilt rises again, water in a plugged up sink, and leaks out in tears that she blots with the back of one hand as she pushes on the oblong brass handle of the glass door and enters the lobby. During the day, at work, she generally is able to leave her anxiety behind, a demanding pet she returns to at night; but today is different. She is venturing out on a limb, for her son.

According to Google, the recruiting office is on the 8th floor, and though she doesn't see it listed in the building directory, she nevertheless enters the first elevator that opens and presses the button numbered eight. The doors close, but the elevator remains stationary. After a few seconds, the door opens again, to the lobby. This doesn't seem to work, she complains to the woman who enters, a woman of her tribe, a middle-ish age, similarly dressed in a well-cut, shower-proof coat, high but not stiletto heels, concealer that doesn't quite cover the grey eye bags. Everyone seems to have something keeping them awake at night. "Try again," says the woman. "You should get a red light. Here, let me try," she says, and does, but no luck again. "Maybe you can't access eight?"

"Thank you anyway," says Lawreen to the woman, who steps out on three. She presses L and rides back down, taps over a shiny black floor to the building directory. No eighth floor listed here at all, though the address was clear, had a map attached. Canadian Forces Recruiting, 8th floor, 1040 Georgia Street. She took a late lunch to do this! Fuck, she says, silently. She is someone who swears not in front of people, but in her mind, in her own company. Tears threaten to flood her eyes again, but she can't let herself cry in public.

While it is too early to return to her office, there isn't enough time to track down a phone directory and find another recruiting office. Annoying and sad. She continues east on Georgia, then turns south on Granville, for the distraction, the exercise, to fill the hour she has taken for lunch. The sushi and crepe shops, the cafés, salad bars, none of them tempt her, but she does look at the street kids loitering in doorways, one of them sitting right on the pavement, between his legs a small dog he's grooming with a comb meant for people. Could be a boy or a girl, a head full of dreadlocks, a loose plaid shirt. He or she should be wearing something warmer; the sidewalk could not be anything but clammy this early in the season, despite the sun. Mattie would not stoop to this. He is clean-cut, university educated. He hasn't asked them for money, not since he left home to share a place with Berk, the overly friendly Turkish boy. So enthusiastic the time she invited him for dinner. A beautiful house, Mrs. ... Can I help you with dinner? He stood in the kitchen talking to her the whole time she whisked batter for the Yorkshire pudding, drizzled beef drippings into the muffin tin, tossed the salad. Mattie disappeared to his old room. She made a big effort for Mattie and his friend, a traditional Canadian Sunday dinner, something she thought Mattie's Turkish friend would enjoy. Then Berk turned out to be as Canadian as any of them, and Mattie, although he had eaten his share and thanked her, and hugged her before he left—hugged her warmly, as she remembers—had not been any more forthcoming than usual about his life or his plans.

She turns left at Robson and walks east again, and in the block before the library she sees the white gleam that pushes Mattie back in the queue of her thoughts. White with black lettering: mobile dressing rooms. Closer, she finds thick twines of black cable duct-taped to the sidewalk, a galvanized steel bucket block-lettered "BUTTS". In the shadow of the library itself, threesomes, couples, all young, all wearing jeans. Gofers, actors. You can't tell the difference unless someone wears heavy makeup, or unless they are stars. Lawreen will not gawk; these location shoots once tested her patience, for the dressing rooms were not as comfortable as those in-studio, and the food served up by catering was frequently cold when it should be hot, or the other way round. She is about to cross the street when a young man stops her. "Excuse me, ma'am?" She hates that. She doesn't feel like a ma'am. "Would you mind waiting a—just a minute." He is wearing a vest in neon green and listening to something on his headset, his eyebrows raised in pause mode. "Okay two minutes. We don't mind you walking through, but they don't want anyone wearing coats."

"Sure, I know. Continuity," she says, tilting her head. "I'll wait, oh, but is Paul on this shoot? Paul Reljic?"

"Paul Reljic? I don't know. You could probably get a crew list."

"I'll just give him a shout later, if I don't hear from him first. He usually calls when he's in town."

She can't see the camera operator from where she stands. The equipment van blocks the scene.

"You know, maybe I'll just cross the street. But if you do run into Paul, tell him Lawreen Webster said hi. Just in case I can't reach him, I mean."

She retraces her steps along Robson, past the shoe shop where she generally stops to look for sales, past the 7-Eleven, the Telus store. A moment of sunny optimism gilds her interior landscape. When she returns to her office she will check to see what films are shooting in Vancouver this week; she will search for crew lists. If Paul is here she will hatch an excuse to meet. But the squall returns, as squalls tend to do in the spring. Matthew.

Could she use Matthew as an excuse? If Paul had shot a war movie? If he had contacts in the Canadian Forces? Mariah would be more plausible. Paul, hi! I heard you were here, and listen. You remember Mariah? Yeah, the cute one. She's in L.A. now. Flown the coop! Yeah, they do have to spread their wings, believe me, I know. Ha, ha. But, well I guess you wouldn't have seen her, exactly, but have you heard of an indie producer named …What was the name? She can't check on Facebook because Mariah has changed her password. Instead she'll open Mariah's IMDb profile page and look up the name of the company before she calls Paul, if Paul is really in town shooting. I just want to make sure it's legit because, well, you know, she's a beautiful girl and you hear these stories. Of course she's experienced, she can handle herself, but still … Oh yes, we mothers …

It has been her identity: Mariah's mother. For years she was introduced not by her name, but by her reason for being on set: this is Jake, Steve,

Mariah, and this is Mariah's mother. No matter how old your kids get to be, that's who you are; you can't escape it. She'll put on that same cloak when she phones the recruiting office again and complains about the misinformation regarding location. Hello, I'm calling about my son. Or, hello, I'm calling about a young man named Matthew Webster. I'm his mother. God! Why does she feel like she has to brush something off her shoulder when she speaks that phrase? No, she won't call. Not until she emails. People email; if she calls she will certainly be referred to the website, or to a menu of choices, none of which are likely to be, "if you're calling about a lost boy, press ..." But when she wakes up her computer by tapping the space bar, she sees a spam warning and a *Hi Mom* in her inbox. From a sender who uses numbers instead of a name to identify himself. Could this be him?

WHEN THEY FIRST SETTLED in New York, Elfie studied websites and papers for news of free events, because Brendan had secured only one class at the school of music and had to bartend to supplement their income while Elfie advertised for students. She found plenty of opportunities to spend more time than money. Art gallery openings; the roof of the Met, where they idled one evening watching smog-filtered sunset approach, daubing smoky oranges and purples on the rooftop sculptures: the glass wall with replicas of dead birds at its base; the huge crocodiles bristling with pointed objects seized from airports. Summer stage at Central Park, music from everywhere in the world, and open air concerts at Lincoln Center where overflow crowds prepared for cement slab seating by bringing their own cushions. If you were too far back to see the musicians, you could find entertainment in human and animal vignettes: once, a pigeon that landed in a reflecting pool as if it had forgotten that it lacked webbed feet.

Food bargains, the market at Union Square. If she appeared to be a serious buyer, a vendor might offer her a French radish, or a cube of fresh bread one week; slices of a heritage apple, or a homemade cheese the next. Elfie made sure never to visit the same stall twice in a month, and to carry a shopping bag, filled with inexpensive potatoes and greens, which showed vendors that she had not come to freeload.

They eyed the lineups on Avenue A the day the Bethel Mission hand-ed out bags of food, but they never got so low they had to join them.

Brendan nicked leftovers from the kitchen of his restaurant, Cucina de Pesce: crusty loaves and vegetables that would otherwise be tossed in the garbage, sometimes a soup. At the end of the first semester he was not only rehired, but offered a second class, plus the opportunity to work with the junior student quartet, which brought an additional stipend. Elfie signed up her first private student, Jane.

It became easier to make basic expenses, but they still looked for entertainment bargains, Shakespeare in the Park, new friends. Jane wanted to learn the violin in order to play with her daughter, who was enrolled in a school music program. The lessons didn't last, but Jane became a coffee pal and encouraged Elfie to try yoga, at a free try-out session. Jane didn't last at that either, but Elfie continued to attend when she could get the money together. She liked the stretching, the breathing, the spiritual messages her teacher, Tara, imparted. Now she has arranged a swap: violin lessons for yoga sessions, not with the lovely, serene teacher, but with Tara's 11-year-old son River, who rings the buzzer and stomps up the stairs on East 10th each Wednesday after school. River, who dutifully courses through the channels his mother has dredged for him, seldom influenced by the immediate terrain. The stair stomping, which neighbours have complained about, is the only sign that he hates what he's doing. Otherwise River is polite; he opens his book, he plays with some competence the song assigned, he sighs. Elfie congratulates him. Very good, River. I bet you want to move onto the next one. River shrugs. Sure, I guess. His eyes wander around the apartment, over the music stand to the brick wall the desk is shoved against. To the Tintoretto on the wall, the bare-breasted woman with her legs open. The desk with its computer, the screen black during lessons. He would almost surely rather be playing computer games, but he dutifully turns the page, "Song of the Wind". "Ok, River, this is the melody," Elfie says, picking up her own violin and playing the tune for him, so that he knows what he's aiming to produce. He listens, his narrow, white face expressionless, picks up his own violin and follows. Some talent, but no desire. You can teach someone, but you can't make them want to learn. Yet she perseveres because she wants to continue yoga once a week.

In the dim practice space that Tara uses, a skylight frames a postage-stamp view of the Flatiron Building and the sky around it—often cloudy, but sometimes, through and above the clouds, a clear section that appears to Elfie like a portal to another world. She arrives early to claim a spot directly underneath the skylight, if possible, but not so early that Tara can engage her in discussion about River. She rolls out her mat, places her blanket, belt and block beside her, lies down and inhales for ten counts, exhales for ten, while Tara chats softly with the other regulars, accepts cash from the drop-ins. Elfie tunes out the live voices and tunes into whatever music Tara has chosen to score the session. Look for the space between the thoughts, Tara advises. But those spaces are flickers Elfie barely perceives before another thought blocks them. Thoughts of Brendan, of the baby. They think it will be a boy; they're already calling him Johann. Should we have Johann sleep in our bed? Should we have a family bed? Brendan thinks it would be derelict to make love with a baby beside them. Or she thinks of Mother, who's in California now, trying to comfort Annette. *I've forgotten how quiet it is here*, she wrote. Just that one email because the dial-up connection is so slow. There has never been anything slow about Mom; it must be driving her crazy. But mostly her thoughts drift to Brendan, who has been in a funk since his team was knocked out of the playoffs.

"Come on, *piccolo mio*. There's always next year."

"Next year it will be some other reason we don't make it to the final."

He expects her to understand, to sympathize, though it's her mother who is the hockey fan, who waited to visit California until she was sure her "boys" as she calls them were not going any further this season.

Tara asks everyone to sit and put their hands on their hearts and start the session with three oms. The vibrations rib Elfie's chest, her throat. Does Johann feel it? she wonders. Hear it? The first position is Biralasana, the cat pose, to loosen up the spine. Elfie can't imagine doing this when Johann is bigger; she can't imagine her spine being strong enough to support a lump of bulging baby, a branch pulled down by a nest. The image makes her smile as her back dips, then arches. For now she feels as if she's barely pregnant. She's still slim; the little fellow is sprouting limbs, features, stretching her insides first.

It's more than the loss of his team that is bothering Brendan, she knows; he doubts himself. An image of oceans merging sparked his idea, the working title, Atlantic/Pacific. The music will be based on the legend of the demon who once kept the oceans apart. Water spirits yearning for one another, pushed by the wind, eventually defeated the demon, which froze into the black rock known as Cape Horn. The demon's anger at his defeat is reflected in the skyscraping waves pushed by gales that defy sailors still.

In the proposal for the piece, Brendan described the way he intended to use instruments from east and west to create musical imagery that would express the difficulty of cultures joining. Ping's violin would repeat a phrase that evoked persistence. But the instrumentation he imagined seems facile to Brendan now, obvious, a new music cliché. People say that the average listener doesn't hear individual instruments so much as the music as a whole, but that is because the composer has been able to blend the elements in his control. Brendan wants to do more than demonstrate his talent for orchestral composition. While the instrumentation makes sense, fusion has become a contemporary commonplace; there are fusion restaurants, fusion film/plays; jazz/classical fusion, rock/everything fusion. Yet to evoke the violence of icebergs crashing, scraping, the gales that blew the spirits towards one another and wore the rock away, he needs more percussion, and to complement the variety of stringed instruments he described in his proposal, he wants diverse surfaces for diverse tools to beat upon: sticks, bones, frame drums, darabukas, tablas. He wants chimes, kettle drums. Not the machine noises that have become fashionable, or the sounds of everyday life more and more composers employ. In his way, in his heart, he is traditional, and it is partly this that is behind his struggle. Can he pull off something as complex as he imagines? When Elfie asks how it's going, he wanders away: "You know I hate it when you ask that." For the same reason, he has been avoiding Ping. It's a matter of waiting for the reality to catch up with the conception, which has happened before, but he doesn't trust that it will happen always. At home he surfs YouTube for versions of various pieces he has admired; he brings his laptop to his borrowed studio. He visits Asian community centres to listen to concerts by masters of the erhu and the pipa, the sitar, the koto. He went through a period of listening to various harpists. He considers cymbals. Turns to his cello as children turn to a comforting blanket, and the water imagery he is aiming to create comes out in long honey strings, bowing that reminds Elfie of the suite he wrote in Milan, which was inspired by the waves curling up the cliffs along the Ligurian Coast.

When she opens her eyes after shavasana, rain is silvering down onto the skylight, splashing into stars as it hits. The rain makes her hungry. Though a wholly un-yoga-like craving, she will pick up deli food on her way home. Pastrami on rye and a side of pickles; coleslaw, too. Brendan may not even notice what they eat, and so far, nothing has disagreed with her. In almost three months she has gained five pounds, but the rounded stomach she is waiting for has yet to appear.

June

Lawreen printed out the only email she's had from him. That was a month ago.

Hey, Mom. Sorry I just kind of like disappeared. We'll talk about it someday, I promise, but to keep it short, everything just got to be too much. I wanted to get away. But I'm fine, and if you were worried about me, I'm sorry. But I'm fine. Just taking a break, thinking about things. I'll get back in touch when I settle down somewhere, okay? Hope you and dad and Gran and Mariah are fine. Tell Gran I'm sorry.

Love, Matthew

No sign of where he is, what he's doing. No opportunity to write back because the 567340@hotmail.com bounced back to her when she tried to reply. But it helped that he wrote. Lawreen is still so angry with her mother that she does not intend to pass on Mattie's apology, but it's comforting to know that he seems to be in control, and if he joined the army, he didn't say. He would have said so if he had. She can't see him in the army; she just can't see it.

Ken thinks he's in Mexico. Remember how he tried to speak Spanish to the chambermaids? What was it he learned to say?

The first out-of-country trip they could afford to take as a family. Mariah was already flying by then, having made a commercial that won a prize, then having to sign an agreement—Lawreen actually signed for her—that she wouldn't take any other commercials, because those were the years when Movies of the Week were frequently filmed in Vancouver, and Mariah was cast more than once as the child involved in whatever story it was. One of them captured an Emmy. That sparked the celebration. The whole family was thriving: Lawreen had arranged flexible work hours, Ken accepted a junior partnership at his accounting firm, Mariah's career was soaring, and Matt didn't provide so much as a speed bump for the rest of the family's forward progress. He seemed happy enough; he did well in school.

They opted for an all-inclusive resort near Puerto Vallarta, a recommendation from one of Ken's colleagues who thought the place good value for money. Three pools. More than three restaurants. Unlimited drinks. The colleague had not mentioned the magenta bougainvillea that fountained over plaster walls painted ochre and peach, the clipped hedges, the trumpet vines, bowls of fruit for the taking. A perfect week. Mariah tanned, but because Lawreen religiously lathered her with sunblock, she didn't tan too deeply. Mattie wandered from pool to pool; he and Mariah took themselves to the gazebo where a cook in a white jacket would make them a *hamburgesa* any time they wanted. Both kids said *hola* unselfconsciously, but Matt actually tried conversing. He learned the phrase for how do you say, *como se dice en espanol*, and would hold up a candy or a drink to one of the maids or the yard boys. When a vendor stopped at the chairs on the beach, Mattie surprised Lawreen by asking, *cuanto cuesta*, and understanding the reply, *diez pesos*. A perfect week.

He could be in Mexico, and if he is, it's clear that he wants to be left alone there. At least that worry is off her mind, for now. Not so much Mariah, who was going to nip home for a visit, then decided not to, and has coyly resisted the hints Lawreen drops about flying down to visit her for a weekend. Lawreen could take a Friday off; it's a quick flight to L.A. They could hang out, as they used to.

"That would be great, Mom. I'd love it! Thing is, I've got a workshop this weekend, can we try for another one?"

Always sweet, but not as forthcoming as she could be. "Oh, Mom; this shouldn't be so hard, but my friend Heidi's getting married. Maybe you could come to the wedding, but I don't know. I kind of hate to ask. She's sort of a new friend? How 'bout next month?"

Too bad about Facebook. Though it is obvious Mariah changed her password, Lawreen still tries now and then to gain access to her page, but only an enticing picture of Mari comes up, and the message, *Sorry, but*

Mariah shares information only with certain people. Rebuked by a Facebook page!

Lawreen is edging the flowerbeds with a crescent-bladed tool as these thoughts tunnel through her head. According to the pamphlet the doctor gave her, and also a website she consulted, gardening calms the nerves. If it doesn't do the trick, she can turn to the mild anti-anxiety pills he prescribed. She has not resorted to them often, so it is hard to account for the sleepiness, the slight disorientation she feels, unless it's the antihistamine she took to control the allergies she has developed. A crystalline Vancouver late spring day. The buzz of Ken's electric pruning shears obliterates birdsong, but not the imagined voice of her daughter. Of course everyone wants to leave home; everyone has to grow up. Lawreen certainly wanted to leave home, and it had been thrilling to set up her apartment, her own place, all to herself. She could have lived there for years, in the West End —something she had dreamed of as a teenager, when she hated sharing a room with Annette, all Annette's junk, Mom's second-hand everything. Barely enough matching plates to set the table for dinner. Escaping that life is what motivated her to save. She was just getting things to where she wanted them when she found out she was pregnant. Not like Elfie, who has been living the high life since she graduated from university. And she graduated from university, which Lawreen didn't.

Inside the pocket of her shorts, Lawreen's cell phone rings. She looks towards Ken, who is wearing earphones, so won't hear her, and instead of asking him to turn off the trimmer, she jogs up the steps and inside the house to answer a caller whose number she doesn't recognize. At least it's not Annette. All Lawreen did was try to be sisterly, to tell Nettie that men who stray once are likely to stray again, so she shouldn't even consider taking Greg back. "Did I ask your advice?" Annette replied, in an unnecessarily snarky tone. Lawreen hasn't bothered calling since then, and when she saw Annette's number last weekend, she let the call go to voicemail.

Normally she does not answer calls from people whose numbers aren't filed in her phone's memory, but with both Mattie and Mariah God knows where, Lawreen has to take the chance. A deep voice, coming from a throat that could be lined with velvet, asks if she's Lawreen Webster. She knows who it is before the speaker identifies himself, but, not wanting to seem too eager, she says, "Yes, this is Lawreen."

"Hey, Lawreen. It's Paul Reljic. I got a message from you."

"Paul! Oh my God, but that was ages ago. I didn't actually leave a message; I just asked one of the PAs if you were working on a shoot I happened to pass. It was nothing. Just thought I'd say hi."

"Well I'm glad you did. That same guy's working on the shoot I'm here to do this week. How's that little beauty of yours?"

"Oh, Mariah. Yeah, well the thing is, Paul, she's gone looking for greener pastures. You know how it is; she's down on your stomping grounds now; she moved to L.A."

"Oh yeah, bright lights, big city, huh?"

It's so easy, this banter, like an old song they both know, any meaning diluted by the forgettable words. She's going to make some coffee to counteract the effect of the antihistamine. For now she struggles through a fretwork of bees buzzing behind her eyes to summon her brightest mood.

"Exactly. In fact I was thinking of asking you if you'd seen her. That's why I wondered if you were on that shoot. I mean, I know it would be a needle in a haystack type thing, but …"

"Well you're right there. There's a million beautiful girls in L.A., not that your Mariah doesn't have a special spark. You outta touch or something?"

"Not exactly that, Paul. It's kind of hard to explain. I'm … Well I can't really discuss it over the phone. Are you busy?"

She brings her coffee into the bathroom and showers for the second time that day and lathers herself with body lotion; fusses with her short hair to create the illusion that a playful breeze has disturbed it. She chooses a mint green sundress with thin straps, a white shrug to keep her shoulders warm, and black flip-flops which display her pumiced and creamed feet and also say, I'm not dressing up for this.

"See you in a bit," she shouts to Ken. He raises his head, nods. He's wearing protective goggles that obliterate the top third of his face, and with the clippers still running and headphones on, he cannot have heard what she said, but it hardly matters. Married for nearly a quarter of a century, they come and go from one another, vaguely knowing where and why. The consistent daily decision has to do with dinner, and who is going to cook, because Ken does, on occasion; or if they are going to bother. If they don't bother, Ken snacks through the evening, a cheese sandwich, a dish of pickles. A handful of nuts. A banana. Cookies. Although he exercises as much as she does, Ken is gaining weight. Not the beer belly some men acquire—he's not much of a drinker—but layers have accrued each year, thickening him. He's wearing safari shorts and a white t-shirt littered with bits of twigs and leaves. Lawreen honks as she's backing her car out of the garage, and as he turns to wave she notices a cut on his cheek, a slash of dried blood.

Downtown she steers into the underground parking lot of Paul Reljic's hotel. More expensive than street parking, but direct, and she won't have to worry about feeding the meter. But she hates underground parking. The oil stains on the cement. The possibility that an earthquake could trap her here. The whole weight of the building? She'd surely die. Another thing, someone could be lurking behind a pillar, as they do in movies. A perfect opportunity for a thief, a rapist.

Her face shows no trace of these concerns as she strides, with as much dignity as she can stride in flip-flops, through the posh, hard-edged lobby, with its indirect lighting, its angular chairs, stainless steel tables, odd arrangements of copper tubing instead of flowers in the waist-high black vases that flank the floor to ceiling mirrors. There's no reason to be nervous; he's just an old movie acquaintance, and she a concerned mother. That she is unhinged, literally off the join that connects her to herself, is something she won't acknowledge. A relief to see him seated on a red lounge chair at a shiny black table. He hasn't made her wait; she hasn't had to wonder if he would stand her up.

"Paul, there you are," she says, as if she has been looking for him, and holds her face forward for him to kiss. It's what people do in the movie business, and while she hasn't associated with movie types for much of the last year, longer, it's easy to slip back into the gestures. She feels the scratch of his three-day beard. The smell of him, recently showered, recently anointed with some men's cologne—subtle, but deep, a leathery scent. She has forgotten that he is shorter than she is.

"So," she begins.

It's girlish, stupid. She's out of practice. On set, her reason for being there grounded her. She and Paul might have flirted a little, true, but only to play. He must do it all the time. The last thing she wants to appear is needy, a gawker, someone who doesn't know what's up. When he asks her if she'd like iced chai, the question sounds as if it is coming from very far away. And when she replies, her own voice comes out more loudly than she intended.

"Chai? That sounds perfect. You read my mind."

Talking will have to power her through the awkwardness; there's no turning back now. She imagines him a client, someone to whom she is explaining the serious business of risk management.

"Thank you for seeing me, Paul. I don't know if you can help, but like I said on the phone, I'm worried about Mariah. She's been evasive. And we've always been close."

"Little birds must fly."

"Oh, I know. And it was time. We encouraged her to spread her wings, but Paul …"

The tears that come into her eyes are real. His head dips to the right.

"She's been vague, talking about indies. Could it be porn?"

"A girl like her doesn't have to do porn. Maybe mama's getting a little overprotective? You know you gotta let go."

He reaches for her arm and squeezes, between the elbow and the wrist, then moves his hand away. Lawreen blinks. She liked the feel of his hand on her arm, a damp, calloused hand. A manly hand.

"No, no. I agree. It's not that. I was just hoping you could give me some names. It's hard to find the indie scene in L.A. on the web. At least I haven't had any luck. If I could check out their websites, if I saw her name."

He's frowning, withdrawing? Thinking her some hysterical woman? She doesn't want this to be over. She breathes deeply, imagines a lazy river. More techniques she found in the pamphlet her doctor gave her. She straightens up, shrugs her shoulders as if saying, what's the big deal?

"Just a website referral, Paul, I'm not trying to play secret agent here, but what are you in town for? Is it big? Have you been working through all the ups and downs in the biz?"

He comes to. The client explaining his perfect claim record. Paul gets as much work as he wants, but that's just it. All he does is work, and as he lists his recent projects she can see that he is one of those people whose way of bragging is to disparage the fact that he is in demand. It spreads to her, this attitude of, I'm beset, but what can you do? She likes it; it applies. They talk and talk, they reminisce about the shoots he worked on that Mariah also worked on. They order a second chai, and then it's evening and if she doesn't leave, he will have to ask her to dinner. One of her flip-flops falls off her bouncing foot. But she doesn't notice because he has his BlackBerry out and asks for her email address and promises to send her some links. When she starts to stand, she has to stab the floor with her bare foot to find her flip-flop. God knows what's on the floor, but it feels sticky. Honey? Bacon grease? She can't clean her foot in public. He is already on his way to the lobby. She toes into the flip-flop and catches up, and when they part at the elevator, he holds her shoulders and kisses her on both cheeks again, as he did when she arrived. This time the touch of his skin on hers flicks a switch as if the power has been restored after an outage. Everything's humming, again. Ciao, she calls, as the elevator door begins to close.

JOHN IS STANDING IN the baggage claim area at the San Francisco International Airport, countrified, but with shreds of his hippie past. Train engineer overalls, a red bandana around his forehead, his white and yellow beard tickling a chest thrust up by the belly that stretches the stripes on the denim. His hairline receded when he was in his forties. Less in front, more in back. When he hugs her she smells laundry soap and man sweat. Is this different? The name John suits the laundry soap. What else will she discover here, in his territory? That he walks more slowly and unevenly than she remembers him doing at Christmas, for one thing.

"Did you hurt your leg?"

"Time's hurtin' it, babe. Knees, you know."

She knew it was going to be John not Annette who picked her up; Annette is too busy to leave the farm in the morning. Shinny doesn't mind because the ride back will give her time to talk to him about Elfie. Always an impatient driver, he carries on a running monologue addressed to cars in adjoining lanes. It is not until he navigates traffic heading north, until they cross the Golden Gate Bridge, that he settles to the point where they can actually converse. He cleaned up the car for her benefit. The passenger seat is brushed, stains covered with a red wool square of blanket, and the dashboard empty of what will collect there over the next few days: receipts, candy bar wrappers, binder twine, a pocket knife.

"Eve and Aidan are doing okay?" she starts, as they pass between the low hills that border the 101 North. Shinny loves the oak trees spread in clumps across the tawny grass. She used to imagine that Africa looked like that, except that the spreading trees would be more exotic than oaks.

"Yeah, I think they're doing okay, considering they're growing up without their mom. 'Course Nettie makes up a lot for that. But you know, is it fair to lay that on her?"

"And you've never heard from Oona? She's just disappeared?"

"Looks like," he says.

Shinny thinks of the people she has known that have dropped off the usual radar, really every kind of screen: her old friend Tina, her old bosses, Randy Stone, then Anthony. Elfie's true father. Now Mattie.

"Mattie, too, and Lawreen won't even talk to me since I told her about his visit. Ken thinks he's in Mexico."

"If they're not worried, you should let it go. He's their boy."

"I just hope he's okay."

"Well of course you do, babe."

"Have you tried Facebook? For Oona, I mean. They've got a friend finder. Have the kids tried, do you think? At least they know her name."

John laughs at the notion of Oona signing onto something as conventional as Facebook, even using a computer. But it's over eight years since he has seen her. Things change, Shinny argues. Maybe, he concedes. They are talking, as they have been able to do easily, for the most part, for the forty some years since they met in Vancouver, Stanley Park, her a young mother, a Lady Madonna, he called her, after one of The Beatles' songs. As they cruise towards the Sebastopol exit, he fills her in on Greg and the cheesemaker's visiting sister, who has extended her stay. A girl in her twenties, a new university graduate, something to do with the environment, who thinks Greg the cat's ass. John can't excuse Greg for walking out on Annette, but neither can he understand what a twenty-three-year-old, supposedly smart, well-educated girl can see in Greg.

"Of course we're biased," Shinny reminds him.

"Damn right we are."

When Shinny first visited John's place it was blossom time; along the highway she saw orchard after orchard, as fluffy and pink as a gathering of ballerinas in tutus. It's later in the season now, not the same flowery setting, and many of the orchards have been felled to make room for vineyards.

"Greg's trading on his folksy farmer image to impress a chick who has stars in her eyes about the country life. Damn it! Will you look at that? The fuckin' gentrification of Sonoma County?"

He bangs the steering wheel with his fist as they pass a hillside barren except for the stripes of young grapevines, a palatial redwood and stone house under construction on the site where a clapboard cottage painted yellow and nearly hidden by wisteria vine used to nestle. It's another world, his territory, and not one that has the power to rile her as it does him, but when she steers the conversation back to her worries about Mattie, John only reminds her that it's typical of her to worry about someone in her brood; that's what it means to brood over your flock. That even if Mattie has joined up, which he hopes not, because no war is justified, more people are being killed in drug wars in Vancouver than Canadian soldiers in Afghanistan. As someone who lives downtown, she should be worried about herself more than Mattie. He drives on, opining as he tends to do, on subjects he can't know much about. The road narrows as forests replace farmland, and he pulls into a strip of town near the Russian River.

"Look there, babe, remember that clock?"

Occidental seems bigger to her, but not so big that it has lost its charm. John tends to forget that she never lived in California, that his memories are not hers, though it's true that she has stopped for Italian food here every time she has visited. He smoothes his ponytail and checks his fingernails and is out the door, opening Shinny's side before she can do it herself.

"I can never pass this place without picking something up, which we could do, or just stay for lunch so Nettie doesn't have to bother."

That he makes it a kindness for Annette persuades Shinny. He leads them to a table in the back of the restaurant and the waitress comes with menus, but he doesn't need to look at something he knows by heart.

"Just bring us two of the house red and your special pizza. You need a salad?"

Shinny lets him take over. He knows what he wants; no change there. The waitress returns with the wine and basket of home-baked breadsticks, which she sets on the classic red-checked tablecloth. John raises his glass to the new grandbaby.

"You're happy aren't you?"

"Well sure I'm happy, but you know."

"You can't be worried about that old business. What scares you?"

Ironically, considering the name he used for so many years, there are no shades of grey for Smokey/John: you tell her, you don't tell her, and the truth that she was conceived during a casual one-night stand, that her mother has been lying to her for thirty years, none of this relates. You do what you have to do and then you do the next thing. The agenda presents itself.

"You think she'll hate you?"

"Do you think she will?"

"You're everything to her. Sorry to say, I wasn't there much."

"I know, but she's been thinking I'm one person, and now she's going to see a side of me she never expected. That's part of it. But her, too. She thinks she's yours. Remember at Christmas? She stood next to you in front of the mirror, looking for some similarity, something that would make her more your daughter. I'm sure that's what she was doing. I was watching from the hallway. I saw her blow her cheeks out. I heard her say, when I get fat I'm going to look a lot like you, Dad."

"Yeah, and then I punched her."

"She'll feel … I don't know."

"Don't get ahead of yourself. She'll be shocked, sure, but she'll come around. You want me to fly out there with you? We tell her together?"

"Now? While she's pregnant? What if it really destroyed her? She could miscarry. She'd hate me even more. Now I know how those lying politicians feel. The cover-up just makes things worse. I should have told her a long time ago but everything was going so easily. It's been so long, maybe I'll just let it go again?"

She's looking for permission, but here's the waitress already, with the pizza. John takes a quick bite, kisses his pudgy fingertips, and sends the kiss to the waitress with an open palm.

"Try it, Shin. I'm not kidding. You haven't tasted better."

The food will be a distraction, and if he has not actually encouraged her to continue the lie, she's comfortable as he can make her feel, as if he has everything under control, that whatever it was will be all right, especially after a feed such as this. It's the way his eyes bathe her, water from a brown, slow-moving river, with gold leaves floating on it, like streams in the fall, like the persistence of the extraordinary in simple lives such as theirs. Like the eyes of their daughter Annette, who is worried to the point of anger when they rattle down the driveway just ahead of the school bus.

"Finally," she says. "Where were you?" When Shinny goes to hug her, Nettie keeps her arms to her sides, and then Aidan and Eve run down from the bus stop and Shinny gives them the maple leaf lollipops she bought at the Vancouver airport. John excuses himself to change clothes, and Shinny realizes that despite his appearance, he dressed for his trip to the city.

"Pretty as ever here, honey. You know your dad. He had to stop at Occidental, he had to order wine. Just one glass. But then another. We should have called. You're doing such a good job here! All these animals!"

John is right; Nettie doesn't look good. Grey wires spring through her hair and she's more pale than she should be for someone who spends so much time outdoors. Pale for Annette, whose skin is naturally darker than Shinny's, than Lawreen's and Elfie's. Ashy bags under her big, round eyes. Above her lip a mustache that will thicken as she approaches menopause. In a white cotton tunic top, which she must have put on for the occasion of her mother's arrival, she looks slimmer than when Shinny saw her at Christmas.

"I have something for you," she says, digging into her suitcase for the hand cream especially made for gardeners. Annette softens with the present; her guard is dropping. Shinny scoops her middle daughter's head down onto her shoulder, grateful that Nettie lets herself be held this time. It is the time for crying, if there is crying to be done. John thinks there is, that Annette has been waiting to let go until Shinny was there to catch her. But no tears come.

"So you're all right, honey? You're managing? It's not too bad without him?"

Annette sighs, and the slowness with which she raises her head makes Shinny think she would like to have cuddled longer. In the distance, the goats thunder down the stony hillside; something has spooked them.

"It's just something in the woods. Could be a dog, a bird. Maybe a coyote. Sometimes they just run without knowing what they're running from. Crazy animals. You can see I'm managing, Mom. It's okay." Why did John think a visit so important? What if Mattie shows up at his

Grandma's apartment and she's not there? What about the job? Sima will be working more, and how will she be able to juggle everything she has to juggle? There's no TV reception here, and the old computer has a dial-up connection. She'll have to be patient, but she'll check every day, her link to Kate, to Kev, to the world she isn't ready to let go, even for a week. And she'll have to do it while Annette is busy with chores, to pretend to give her middle daughter the whole of her affection. It's why she came. Yet the week begins to feel as if it will pass too slowly; this shallow bowl surrounded by forested hills, more a stockade than the pastoral scene it appears to be. She waves a fly away and takes a deep breath. It reminds her of Meadowvale. Grandpa's farm, his cows. The vomity smell of warm milk. Manure. Grandpa listening to Beethoven on the radio in the barn. Elfie's musical gifts could have come from him.

"Sometimes it's not okay, though. Well, what can I do?"

As if she heard Shinny's thoughts, and like a patient who calls the doctor with a complaint that is groundless by the time of the appointment, Annette wonders aloud if she really feels better or only thinks she does.

THE LANDLORD KNOCKED ON his door yesterday to ask his plans. "Hey, Randy, if you stay the more I need cheques."

"Yeah, sure. I'll check with my boss. Let you know this afternoon?"

The landlord, Ali, a short, tidy man wearing a blue-striped business shirt whenever Mattie has seen him, says, "Sure man. End of day is fine."

Now Matt has to decide if he wants to continue hiding out here for a few more months or move on, but where to? That's the problem. This empty apartment feels like home. When it isn't raining he can see Mount Seymour across the Inlet, and the container loading dock, the big ships waiting for loads. Maersk. Hanjin. CNB Sakura. At certain angles, the cranes make Ts, some of them with long stems and disproportionately short crossbars. To the left, the Sea Bus shoots across the Inlet, from south shore to north shore and back all day, a waterborne boomerang. To the right, beyond the grain silos, cars and trucks stream over the Second Narrows Bridge. The mountain range behind all that, sometimes purple beneath a blue sky, sometimes black shapes in a night that is never entirely dark.

No one has spotted him. He got his Mom off his case by writing her from an email address he deleted immediately. Kate and Grandma are getting along; he has to stop himself from writing too much, though. Kate's going to school, and she's got friends, and a boyfriend, though things aren't going too well with him. Why would she spend all her time writing to some old lady she's never met? Once a week is lots. Too much.

He thinks that he is free of Berk, because Berk has not been able to get through to Randy Phlueger. Matt's the one that made their set-up work; Berk is too lazy, by nature. The talker, the connection, but not the one who made it work.

Berk. Who knew? They met in college in Vancouver, Berk there because of a deal he'd made with his parents, Matt because, at the time, he believed that a degree would set him on the road to somewhere, destination unknown, but he would discover that, his advisor promised, if he enrolled in a variety of courses. Everyone gave him ideas, his mom's and dad's practical: follow Dad into the accounting business. Except that Matt didn't like math as much as his dad did, and he wasn't as good at it. Try anthropology, Auntie Annette suggested. You study people. Okay, so he did, and it was interesting, for a while. Like the tourism program he tried, at Gran's suggestion. The graphic arts his sister Mariah thought might interest him. Too bad he didn't have a talent for art, because he liked the kids in the class, some awesome artists. Berk sat next to him in a required English course, whispered comments about the young teacher, and tagged along with Matt at breaks. Matt didn't mind. College was supposed to be a chance to branch out. Berk came from Alberta; by hanging out with him Matt wasn't branching too far, but the shine in Berk's eyes when he talked about his past suggested more than oil wells and cowboys. To encourage Berk to continue his education, his parents paid half his rent for a ground floor apartment on the east side of Main, walking distance to the college. When Berk suggested that Matt move in with him, Matt saw the logic. He'd never get a better deal.

Does he wish he'd never got mixed up with Berk? Yes and no. He definitely found something he was good at, and made awesome money from the start. But here he is, not even two years after they started their business, hiding out. Wondering if he should leave the country while he has some money, or join the Forces. Fight fear, fight distress, fight chaos.

Thing is, if he joined the army, he'd have to fill out some kind of application. What in his recent history was legit? How was he going to account for the time? Could he make stuff up? Would they go for it?

Matt can't relax because while most of his old associates knew him only through the 'net, Berk knows him in 3D. He has to have recovered and might persist until he tracks down his former partner. Unless laziness prevails. Matt keeps an eye out, because of that time he found himself in a park near his building. Literally came to consciousness on a bench in the small park he often cuts through on his way home from the bars. Why was he still here under this mousy sky? It was really late, or really early, depending on your perspective; light had begun to shred the murk above the bridge. He heard something drop to the ground. Matt shivered, stood and almost slipped on the gluey mud at the base of the bench. Somebody behind him called, hey. A big man, in a flopping coat, carrying a big black plastic bag. Matt started to run but the man called again. "Hey, it's okay. I didn't mean to scare you." Turned out he was scattering chocolate eggs for a sunrise service that included an egg hunt for kids. The man himself volunteered the information and offered chocolates wrapped in shiny pink and gold and aqua. Matt opened his hand, nodding, as if he'd never had reason to worry. The man blessed him and wished him a Happy Easter, and Matt continued across the grass to his street and into his building, thinking, what the fuck!

He doesn't drink much because he saw what it did to Berk. Indiscriminate talk, taking stupid chances, making stupid choices. But maybe that night he drank more than he intended. It spooked him, waking up on a park bench like some rubby in Pigeon Park.

Fight fear, fight distress, fight chaos. The Forces promise a lot; would they deliver?

OUT OF THE BLUE, Lawreen calls. "Saturday Afternoon at the Opera" is broadcasting *Il Trovatore* this week, the opera she and Brendan saw at La Scala their first year in Italy. Azucena is singing the passionate "*Condotta ell'era in ceppi*", vowing revenge for her mother's death, when the phone rings.

"Hey little sister, how are you feeling?"

"Lawreen? What a surprise! What's up? Just a minute. I'll turn down the music."

"Is everything okay?"

"Seems to be. I had my blood test, and no sign of any trouble there. No morning sickness."

"I was just thinking of you all alone."

"I'm not really alone."

"Away from your family, I mean. But you must be used to that. Is Brendan supportive?"

"He's good. You know, busy. In fact right now he's at his studio. Not his, really; a friend is letting Bren borrow his place while he's away. It's hard for him to work here. He's got to make the most of the summer because when school starts he'll be busy with students, then the baby will come."

"And then you'll really be busy."

She laughs, but it's a huff more than a trill of pure joy. Elfie braces herself for something mean. It's a habit. When she was little, Lawreen had a way of blindsiding her.

"How are you, and Ken, and Mariah? Any news from Mattie?"

"I hear from him now and then, can't really call it news. It's like he's a hostage. Just wanted to let you know I'm all right. That's about all he says."

"But not in the army? Like Mom thinks?"

"Don't talk to me about her. And don't tell her that Mattie has been in touch with me."

"You're still not speaking?"

"I have nothing to say to her."

The voice of Elfie's oldest sister is wind and brass, blats, trills, the occasional squeak.

"But everything else is okay? Mari still doing well? I Google her every so often, and sometimes she emails. She found some cute baby clothes she wants to send."

"I thought I'd see if you have any news to pass on when I see her, but you two are in touch?"

"Not often. But it's always good to find her name in the inbox."

"I miss her. I can only stay for a week, and she's busy, but, well, there are a few people in the biz that I know from here."

"She'll be glad to see you."

"Hope so, but I don't want to tie you up, Elfie. Just thought I'd check."

"Thanks. I do feel far away from everybody."

This is Lawreen's opportunity to pick up on the faint break in Elfie's voice; they could move closer, bonded by the experience of motherhood now, though at opposite ends of it. But instead, another huff through the earpiece.

"That's because you are, girl. Not for the first time, either. Take care. Ciao!"

That's that. The surprise call like one of those plastic rings with a fake stone that you find in a Christmas cracker. At least she didn't encourage Elfie to open up, then attack, as she used to do. Lawreen is mellowing, despite her impatience with their mother. At least she's in touch with her son. At least Mattie isn't in the army, as far as anyone knows. Why would Mattie even consider it? Nobody in their family has gone to war. She doubts Johann will either; maybe by the time he is old enough there won't be wars, or if there are, they will be fought by robots, not boys. Although she and Brendan will not know for certain until Monday, they are both sure that Elfie is carrying a boy child. The position of her small protrusion, the results of the string over the belly test, but mostly intuition have contributed to their conviction. Neither will mind if they turn out to have guessed wrong.

"Johann Sebastian Gill?"

"It doesn't have to be Sebastian. His middle name can be my dad's or your dads, or yours, or something totally different."

"Johann Smokey?"

"Or Johann Christoph. I told you Dad doesn't like to be called Smokey anymore; his real name is John. But you're right, Johann John wouldn't work either."

The only side effect of the early pregnancy has been sleepiness. After supper most nights, she can't stop herself from sinking onto the bed. Tonight Brendan joins her, drums some kind of beat on the pillow—da-da-da, daa-daa,daa, dum. He shaved his mustache the first hot day, but kept the habit of stroking his upper lip, which he does now as he stares out the window to the big elms that line Tompkins Square. Curtains of rain between claps of thunder, lightning that must be striking the city somewhere though they can't see the bolts, only the flashes, from here. Wind making a blur of the leaves. Rain blows in through the screen, but it's too muggy to close the window. Elfie doesn't mind. "Bren? I think I'm going to nap for awhile." She feels him lift off the bed, the soft pucker of lips on her forehead. He's going out to a bar, to watch Game 7 of the Stanley Cup playoffs. Not his team, but after tonight there won't be any more hockey til October. Too bad Mom isn't here to join him. Hockey is one of the few things they have in common.

Very sleepy, yet sleep doesn't submerse her. She floats just below the surface where random images form and mutate; the baby, his big head; a sharply defined small man riding a bicycle; lilies so close she can detect the shining wetness of the pistil, which quivers in the centre of the rougher textured stamens. Something is sizzling on the stove at the back of the apartment, in the kitchen, or maybe it's the rain. Or could it be applause? The tentative beginnings, when the audience doesn't know if it's the end of the piece or the end of a movement? Strange Lawreen, so protective of her angers, so deeply dissatisfied.

Then, like a shelf you drop off after wading a distance out from shore, she's asleep, and she doesn't wake until early morning. The rain has stopped and the temperature fallen. Brendan has pulled up the quilt she folded at the bottom of the bed. She slips away from him and starts for the bathroom, the street lamp and the general glow of the city allowing her to find her way without turning on a light inside. Sleeping more, peeing more. She has not felt the baby move yet; according to her pregnancy guide, it's still early. But maybe that's why anxiety has been knocking now and then, not the stranger it used to be. Or maybe it's hunger. By the light of Francisco's restaurant downstairs, where busboys are cleaning up after late diners, she puts bread in the toaster and roots in the fridge for peanut butter and milk. She and Johann will eat peanut butter sandwiches together in the park across the street. If they stay here. Which isn't certain. Either Johann or Johanna. It won't matter to the list she's been compiling, things they'll need—a crib, a stroller. Lots of diapers, because she intends to use disposables only when they travel. Blankets. Undershirts. She has little experience with babies, but all the lists she's seen on the web include undershirts. A bunting bag, so she can take him for walks in winter. Oh but where will they leave the stroller? She won't be able to carry it up and down with the baby in it. But maybe they'll move, and if they do, they will have to choose a building with an elevator, or an apartment on the ground floor. Closer to Brendan's school, too, though she likes this downtown neighborhood. She'd miss it. Francisco's busboys and waiters have finished. Aside from car noises, an occasional dog bark, the neighbourhood is as quiet as it gets in summer.

AIDAN AND A FRIEND have been riding the friend's dirt bike most days, speeding it up and down the gravel drive, laughing and hollering over the whining, blurting engine. The ranch is only genuinely quiet when Aidan is sleeping.

Annette has begun to sterilize the milking equipment at night so that she has time for a morning cup of tea, which she drinks on the deck looking out at the dribble remaining in the creek; the pasture, which is already brown as the oak leaves in fall; the flower bed that Mom cleaned up when she was here, which is dry, too, only the hardiest brown-eyed Susans able to survive without being watered, which Annette does not have time to do. The newest babies stay close to their moms but in an adjacent kid stall at night, and they are clamouring for reunion by the time morning blanches the sky, making silhouettes of the trees in the surrounding forest. Annette ignores the bleats and picks out one of the three does, Molly, the only pure white of her Lamanchas, and leads her to the milking stand where grain distracts her from her anxious twins long enough that Annette can wash her udder and squirt milk into the waiting stainless steel pail. Though she's milking once a day, she still gets over a half a gallon from each of these three, and the same, more or less, from the other lactating does in her herd.

Before she starts on the does whose kids are mostly weaned, she lets the recent babies and moms reunite, a high watching goat love in action, the kids vaulting over the earth, half birds, defying gravity until weight and age pull them down; the moms bleating with slightly toned-down joy having to do with relief from their swollen teats. The two sides of hunger. The best thing about this time of year is that she is finished milking and cleanup by 8:00, when everything has gone according to plan, and in summer it mostly does. She has time to fix herself breakfast and take it out to the deck to eat, scrambled eggs and toast today, and more tea, in the cool shade the house throws over the deck until noon, when it is too blazing hot to sit out here. Greg intended to install an awning, or an umbrella, but it was one of those things he never got around to. She's going to do it herself. Dad offered, but she doesn't want him to strain himself trying. He's admitted to arthritis. His doctor has suggested a knee replacement. Dad can't see walking on plastic knees, but it is just a matter of time, she suspects.

Although Greg has called a few times, she deletes his voicemail before she can hear what he has to say. At her angriest, Annette considered switching cheesemakers, or making cheese herself, but the effort she put into the process exceeded the lumpy results. Josie knows what she's doing. Annette hates the image she can't drive from her head, of that girl, Josie's sister, gripping a roll of herb-crusted chevre like she must grip Greg's cock. But, as Dad reminded her when she told him she was considering a switch, Josie didn't spark the trouble, and she has developed a market that returns Annette a consistent, if small, monthly income. It would be foolish to let Greg's lapse in judgment change that. Sometimes Dad uses phrases, lapse in judgment, that don't sound like him but like someone else in their family, Lawreen, maybe. Generally Dad tends to tiptoe around the Greg issue, as if by criticizing Greg he would be betraying a fellow member of some exclusive men's club.

Here she is nearing forty. Who knew she would end up like this? But who ever knows? Even her anal sister's plan for a perfect life was interrupted by the unexpected conception of Mattie, who is still interrupting what Lawrie thought would be a peaceful middle age with his erratic appearances, or disappearances. Annette sips from her big mug, making the tea last, fingers toast crumbs onto her tongue. A black hawk is circling, cruising for a feed, but her kids are safe. Only once has a bird bothered a baby, and that was an orphan whose mother died giving birth. Annette's first death. She ran out waving a broom at the sky. Get out, get out, she screamed at the hawk, though it was doubtful that the hawk was strong enough to snatch the bleating kid right out of its pen.

She hears a truck motor and reluctantly stirs. It's Greg's, old Ford bouncing into the yard. More than disorienting. Anger complicated by the realization that she has not yet dressed; she's wearing barn-soiled pajama pants, bare feet; her toenails are rimmed with dirt from the inside of her boots. She hasn't yet brushed her hair, washed her face, cleaned her teeth.

"Hey there," he hollers, stepping out from the truck, which he has parked in the space where he used to park it.

"Did you leave something?"

It's obvious that he has spruced up for this visit. With damp, combed back hair he looks like a greaser going to court. His shaved face exposes an upper lip that's long, a closed zipper of a mouth. A different man than she fell in love with; different, too, from the man who betrayed her. He pushes his sunglasses up over his forehead. Ridiculous to be wearing them this time of day. Does he think he's some kind of stud?

"Looks good around here. You managin' okay?"

She shrugs, waves her hand around.

"Okay y'are managin'. I didn't mean to say otherwise. You mind if I come up there and talk for a spell?"

"About what?"

"Well, things. You musta got my messages. I wouldn'ta just showed up here but you never call me back."

"I just finished milking. I'm not even dressed yet. It's not a good time."

"Well ..."

He takes a deep breath, turns to the side. "When is a good time, you figure?"

"It depends on what you want to talk about."

He hasn't been back since March, not when she's at home. If he snuck back when she wasn't at home, she doesn't know about it. There was the big blowout, both of them yelling; Greg admitting his affair with the cheesemaker's sister, whose name Annette will not pronounce; her telling him to get his things and get out, for good. Him gathering clothes, CDs, some books and tools, while she crouched in the barn, out of sight, swallowing sobs until her throat ached, wanting to smoke, drink, do something to numb the hurt-fed rage that made her want to beat him up, him or someone. Twelve years and he cleared out in half an hour, sped off in the truck. She was going to have to buy another truck, she thought then. But she would force Greg to give her half of what their Ford was worth. He took her self-esteem, her happiness; she wouldn't let him get away with anything else. This is her land, hers and Dad's, and Dad helped them build the house. She owes Greg nothing. Those light blue eyes. She used to love it when he squinted and those slivers of blue flashed through his tanned skin. This is when he'd be spouting philosophy, something that impressed her at first, but which she came to realize was dope talking. Those eyes don't affect her now. She's standing above him, on the deck of her own house, on her own land, and he's down there wanting something.

"All right, I get it. You're not ready. But it's not over, Annette. Not what we started isn't. I'm leaving town is what I came to say here. My mama's sick. Cancer. I'm on my way over to Utah. By myself. I'll leave you a message whether you answer it or not. You used to like mama."

He gets back in the truck before she can reply, glances up at her once more before he starts the engine, then looks across his shoulder to back out and around her newer, if smaller, truck. She can send a note to his mom in Utah. What happened with Greg doesn't have to affect her relationship with that big, fat, sweet woman who taught her how to make butter. Delores. The times they visited and Delly reminisced about her parents, who had homesteaded hard land that had none of the virtues of Annette's small spread in northern California. But the standoff with Greg has already affected that relationship; Annette hasn't talked to Delores in months, nor written. The poor woman doesn't use a computer. Doesn't want to use one, despite Greg encouraging her. Cancer? The sun has made it over the roof line. She hears voices from Dad's house. Maybe Aidan's friend will stay home with his bike today, or Dad will take the kids somewhere and she can recapture the peace she felt before Greg showed up. But first she will take a shower. Dad once said that she was letting herself go. He didn't put it that way, he said that she puts more care into her does than she puts into herself. Funny how you don't think of how you look until someone reflects your appearance. The cheesemaker's sister, younger, no doubt prettier, more feminine. When Annette met Greg at Dad's, when Greg was dealing, she and Greg had liked their similarities, both big people, both with full, dark brown hair, both with long feet and broad hands and big appetites. Now they've both lost weight. She's going to have to get herself some new clothes that fit better; at least pajama bottoms she doesn't have to hold up with a safety pin.

But here's Dad hobbling down the slope.

"Nettie? You up there? I got to talk to you. Poor Elfie got some bad news."

THE STREET IS BLOCKED OFF. A big canvas shell has been erected behind a temporary stage. Kiosks sprung up along the edge of the park offer roasted corn and potatoes, crepes, tube steak, hamburgers with fried onions, lemonade, gelato. Still morning and people are already drifting onto the grass field to anchor their chosen spots with canvas and plastic lawn chairs, picnic coolers, blankets, sleeping bags, elaborately patterned fabric from South American countries.

Shinny chooses the walkway through this mélange to the seawall, intending to walk west, beneath the Granville and Burrard Bridges, along the path that scallops English Bay, towards the inukshuk that marks her customary turning point; the inukshuk based on the Inuit stone statues that look like a man with his arms outstretched, to guide lost travellers in the Arctic. But the sight of three actual men stops her. Tahir and his friend Sayed , the same man Shinny first saw when his SUV crashed into the delivery van outside the store, and a third man, all three wearing sunglasses though the overcast has not yet burned off. They're standing at the moon pool, a temple-like structure with six concrete pillars supporting a circular cement band at the top, around which are printed the words, *The moon circles the earth and the ocean responds with the rhythm of the tide.* Graduated cement platforms on the perimeter suggest resting places for Gods and Goddesses, but the men with Tahir are not admiring the possibilities or looking at the marine life the receding water exposes at the bottom of the pool, nor the chip wrappers and stir sticks that collect among the rocks before city parks staff can haul the garbage away. They're arguing about something. After much heated debate, says the news anchor in Shinny's mind. Tahir's head is down; Sayed waving his arms, the third man thrusting his face towards Sayed. Shinny steps off the path, behind an exhausted shrub drooping wrinkled brown flowers. Crazy. She feels like a spy. But something is going on. If she knew their language she would understand, but now she has only association and tone as clues. Before Tahir can spot her she walks west, to where gleaming aluminum letters reproduce a greeting in the Chinook dialect, from an Indian chief who had no idea what the white men were bringing to these shores. "Here you begin like new," he promised. "Come to time where people talk different but good together ... You begin live like Chief. World same like in your hand."

She repeats the words unconsciously as walks beneath the Cambie Bridge, here you begin like new; past the dog park, past the casino, registering none of this as she continues toward the geodesic dome that houses Science World.

Tahir's friend Sayed has been too much in the picture. Could the two of them be a sleeper cell, plotting some kind of terrorism? Gentle Tahir? So quiet, so responsible. Yet what would a terrorist look like, be like, if he were in sleeping mode? He would have to fit in. He would have to become part of his new community, as Tahir has, develop trust, yes. He has done that by running a small, stable, innocuous business. What's suspicious? Envelopes have changed hands. Sima said that Tahir sends money to the people in their old village. The envelopes must contain donations. How else could he have come up with the $5000 he sent in the MoneyGram she found last month? But what if it's instructions, or payment? She has seen enough spy movies to know how easy it is to convey information in a document that looks innocent, but which may be code for "blow up this plane". If they are a terrorist cell operating right in her ordinary Vancouver neighbourhood, then the war over there has come closer. Now she could be in as much danger as she has imagined Mattie to be, though she doesn't know for sure that he's joined the Forces, of course, or that, if he has, he has been offered as a sacrifice for Afghanistan. Even if has been sent there, not every soldier is killed or even wounded. But if there are terrorists here, he would be better off trying to rout them out at home, where they could be an immediate, not just a potential, threat. Signs on the sides of buses say, Report the Suspicious, Not the Strange. Is she being irresponsible? If she reported Tahir she would lose her job, for one thing, but what is a single job compared to the safety of an entire city—an entire continent, for that matter?

The day is warming up. She rests in the shade beneath the Cambie Bridge and watches dog owners throw balls for their dogs, who, remarkably, chase the exact ball meant for them, like hockey players who aim a puck to a team member right across the ice, through and past the sticks and skates of the defensemen.

The three possible conspirators are no longer gathered by the moon pool when she returns. Whatever their business, it's finished. The tide is out, and a Starbucks cup bobs in tendrils of water slipping around the rocks. A crow is picking at the carcass of a dead rat. Graffiti on the cement pillars of the temple says, in black spray paint, *Be bold, free, truthful.* She continues across the brick courtyard of the old Roundhouse to Davie, to buy a newspaper from the stand outside Tahir's store, not for the news, which she doesn't need, having listened to the radio, clicked on the TV, scanned headlines on her personal Google page, but as an excuse to enter the store. Tahir is standing at the postal counter, efficient and impassive as always. She hands him her coin.

"No need for pay," he tells her.

"Well thanks, Tahir. I guess I'll see you tomorrow? Usual time?"

He nods; the responsible small businessman. She can't imagine him attaching explosives to himself, but maybe financing someone who would?

The music has started, the park is now thick with people. On the grass at the side of the stage, dancers gyrate inside hula hoops. It's a samba band, the trumpet solo clear, the sound bright as if bound with shining cellophane. She could hear just as well from her apartment across the street, but lingers in the crowd enjoying the distraction of the buzz, expecting to see someone she knows. Maybe him. The green-eyed piano player. She circles the crowd in one direction, then the other, drawn to tall men with grey hair, though he could be bald. She looks at bald men, too. Nothing, though a good part of the crowd is the right age. Here's Irene, in her customary white; even her canvas chair is white. Winking, she passes Shinny a silver flask. Irene is feeling better, no doubt, because just mere weeks ago, when Shinny stopped at her table outside the market to say hi, Irene claimed that widowhood was killing her. She had passed the shock stage before she knew she was in it, then had gone through a brief period of determination, because Stan would have wanted her to move on, to live it up, she said; but what could she make of a life without him? Nothing. Which is how she had landed in a shithole of despair. Mind if I smoke, she had asked, and Shinny couldn't deny her, not after the shithole of despair remark. Smoking released memories, where she and Stan might have been this time of year, were Stan still alive. The resort circuit. Casinos. No dives, though. Some people complained about the motel life, but Irene and Stan liked it.

"I'd haul a few scarves out of my suitcase to gussy up the place, candles to light when Stan was finished for the night and we'd loll around the bed, having a nightcap or two. I could count the nights we didn't do it," she said. "We were hot for each other 'til the end. But when he got sick he couldn't get it up. His doctor wouldn't prescribe Viagra. Not in Stan's condition. That fucking doctor!"

It's too loud for any kind of conversation now. The vodka in the flask stings Shinny's throat, loosens her. Irene gets up and starts bobbing her head to the music, spike heels sinking into the grass too deeply to allow real dancing. The music is so infectious Shinny can't help moving herself, but she faces away from the stage, disciplining herself to scan grids of people. It's the perfect place. Because who says he had to be a classical musician? Who said classical musicians can't like jazz? Will she know him? Will she see him and connect, will it hit her like her mother used to say love would do? You'll know, Sharon. You'll just know. But she has never "just known" in the way her mother seemed to mean. Not even with Smokey, John. That night at his house last month, after the kids were in bed. She loves John, yes, but with a different kind of love; desire doesn't come into it like it did when they first met. He's fat now, no getting around it with generous euphemisms like portly or stocky or just big. So different than lanky Glen, who was more wrinkled from all his time in the sun, but had all his teeth and a quieter way about him than Smokey, who urged her to have another glass of wine before she left.

"No, no. I don't want to kill myself walking down there. Do you have a flashlight?"

"I'll walk you down, if you have to go."

"Shep will make sure nothing gets me. If there is anything. What gets the goats?"

She leaned over his chair, to kiss his forehead, as if he were another child or grandchild. He pulled her into his lap and cradled her head on his shoulder. It was nice, being held by a man. His pillowy front, could she accept it for comfort? Could she somehow see it as sexy? His arms firmed around her and his cheek slid along hers; he wanted a kiss, which she gave, briefly, not wanting to be stirred just yet, not wanting to know if she still could be stirred by him. At least she'd know what she was getting, unlike the men on the dating site. But still, to get into bed with this man again … She wriggled up and out of his arms.

"Where did you say the flashlight was? Don't get up. I can find it."

THE DAY FOLLOWING THE jazz festival, Tahir is not at work. Hassan is working the cash register, Sima the postal station. When Shinny arrives, Sima tells her father-in-law to go; Shinny understands that much, but not the words, just sounds to her really, that rapidly follow.

"Everything okay? Is Tahir sick?"

Sima has a way of combining a frown with a smile. The eyes narrow, the head tilts, the corners of the mouth turn up slightly. The plump, tan cheeks, the sleek eyebrows. A pretty woman aging. Although she doesn't wear a veil to work, a hijab, Shinny can imagine one covering all but the top portion of her black, black hair. A veil and a robe instead of the pink-checked skirt she wears, the white blouse into which amber beads are stitched, around the neckline. Sima said once, in Canada, I do everything in twos: two sets of clothes, two kinds of food, two languages.

"Sick? Tahir? No, no. Just very busy now. Much to do."

Like what, Shinny wants to ask, without pushing it. Sima is easier and she can't be one of those radicals, not with her Western way of dressing. Whatever Tahir is doing Sima assumes that Shinny knows about it. So maybe there are no real secrets, only the vague misunderstandings that are a predictable consequence of the language barrier. This eases her anxiety while whetting curiosity.

The stage has been taken down, workers are piling metal poles into trucks, rolling cable. Shinny observes from her balcony that activity and the many gulls that dive and circle over the creek, related in that they're the same species, but strung out against the wistful twilight as if they need that much distance from one another to maintain their distinctness. She sits on the balcony and watches the birds and the various boats plying False Creek, the dragon boaters; studies the darkening sky as it absorbs the wan clouds, and listens to the women who have reclaimed the park now that the jazz fest is over. They call their children with an urgency that needs no translation; the children call back, in English. No, mama. Not yet.

When she picks up the phone to call California, there's the bleeping notice of a message. Elfie, her voice like Annette's the day she called to report Greg's abandonment. Mo-om? I need to talk to you.

What? After 7:00 here, so after 10:00 in New York. Too late? But if she needs to talk ...

"Hello. You've reached Brendan and Elfriede, and we're not here now. Of course you know that by now. Leave us a message. Ciao!" Brendan's smooth voice. And a few cheery notes on the violin. Elfie's touch. But what's the problem?

II

July

If you didn't have to move forward, if you could choose a time and dwell in it, Elfie would select the moment she woke from her nap, July 4th. Hair damp. Pink cheeks spotted with the cinnamon dots of her freckles. A cool shower. The barely moving air of late afternoon sifting through the bathroom window screen, too humid to really dry her skin. Choosing a sundress she bought because it hangs simply from the straps at the shoulders and will accommodate her expanding belly. Packing cheese and grapes, a covered bowl full of watermelon chunks. A bottle of wine for Brendan. They were going to join their friends on the roof of Ping's apartment on the West Side to watch fireworks explode over the Hudson, to celebrate the city's 400th birthday. The sky sparkled, they laughed at the booms and snaps, the predictable 1812 Overture. Ping, Brendan's friend and mentor at the school, cherishes irony. He countered the traditional music blaring out from a public loudspeaker with a CD from the Hard Rubber Orchestra. Although they could barely talk over the discord, everyone looked happy. Brendan animated, the almost vertical dimple in his left cheek deepening the more he drank and laughed, the lock of hair he let fall on his forehead because she once told him it looked sexy and licked the join of his perfectly square jaw. Since that joyous July night their lives have been whipped by blades of regret, doubt—anger, too. After the first days, the tears, the comforting, he hardened. It's not meant to be, Elfriede. I feel as bad as you do, but we shouldn't drag it out. It will just be harder if we do. We can get pregnant again.

She imagines tiny valves opening, like the sea anemones she used to poke at the aquarium in Vancouver. Johann's heart is beating more quickly than the sea anemone's muscles contract; she's tuned in to the extent that she can feel it, even hear it when she puts a glass to her womb. She can hear him, and, at this stage, he can hear her, them. Can he understand what they say? Was he paying attention when his father said, it's not meant to be?

The day of the ultrasound they expected to find out whether their child was Johann or Johanna. Then they would announce the name, though someone once told her that African babies are not named for as long as a year, because many of them don't survive until their first birthday. Boy or girl, that's all they wanted to know. Why should shadows have darkened the day? Particularly that shadow. But yes, it's a boy, and Brendan squeezed her hand. They were right. Their instincts spot on. They mustn't forget that, she tells him.

Today there is enough of a breeze that none of the garbage smells that brew in the summer and bubble up on sultry days flow over the windowsill, onto the bed that has become Elfie's nest. It's the fear that keeps her here, fear skulking like one of the rats that populate the city, that dart out from cracks between the buildings, crossing the walk right in front of you, making you trip in your hurry to avoid them. She walks more slowly; she both wants and is wary of sex. She has seen Johann, she can feel him fluttering in her womb. Will he make it? Should they give him a chance to try? He could die before or during birth, and if he survives the pregnancy, he almost certainly will need immediate surgery. Elfie clings to the uncertainty. If he might die in the womb, he might also live; if he might die at birth, he might also squall as infants do to announce their needs until she swaddles him and gives him suck. And then they will see.

Brendan wants it over. He has enough on his mind. That's what he's been thinking, she knows; at the same time, he's grieving with her the loss of a fantasy that had a very good statistical chance of becoming reality. In couples their age, there's a 1 in 45,000 chance that a child will be born with a heart defect such as Johann's. The odds climb to 1 in 10 if the genetics are wrong, or right. In their case there isn't an apparent genetic connection.

Echocardiography confirmed what the ultrasound suggested, and the kindly doctor, a middle-aged Iranian woman, spoke to them in her office. A sparse office, with a computer on the walnut desk. An abstract painting on the wall. Shades of white and grey. A streak of black. Some couples in their position choose to abort. Considering the medical implications should Elfie carry the child to term, an abortion could be performed here, safely. Elfie has read of in utero surgery. Is this possible? No, said the kind Dr. Radan. Only rhythmic anomalies are so treated. Brendan scowled. Rhythmic anomalies characterize the piece he's working on. Tablas, bodhráns, congas, the various timbres of water on rock. Kettle drums barging through the liquid flow of a cello phrase. Polyrhythms. Why not? If a variety of rhythms characterizes music, why not human life?

The doctor typed something onto her computer; appointments for more tests, including amniocentesis. Someone is going to invade Johann's space, their privacy, with a needle Elfie resists picturing. She will need Bren, but he dreads sitting alongside her, watching the steel point pierce her womb. Still, if the child has multiple defects, they should know. Knowledge informs decisions. They are rational, well educated people. She feels guilty. She has done something wrong. Why else would this have happened?

Though they haven't said so, Brendan's parents must blame her. Brendan paced as he waited for them to pick up their phone. He paced while he explained the reason for the call; he continued pacing while he listened, and Elfie waited. Brendan nodded, he said uh-huh. He said what the doctor said, a hole that could be nothing, that could be treated at birth, that could compromise the baby's chance for a normal life. No one knows for sure. He handed the phone to Elfie. So sorry, dear, said Mrs. Gill, but no trouble in our family, not as far back as we know. All strong hearts in the Gill family. Did you talk to your parents?

Of course she did. Immediately after the echocardiograph she dialed her mother, who was out. Where was she? When she called back, and learned the sad news, she cried, Oh Elfie, I'm so sorry, so sorry. Which made Elfie cry, the two of them on the phone, trying to have a conversation through tight throats, sniffles. I don't know, Mom said. How far back do you have to go? I could call my sister. Maybe she knows something. Aunt Carol, whom Elfie met maybe once, twice? I'll let you know what I find out. For now, I don't think so. My mother died of a heart arrhythmia, but it wasn't caused by a defect.

"Oh Elfie, I'm so sorry," she repeated.

"I know, Mom, but it's not your fault."

And then Dad, who also didn't know, but as far as he did know, there were no problems in his family. As far as they can determine, there is no genetic cause for Johann's faulty heart. It has malformed on its own, and the outcome is as enigmatic as the cause. Elfie knows what she hears. A little flicker, a hummingbird's wing beats, the tick and tock of her baby beating the minutes until she delivers him into the world. She is the watchmaker, and the lens of Johann's potential handicap has sharpened her attention.

It's past noon. Brendan left before Elfie got out of bed to make tea, toast, to swallow her vitamins. She has cancelled her lessons, even Hilda, because she can't concentrate. Everything okay, dear? Hilda asked on the phone.

"Oh don't worry about me. I'll call you when I set up my new schedule."

She imagines them, her students, suppliants, looking up at her, shoulders slumping so that their fiddles and bows hang from the ends of limp arms. She can't handle them right now; she can't detach from this drama and smile, listen patiently while they saw through "The Song of the Wind". The effervescent Hilda; the retired ambulance driver, Brian, who is determined to play "Danny Boy" next March 17th. But the days get long. She grabs the phone and dials, supposing Annette will be outside with her animals, and is grateful when she hears her sister's voice.

"Oh Elfie, I was going to call. I just feel so bad for you."

"Thanks, it's sure not what we expected. Anyway, I thought you'd want to know what's going on, but I guess Dad told you."

"Yeah. Do you know what you're going to do? I mean …"

"I know what you mean. We've got amniocentesis tomorrow. If everything's okay as far as that goes, I mean, if it's only his heart, I don't know, I'm thinking of taking the chance. Brendan isn't as optimistic. He feels we should think of the kind of life Johann would have."

"Johann?"

"It's the name we picked. I know it's too early."

"Brendan has a point. Not that I'd ever tell you what to do. It must be so hard. It's easier with animals. If something is wrong with a kid, the doe spontaneously aborts."

Elfie traces a lizard skin pattern of cracks in the paint on the windowsill. Considers that what Annette has just told her actually supports her instinct.

"So maybe it won't be as bad as everyone is thinking; maybe if it were going to be that bad, I would have had a miscarriage."

"Maybe. On the other hand, humans are so screwed up with drugs, it's not the same as with animals. With animals it's simpler, more natural, right from the beginning."

The purity of the country. Brendan would be bug-eyed with impatience at Annette's self-righteousness. Luckily he's working again, on paper and on the computer program he uses; luckily he can't hear Annette talk about the increase in production since she has cut down to once a day milking; that what seemed like a convenience has turned out to have been the right thing to do. Oh yeah, Elfie is tempted to say: does that go-with-the-flow philosophy apply to Greg leaving? If she were Lawreen she would say it, but Elfie does not want to wound Annette. Although she has envied Nettie's closeness to their father, she wouldn't otherwise want Annette's life, not as a meal, only a snack now and then. She has pictured Johann playing with the goats, like Heidi in the story she read as a child. Heidi and her grandfather. Heidi drinking goat's milk. Elfie loved the old book she found on the shelf at Grandma Shinnan's.

"Anyway, you know, with goats, they don't have the complicated emotions we have. They just accept what's meant to be."

"Too bad we're human."

"That's not what I meant, Elfie."

Elfie knows this, but she thinks, how can you know what's meant to be until you get to the end of the story, wherever that is.

WEED EATERS WHINING, WAKING him. Pounding. A building going up on the next block. The splat splat of a nail gun. More pounding. All you hear about is financial hard times, bailouts, corporate crooks, but construction hasn't stopped. The hour doesn't matter, Mattie doesn't have to be anywhere, but he checks his cell phone out of habit, falls back on his air mattress and dozes. Because he keeps the blinds rolled tightly shut, his apartment escapes the blast of sun that would otherwise begin to heat it as early as 6:00, when the sun strains over the mountains and starts its crawl across the sky.

He wakes again, though the weed eating is finished and the pounding stopped. Confused, thinking he slept the whole day, he checks the microwave and sees that it's lunchtime for construction crews. Exactly noon, as BC Hydro's "Oh Canada" whistle affirms. Not that he has much to do. The days have assumed a rhythm dominated by frequent spells at the computer, which he powers up as he passes it on his way to the fridge. A big glass of water first, and then he shakes himself like a dog, as if the water has seeped out to his skin, and reaches for the carton of Tropicana. Now he's awake.

Looking through the slats of the cranked-open blinds, he counts four freighters at anchor in the Inlet. He squints and cocks his head and three big orange Ts form from various crane configurations. Another ship is docked alongside the grain elevator at the east end of the Inlet, a cruise ship pulled into a berth at Canada Place. His sliding glass door opens to a small balcony, but he never steps out during the day. He can see just as well from inside, a view that is the same yet different from day to day. There might be more ships in the harbour; there might be a float plane zooming off. Now that summer is here there are tour boats, too, and the mountains across on the North Shore are losing their snowcaps. It has been hotter than usual the last month: one day of rain, real rain. A haze has developed over the city. Something you don't see much, that brown veil slung across the horizon.

He's doing okay on his own. He has a stable of people and they've all got their place in life. He checks their emails daily, their Facebook and MySpace accounts. One of them has a Twitter account. Some of them write to him and he writes back. He has the highest level of security on his computer, and at the end of the month he's going to sledgehammer it and start over, because the main thing is to avoid detection, and he has succeeded so far. You have to establish priorities, something his parents and teachers told him all through school. Establish priorities, Matthew. You can't do everything. The priority is to remain undetected, worth any money—he still has a bundle of that—and any effort.

He has to answer an old note from Gran to Kate, asking about her soil. How much should Kate say? He'll think about it. Old Gran. She knows things he wouldn't have thought she knew.

The headings at the top of the screen become abbreviated the more windows he opens. What's fun is having one of his characters, Mike, say, post to another, Kate or Beetle, and watch Mike's post instantly appear on Kate's or Beetle's home page. Mike tends to post his game results, his thoughts about the weather. He and Beetle are unlikely friends, but that's how Facebook works. Matt has never turned down a friend request for any of his people. And they are law abiding, even if one of them, his adolescent nerd Beetle is sometimes tempted to use what he knows. Last week, for example, he wrote on Godfather1022's wall. *Hey, G-dad. There's this cool way to get money out of my Mom's bank account. It's just sitting there waiting for me to do it. I wouldn't take much. But I know how!*

Matt replied: *Beetle, you're smart. Too smart to post a question like that on FB. Use your smarts for something to help your fellow men and women. You might be able to invent world peace. Any bank account tampering could get to be a dangerous habit.*

Having paid Ali another three-months' rent, again in cash, Matt is safe here for the time being. It's like being on a desert island; the sea is the city of Vancouver and the island is this apartment. At night he takes the stairs down to the street and swims out for supplies, that's how he thinks of it. Up to East Hastings, to a discount grocer that stays open late. Most of the time he wears a hoodie and keeps his chin down and coughs as if he's sick. People keep their distance. There are rumours of a killer virus related to pigs that is making its way around the world. They're used to him in the grocery store now, the man who might be the owner or a long-time em-ployee, maybe Vietnamese; he's small and his English isn't so good. Matt buys cereal, cheese, instant noodles, bread, milk, Kit Kat bars that more often than not turn out to be stale. Last night he bought a big plastic box of strawberries, which he remembers now. The strawberries aren't as red as they looked in the fluorescent store lighting, but he slices them over the Cheerios anyway and pours on milk, empties two packets of sugar over them. He collects sugar packets from restaurants. An old habit, from when he had an urge to get away with something but he wasn't sure what.

While he's eating, he thinks: he hasn't tried anyone Asian, or from any other country. All his people are white. Could he pull it off? He could get the raw materials. He could get the basics, but then what? What do these people do? Who do they know? What sorts of things interest them? Food. That would be easy. There are so many ethnic restaurants and grocery stores in Vancouver. He could get the food down. But what would they post about on Facebook? How would they talk?

There was a boy in elementary school, a small dark kid from Bangladesh whose father worked for B.C Ferries. The kid invited Matt to a birthday party at his big, pink house with a white iron fence around it. The tile floors gleamed. His mother wore a shiny green sari and spoke English, but like she had a bean in her mouth. There were a lot of kids from Hong Kong in class, but Mattie never got to know any of them, and anyway, they were like Berk, from a foreign country, but not so you'd notice, except for the food they sometimes ate. Mooncakes for holidays. A teacher once brought some in and divided them up, so that all the students could try a piece. Disgusting.

Berk's parents truly were different. Matt visited them the first time for a holiday dinner. A feast, Berk called it. My parents want me to invite a friend for Seker Bayrami.

"Seker what?"

"Chill it, man. A holiday feast, for the end of Ramadan, lot of desserts."

"So, like Muslim?"

"Yeah, but it's no bigger a deal than Christmas. Do you want to come or not?"

"Sure, I'll come."

This was just after Matt moved to Alberta, before the business really developed. He'd known Berk for about a year. A strong guy, taller than Matt, so over six feet, and thick necked, Berk wore his black hair short and kept himself shaved. He didn't have a fat face so much as planed, as if there were no bones underneath the smooth whiskey-coloured skin. His teeth were perfect, white, a little small for the rest of his face. When he smiled his gums showed above them, and he smiled a lot, topaz eyes narrowing as his flat cheeks slid up to his eye sockets. Berk liked to walk around naked when he was home, no matter who was there. Thus Matt knew that his friend waxed his body hair, that the lack of apparent structure in his face continued through the rest of him. That his package was average to small and he hadn't been circumcised. Matt didn't want to gawk, but he found it impossible not to at least glance. Berk was almost inviting him to; look but don't touch. Not that Matt would have considered it. Berk had a way of suggesting possibilities, though, other options for being Matthew Webster. A great dizzying plain would form in his imagination. He didn't want to get lost out there and so he disciplined his gaze, remained the observer he had become so good at being, and saw that only at the knees, the wrists, fingers, the ankles and toes was it clear that Berk had a skeleton. Berk's father worked in the oil fields at Fort McMurray and returned to Edmonton, to his wife and his small, black-garbed mother, on weekends. His wife had a permanent smile and wore a scarf on her head—a hijab, Berk told him, in a scolding tone when Matt asked if Berk's mother always wore the scarf at home.

These were the kinds of things he would have to know if he were going to create the identities of foreigners. The names of the food, too: the shish kebab, the pastry that reminded him a little of the mooncake he had thought disgusting when he was a child.

He has been standing at the kitchen sink as he eats, looking at the same vista available from the sliding glass balcony doors. A couple of boys are having a water gun fight in the backyard of one of the houses across the lane. Next door to them, a woman on her deck hanging clothes. Although all his windows are closed and the air conditioner is running, he can almost hear the squeak of the line as she forces it through the pulley. The thing about summer is, it doesn't get dark until after 9:00, so he won't be going out until then. His days at the computer are longer, but he has a lot to handle. This new guy, Kevin Decoste is a member of the Princess Pat Canadian Light Infantry Regiment, from CFB Edmonton. Younger than Matt himself, Kevin's a kid who joined the cadets in his hometown of Cochrane, Alberta, a kid who grew up on a ranch and rode horses as naturally as city kids ride bikes. Matt found a picture that doesn't really show a face, but more a profile of a guy in the Forces beret, looking out at a desert sunset. That's the picture he uses for Kev's profile. Kev's got a girl, too. Somebody from Cochrane. Today he starts the letters between them, the emails. The girl's name is Jennifer and she was all for Kev joining up, but she wants him to come home safe so that they can get married and start a family, and build a house on the Decoste ranch. Everybody calls him Kev.

Mattie doesn't have an account for Jennifer yet, so he has to create one, a Hotmail or Gmail account. He switches from one to the other, and for Jennifer it's going to be Hotmail, because Kev has Hotmail. Then he can set her up on Facebook. Matthew is feeling more confident about girls since he's had Kate going. But he should think of a less common name. Except that a girl from Cochrane dating a soldier like Kev would be a Jenny, or something just as common. But the name gives him the same trouble he had with Kate. He tries Jen90, but it's not available. Modifications like Jenny90 and Jennifer90 are taken too, which just goes to show how many Jennifers were born that year. So he tries doing it backwards, Nnej90, and it works. Password, Lovekev. Done. He makes a handwritten note in the spiral pad he keeps by the computer, because he wants a backup. His memory is good, but not so good that he can keep everyone's password straight, and he never goes for the "remember me on this computer" choice, because it could land him in trouble.

Dear Kev, he starts. *I miss you, honey. Mom says I should watch the news so I can keep track of what's going on over there and maybe I will someday but they never tell you what I want to know just about how many people got killed that day and stuff like that. Tiana and me went to the mall in Edmonton with her parents and it was fun but not as much fun as when you and me went there and I'm getting tan to because of working at the park this summer Mom says I have a gift where kids are concerned and I should get my preschool teaching papers and maybe I will but I don't know.*

What do you thin Kev?

We are prayin for you every Sunday at church and the other boys from our town and meanswhile I love you honey.

A squeeze from yer Jenny

Kev gets this immediately at his Hotmail address, and after a long day in the field, patrolling a district on foot, nervous that an IED could blow up at any time, he writes back, though Matt saves the letter as a draft until the appropriate hour, considering time zones. When it's morning in Alberta, it's suppertime in Kandahar. If Jen's writing in the evening, Kev won't see her mail 'til the next day.

*Hey Jen baby. You know I kinda agree with your Mom. U do have a way
with kids and animals 2 like that colt that one time that got so scared and you
calmed it down jus talkin to it Wish u could talk to me like that. Mayb on the
phon they say we can make calls and such once a week I'm good though. Sure
hot here and way hooter that it gets back home, I'll tell u that. Buut I may be
ere in winter too when it gets way colder than home too but I have to see it to
beleev it*

    *Miss u 2 baby and thinking of when we go back to that mall and how I'm
going to surprise you with something there U talk to the pastor yet about the
wedding?*

It occurs to Matt that maybe emails from Afghanistan are censored.
Like, would soldiers just be able to open a Facebook account and message
anyone they want? Have their own Hotmail account? It didn't used to
be that way in war, he knows, because when he was working on his family history back in elementary school he found out that censors actually
cut words out of letters or black them out, so if the enemy intercepted a
letter, the location or plans would not be revealed. He checks the Canadian Forces site that has become an important resource for handling Kev,
but he can't find anything about rules having to do with communication.
That's the thing, it's a good site, but it only goes so far. Like other sites on
the net, you get basics, not so much below the surface. That, you really
have to hunt for. It's only 5:00 or 6:00. Actually 5:37. He's got loads of
time to develop this, but he's feeling a little cramped.

In the harbour, one of the freighters is steaming out, guided by a couple
of tugs. A helijet is landing close to the cruise ship terminal with its fake
sails. He makes himself two grilled cheese sandwiches, which he stands at
the window to eat. Since he's out of coke, he drinks water from the tap to
wash down his lunch. He'll pick up more Coke when he goes out, more
milk, more butter. He feels like a doughnut, too, so he'll have to track
down a Tim Hortons. Maybe pick up something frozen for tomorrow.
Two trips then. One to get the stuff and come back with it, another to go
out for his nightly stroll. The people who work are coming home. He can
hear the whir of the elevator as it lands somebody on his top floor; the
slam of doors. The building acquires energy it has lacked through the day.
At least it feels so to Matt. Could he live his whole life like this? He's heard
of solitaries who find whatever company they need in bars, like he's been

doing. Who knew there were so many places to drink? Not that he drinks much, and he never stops in the same place more than once every two weeks—though it wouldn't be surprising if he did so by mistake, because once you walk in they're pretty much the same: dark, beery, worn carpets, ripped vinyl chairs or booths, usually red—because then he'd be a regular somewhere and if someone was looking for him, they'd spot his pattern. It must be how spies live, but he's not a spy and he's not exactly a fugitive, because he isn't the one who did anything wrong. Okay, maybe he took stuff, made stuff up, but Berk is the one who sold it. He was an accessory; maybe he could be in trouble for that. Well, okay, he could be in trouble; but he tries to not think about Edmonton, except as the base where soldier Kev trained with the Princess Pats, the base he left from, with Jenny waving goodbye, crying, blowing kisses.

His family knows nothing. He's written just that one email to Mom, and that because he doesn't want any of them going to the police, reporting him missing. Then there's Kate and her pen pal type thing with Gran; he could use that if he had to. Get news to Gran through Kate. For now he'll let things roll, maybe write to Mom once more before he smashes this computer.

The next time he looks at the time on the screen it's 8:29. What happened to the last two hours? Who's this new guy on his screen? Robert? Another side view, of a thirty-year-old with a beard, a plaid shirt. His profile says he's a teacher. Spooky.

IT'S KEN'S TURN TO cook tonight. He's making pasta with homemade pesto, something that he has been experimenting with. His last few meals have all featured some version of homemade pesto, different greens, different nuts. Walnuts this time. Pasta is a staple with him, and his backyard herb garden has thrived. The kitchen smells like fresh basil and garlic. Lawreen sits at the kitchen table watching him chop and stir, knife up bits to taste. He opened a bottle of wine and poured her a glass, so she's sitting here with him, although the point of trading off cooking is that one of them can stay out of the kitchen after work. But it's okay. He doesn't need her to talk to him; maybe he doesn't even need her to be here. Maybe she is putting this obligation on herself. Out of guilt. A month has passed.

Ken has noticed neither her yearning nor her frequent trips to the computer, to check email. They have kept up their every ten days to two weeks sex and, true to the Cosmo article she read about the effect of affairs on a marriage, it's been better than it was for some time. She has done things for him that she stopped doing years ago, except on special occasions, like their anniversary. Nothing too exotic; she doesn't want to arouse his suspicion. But some light fellatio to start before she feigns reluctance and pulls away. Which has encouraged him, and that's good, because oral has always been more successful with her. More of a sure thing. Maybe thinking that tonight's the night, Ken spontaneously turns around and grins. "You're going to love this," he says.

She smiles, sips her wine. She's dreaming of California, of Paul. Maybe she and Paul could meet in San Francisco. Lawreen could combine a tryst in San Francisco with a visit to Annette, whom she hasn't visited in years. That way Ken wouldn't suspect anything. Oh, just quick trip down to visit Nettie. You know it's been hard for her since Greg left. She imagines Ken nodding in agreement.

Lawreen and Paul got together only once, but he promised to call her when he returns to Vancouver, and that could be this fall. Meantime they email. Reluctant to overwhelm him, she limits herself to once a day and sends jokes, cartoons, some inspirational sayings. She likes the zen-flavoured words: you're in exactly the right place, with exactly the right people; there's nowhere you are that isn't where you're meant to be. Or was that a Beatles song?

This is her first affair. Almost twenty-three years married and she has never cheated, and she doubts Ken has. She pulls focus to a long shot, and sees her husband smaller, in his usual summer shorts and golf shirt, bare feet, glasses on his head for cooking because his vision has changed; cooking is somewhere between near- and far-sightedness, meaning the glasses go up and down. He nods his head to his Michael Jackson CD. Michael Jackson is everywhere since he died last month, just after her trip. Paul wrote to ask if she had seen MJ's first moonwalk? Does she remember where she was? It was March 1983. Yeah, she saw it, on TV. Elfie was a baby then and Lawreen was babysitting while Mom worked late; who knows where John/Dad/Smokey was. She pours herself more wine. She was never a big MJ fan like some of her friends. But now she misses him like she misses Paul, Mariah,

Matthew. All this loss. She's going down; she can feel it and she has to stop herself. She hasn't been down for weeks, not like she was in the spring. She could take one of her little pills, or half of one.

"Have you heard from your sister?" Ken asks.

"You mean Elfie?"

Because Elfie is whom everyone is thinking about, nothing new there. She has been the centre of attention since she was born, first because she was the baby, then because she turned out to be so talented and did glamorous things such as live in Europe, visit famous places the rest of the family has only heard of. Not so glamorous is the possibility that her baby may be born with a heart defect.

"No, I haven't heard from her. Annette said that Mom is thinking of going out there. She definitely will if Elfie goes ahead with an abortion."

When Mom called to report Elfie's sad news, she talked to Ken. Lawreen is still angry with her and has not told her that she hears from Mattie, not that she does hear too often. Which reminds her, she hasn't checked email for hours.

"Are we close, Ken?"

"I'm going to wash the salad greens and heat the bread. Maybe twenty minutes?"

"Okay, I'll be back. But no bread for me. The pasta's enough."

"Carbs are good. You work out enough. Hey, I saw a deal on that new gym. We could get a couples discount."

Lawreen is out of the kitchen and up the stairs to her bedroom, to the drawer where she keeps her pill bottle, before his sentence ends. She breaks the small pill in half. There. Now, just enough time to log in and check her email and log out quickly in case Ken gets curious. Nothing from Paul, nothing from Mattie. But this from Mariah. *Mom, I got the part! Not much, jst one line, but it's a speaking part in a series, Lost Again. Maybe they'll do something more with the charactger. Knew youd want to know. Dont try calling this weekend. Im gonna be gone.xxxxMari*

"Ready!" Ken calls.

Was that twenty minutes? "Okay," she hollers. "I'll be right there."

She enters the kitchen smiling. "Mariah got the part in the new *Lost* series!"

"Well we told her it was going to take some time, didn't we?"

He has lit the tall candles she keeps on the sideboard, that she was saving for company. But they don't have company often. She bites her lip. He's only trying to create a mood, make it nice.

"Looks great, hon."

"Try it. Tell me if you can taste the walnuts."

"I like the walnuts. Deepens the taste, but you know, Ken. It might mean me going back there."

"To L.A.? Lawreen, she's grown up now. She doesn't need you on the set. Probably doesn't even want you on the set. Not to say she doesn't love us, but little birds fly, like they say."

He smiles his nice-guy smile, lifts his eyebrows, his glass, which he toasts to her. His fingertips are green from the basil he's been chopping. This is my life, she thinks. This is really it.

August

Shinny should have flown to New York immediately. Instead she cringed, her neck crawling with cold shame as Elfie softly wailed into the phone, what should I do, what should I do? Cowardice has kept Shinny in Vancouver, dealing with Elfie through wires that connect her to the internet, the phone. The abortion is scheduled for next week, though there's still a chance that Elfie will keep the baby, and that the baby will be all right; either way, Elfie wants her mother. But what a terrible time to leave. Crazy that elections in some far off country, where people are going to have to travel by donkey to vote in a polling station that's housed in a tent; crazy that she should be torn because of something happening so far away. Of course she should fly to New York. There's no question. She's looking for excuses, and yet what happens in Afghanistan could determine Mattie's fate, and the fate of the soldier who contacted her out of the blue, Kev, whose last email popped into her inbox this week: *I was having a little bit of a discussion with a visitor yesterday about my decision to join the Canadian Forces Thelady I was talking to said shesupported my decision but does not like the armyI told her that Canadian soldiers serve and stand on the front line or standon a wall to protec ther and the rest of Canada's population while they sleep, andwe need to do that. I also told her about the bumper sticker I saw that reads 'If you don't support our troops, feel free to stand in front of them'. Interesting caption eh? Heythanks for the thought but Im going to be moved can't sayw here, so don't send cookies. Mymomsent somethingand Jen so it was like Christmas here.Sorry I still haven't runcross your Matthew.*

This month another Matthew, but a Mathieu, another Quebecer, killed in an ied explosion. So many Québécois, it seems, like goalies. Most of the best goalies are from Quebec: Martin Brodeur, Roberto Luongo, Marc-André Fleury. That's fate for you. Born with the body and the reflexes of an athlete, a boy can become a star in the NHL. If not, there's always the Forces and the possibility of early death.

When Shinny handles the sundries counter, she sees that the flow of MoneyGrams to Afghanistan has continued. For tractors, or guns? To people there who are supporting which candidate? The man with the pancake hat? The turban? The one who wears that beautiful green cloak? Sayed, and people she doesn't recognize, step into the store, and Tahir leaves. The men, always men, meet at the park, she supposes; never for long. When he hustles back into position behind the counter, Tahir is reticent as usual. If they are plotting some violent act, here or there, her absence may slow them down in that Tahir will have to remain in the store and tend to business. But it's still unclear to her what they are doing. In their most recent brief conversation, as Shinny was arriving and Sima leaving, Shinny remarked on Sayed. Is he a relative? she asked. Sayed, no, Sima laughed. Maybe a godfather? Like to help Tahir. That funny frowning smile, which means what? Even if she knew the language, Shinny would remain in the dark culturally. Sayed is helping Tahir, who is helping people back home, but helping them do what? Sayed obviously has more money than Tahir, but where does his money come from; where does it go? The money and the impromptu meetings of men in dark glasses are the only signs that something may be up. North Americans used to send money to Ireland, but the IRA kept its nastiness on the other side of the ocean. No wonder that when she looks on the web for advice regarding suspected terrorism, the first sites to pop up are from the UK. Though not much help. Among the listed causes for suspicion are vans, multiple mobile phones, fake-looking passports, computers, chemicals and fertilizers. Someone carrying a suitcase with vague plans for where they are going. Chemicals and fertilizers? And what self-respecting terrorist would use a passport that's obviously a fake? Uncertain of the need to report Tahir and his cronies, the consequences, she has done nothing. Her uneasiness has played beneath her work hours especially, like the faint ticking of radiators when the thermostat kicks in and the electric coils begin to glow red.

The uneasiness is with her even as she stands in the security lineup at the airport. Back to the U.S., that bastion of freedom. Who said that? Some American newscaster she heard when she was living in Washington, no doubt. But the phrase has risen to her mind like letters beneath the fingers of an expert typist, and flown onto her mind's visual display. Free or not, the country whose legal space she enters when she passes through customs at the Vancouver International Airport is more of an actual bastion now, despite the changes people expected Obama to bring. Still, she is as stoic as everyone else who automatically takes off jewelry, empties pockets, removes shoes and steps through the booth to be scanned before passing security. It's the second time this summer that she has handed her passport to a U.S. border guard and said she was going to visit her daughter. Except this trip is a truth mission, not that the squinting border guard has to know, or would care once he has determined that she is no threat. Not to him anyway. Not to the U.S. of A.

She must try to get Elfie to remember how it was when she was a girl. Didn't she ever feel impulsive? But the times they lived through, so different. Shinny had not planned to raise children single-handedly; she was a parent before she could plan at all. And now there is Barack Obama to prove that the children of single parents can be whatever they want to be. Oh, but the lie. Barack Obama's mother never lied to him. How could she? Barack inherited his father's skin colour and facial features. Elfie's inheritance has been easier to conceal. Now the cover-up has become worse than the original act, as with President Clinton and his chubby girl lover, Richard Nixon and the burglars at the Watergate Hotel. Shinny's one night with the green-eyed man who had a grand piano in his apartment amounted to nothing compared to the decades of pretence that followed.

Thick air between the airport and the shuttle van, then air-conditioning. Traffic thick, too, even at this time of night. A ball game just over. The driver talks to another shuttle passenger about the team's season. Shinny can't think of any baseball player's names; it's not a sport she follows. Mahmoud Ahmadinejad. Basra, Hamid Karzai. Evgeni Malkin. Maxim Afinogenov. Abdullah Abdullah, Ramazan Bashardost. Alexandre Peloquin, Charles-Philippe Michaud. The mantra calms her, names like orderly ramparts she must climb up, step down, until the shuttle van brakes in front of Elfie's building on East 10th.

Late, well after 11:00, but here's a mother wheeling a baby down the street. The mother is speaking Spanish to her baby, singing a little Spanish lullaby, unselfconsciously. Brendan answers the buzzer and meets her at the outside door, takes her case, briefly kisses her, on both cheeks, which is disorienting; Shinny never remembers that he's going to go for the second cheek. Elfie stands at the door, her white t-shirt stretched over the faint mound that will be Shinny's third grandchild, if he survives. If Elfie aborts him now, it will be like killing an actual child, whose heart beats between them as Elfie leans into her and digs her chin into her mother's shoulder, as she used to do, and the tears her condition and her situation replenish with such regularity fall onto Shinny's collarbone. Brendan excuses himself, mumbling some reason that Shinny doesn't catch. Whatever reason he has to go out when it's nearly midnight is just an excuse to leave them alone, these two weeping women, Shinny trying to comfort with words she used to use when Elfie was little, aw honey, it's going to be all right. There, now.

"Mom, do you really believe it's going to be all right? What's going to be all right? Me, us, the baby?"

"Didn't they say there are operations?"

"So you think I should just go ahead? Hope for the best? What about Johann? What kind of life will he have? That's what kills me, Mom, thinking of him. Watching those kids playing basketball across the street, no matter how hot, knowing Johann won't be able to do things like that. If he makes it through the birth."

She's up now, gone to find Kleenex. Shinny follows her to the back of the apartment, turns on the too bright overhead kitchen light. Looks for tea. Remembers the gift Lawreen sent with Ken, who drove Shinny to the airport. Is she still mad at me? Shinny asked him. She's mad at something. I can't get through to her. But she sent this for Elfie. I told her you wouldn't be able to take it in your carry-on. She said, then tell her to check her bag. Do you mind?

"Look, Elf. Your sister sent you a present."

"Thanks."

Elfie is too upset to appreciate the basket of soaps and lotions. Her pretty face is blotchy, the whites of her eyes red, which makes the green flash like the arrow on that elevator. Of all the images that have stuck in Shinny's mind. She can't tell Elfie tonight. It's too late.

"Do you have some herbal tea, honey?"

"Don't make tea. It's bad enough as it is getting up in the middle of the night, walking all the way back here. If I drink tea I might as well just stay in the bathroom."

"Lie down then, let me rub your neck. Okay? We have a lot of talking to do, but I think we should wait 'til tomorrow. You need your sleep. It's late."

"I know. I am tired, but we have to decide really soon, Mom."

The apartment is so narrow there is little room to pace across, only back and forth the length of it. The street lamps ensure that it is never wholly dark, especially here by the window where Elfie lies on her side while Shinny massages her upper back; feels the knots that express her daughter's indecision, each knob a what-if. She lifts Elfie's golden hair, naturally red-blonde and wavy, and smoothes it off her neck and presses three fingers into the cords unyielding as wire rope. Elfie lets herself be soothed; it's why her mother came, in her view, to be with her for the procedure, unless she decides not to have the procedure. It's booked. Three days from now Elfie will be admitted to hospital and her little Johann, her damaged baby, will be what they call evacuated, as if he were someone threatened by hurricane or wildfire instead of some vague malformation that could turn out to be nothing but a nuisance. If only she hadn't named him, Shinny thinks, it might be easier. If only there weren't those ultrasound pictures that show the big head, the fingers and toes already formed. It would be easier not to think of him as someone who would grow up and become a human being with his own personality, his own quirks of appearance. A fan is blowing between Elfie and Brendan's space and the rear of the apartment, just outside the kitchen, where Shinny is bedded down. The white noise and cool air encourage sleep; she drifts off, but then Brendan comes in, trying to be quiet, barefoot, tiptoeing. One thing for sure, she's going to tell Elfie alone. Elfie can do what she wants with the information, but Shinny does not want to reveal her past before Brendan's gaze. It would cap his opinion of her as a lightweight, justify it.

Her troubled sleep, the time difference; Elfie's worry-chiseled expression, the grid across the forehead, the way the freckles squeeze into a sandy island at her temple. Shinny wishes they could go out, to the park across the street or to Central Park, which is less crowded than she would have thought. The time Elfie took her there, on her first visit to New York, there were benches, walkways, entire empty swathes of grass, a kind of miracle in a city with so many people. She folds her bedding while Elfie boils water for tea, which she brings to the small table in the kitchen. It's so small she won't be able to squeeze in if her pregnancy continues, but they are a family that discusses important life events around the kitchen table, as if it is a fire and they the members of some ancient tribe.

They've already talked about the facts of the situation on the phone, the apparent malformation that indicates but does not guarantee a heart defect that will require immediate postnatal surgery, or the possibility that the child will be born dead, or will live for a short time only. There's also a chance that the perceived—and her doctor emphasized perceived—malformation will be something to watch as the child grows, something that will correct itself. When Elfie explained it to Shinny, she said, it's heartbreak now or heartbreak later. A good chance of it, anyway. We weren't sure we wanted children now anyway, but now that he's here. God! What should I do?

Before they can address that question, Elfie has to know the truth. Shinny swallows a mouthful of hot tea.

"Honey, there's something I need to tell you before we decide anything. I just want you to listen. Are you okay? Do you want me to make you an egg? Like I used to?"

ELFIE HAS BEEN IN the bathroom for so long that Shinny is pounding on the door. Pounding, not knocking, partially because the door is so heavy, to bar potential thieves seeking entry from the fire escape, more so because she is worried, guilty. But Elfie is not thinking of her mother, or even her child. She has not been thinking at all. The last twenty minutes she has been standing in the arrivals area of an airport she never expected to visit, where people speak the same language but their accent is different, the scenery outside the window familiar, but a season out of sync. She wishes her mother would leave. But she just got here. Can she throw her out? Let her find herself a hotel, or just pay the difference and fly home early?

"Elfie? Say something!"

"Something! Now please let me be."

Elfie sits on the toilet lid, looking out to the rooftops beyond the metal grid of the emergency exit. Air conditioner hum, drip; traffic; muffled music from a boom box set up next to someone sunbathing on a deck chair. A lemon-coloured umbrella, pots of tomato plants with pendulous yellow and red fruit bending the stems.

"I wouldn't blame you for being mad at me," Mom said, the forward cline of her body imploring forgiveness. When she reached for Elfie's hand, Elfie pushed the table right into her, because she had to, to extricate herself from her chair, but she didn't have to push it as hard as she did, though Mom seemed to accept the assault, to be ready for more. Mad? Anger doesn't begin to define her emotions. Dad, Smokey, John, whoever; that big, funny guy is not her dad now, but her stepdad, like he's Lawreen's stepdad. He lied to her, too, though Mom is taking the blame. Elfie wants her out of here before the whole visit, which was supposed to be about Johann, begins to turn on Shinny's guilt, the big lie; they are going to get to that, but not first, not now. Can she say she always knew this would happen? She can't. It was Lawreen who felt she belonged in the wrong family. Elfie has never questioned her parentage because Mom had ready speculation as to the source of the freckles, the sandy hair, the eyes that are sometimes a bottle green, sometimes the darker olive of the sea when you look down into it from a dock. The music. Everything can't be explained and now even less can be. Unless she finds him. Him, who never knew of her existence. Sweat dribbled from under Elfie's breasts, trickled over her mysterious child as she stared, incredulous, at her mother. Shinny was trying to make it seem like some sort of miracle. "A piano, honey. A grand piano!"

But he didn't play anything on it. There was a time in school when kids talked about seeing their parents "do it", some with wonder that their parents should have sex lives, some disgusted. Elfie was not able to add to those stories. But her mother has just sketched a picture for her. "Don't you see, honey? I was still young. I was lonesome. It was the Sea Festival and so hot that summer in Vancouver." Fireworks! Elfie squeezes her eyes shut, which does nothing to erase the mental image. She watched fireworks just a month ago and thought of Vancouver, skies cloudy with smoke from rockets and scintillant fountains in the unreal reds and greens she used to anticipate with such excitement when she was little and Mom herded her three daughters down to English Bay with a picnic, hours early, to claim a good log from which to watch the night's show. The same log where she sat with him?

When she hears nothing for ten minutes, Elfie opens the heavy door and steps into the kitchen. Mother is gone, thankfully. Not for good, of course. Her bag is still crammed into the corner by the couch, her sweater hangs from the knob of a chair. The creaking planks reassure Elfie that not everything has changed, only become more complicated. An unknown root contributing to Johann's characteristics. He might be tall and freckled like his grandfather and be forced to live with a heart defect that runs in his grandfather's family. The doctors can make a firmer prognosis if they know the family history, but even then they won't be able to predict with certainty whether the baby will be healthy.

"So what do I do?" she asked the doctor.

"You listen to your art," said Dr. Radan. Because she did not aspirate the h, she said art, though she meant heart.

This is what Elfie remembers. You listen to your art.

She lifts her fiddle out of its velvet bed and tunes it automatically, and plays the first notes of Bach's B minor partita. Each note of each phrase draws her to the next note, the next phrase, and in her mind she is playing for her father. But she isn't concentrating. She's adding portamento where J.S. never intended it. Stupid. She puts the instrument down. Mom was supposed to help her but she has made the situation worse. Not only does Elfie have to make the hardest decision of her life, almost immediately, she is not the person she thought she was. Summer dog days in New York and she's shivering.

Hours later she is sitting at the computer when the entry buzzer rings. It has to be Mom because Brendan has a key. Elfie considers ignoring her, but knowing her mother, instead of walking away, she would likely call the police. My daughter was distraught, officer. She'd just got some bad news. I'm afraid she might have hurt herself. And she's pregnant, officer. God! How she can lean on people. Elfie used to think it funny. People responded to Shinny's panic over whatever situation, and helped. Would that beseeching expression work on a New York cop? Elfie doesn't want to risk it. On the third ring of the buzzer she presses the button that opens the downstairs door and unlocks the inside door, returns to the computer, to the Vancouver pianists page she opened in the directory of studio musicians. She knows his approximate age; she knows when he lived in Vancouver. If she saw a picture she could ask Mom to look at it. Another page she has opened is the site she has bookmarked, on abortion. She has read about the procedures, the possible complications. She has read that the latest safest opportunity to abort a child is twenty-three weeks; at that point an abortion is more like delivering an actual baby. It's also true that he could die in the womb at any time.

Elfie doesn't look at her mother when Shinny tiptoes in, knowing that the full-on sight of her will impel her to pull Shinny's hair, throw something, hurt her mother as deeply as her mother has hurt her.

MATT IS GOING TO have to make a move by the end of the month. He's ready, if he still does not know what's next. In the height of this hot summer he feels like he's in prison, not that he was such an outdoors guy before. Last summer, in Edmonton, he rarely went out during the day, and at night, if you stayed out long, mosquitoes found you. Berk wanted to fish. He used to fish with his dad and his dad loaned them his boat. By the time they got to the lake it was 6:00 or so; the fish rose at dusk, Berk said. He had a cooler full of beer. Joints. Matt didn't smoke but he drank beer to fight boredom. He thought of boating with his Gran when he was a kid. His Dad, Ken, liked city sports better than the bush. They camped as a family maybe once. Or did they camp at all? No, that was with Gran too. Dad likes tennis, golf, his train hobby. Matt used to like to watch his dad play with the train, put the track together, buy or build little stations for it. Help your dad with his train, Matt. All boys like trains, Mom used to say. But Dad, while he welcomed Matt into the basement where the tracks looped around storage boxes, a dehumidifier, the exercycle, didn't talk much while he tinkered with engines, painted backdrops for the pretend scenes his train would pass through, nodded his head to music from the '80s, from before Matt's birth. Happy to have his son around, not unhappy if he left. See ya later, Dad. Yeah, okay, Mattie.

His plan has worked. In all these months no one has spotted him. His only contact other than casual conversation at stores and restaurants has been with the couple of girls he picked up. Neither of them were like

Laura, nor Kate. Just girls in a bar, one of them a quick talker, funny, tall with short dark hair, a tiny rhinestone at the side of her nose, and a sarcastic comeback to every question. He might have liked her, but she didn't seem to care if he did or he didn't. He couldn't take the chance of seeing either of them again. If he bought it here, just died on his foam mattress, he'd be one of those people whose bodies are discovered because somebody in the building smelled something rank. Maybe he would be completely decomposed by the time they found him. A skeleton. Who was he, the police would ask. He'd have teeth. They'd be able to search dental records. How they do that, Matt can't figure. Go through every dentist in the city? No, somebody would have to report him missing, and he's taken care that nobody does that by writing his Mom. Just a couple of times, but enough to keep her off his track. And Gran, but Gran knows him as Kate Babcock, a sort of nature girl who is trying to grow herbs. Kate knows Mattie, but hasn't seen him much lately, though he has messaged her on Facebook a couple of times. Gran always asks about him. Kate takes awhile to answer her emails and she always calls Gran Mrs. Shinnan, which is funny, because Gran never got married—to anyone—but she doesn't correct Kate, which makes Mattie wonder if Gran has been rethinking her life now that she's getting older. Kev the soldier writes to Gran, too, but not so often. He's especially busy now that Taliban activity is cranking up ahead of the elections over there. In every email Kev reports on Matt, that he hasn't seen him, hasn't heard his name. But it's weird, because Matt thinks Gran should know that he's not in Afghanistan. Mom should have told her. Unless Mom thinks he's there, too; but why would she? He's never said he joined the Forces. Of course he has not said what he's doing, just that he's all right. As he recalls. He can't check sent mail because he destroyed his first computer and deleted the Hotmail address he used to write Mom from as soon as the site let him do it.

It was easy to get his people back; he can access Facebook from any computer as long as he knows their passwords, and he has the little notebook where he keeps their info. It is dangerous and inconsistent of him to keep such a notebook even though he has found an ingenious hiding place for it. He's got to throw it out. He actually took it with him to the waterfront with the intention of setting fire to it, then discovered that he had no lighter, no matches. These breaks are happening more often. He thinks that they're happening more often. The problem, memory—losing big patches, hours, a whole night once, and that was as freaky as the event with the human Easter Bunny because when he came back to himself he was heading down Hastings Street, dressed in sweats, t-shirt; couldn't remember leaving the apartment. After that episode he installed a complicated lock on his door. If he's sleepwalking, he shouldn't be able to unlock it. It's best if he sleeps through the daytime hours, air conditioner blasting; he hasn't heard of daytime sleepwalking, and the longer he sleeps through the day, the easier it is to wait for night.

He enters Kate's username and password and opens her inbox to read Gran's last email.

Dear Kate,

I'm glad you're having good luck with the basil. If you have room, maybe you should plant some oregano and thyme, too. That would give you the main herbs for Italian sauces, and wouldn't that be nice to just use your own herbs? Mmm.

Like I said, we didn't grow many herbs for cooking. It was all about healing with Glen. He was that kind of man. He liked to farm and he liked to do good.

Ask me whatever you want and if I have the answer I'll write back. I'm glad you at least heard from Mattie. The next time you write, tell him his Gran misses him and would love to hear from him sometime.

Sincerely,

Sharon Shinnan

It's too soon for Kate to reply. Kate always starts her notes with a sorry, but … She's a procrastinator. A nice, well-meaning girl, but she tends to put things off. Mattie wonders if Gran sees the inconsistency, a procrastinator who grows her own herbs. He sees it, but it's too late now. After living with her for a couple of months she's real to him. Well, people are inconsistent. Take Mariah. She always played the beautiful good girl roles, won parts in Disney shows, on Nickelodeon, and she has always been generous with her family. Matt received big cheques for presents as soon as she could access the money she made as a kid. She invited him to the set, thinking he'd like the glamour, which wasn't really glamorous, she said, just a lot of people doing their jobs. Mattie went with her once but found it too slow. The repeated effort to get everything exactly right.

He's got Mariah on Facebook through his soldier, Kev. Kev is a fan; he has seen her movies and found her on Facebook and asked to be her friend, and Mariah accepted. She has hundreds of friends. She must accept everybody, and she seems to join every group people want her to join: video game fan clubs, movie site fan clubs, Relay to End Breast Cancer, Let's End Puppy Mills. Actors Against the War.

Kev questioned her about this. *So what war are you against?* Mariah eventually answered with a single line: *all of them.* Kev doesn't let up. He wants to know if she's aware of what the Taliban have done to women in Afghanistan. This one she doesn't answer. Kev writes again, just a question mark, directly on her wall. Someone posts a Support Our Troops image in a friend feed. Somebody sends the image of a belt, with the line, support your pants. Mattie follows the chatter on his sister's page, about pounding tequila shots, about working out, about one of her friends, the most consistent "feeder", who posts her daily mood changes, her state of health. But what gets his attention is a reference to seeing Mariah in a small film. *Babe you're beautiful—all of you.* Mariah returns the comment, with a *Shhh.*

Some kind of underground deal? Something secret? He clicks into the Internet Movie Database and enters Mariah's name. There he finds a list of her films and TV appearances, the latest being earlier this year, a small part in the TV series *Lost.* But she was making that last year, before he dropped out. He remembers because she was excited and so was Mom. "*Lost*"! A big hit. According to this IMDb list, she hasn't, not yet; nor has she appeared in anything since then. There's only that one listing.

Kev posts another message on Mariah's wall. *Hey, I'm hungry for more movies. What's the hush, hush one. Is it on DVD?*

Mariah changes her profile picture often. The current version shows her with a little dog. Her blonde hair is flopped over her cheek and she's wearing big sunglasses so you can't see much of her face, only that big smile everyone loves, the straight teeth she never needed braces for, the nose turned up just enough to have swung her those parts in the Disney shows, and hands with nails so long she must have to be careful not to spike her pet. *Me and Topo*, is the caption.

If it's porn she was doing, Matt can probably find it. The question is, does he want to see her in one of those poses, exposing her—thing? He can't say cunt in connection with his sister. He won't go there, though he's curious. He's got to keep himself busy, that's the trick.

Six o'clock. He gets up and stretches, checks out the windows, the one in the kitchen, over the sink, the sliding glass door, which he opens to see if the temperature has dropped, and it has. He could turn off the air conditioner, but the low buzz of the motor is company for him. With the slider open he can hear the traffic sound that's like a carpet, always there but something you never consciously register. The breeze coming off the water brings a sour tang smell from the granaries. He counts the freighters at anchor while he drinks from a can of Coke. As long as he's looking every day anyway, maybe he should find out if there's a job counting boat traffic. They probably have someone doing that at the port office; somebody would have to be keeping track. But is anyone really watching as much as he has been? What if a spy boat were to slip under the radar, if there is radar, which there must be. What if some enemy boat—a terrorist boat—somehow drifted in at night and sat at anchor, half hidden by container ships? The guys pack it with explosives. Set the timers. Row across to the North Shore, or to the south shore, to the little beach down the block. Or maybe they'd swim.

He has already given Ali his notice. Now he needs a plan. He stays in the shower until the water runs cold, thinking that the pressure on his head will give him an idea. He has cash, but it won't last forever. Maybe he should go visit Mariah. She'd have a place for him, and maybe an idea, too. Or Annette. He has a passport with his birth name on it, Matthew Webster. He pictures himself at the border, handing over he passport. He'll tell the border guard he's going to visit his sister in Los Angeles. He has her address. Of course, he'll be in the system, then. As far as he knows, no one has any record of Matthew Webster doing anything official since late January. In a sense he'll be coming out. Coming out and going out. It's a definite option.

He leans his forehead against the back wall, beneath the showerhead, so the water hits his back, and deals with the erection he gets every time he steps into the tub. How could he have a girlfriend though? Maybe he'll run into that tall girl again, the sarcastic one.

Finally dusk. He pulls clean jeans off the stack on the floor by his mattress. A plain brown t-shirt, a brown hoodie with an abstract logo on the back. He's checked it out on the web to make sure it isn't a secret code. He doesn't want to become a member of some club he didn't know about. He logs out of all the accounts he's been into: Kev the soldier; Kate Babcock; Beetle, who tends to write him everyday, conversations about technology that keep Matt sharp. Before he closes Kate, he checks her inbox to see if Gran has written again. No.

Almost nobody between his street and East Hastings. Schoolyard empty, lights burn irregular white discs on the playground. A couple of kids practicing wheelies on the street. An old woman shifting heavily from leg to leg, as if she is more machine than person. Maybe she's got a fake leg. Hastings is busy, as usual. It always hits him like a blast after his solitary days, the buses, the trucks, motorcycles, cars, some speeding. The stores. The Laughing Bean Coffee shop, the Lotus Garden, where he gets his take-out beef and greens. From here you can see the downtown buildings with their lights promising something. He lets himself look for only a second because the Community Policing office is across the street; he pretends to be very interested in the Humans for Responsible Reconstruction window display he passes, and the people, an old Chinese man leaning on a cane and shuffling, girls in pairs or threesomes, bare feet in flip-flops, painted toenails, toe rings, ankle bracelets, tattoos, some of them. He looks up briefly to check out their lipsticked mouths, dark eyes made darker by heavy liner, mascara. Not so much with the Asian girls, many plain, in clothes unremarkable as his own, but some—especially near Main Street—tattooed, pierced, dressed in black skinny jeans, leather jackets, even on a night such as this.

Iron grills protect the windows of the corner stores, and the big ceramic roosters with thick red combs and molded blue tails that sit on dusty window ledges. Just around the Como Market he encounters the first panhandlers. He puts his head down, walks right past. Then the Filipino phone place. He thought of keeping a postbox here. It would have been perfect in the days when he and Berk were running the scam; he can't help but mentally record it as a possibility. All the possibilities for anonymity. This store especially weird, a kind of mailbox/phone station/pet shop. One night when he passed, it looked like some yellow birds, maybe canaries, had escaped from their cages. Along with the chirping there were knocks, like cinders on glass, as the birds tried to fly through the window. He couldn't see how many stunned or dead ones had collected on the floor.

His steady, medium pace, his inclined head, pocketed hands declare him to be a person who is self-contained. He's in his own world and if he encounters others, it's as a passenger on a cruise ship, visiting an unknown port, glancing at his surroundings, glancing away if another pair of eyes seek engagement. Koko Japanese. On Lok. Smells of exhaust, of french fries from the A&W. Eagles in the Sky Association. Weeds grown up around small trees meant to beautify the street, but there isn't much beauty here, unless you count the funeral chapel and its Band-Aid strip of green lawn. Empty buildings plastered with posters for video games and movies. Long Hong Auto Repair, the stink of burning feathers at the chicken processing plant. He walks past the bleak area on either side of the rail overpass, the B.C. Sugar Refinery factory he visited on a school field trip, stops to glance at the lighted orange cranes that stand out like dinosaurs against the black shapes of the mountains, the lights of Grouse Mountain. Past the Astoria Hotel and into the poorest district in Canada, where the buildings are empty or covered with grills that all but mask their purpose. Druggies collect like wastewater at the bottom of a clogged up gutter; crazies wander, stop people to rant about something that has meaning only to them. Panhandlers multiply, and girls wearing not enough clothes, even for a summer night. Having walked this route several times a week for months, in a hooded jacket first, now lightweight hooded sweatshirts, Matt knows how to shrink inside his clothes to become invisible. And soon the street is livelier; maybe crackheads lend the energy. People talking loudly, some yelling; others walking as though they've got somewhere to go. It's safe to raise his head now and look out at the scene he passes on his way north, towards the waterfront, to an artsy bar with miniature Christmas lights in red and blue and lots of mirrors; so dark that it's unlikely anyone will spot him. Last time he chanced on the opening of an exhibit. He walked in like he'd been invited, a video was playing, of animal deaths. Gruesome. Lions nonchalantly munching on antelope parts, a boar chomping on a piglet, a fox tearing at a rabbit. People were fixed on multiple video screens, no chance they'd be looking at him. Waiters came round with trays of free food. He bought a beer and made it last. You never know what you're going to run into at this place, which makes it a change from the strip clubs further west.

Before he turns in at Powell Street, he notices the lions guarding the bridge to the overpass at the harbour. Crab Park to the left. Gran used to drag him down here to sit on the bench she donated in her mother's memory. The memory bench. Could it help restore him? When they sat there Gran would tell him stories of her childhood in Meadowvale. She believed that he had invented a family history because he didn't know the real stories, and he didn't try to explain but let her dredge up the special occasions, the birthdays, the Christmases, the Easters; churchgoing, the hymns that got sung. The foods her mother cooked for each holiday. She made it seem as if there was a real order to lives then, yet she had rejected it. And she had it wrong about his motivation for writing that family history; it wasn't because he didn't know the truth, at least the outline of it—it's that he thought the truth boring.

He hasn't hung around Crab Park in years; the bench may not be there anymore. There may not be any benches now, because bad as it was in Gran's time of visiting, when she would have to clear the area of condoms and needles before they could sit down and relax, it's got to be worse now. He walks past the lion on the west side, out to the highest point of the bridge's modest arc. It's a windless night. Typically cool by the water. Smelling of creosote and seaweed, that metal trace of salt. Benches arranged like the driftwood logs are spaced on the public beaches in Kitsilano and Point Grey, with enough room for a person to sit by himself and think, but not so much that he can stay that way forever without someone becoming curious. As he remembers, his great-grandmother's memory bench sat closest to the shoreline. It would be funny if Gran were sitting there now, he thinks; but no. She wouldn't be crazy enough to risk it this time of night, with the park almost empty. Only a couple walking along, weaving along, stopping to kiss. He turns away. They're a couple of drunks.

ANNETTE IS STANDING ON the paint-spattered stepladder, screwing hooks into the fascia board every ten inches. John is setting grommets into the canvas sailcloth she found at a thrift store. Making use of found things is something Shinny encouraged, that made a scavenger of Annette. Delores passed the same tendency onto her son Greg.

"It's why there's so much junk up in the loft, Dad. His mother taught him to scrounge, even more than Mom taught us. A use for everything, she used to say."

"How is she?"

John has never met Greg's mother, but Annette keeps him posted. She spoke to Delores on the phone just this morning, the most recent of several calls.

"Some of those churchgoers? They almost make you want to try it. She's in good spirits."

"Not me. My church is right out here."

Not even 11:00 and already too hot to be working in the direct sun, but the whole point is to create shade for days like this. It's a project they should have done in May. Annette is wearing cut-off jeans and a stained yellow tank top, and sweat is streaming from her armpits down her sides. She needs a break.

"Not me, either," she says, stepping down to the deck, onto the canvas, which mounds like lumpy potatoes spread over the deck. "But it's good for Delores, Greg thinks, and I do too. Her pastor visits her every day and reads to her from the bible; my flesh and my heart may fail, but God is my strength. Stuff like that. She's going out like she's leaving on a trip, destination heaven. Greg doesn't like the pastor so much, but he likes it that his mom is peaceful."

"So you've been talking to Greg?"

"Of course we've been talking; Greg's the one who answers the phone. Delores is in bed."

What Dad really wants to know is if they're talking about reconciling. They haven't been. But they have been talking. Greg calls at night, asking, are you busy, and then just rambling, as if he's stoned, though he claims he hasn't smoked since he crossed the California border. It's just that his mother's last illness—that's what he calls it, mama's last illness—is making him philosophical. Not philosophical like he used to be, with quotes from album covers; they have talked about death and afterlife and, lately, life, how big and full it is and how a person should now and then review missed opportunities. Annette supposes that he is justifying his recent behaviour; nothing an opportunist likes more than an opportunity. Or maybe it's just that Delores has lung cancer and Greg has looked at pictures of the respiratory system, that his head is filled with images of branches branching out from branches. Annette lets him ramble. She's an unlikely person to comfort him; anger still burns in her when she thinks of the cheesemaker's sister. But it seems the cheesemaker's sister has left town. Annette needs to know whose decision that was. If Greg realized that he made a mistake, okay, they would have a place to start. If the girl dumped him, then Greg's return would be to someone who is his fallback; she couldn't accept that.

Dad's concerned, she knows, or at least curious, but his main worry has been for Elfie. Elfie is wavering on the abortion, though every hour, every day will make it harder. If she waits any longer, she won't be able to decide; she'll have to have the baby and hope for the best. When one of the does spontaneously aborted last year, Annette traced the cause to an infection. The tiny fetus lay on the ground, bloody and malformed; you wouldn't have known it a goat fetus by the look of it. The doe, Kathleen, bleated until Greg took the fetus away. That was it. But one farmer Annette knows had a pygmy doe that got out of her pen while in heat and was bred by a full-sized buck. The farmer had to take the chance that the doe would successfully birth a kid larger than usual, that could be too big for her, that would hurt her or require a C-section, or give the little pygmy medicine that would induce a miscarriage. He decided on the medicine. Is the Elf up to that? Annette doesn't know her sister anymore. Never much did. A skinny, freckled girl with pretty hair, green eyes that got greener, truly glittered when the whites of her eyes reddened with tears from crying or allergies. She used to insist that the family celebrate every birthday with party hats and streamers, in blue for Lawreen, yellow for Annette, pink for Elfie, everything the same, every year. After Annette got hit by a car on the way to middle school—more grazed than hit, actually, but her collarbone fractured—Elfie appointed herself nurse, carried snacks to her injured sister on the couch, changed the channels on the TV, dug comic pages out of the stack of papers on the back porch. A few years later, the summer Annette was so depressed, before she and Dad drove down to California in his Jaguar, Elfie demanded that her big sister hold herself together. Not in so many words, but by asking Annette to take her to the beach, to help her braid her hair, to taste the cookie dough, to surprise Mom by painting the coffee table. God, she'd actually got Annette to do that! And a big reason was that Elfie could cry instantly if she didn't get what she wanted. Annette pictures her sister's face, the lines that etched her forehead from the time she was young. Those red and green eyes. Yet you couldn't call her exactly spoiled. When Dad came to visit he distributed presents evenly, everyone got something the same size or value. That's after he moved away. She can't remember the years when they lived as a regular family, Mom, Dad, three girls, for even then he came and went. It was Mom who pushed through the back door every night after work, carrying a plastic bag with whatever she'd brought home for dinner, or leftover decorations from whatever holiday had just passed. Promotional items from the store. Packets, usually, of gravy or dips, cookies, if they were lucky, or new flavours of potato chips. "Did anyone think of starting dinner?" she would ask, though by anyone she meant Lawreen. "I'm not the servant around here," Lawreen would snap. "No, you're not, but you are the oldest."

When did it start, when Lawreen was twelve, thirteen, fourteen? Mom and Lawreen fighting, calling a truce. Sitting next to each other on the couch, touching. Annette never sat that close to her Mom. Mac and cheese. A lot of baked potatoes, frozen broccoli, frozen peas, applesauce from jars. Mom driving her or Lawreen to the laundromat to wash and dry their clothes; out to Meadowvale one weekend a month to visit Grandma Shinnan, another ritual Elfie insisted upon. Taking them to Stanley Park. The time Lawreen wanted them all to wear blue for a photo. Lawreen envisioned a paint-by-numbers world straight from the pages of magazines like *Chatelaine*. But they all went along with her that time, and Mom took a picture of them with her Kodak Instamatic: Lawreen taller than her mother, wearing the magazine cover smile she had practised in front of the mirror, a navy mini skirt and a baby blue blouse with frills down the front, her hair styled to look like Princess Di. Annette almost as tall, wearing denim capris and her favourite blue sweatshirt, dark hair springing out like bushes on either side of her head. Lawreen said that she should have smiled, but when a young teenager, Annette didn't smile for years. Elfie, of course, the darling in a little flower print dress with a skirt she could twirl. Baby teeth still, which showed between her full lips, holding her sisters' hands, one on either side of her. Lawreen wanted one of them standing and one with them sitting on a bench in front of the duck pond, oldest to youngest. Take another, take another, she urged Mom, wanting to make sure there would be at least one that turned out. A passing stranger asked Shinny if she wanted a picture of herself with her daughters, and she said sure. But in the only one that includes her, Mom is looking off to the side, laughing, her platinum hair still big. She's wearing blue, too: her usual blue jeans. These were the days before digital cameras, when you knew if your photo succeeded only if you used a Polaroid instant developing camera, which they didn't have. Lawreen got her picture and made copies and framed them, and gave one to everyone for Christmas. Of course she chose the one that showed her looking her best.

The whole summer has been hot; morning fog burns off more quickly than usual for this near-coastal neighbourhood. The NPR station Annette listens to credits global warming. People in Sonoma County have been worried about fires, even here in the middle of the redwood forest, especially here, although the worst fires have been in the southern half of the state. If the redwoods go up, think what we'd lose, said the lady in the feed store last week. So be careful out there, hon.

She splashes water over her face, avoids the mirror, fills two glasses from the pitcher in the fridge. "You doin' okay, Dad? Need anything?"

"Doin' good. As soon as you're finished with the hooks we'll fit the grommets over. We just gotta hope our intervals match."

"They will, Dad. I used the same measuring tape."

It's time to get back to work. She wants to finish the last few hooks and drill screws into the deck railing. The sail will make a kind of tent more than an awning, but she isn't fussy; shade is the point, another is manageability. Eve wanders out from where she's been playing inside.

"Net? I'm hungry."

"You just give us a sec, babe. Soon as we're done here, we'll go home for something."

Dad never assumes that his kids are hers. Always respects that this is her house, though he and the kids are here much of the time, even more since Greg has been gone.

"There's lemonade in the fridge, Eve, and peaches in the bowl. Crackers in the cupboard, the kind you like. Just help yourself."

In shorts and bare feet, her legs scabby with healing scratches and mosquito bites, her toenails painted black, Eve resembles Annette as a child. Dark haired, big boned, like their father. Oona's delicacy passed to her son, Aidan, who, at twelve, is as tall as Annette and slim as a rake handle, elusive in nature and as fair as his mother. Eve is the same age Elfie was when Annette left Vancouver. Her stepsister, or half-sister, though she knows Eve better than her real sister, whom she sees only at holidays when the family gets together in Vancouver. Since university, Elfie has seldom visited the farm, and Annette has never been to New York. It's the last place she can see herself. They email, they talk on the phone, especially when there is some kind of problem, as now. And some sisterly closeness revives. Elfie called to announce her pregnancy, full of plans. That's before she knew she was carrying damaged goods. She said she wanted Brendan to look for a job opening on the West Coast so that their little Johann— bad luck to give him a name—could get to know his family. "We'll bring him to the farm because I want him to get to know his grandpa and his auntie. You know how kids love animals."

"Brendan won't though. He's never wanted to come."

"He doesn't have to come. Or he could stay in San Francisco while we come. Maybe a week every summer."

Elfie had it all planned. But if Johann makes it to term, he might not survive infancy. He might be born with severe disabilities. Annette can't understand what Elfie is waiting for.

"Dad, don't you think the Elf is just torturing herself?"

"Just a sec, Net. Can you hold the other end?"

She screws in the last of the hooks and slides the ladder down the deck. Dad holds up the sail and she slips the grommets onto the hooks. A simple plan, but it's going to work, she sees. Luxurious shade.

"There. You got your awning, girl."

Eve brings her bowl of crackers outside and sits cross-legged in the middle of the deck, which would not have been possible half an hour ago, when the sun forced the last vestiges of resin to sizzle out of the old boards. Annette scoots a couple of deck chairs over and ducks inside to fetch beers for her dad and herself.

"Here's to full sail ahead, Dad. Thanks!"

"It's my pure pleasure, sweetie. Two sweeties."

"Fifty percent of your daughters, Daddy."

Eve is good at numbers and she likes being part of a group. Dad snorts and raises his eyebrows and Annette senses some reluctance to agree. Oh no. Will some woman show up, claiming to be another of John's daughters, a girl conceived when he called himself Smokey? He has never tried to hide his hippie past; he believed in free love and would say that he still believes love should be free.

"Well I guess you could say so, Eve, or a hundred percent of whole daughters, fifty percent of the whole shebang."

"What do you mean, Daddy? We just started percents."

"Never mind, sweetie pie."

He's taken off his red cap and his hair spreads over the suspenders of his overalls. He lifts his beer and drains it, and signals for Eve to get him another. When she's gone, he turns to Annette.

" Guess you've heard by now, from Elfie."

"What do you mean?"

"Your Mom hasn't told you? Well forget it then."

"You can't do that, Dad. What was Mom supposed to tell me?"

He hoists himself up from the deck chair, wincing and blinking, reaching his hand round to the small of his broad back. "Damn," he says. "Now I've gone and done it."

"Dad!"

"Well she'll tell you sometime, now it's out. Thing is, Elfie had a different father, Net. Brief affair your Mom had long time ago."

"Are you kidding? Mom? When? You're not her dad then?"

"You know, Nettie, dads are the ones who raise you, or do their best considering the circumstances, like I tried to do with the Elf."

As if she has eaten too much, she's full, breathless, finding it hard to swallow. Shock, yes; some pride, yes—she and Eve are Dad's only real daughters! Instant anger at Mom, for keeping this a secret.

"Are you sure, Dad?"

"Darlin', it's not something I'd make up."

"So who was he? Why didn't they get married? Why did you pretend all these years?"

"Pretend what?" Eve is carrying a beer for dad and a glass of lemonade, with ice, for herself. She sets it down and returns with her bowl full of rice crackers this time, and raw green beans.

"Oh, just a little something happened a long time ago, baby."

Annette, too, finds herself downplaying the situation for Eve, and later, after Eve and Dad have gone home, she wonders why. She thunks the milk pail into the drainer. The smell of bleach is killing her tonight and she tears off her gloves and leaves them on the counter. Goes out to where she can hear the muffled sound of maas. Almost trips on the tools she left on the deck. Shit! Does Lawreen know? She didn't have a chance to ask because of Eve sitting there munching, daydreaming. Without communicating, not so much as a purposeful glance, they independently decided that Eve doesn't have to know the details. Which is stupid, Annette thinks, because they are more or less perpetuating the lie. WHY DO WE DO THIS? She's got to call Lawreen and slide into it, in case Lawreen already knows, as she must. Wouldn't she? If she does, why didn't she tell? Was it one of those secrets Mom confided in her oldest daughter late one night after Annette was in bed? Is it going to turn out that they excluded her again?

September

Another note from Mattie, no more informative than the previous two, but he's alive and apparently well. As with his earlier notes, he tells her not to worry and Lawreen is happy to oblige because she has enough to worry about. Now, of all things, Mom. And the mortifying suspicion that she is the only one of the three daughters who did not know about Elfie's true father. Then Annette called, nervous about something, and Lawreen sensed that Annette too must fear that she had been left out. For a disloyal instant, Lawreen considered pretending she had known the truth all along. If they were younger, she might have carried through, but Nettie is on her own now, with all those goats to look after, plus Dad and his kids. She can't do it.

"She didn't tell me either, Nettie. I think the only person who knew was Dad. God, can you believe it?"

"So tacky. And I'm mad at him, too, for going along with her. I mean if they'd stayed together that would have been one thing."

"They were on their own little island."

"I just hate it that they lied. Have you talked to Elfie?"

"If you can call it talk. She thinks she's going to find him. She was crying one minute, rattling on the next about her ideas of who he is, where he is. The girl's a mess."

"She should have gone through with the abortion. Funny, somebody as worldly as she is. To me it just makes common sense."

It's warm enough that Lawreen is standing on the patio as they talk. The yard is more beautiful now that rain has sprinkled the flowers, the rows of chrysanthemums in yellow and bronze almost tall enough to make a hedge along the short brick walkway to the back lane. The bird feeder Ken installed earlier in the season attracts birds whose names Lawreen doesn't know, but she likes it that they come. Why do such simple things seem like such unique achievements? Oh but she's feeling light-headed again. She has to sit down, and she has to make sure she doesn't say out loud what she's thinking, that what's common sense to Annette might not be so obvious to someone who is pregnant. Because putting those two words in the same sentence, abortion and pregnancy, recalls the thrashing around Lawreen went through twenty-three years ago. She didn't want a baby; she didn't. But the one inside her persisted in growing fingers, veins, hair, skin even as she thrashed. It was Mom who more or less talked her into letting the pregnancy continue, giving the fetus who became Mattie a chance at life. Then, of course, Ken, who proposed, who held her and let her cry and promised her the life she dreamed of, which made her cry harder. Did Dad, or Smokey as he wanted them to call him then, did he say the same to Mom? Is that why she went ahead with Elfie? Hard to believe.

"I don't know, Annette. It's hard to see into another person. I'm just, well, this whole thing…"

"What? What, Lawrie?"

"Don't you feel like the world just tilted? What else is she holding back? What if Larry wasn't really my father? I don't know, it's dizzying. I can hardly get my breath sometimes. "

"Are you okay, Lawrie? Have you seen a doctor? Talked to anybody about this?"

"I'm talking to you. Anyway I have to go. I'll let you know if I hear anything, and you do the same, okay?"

"Sure. Take care. Thanks for calling."

"You're the one who called."

"Oh yeah, I forgot."

After Glen died and Mom moved back to Vancouver, Lawreen invited her over for dinner every Sunday. Mattie and Mariah were still home then and sometimes, in nice weather, Mariah would join her mother and grandmother for a walk through the University Endowment Lands, or a drive down to the beach. Shinny seemed smaller. Skinnier than normal, her throat scored and bunched. What did I expect? she would say. It wasn't as if he was a young man, and then she'd tell the story of finding Glen fallen in the echinacea flowers, the picture of that moment locked in her brain like an image locks in a digital camera. But after the first few months, when the same words began to replay, Lawreen would catch Mariah's eye: they had to do something with her, they had to keep her busy. Shinny rejected every idea Lawreen proposed: take a course? For what? Meet some new people. I've met new people, Lawreen. It's just that I don't go out much. But she managed to drop in, unannounced, at least once a week, close enough to dinner time that it was clear she wanted to be asked to join the family. She always had a good excuse, a special she found on eggs or apples or something, always something perishable, that she thought Lawreen could use. Once she offered as the reason for her sudden appearance a five pound block of cheese with two days until its best before date.

For the first year it seemed that an aging Shinny would grow more and more dependent on her oldest daughter, and one week Lawreen just blew. "Mom, you have to get over this. You have to move on. You'll end up in a nursing home at this rate, because I'm still working. I couldn't take care of you."

Surprise turned to guilt on her mother's face. She didn't cry, though, which was a relief. She stopped calling most nights a week, and she offered to cook dinner at her place one Sunday. Then she got the job at the post office. Hallelujah, said Mariah. Don't be mean, Mattie told her. What do you know, computer-head? You never come out of your room.

Since then it has been no different than it ever was between Lawreen and her mother; they argue, they get over it—until Shinny confessed Mattie's visit. Lawreen has been letting her mother stew. Letting her think Matt might be in the army, might be in Timbuktu, wherever that is. Now this. She never considered that her mother could have a life she didn't know about. A lover? He might not even be dead, like Larry Blake, Lawreen's father, if indeed he was her father. Meaning that there might be some happy family reunion at which she will be the outsider. No wonder the world feels tilted. Like the old person she fears becoming too soon, she leans on the broom she was using as she climbs the few steps from the patio into the house.

Where did Ken say he was going? When did he say he was going to be back? She looks on the whiteboard attached to the fridge, where they leave notes to one another. Nothing. It's Saturday. He could be anywhere and he must have told her where he was going because he's good about that sort of thing and she likes that about him. If Paul returns to Vancouver, she will know just when to meet him, when the coast will be clear, so to speak, because Ken is so predictable. Not that she should invite Paul over here. No, the twain shall never meet, someone said. Maybe Mark Twain? Wouldn't that be too obvious? She'll look it up and while at the computer she can check her email, though the emails are less frequent, and now the show Paul had been hired to work on this fall may be canceled on account of the Olympics. What one has to do with the other she doesn't know, and Paul hasn't explained, but if she doesn't stay hopeful, Lawreen fears she will end up where she was in the spring, flat, disconnected, her head simultaneously airy, vacant and somehow full of hard, insisting thoughts she does not want to think.

Her mother had an affair, why shouldn't she? The only thing is, Lawreen isn't satisfied to keep it at one night, like Mom did. It seemed they were starting something real that night in L.A. That night. How often has she revisited it? Paul showed up in jeans and a t-shirt, glasses on his head; everyone perched glasses on their heads in L.A., and casual was the trend. Lawreen hadn't packed jeans; jeans reminded her of her mother, though Mariah's jeans must cost hundreds while Shinny most likely bought hers on sale at the Work Wearhouse store. Lawreen wore white capris and a sheer, floral top, pushed her sunglasses up over her forehead as if she did it every day, as if it were no big deal to be riding in the passenger seat of Paul's classic car, not the sporty model Lawreen had envisioned, like Mariah drives, but a big old thing, rose and cream, polished to a deep gleam.

"My first love," Paul explained. "Do you know what this is?"

A big, heavy car, a Chevrolet, she knew, because she recognized the logo, but Paul had to explain that it was a '57 Bel Air. She would not have imagined Paul a classic car fanatic, but he didn't obsess about it. In fact once he'd parked his baby, as he called it, in a safe parking spot, he didn't refer to the car again until they left the restaurant, a Mexican-Asian fusion place, with lemon grass chicken burritos that Paul insisted she try, so spicy she drank an entire pitcher of water. Paul offered to drive her around, show her some sights. He lived in Santa Monica, and it was clear from the big green signs on the freeway that that's where they were headed.

"Scoot over. I'll show you how teenagers used to cruise when your parents were young. That's right, now unbuckle my seat belt and stretch it around you. You know the original model didn't have seat belts? I had to get them installed. That's right. Now we're cruisin', sweetheart."

Parents? Her mother and Larry Blake?

Right! Ken is golfing, his firm's annual outing; drinks and dinner at the club afterward. Somebody's club. A club Lawreen aspired to join at one point. Considerate Ken said that he wouldn't be late but she shouldn't wait up for him. She rummages through the cupboards for something to eat. Dried apricots, rice crackers. She isn't hungry, but if she takes another bath her skin will dry out. With nothing to do, she slips into bed, but she can't sleep, and the pill she swallows does little to relax her. Something is missing, something she needs, but all she can think of is taking another pill.

For Elfie's sake, Shinny is doing whatever she can to find her father. Immediately after returning from New York she visited the apartment building she entered with him that summer so many years before, which is still standing, with an elevator that still works, the arrow pointing up still green. But what floor? The manager winced at her questions, lifted a paw-like hand to his bulgy cheek. Sorry, lady. No history here. Not like library.

Buildings last longer than the people who lived in them, the land beneath forever absorbing bones, arrowheads, oil tanks, foundations from houses long gone. She can't read the earth, but the library, okay, that was a good idea. Between the library and the City Archives, with the help of a young clerk compelled by her urgency, she discovered who had owned the building. It is a matter of life and death, she told the clerk. Do you mean life or death, he asked. It could mean that, yes, for the baby. The clerk showed her how to use the microfiche machine; suggested the public records she should examine. But to get a list of tenants, she would have to ask the former owner to search his private files.

A squat building set bunker-like into a low hill at Vanier Park on the edge of Kitsilano Beach, the City Archives stored old newspapers and photographs that recreated the past in her imagination. A big headline in

The Province reminded her that Mount St. Helens erupted the same year she conceived Elfie, but in May. Then it got so hot. The weather corner on a front page from July confirms her recollection: a torrid summer, just as this one has been, but worse because of a brewery strike. Driving back to the city from Meadowvale, where it was always hotter, the air as if ironed, Shinny had considered going to a movie. With Lawreen and Annette at her mother's, she had a rare night free. An air-conditioned movie? She picked up a paper on her way home and looked at the listings. Ordinary People? The title had to be meant ironically, because who would pay to see a film about ordinary people unless they were ordinary people made glamourous by some extraordinary event, to make the point. The clothes she washed and hung to dry before driving out to Meadowvale, the white cotton pants, the white cotton top from an import shop in Gastown, a white sweater for when the night cooled. No chance that Annette would wipe her face on her Mom's shoulder, or that Lawreen would spill something on her. You don't meet people at movies, only delay the loneliness that sent you to the theatre. She had to take a chance and so she parked near the Burrard Bridge and walked across with the gathering throngs, slowly, because it was humid still, at twilight; sweat pearled her forehead, her upper lip. By the time she reached Beach Avenue, the sun had set. The seawall around Stanley Park had been completed earlier that year. Maybe she and the girls would walk it, stopping at various attractions, Lumberman's Arch, the statue of the swimmer in the water, which Lawreen thought a mermaid. Lost Lagoon. Where Shinny first met John. She had wanted a man then, too, a father for Lawreen, someone to replace Larry, who might not have been steady in her life even if he hadn't tumbled off that railway bridge. John hadn't turned out to be steady either, not as a live-in husband and father.

Odd that she felt guilty before she even met Mr. Green Eyes. John, or Smokey as he called himself then, wasn't faithful. In those liberal days, he thought people should be free. You didn't have to talk about it, you didn't have to hurt anybody's feelings, he told her, his eyes big as they could get, a pair of raisins thumbed flat behind his round glasses—John Lennon glasses, the kind he still wears. That expression meant that she should stop her questions or she was going to learn something she might not like.

He shouldn't have told Annette about Elfie's true father. Shinny want-ed to do it herself, but John let the revelation slip. Don't know what I was thinking, babe. A rare email, a one liner from Annette, followed. Thanks for keeping me in the loop, Mom. Shinny pictures the twist of her middle girl's head, her raised chin, the tears that would have come into her eyes at one point, earlier, before she wrote the email. Saying she's sorry won't help, either. They all seem to hate it when Shinny says she's sorry, but isn't it better than saying nothing at all? Who lives a life of no regrets, nothing to apologize for? She doesn't regret having kept Elfie; her regret is the lie. Lies are the poison in the sludge of the past, and when it hits you like a toxic wave in a horror movie, all you can do is say sorry, and that doesn't change what has been done or stop the wave from engulfing you. The best you can do is to keep your head above it and try not to inhale the worst of the fumes.

All her girls are mad at her. Their anger has darkened the season like the sulphur-edged puce clouds that collected a few weeks ago over the mountains. Thunderclouds. Rare in Vancouver. Then puffs of brightness made a blueberry smear of the sky and a slim white branch of lightning pounced on the city. That was like a horror film, too. The rumbles moved closer until the thunder cracked directly above and the downpour started. She could hear squeals from opened windows. An unusually spectacular storm in a hotter than normal summer following a colder than normal winter. It has been one of those years.

The man who owned the West End apartment building where Elfie was conceived in 1980 died ten years later. She found out that much and phoned his son, who might have kept the records; he hasn't called back. What else can she do? Keep referring to him as Him, or the green-eyed man, like the one-armed man killer the fugitive kept looking for, in the old TV series? Kept looking for, but never found. She has searched the his-tory pages of the UBC Faculty of Music on the internet, studied pictures of the Vancouver Symphony Orchestra in the early '80s. But why does she persist in thinking that he was a classical musician? The Smilin' Buddha was big in those days too, Joey "Shithead" and D.O.A. Punk. Except he didn't look punk. Is what she remembers true, or has imagination tam-pered with memory? She thinks his hair was short, that he was freckled, tall, slender. But he would be thirty years older, no longer slim.

She returned to the archives, to the clerk with his three-day beard and pierced ear, his long sleeved t-shirt with French words written across it, who appeared too hip to be working in a bunker filled with old papers. Yet his enthusiasm for the past and his knowledge of how to access it said he loved his job. He squinted into options. How about a backwards directory? With the address of the building, she could search the tenants that way. The public library might have backwards directories from that year. Of course she would need to know the name.

"That's the problem," she confessed. "I don't know the name."

"I wish I could help," said the clerk.

She believes he meant it. He wanted to help, but he needed the name. The name. A phrase she saw printed somewhere years ago recurs in her mind: every child has the right to a name and a nationality. If Johann survives he will have a name, but there will be a blank space on the family tree. She can't put just any name in the space; it has to be a name that identifies his tribe. Oh, you're one of the Shinnans, people say, or the Singh-Gills, or the Browns. Names shelter people, offer belonging. That slang word "handle", as if a name is a way of opening a person.

Posters and ads from old businesses framed and mounted on the cement walls of the reading room distracted her. Old newspapers. An owl on the advertisement for the Wide Awake Furniture store on Hastings Street. The front page of The Vancouver Sun announcing the collapse of the Second Narrows Bridge. That event only fifty years ago, but already history. The present becomes past as quickly as the digits flick over on a watch, becomes part of the compost out of which the future grows. Tahir said as much about the election results. Election results are still rolling in, said the newscasters. But Tahir didn't need the evening news to learn what was happening in his country. His candidate came in third. Although the tally is not final, there is little chance that Bashardost will leap past Karzai.

"That Pashto thief," Sima said.

"They have it against us for centuries."

Apparently it takes anger to activate Tahir's vocal chords, because yesterday he talked more than he has talked in Shinny's presence since she began working for him.

"Centuries of trouble. Then Taliban try to kill us all, the Kuchis graze our land."

What will this mean for the war? Four more soldiers, three from Quebec, died in September; the latest, a private, as Mattie would be, if he's there. Still no word from him, and his mother isn't speaking to her. Only Kate to tell his grandmother that Mattie is still alive, posting messages for his friends. Mattie is Shinny's personal concern, but Sima, no wonder she can't smile without grimacing—all that inherited anguish. Centuries of it. Shinny has been trying to go back a paltry thirty years.

She is standing at the window, her thoughts more vivid than the first yellow leaves on the trees in the park when the phone rings. She tenses. Will the change of seasons bring a change of luck?

"Sheeny? This is Tahir. You work early today? It's okay?"

He has lived in Canada for as long as he lived in Afghanistan, and still he talks like his relatives. He needs more Canadian friends. But his voice is a relief.

"Sure. What time?"

He wants her right away. Something has come up, and when she gets to the store she sees that the something has to do with Sayed, who is dressed in a suit and carrying a briefcase.

"What's wrong?" she asks.

"No worry. I'm back in maybe two hours. You handle everything? Sima comes on train, after her class."

"I'm sure I'll be fine. Go ahead."

As Tahir and Sayed wait for a car to pass, then cross the street, Shinny imagines them in dusty turbans, or pancake hats, standing on a rutted road along which squat cement buildings resemble broken tombstones. Now that their candidate didn't win, will they try to get what they want some other way?

Sima hurries in at the expected time and takes her place behind the counter. As usual she looks tired. Her greeting smile has that same tinge of worry, of sadness that is, if anything, more pronounced today. Deep lines web out from eyes that, like her brother-in-law's, like Sayed's, are teardrops turned on their sides. It comes from them being Hazara, Sima explained, when Shinny asked about this similarity. It is how many Hazara look. Although she has not been in Canada as long as Tahir, Sima speaks better than her brother-in-law because she has been working on her English. Her husband does not like her going out; he does not like her working, he does not like her taking ESL classes, but since he cannot support her and their children, and since Tahir cannot do everything, they have reached an uneasy agreement. Nasir stays at home with his mother and the girls; he can cook, he can weave. All he needs now is the hijab, Shinny thought when Sima described her husband, but she didn't say it. People who take their gender differences so seriously would not see the joke.

"You didn't have to hurry, Sima. I would have been okay."

"Yes?"

"Sure. If you need to be home, I don't mind handling the store. Tahir will be back soon."

"Thank you. Maybe not, I think. Is not good for Sayed. He need the friend. If not for Sayed, Tahir cannot do this store. Sayed help with money to buy. Now somebody tell RCMP Sayed is bad. Tahir goes for him to questioning."

"The police? But why?"

"For suspicion, I do not understand. The terrorism, I think."

"Who would do that?" Shinny asks, as if she never considered doing so herself, as if she too did not find the frequent meetings between men wearing dark glasses worrisome. And Bashardost. He seems an honest man from what she has heard on the news, read on the internet, but is he, really? Anyone can write on Wikipedia. What does she know? Truly, nothing.

"Nobody know. Could be anybody. You notice signs on bus? If you see something, say something? That person who tell RCMP. Who knows that person saw what?"

"Oh Sima, and with all you have to worry about. But if he didn't do anything, it will be okay. This is Canada."

That pained smile again, a touch of condescension. In her own country Shinny disappears in the crowd; she has never been suspect, she has never been an immigrant from a country known to have links to terrorism, that now common phrase on the news.

The conversation that has more or less flowed around the comings and goings of customers wanting stamps, forms from Shinny, pop, magazines, candy, cigarettes from Sima, pauses again when a man with a baby bound to his chest enters and stands in front of the magazine rack, studying the selection. He's a Vancouver Canuck, one of the best defensemen. He chooses a *GQ* and a newspaper and a large chocolate bar. The baby continues to sleep on his broad chest. Sima rings through the purchases without looking into his face. Many of the team live in this neighbourhood during hockey season, and it's usually a thrill for Shinny to see a player, especially after a big win, when they swagger a bit. But Sima doesn't know that her customer is a famous hockey player. She doesn't know hockey. Doesn't care. Does she think Shinny is the one who reported Sayed? She did ask about him, and she also Googled sites for information on what to do if you thought someone might be a terrorist. That's as far as she went, yet Shinny feels guilty for even thinking those disloyal thoughts about the man who financed this little store's beginning, meaning her job.

All these things you can't know. How you start out sure, then gradually become more uncertain as you get older. Yet stones are somehow more entrancing, mysterious, seen through water than when the tide goes out and you can walk on them, and the barnacles are nothing more than something to crunch beneath your feet, the fingers of kelp something to avoid or slip on.

HERE HE IS, AT the train station in Vancouver, which is also the bus station. It's 6:15 AM and Matthew is booked on the next bus south to Seattle. He has his actual passport, a bank draft made out to him, in his real name, for $10,000, a story in case he's searched and the border guard asks what he's doing with so much money. The story? It's a student loan he just got. He's going down to the States to visit his sister and begin school at Sonoma State University; the bank draft will start a new account. He has his sister's address in Los Angeles, also his aunt's, Annette's, whom he'll visit before school begins. This is what he has rehearsed, repeating it to imaginary border guards so often that he's on the brink of believing it himself. Matt has mastered pretending, but he usually does so at a desk, in front of a screen; he isn't as good in the flesh, he hasn't had as much practice. So as he sits on the wooden bench, half-consciously tapping the rubber sole of his running shoe on the spotted terrazzo floor, smelling Egg McMuffin and coffee from the in-terminal McDonald's, he tries to zone out. If he's convinced of the story, there should be no sweat at the border. Matt chose the bus as a way of crossing because he thinks it must be easiest to go in a crowd. Maybe the border guard climbs on the coach to inspect passports. Punching something as he goes, like a ticket taker. Matt has not considered what he'll do if there's any trouble, doesn't even let himself imagine the possibility. Part of the reason he has been writing to his mom has been to avoid trouble. It should be okay. He is Matthew Webster, formerly of the University of Alberta, Edmonton, traveling south to visit his sister and his aunt before continuing his studies at Sonoma State University, in computer programming and psychology. Plausible, because Sonoma State is known for these specialties, but he doesn't know anything about psychology. If he's questioned, the safest answer will be something related to computers, which he does know about.

If anyone remarks on him looking pale, he'll explain that he is dangerously sensitive to the sun. That he has to stay inside during the day, or use heavy-duty sunscreen. He has kept his hair cut short. No mustache, no scruffy beard. A beige golf shirt. In the mirror he looks like a Jehovah's Witness without the suit; his appearance will get him through the border. He knows how to be polite, deferential. It shouldn't take long.

The departure is announced and Matt walks out to Bay 3, where a Quick Shuttle bus is boarding for Sea-Tac Airport. He's going to fly down to L.A., he plans to say, and everyone knows that it's cheaper to fly from Seattle. His sports bag is loaded with clothes, a couple of books on computer technology. He also has a backpack with a blank notebook, a water bottle, a graphic novel to read on the way down, something Matthew Webster would bring. An iPod with pop songs. Pink, Britney, Metro Station, Rihanna. Nothing political. He first imagined himself as this character, Matthew Webster, then bought props to detail that identity. When he nods to the bus driver taking his ticket, asserts that he does have a valid passport, and makes his way to a seat midway down the aisle, he perspires a little, but it's seasonal, honest sweat.

After sledgehammering his computer and throwing the pieces into a dumpster at the back of his building, he didn't much care what was left in the apartment. He did check to ensure that nothing he left behind could be traced to him—but what was there? A blow-up bed with a set of sheets, a blanket; a few dishes—he walked out of the apartment before daylight, feeling like a turtle that has moulted its shell. During the walk from East Hastings to the train station on Main he actually felt the air sting his skin.

He had planned all along to move at the end of the month, but he didn't think Berk would be the guy to vault him over the border. Not after six months in hiding. Berk is determined to a degree that stuns Matt. The news came through Kate Babcock.

Dear Kate,

I think pots are a good idea. For one thing, you can bring them inside when it gets cold. Some of your herbs might even last through the winter. Oh, by the way, if you see Mattie, or write him again, tell him that his friend Berk called. He was passing through Vancouver and remembered my name, which is amazing. He said he hadn't heard from Matt for a long time. Well I don't know about you, but I said to Berk that he can join the club. I wonder if you ever met Berk. A nice young man. Very polite. He said he had an accident awhile back, and he had to go to his physio appointment, so he couldn't come over. I did invite him. Well you know I'm thinking that I might try some pots, too. I have a balcony. But that's going to have to be next year.

Yours,

Sharon Shinnan

CLOSE. REALLY CLOSE. BUT physio six months later? For real? With Berk you never know. His most consistent characteristic is evil. Funny the way evil shows up, without the horns, the pitchfork, but with radar that can zero right in on a person's dark side.

The bus stops at a couple of downtown hotels and heads out Cambie Street towards Highway 99, which leads to the border. Can't happen soon enough for Matt. No one has sat down next to him, but the bus is full enough, a couple in the seat just ahead snoozing, wrapped around one another. He closes his eyes and leans his head against the window. Matthew Webster is tired. He has been preparing for this change, saying goodbye to family and friends, selling off things he won't need in California. He's had to talk to Kate, the girl he's been seeing for a couple of years, since they met at the University of Alberta. Actually, if Kate had agreed to marry Matthew, he might not be making the trip today. But Kate has a mind of her own, like a lot of girls his age. She's into organic gardening and herb growing. A wholesome sort of girl. That's what Matthew Webster likes about her. It might not be over. Kate has promised to write, and he probably won't stay in California; after all, he's a Canadian. But still.

If he doesn't pull back and realize what he's doing, he can get so caught up, Matthew Webster's emotions start working on him: rejection, being dumped by a girl he thought he'd like to marry. He can get lost in the Matthew Webster he created. And that's okay. Because here are the exit signs to White Rock and Crescent Beach. Border just ahead, and traffic not too heavy this time of day. He can sink back into Matthew and think about Kate, whom he imagines to be pretty, fair, like Aunt Elfie, and slim like her. Mom is blonde, but not really, not anymore. She colours her hair and so does Mariah. He doesn't know what colour their hair would be if they let it grow out. Kate is a natural blonde, like Elfie, and doesn't have much in the way of tits; that's like Elfie, too. Not the dancers in the clubs he went to, on the Downtown Eastside. Those girls all had big breasts, probably most of them fake, and would touch them while they slithered on the floor or around the pole that stood in for a big dick. Matthew Webster has visited those places, sure, but out of curiosity. As a guy he's the more straight up type, like his dad, Ken Webster, who's an accountant and a husband and a model railroader.

The bus driver announces the drill: everyone has to get off the bus, with all their luggage, and go through customs one by one, inside a building where bus passengers are supposed to be fast tracked. They are instructed to have their papers ready so that processing can take place quickly. Once everyone has been cleared, they will board the bus on the U.S. side and continue on to Sea-Tac.

Since he sat midway down the length of the bus, Matt is in the middle of the queue that forms inside the U.S. Border building. Everything is serious here. People stand in lines; half walls and roped off sections keep everyone where they are supposed to be. The uniformed customs officers at counters you have to file through have guns at their hips; they listen for suspicious answers to the standard questions. Where do you come from? Where are you going? How long do you plan to be in the U.S.? At the last minute Matt decides to change his story because he heard one of the officers ask another passenger if he had a student visa. Mattie doesn't have a student visa. His cashier's cheque is folded inside a piece of paper in his jeans pocket. No one will know he has it unless he's searched, and there's no reason for anyone to search him.

He thinks of Kate. Bites his lip. When will he see her again? Sweet Kate, her fresh face—she gave him homemade jam, she baked cookies for him—keeps him in Matthew Webster, whose turn finally comes.

"Where are you from?" the officer asks.

"Vancouver."

"Where are you going?"

"I'm going to Los Angeles, to visit my sister, Mariah Webster. She's an actress. Maybe you've seen her on TV? She was on *Lost* last season."

This is more talking than he's done in months. He's nervous. Kate, Kate, Kate; Matt thinks her name like a prayer.

"Oh yeah? How long are you staying for?"

"Two weeks. Gotta get back for school."

"Oh, yeah? Where do you go to school?"

"University of Alberta, that's in Edmonton."

Matthew Webster thinks about his dad, about the sturdy locomotive that chugs through plywood fields painted blue and yellow. This border guard is about his Dad's age, and he speaks with a mild twang. A mustache, a double chin, though he's trim; he must work out. He inspects Matthew Webster's passport, fiddles through his backpack, pulls out the graphic novel, *A Distant Neighborhood*. Mattie has bent and otherwise manipulated the book so that it looks as if he's been reading it.

"You know that one?" Matthew Webster asks, with a little smile, a Ken Webster smile on his face, a do-no-harm, sorry, I-guess kind of smile.

The border guard puts it back, hands Matthew Webster his backpack and turns to the person behind him.

"Next?"

He's in! Or out.

BRENDAN IS FROWNING AT score sheets spread over the desk. The music is leading him away from the formal structures drilled into him at university and after, when he studied in Europe. Moving from computer to cello to Elfie's violin, he tries to let himself follow the music's lead, yet wonders if it is teasing him into another blind alley. The players must have some liberty to improvise, as is part of the musical tradition of India, for one, of jazz, for another; Ping is expecting some freedom and looks forward to the spontaneity the other performers should offer. But is the base strong enough to support the constructions of musicians Brendan hasn't met, may never meet? What a contradiction, precise notations for improvisation? Chopin used to improvise, then try to catch on paper the spontaneous flow from his fingers.

Elfie is sitting on the couch, talking to Annette. September and still humid; the whirring fan drowns out voices and other noises from the street.

"I haven't talked to Mom either. How could they be such hypocrites? I don't know. The other thing is, I barely have time to talk to anyone."

"Oh, sorry, Annette. If you have to go."

"No, it's okay. Everything's cool. I don't know, Elf, I'm just so sorry. I can't imagine what it would be like. But you know, you're still young, you could have other kids."

I don't know, Annette says. She says it a lot. And, I can't imagine. It's true Annette can't imagine what it would be like. She has never been pregnant. Never wanted to be, as far as Elfie knows; Annette wasn't the best person to call. But she had to talk to someone, and definitely not Mom and definitely not Lawreen, who sounds spacier and spacier. Now Lawrie thinks that their mother is holding something back from her, too, that maybe she has a father she doesn't know about, that it was just convenient for Shinny to blame the pregnancy on the famous and long dead Larry Blake.

"But it will be pretty hard, won't it? I mean, almost like the real thing? I don't want to say you should or you shouldn't. It's such a personal decision. Man, Elfie. I sure wouldn't want to be in your spot."

Annette is right. At this stage in her pregnancy, the abortion won't take a few minutes, but a few days, at least two, before the child she has been calling Johann will be gone from their lives.

"Maybe you shouldn't have named him, Elf. It's probably harder."

"I know, I know, but I did."

Annette is sympathetic, but the breadth of the continent doesn't begin to equate the space between them. Go with your heart, that doctor said; Elfie's heart says yes, that she should trust his, her baby boy's, heart.

"I'll let you know what happens."

"Good luck, Elfie. I'm real sorry you're having to go through this."

Brendan doesn't turn. He doesn't come over and put his arm around her. Although he is wearing earphones, she can hear leaks from "The Moldau", which has become part of his regular playlist along with the work of a contemporary composer, Oliver, from B.C., and Cage's "First Construction in Metal". How he'll put all this together, how he can think at all, is a mystery to Elfie. It's different for men, unless he's channeling the stress. Classes have started to squeeze his time. Since they got the news about the baby, he has compartmentalized to the extreme, but she knows a bit of what he's thinking by the music he listens to, this stirring and sentimental piece that is very unlike what he described, and sampled, for his winning proposal. It might be the watery beginning that intrigues him, but the lush sweeping strings? The peasant dances? Isn't what he's trying to do the opposite of the nationalism that inspired Smetana over a hundred years ago? Now "The Butterfly Lovers," again with the flutes simulating the trickle of water, violins playing a melody using chord structures and patterns from the Chinese tradition, modified for Western instruments. This piece also based on a folk song about a legendary river, also melancholy, lush. What is happening to them is coming out through his music. Maybe this is what he is trying to fight, or manage at least.

Elfie has had no luck finding her father. She discovers a promising name in some directory and Googles it, looks for pictures. She can't find a red haired, freckled pianist from that era. Not in the classical genre. Mom said he was younger than she was, so in his fifties now? Has there been a famous red haired pianist? Maybe not famous, it doesn't matter. Lawreen is the one who likes to fantasize about a heritage loftier than what came through their mother. So little to go on! Green eyes, a grand piano. No matter what she decides about Johann, she won't stop looking until she finds Johann's grandfather, or learns that he's dead.

She waves to Brendan. "Could you take your earphones off and turn that down for a minute? We have to decide, Bren. I just wish we didn't have to do it before we know what only my father can tell me."

Barefoot, bare legged, in shorts and a white t-shirt, he stands, stretches, strides over creaking planks to the kitchen, returns with an apple.

"What if you do find him, though? What if you find him and surprise him—hey, Dad! And it turns out that his family has all died of cancer, not a heart defect among them. Then we've waited, making the abortion harder and more dangerous, for nothing."

"Except I would have found my dad."

"Who you lived without for your entire life."

"Because …"

"I know, because you thought you had a father. Elfriede, we've been over this too much. Don't cry."

"I can't help it. Women get emotional when they're pregnant and this situation just makes it worse. I know you want me to abort."

He hits the back of the desk chair, which smashes the desk, waking the computer.

"We didn't even want a kid yet. Now all this drama!"

"Don't call him a kid, like he's a stranger."

"Don't make him what he's not. We have to accept that it isn't meant to be. I don't want you to wait anymore. The hospital has a spot for us this week."

"I don't know if I can do it. Look, he's right here! If you let yourself think about him. He has arms and legs, he can swallow. He's almost a pound."

A Bollywood number, "Bulleh Shah", blasts out from the computer speakers, the brightness, the infernal tambourine. He doesn't have to say with any more emphasis that the conversation is finished.

Can the marriage bear this uncertainty, this tension? Lately it has been doubtful, though when he takes her hand there is still voltage between them. They have been one of those lucky couples who reach for each other every night despite what has happened during the day. Except she's been feeling so fragile, feeling Johann is so fragile, that she has resisted Brendan's touches under the sheet. That must be part of his frustration. There's one more ultrasound tomorrow. She looks pregnant and is wearing clothes that emphasize her belly's roundness. She loves the attention she attracts when she walks down the street, eyes that glance at her middle before moving up to her face. How could there be anything wrong?

"Bren," she shouts, "if the ultrasound shows that nothing has changed, I think we should go ahead, take a chance. If it's clearer that the defect is serious, I'll have the abortion. And it will be the end of it. I promise."

He kills the music, stares at the reproduction of Tintoretto's *The Origin of the Milky Way*: cherubs, birds, the father placing the child at the mother's breast, the bright blue background, the points of golden stars. They brought it back from Europe, and when they could afford to do so, Elfie had it framed and hung it on the brick wall. Brendan has been letting her take the lead from the time she found out she was pregnant. He would really rather not be thinking about it all, but working. It's like hearing something in the distance, trying to get closer, but running in quicksand. It's out there, he complains, but he's not getting closer, and time is getting short.

She believes that he sees her, their situation, as the obstacle. The threads of his piece resist his attempts to weave them. Chaos, discord, but not the intentional chaos he is striving for. He respects deadlines, he is strict with himself in that sense, no patience for procrastinators. He's battling on to deliver the score when he said he would. And while he was as intrigued as Elfie to know that her biological father was probably a musician, he's come to the point, she knows, of not caring if the man was a musician, a mass murderer or a plumber. The despair in his eyes, the way it pulls his face down, actually sags it, and the whites of his eyes, which can be yellowish when he's tired, that awful colour of a dried mustard smear. Everything's a what-if with her now. What if Brendan is sick with something? How could she handle a sick husband and a disabled child? He stops pacing and stands with fists on hips, arms making triangles that jut out from his body.

"Okay, so say I agree. We wait until after the test tomorrow to make the final decision. Will you stick to that? What about all the medical science you've thrown at me? They can do anything? Even before the birth?"

"I promise, I won't change my mind after tomorrow. The picture should be clearer. It might be that everything's okay and we worried for nothing."

"It's not okay, Elfriede. I know you want to believe that, but you have to be honest with yourself. There's a hole in his heart. Maybe not big, maybe not so bad, but you can't start thinking it's all going to disappear. It's going to cost money to fix it, and sure, my parents will help, but I've got to keep my job, which means this," he waves an arm, as if he can just summon his idea, vapour about to materialize, "this has to be the best."

"Don't you think I know all that?"

Tara, her yoga teacher, has counselled her to breathe deeply at times of stress, to step back, remain uninvolved, follow the breath. If it weren't so sticky out, if people didn't keep pushing her. But she tries, standing at the kitchen window, where smells of garlic rise from Francisco's patio. If she lets them take Johann, people like Francisco and his staff, and the clerks at the grocery store, her students Hilda and Brian, Tara and her yogis are going to want to know what happened. Lost the baby, I lost the baby, she'll say, guilt stabbing her, the word "lost" implying negligence. Their happy expectation will freeze, then shatter, as if someone has stepped on it, and the new expression will be fragmented, uncertain. Well you can try again; that's what everyone says, you can try again.

That night Brendan thrusts hard, from above, resting on his elbows; from the side, his left hand caressing her swollen breast, teasing her nipple. Sex is not supposed to dislodge a fetus, and if they do accidentally dislodge Johann, then it will be decided. She's sure Brendan is thinking the same thing, that this is him holding a finger in the wind to determine which way it is blowing, and then she can't think anymore. Orgasms are good exercise for the womb, for birth preparation; but these waves are small tsunamis, like the contractions she's read about? Is that what's happening? Whatever, there's no chance of finding higher ground; the sheets are wet, her legs are wet, the pillow is wet, Brendan is wet and she can't tell if it's tears, or humidity, sweat or semen, or the amniotic fluid that proved Johann has no chromosome disorders, only that vacant space, like the eye of a needle, in the left ventricle of his nut-sized heart.

DAD IS HAVING A party, but Annette is not invited. Music fans out, old hippie music. The Grateful Dead. People climb into trees, into the pasture, to commune with the goats. Wild animals galumph into the yard, a big white bear, a dinosaur without a tail, a leopard slinking. Dad's house is closer; she can see people dancing on the cement pad at the bottom. Dad is dressed as Santa Claus and people take turns sitting on his lap. Now Elvis is playing, "I'll have a blue Christmas without you." The leopard and the white bear just sit there. Neither one of them seem to be interested in the goats, who run up and down the pasture, maa-ing. Finally Dad shouts something to the dinosaur, and the dinosaur galumphs further down the now steeper but shorter slope. He is tall enough to look directly at Annette, who faces him from her deck. His eye is amber, and his pupil consists of concentric rings, sucking whirlpools; his breath carries the dregs of everything forgotten. As she comes to, the dinosaur has turned into a horse that's chewing on the rail of the deck.

She wakes. A horse? No, it's Shep. Black ears upright triangles, eyes bright, whitening muzzle around a worried mouth, and he's scratching at her door. Something wrong? She sits up, reluctant to leave the dream, but already the dream is going wherever dreams go. It's almost daylight, a sky the shade of the dull side of tin foil glazes the window above her bed. Weird dream, but she has to shake it off and get going because after she milks and feeds, she will drive into Santa Rosa to fetch Matthew. Funny he made it down here.

"Annette? It's Matt," he said on the phone yesterday. Out of the blue. "I'm in San Francisco. Is it okay if I come up and hang out?"

"So you're not in the army, then? Thank God. You've got everybody worried about you, Matt."

"Yeah, well, I'll talk to you when I'm up there, if it's okay that I come, I mean. I think there's a bus to Santa Rosa."

"Or I could drive into the city, or Dad could. Your grandpa."

"Aw, I wouldn't want to put you out. But don't call Mom or anything. Okay? Like I said, I'll fill you in when I get there."

He would have come all the way, but there isn't a bus that stops in Sebastopol. Annette doesn't mind; she needs a trip into Santa Rosa anyway. With her milk totes and bucket clanking, she steps into the gauzy air of morning. Shep treads behind her to the barn as usual, stands at the fence while she fetches a doe, follows her to the milk stand, where he collapses onto the straw littered stall floor.

The strange dream is vanquished by the day thoughts that occupy her, about her nephew, her shopping list, which she made last night and tucked into the visor of the truck. Matthew was growing in Lawreen's womb when Annette left Vancouver, and since she has returned only for holidays, and he has not visited the farm with his parents more than a couple of times, Matt is a near stranger to his aunt. Always a nice little boy. At Christmas she saw that he had grown out of the gawky teen stage, still a nice kid, but not much of a talker. Hey, how you doin', he would say when they ran into each other in Lawreen's house. Greg offered him a smoke, but Matthew didn't smoke. He wasn't pious about it, he just said no thanks. He kept to himself, but you couldn't call him antisocial. He helped clean up after the big meal; he sat around and listened to every-one's stories. Drove people through the snowy streets in his friend's SUV.

She finds Matt standing right outside the Greyhound station, on Santa Rosa Avenue, which is considerate of him because she won't have to worry about leaving the supplies in the back of the truck, not that thieves would be tempted so much by sacks of alfalfa, diatomaceous earth and the case of bag balm she picked up because it was on sale. He's got a backpack and duffel bag, which he throws on top of the farm supplies, and climbs into the cab. Annette holds her face forward in case he wants to kiss her, but he's fiddling with the strap on the seat belt, apparently not comfortable with a kiss.

"You're travelling light, Matt, and it's a big surprise that you called, but I'm glad you did. Are you hiding out?"

She means this as a joke, but his twittery laugh convinces her that he probably is.

"No way. Just trying to see the world. Thought I'd start with you, then go stay with Mariah. If I have any money after that, I might head into Mexico. But I don't want to be tied to any plan, so I've been laying low. I mean as far as the family goes."

"Your Mom is worried about you."

"Yeah."

"But I guess you've been in touch with her."

"She knows I'm okay, but like I said, I'm trying to lay low, just be free. I've never done it before. Thought I'd give it a try."

"Well you can stay with me as long as you want. I could use the help. Greg's been away."

"Oh yeah?"

She said away, which surprises her. But it feels right. Delores is un-conscious now. Annette talked to her for the last time a few days ago. If I don't talk to you tomorrow, remember I love you. Delores replied, Oh sweetheart, you sweet girl, I'll still be here tomorrow, so Annette said that she would talk to her then, and she called, as she has every day these last couple of weeks, but Delores couldn't talk. Greg answered, as usual. She's in a coma, he said.

"Are you all right?"

"It's kinda strange," Greg said. "I feel peaceful. I feel I've worked a lot of things out just bein' here. She's a unique woman, Annette. I've been lucky to have her as my ma. She's not afraid, Net. She's got a clear picture of what she's heading for and she's ready. You know, I may not smoke anymore. I'm doing okay without it. No more fuzz on the scene, no more easy justifications."

"I know," Annette said, which she did. She'd left off smoking herself for the most part. But how would it be with Greg straight? He hasn't been straight since they met.

"I'm not promising anything. "

"You don't have to promise anything to me."

"I'm talking to myself. I'm not making any promises to myself. It's one thing to be here, with her, another to be back there."

Annette didn't say, so you're coming back? Because she didn't want to sound needy. She has been managing fine, and now she has someone to help, if Matt helps; if he stays long enough to help, if he can do anything practical. He's jiggling his head to some music only he can hear, and he's not plugged into an iPod. They pass a vineyard, where harvest has started. One of the local farmers is trying to make a festival of it, but the biggest, most established vineyards, east of Santa Rosa, draw most of the tourists.

"They're harvesting the grapes," she explains, pointing to the people in the rows, most of them Mexican, most of them wearing ball caps. Big plastic tubs on the ground, a tractor with a wagon attached. Clusters of pale green. If it were Lawreen's vineyard, she would want the harvesters to wear straw hats, and maybe sing. She's the kind of person who would sign up for a grape camp herself, put on her own ball cap and gloves and join the other city folk who want a harvest experience, to eat and drink themselves silly for a week for only a few thousand dollars. Yet this feels a disloyal thought with Lawreen's son in the car. He doesn't seem to want to talk, but he's still nodding his head and the corners of his mouth are turned up. When she was at the age when she didn't want to talk, she didn't smile either, and before she can decide whether or not it's important to draw him out, they are nearing the farm, which he remembers.

"Hey, the driveway's coming up, isn't it? Just past that sign there?"

"Matt, you remember, and you've hardly been here."

"I remember things all of a sudden. They just pop into place."

He is sitting forward in his seat, anxious or maybe just excited, which is cute, considering his age. Could he be someone who will follow her into the country life? She brakes for the turn into the gravel driveway, liking the homey crunch beneath the tires, the brush of the scrub oak leaves against the sides of the truck, the sense that she is dropping into a slot the perfect size and shape for her. She drives slowly, giving Matt the chance to smell the trees and appreciate how far into the forest they're going. In the old days, Dad had to have a long driveway; he needed to know when someone was coming. Then the state police started using helicopters to look for crops, and growers had to become more inventive. The vegetation thins where the driveway begins to open out into the circle that skirts the barn and the house.

"Wow, it's different," Matt says.

But he doesn't say how. It's that exhausted late summer look, before the hard rains begin; everything yellow. Even the green leaves of the willow and the oak and that big magnolia dad bought her to replace the cherry tree the goats nibbled at, even those are jaundiced, like an old person's skin, a sick person's eyes, a hardening lemon rind. Matt stands by the side of the truck, obviously pleased, his fingers flexing on the grip of his plain black duffle bag. His skin is oddly white for this time of year, his blue t-shirt dark against his spine where sweat has dampened it. Could he be sick? Is this a goodbye tour? No. She's thinking like her sister.

"Come on in, Matt. You can have the room I call the study, even though I don't do much studying. The computer's in there, and of course a bed. It used to be tough to get you off a computer, so I figured it's the place for you. Anyway, I don't have another room with any kind of privacy."

He follows her up the stairs, in through the sliding glass door off the deck. Needles and fallen leaves have collected in the creases of the sail awning. They're going to have to take the sail down eventually; maybe while Matt's here. When she told him he could stay as long as he wanted, she thought he'd let her in on his plans, but he accepted the offer with thanks only.

"I haven't done too much to the house. It must be pretty much the same as when you were here last, right? Here's the kitchen, help yourself to what you need. Everybody pretty much serves themselves all day, then Dad, your grandpa, or I cook dinner. The bathroom's back there, and my room. Here's your room. I'm going to go out to check the goats. Come out when you're ready."

"Okay," says Matt. His eyes are shining; couldn't be tears. Might he be on something? She doesn't want to pressure him, but eventually he'll have to explain what's behind the hush-hush.

The girls see her standing at the fence and thunder down the slope, anticipating food. Cleopatra's classic Nubian call and the more stuttery bleat of the Lamanchas shatter the silence. Annette had another Nubian, Zoe, but Zoe's lovely long ears flapped even as she convulsed and died before they could get her kids out of her. Nubians are less reliable, she found. It was Dad who initiated her to goats. When she first moved down here, all her worldly possessions in the trunk of Dad's old Jag, he had a big herd and a young couple to help him. Green, but wanting to please, to show him she belonged, she tried playing with one of his bucks, William, who typically peed all over himself and often her, and got boners whenever she tried to touch him. That left her wise to bucks, that experience, sore ribs and a broken toe and a purple-brown bruise close enough to her eye to qualify as a shiner. When she developed her own herd, selecting her favourite does from the goats Dad wanted to sell and adding the beautiful Cleopatra, before she knew Nubians, she kept Willy and added Bob, but she left their care to Greg, who griped about their smell, but found their one-track minds and their forceful rutting admirable. Such studs.

Carmen, the leader of the Lamanchas, lifts her chin to the side, inviting a scratch from Annette. Goats like their chest and shoulders to be scratched, more than their head. They can see all around them, but not something that arrives from the top; they startle if she reaches in to scratch their heads as she would scratch Shep's. Marie, Loretta, Kathleen and the others jostle Carmen, but gently, knowing who's boss. The kids born earlier this summer scamper down to see what's up. Annette feels like a mama with a big family and an exaggerated, tear-holding-back smile spreads across her face. She sniffs. Must be that she's missing Greg. No. It's the simple honesty of the connection, her and her goats. She could never lie to them as her mother lied to her; she could never, would never, betray their trust in her by hurting them, like Greg hurt her.

He GOT OFF THE bus in Seattle; that much he's sure of. Five days later he came round to himself in a motel on the Oregon Coast, a place called Coos Bay. Smelled of wood pulp and rain soaked into carpets, soaked into everything. Walls of fake wood paneling, a stained, olive green lampshade teetered atop a brass stand. Matthew Webster's backpack sat on a blue leatherette chair beneath the window, the duffel bag on the floor. A can of Coke on the bedside table, a half-eaten bag of Doritos. He hates Doritos, the way the cheese coating stains your fingers. He checked his hands; they were clean. A receipt on the dresser showed that he had checked into the motel two nights before. The bathroom had a soapy air, as if he had showered before he went to bed last night. Thin, white towels on the floor. Plastic wrapping from a disposable glass on the sink. Okay, last night he showered and brushed his teeth with a brush that's his, from his kit, but where had he spent the other three nights? In the mirror he saw that he had shaved, and that scared him, the idea of bringing a razor so close to his throat when he was unconscious, or the equivalent. Toenails, finger-nails, hair, all growing without him being there for it. Going through the motions life required, shaving, eating, showering, but like a sleepwalker. What else? A true black space existed between Seattle and this mill town. Did he take a bus again? Had he flown? No, you couldn't go through security, air pressure changes, all that, without waking up. Could you? It was like files he had neglected to save before shutting down, and now that he had powered up, he regretted the information lost.

This was the worst yet. No idea how he got there, when he got there. No idea what he did on the way, said on the way. He thought those epi-sodes would stop once he got out of Canada; sites he found on the web before he left Vancouver explained the brief periods of amnesia as stress-related. Thing was, he couldn't take a chance on it not happening again. He had to hang onto himself, and his best chance of doing that was to be with people who would ground him. His vague plan of visiting his aunt became firm. From Coos Bay it wouldn't take more than a day to get to San Francisco.

In the few weeks he has been here he has turned on the monster, old-style computer only a couple of times. The slow dial-up connection es-tablishes with a techno-pop dance number kind of sound. It's as if all his people went on vacation, some wilderness trip where you don't have electricity. Or died. Kate, Kev. Beetle, Robert. The bulky monitor sits on a shelf just wide enough to hold it, the keyboard and tower on a lower shelf at the end of the daybed Annette assigned to Matt, so right there, in his face the minute he opens his eyes, which is early because he hears Annette clanging around with her pails and totes. She expects him to help and he does help, but he can't see himself milking, not yet; maybe never. The girls, as she calls them, fidget when he enters the barn. They can smell his fear, just as dogs are supposed to be able to do. If he got right in there, at the milking stand, one of them would kick him in the face, probably, or he'd pull on the teat too hard. Mammary glands, like the tits on the girls at the bars he used to hang around; like any girls, though you'd never connect nanny goats with girls.

Instead of actually milking, he washes the milk pails and the totes with Clorox, and Annette appreciates this, thanks him every time, because her hands are wrecked. Now his hands are getting wrecked, if wrecked is what you can call their unnatural whiteness, the walnut-shell pattern at the ends of his fingers. She gave him gloves to wear and he's going to have to start wearing them because he's washing the dishes, too, and at night, after supper, there's a counter full of them. It's a new world, a new life, and the best thing about it is that he has not vanished again and if he did there would be someone who noticed.

He has helped with the washing and sterilizing; set the table for dinner when Grandpa and his kids come over, which is pretty much every night; played catch with Aidan, who groans when the ball goes way off, but seems keen to let Matt keep trying to snare it in the glove. Annette wonders if Matt needs glasses, but Matt thinks he just needs practice looking at things farther away than the screens he has been focused on. He has joined in Eve's pretend games, something he is good at. Everything in his old life seems very far away: Berk, Vancouver. The scams. The possibility of being found out, or losing himself. No wonder Grandpa chose this place. He doesn't need a hide out now because he's not doing anything illegal, but he was growing marijuana when he first moved here, and he doesn't mind telling Matt about those days. An old timer reminiscing. Weird. But he's a cool guy. He doesn't ask too many uncomfortable questions and has agreed, like Annette, to keep Matt's presence here a secret until Matt decides what he's going to do. Matthew Webster is filling out with the actual, not the imagined, building an identity in the tangible world. The easygoing nephew, grandson, cousin. How he's related to Aidan and Eve he isn't sure, but they don't seem to care. Before school started, Eve sought him out first thing in the morning. Cute, pudgy little Eve in stained shorts and t-shirt over a chest beginning to bud, runners fastened with Velcro, no socks, a rim around her lips, from grape juice; hair like her dad's and a little nose and hands that are dimpled, smooth-skinned, tan; dirty fingernails.

"Let's pretend that the goats are wild horses, okay Matt?"

"Okay, then what?"

"We have to go catch them and bring them in."

"I'm not so good with the goats, Eve. They don't like me."

"We're just going to pretend to go get them."

"Okay. What do we do?"

More than anything, Eve likes to talk. Her chatter replaces the Vancouver sounds of traffic, air conditioners, voices from computer-streamed talk shows and sitcoms, movies. When Eve goes to school, it's really quiet, but Matt is able to handle it better. Eve has been a good bridge; Grandpa talks a fair bit, too.

"What are you now, Mattie? Twenty-two? Plenty of time to figure things out. Just put that army idea right out of your head. You gotta give up torturing your grandma, too; she not only misses you, she thinks you're in Afghanistan, son."

"Mom should've told her I'm not. What's up with them? Why aren't they talking to each other, Grandpa?"

"Some mother-daughter mystery. It's bound to blow over, always does. Meantime, tell ya what I'd do, I'se your age, though. You're pretty good on computers, right? I'd get me a web business. Live somewhere off the beaten track like here, keep yourself in touch with people all over the world."

"Good idea," Matt said, inwardly quaking with a combination of paranoia and hilarity. It is just the career he has been trying to put behind him.

Then, at dinner last night.

"You give any thought to that computer idea, Matt?"

"Yeah, I've been thinking about it. Thing is, though, Grandpa, you need a high-speed connection for stuff like that. I don't know how far away you are from getting that here. Will you ever get it?"

"Always something else you have to get. Well you can stay here as long as you like, son, but there isn't much work. Go over to Occidental, get a part-time job in the hotel, maybe."

"He'd need a car for that, Dad. I can't spare the truck. Do you think you can spare yours?"

Annette is less clear about him staying, Matt thinks. She lets out one of those big sighs, as if she's saying okay, I guess I can't do anything about this, when she squeezes around his stuff to use the computer, which she doesn't do often. Yet she's happy when he brings the clean milk pails to her in the barn in the morning. Her best time of day. Sometimes she doesn't get dressed but heads out in her pajama bottoms and an old plaid shirt, her hair wild around her head, sleep in her eyes. The goats can tell she's in charge and she talks to them while she wrangles them into the stand, while she's pulling on their bulgy elongated udders, the pointy teats, while the warm stream squirts into the pail. Matt brought coffee out to her a couple of times and she said, Mattie, you're so sweet, but she drank just a swallow. Now he knows she prefers tea.

She isn't kicking him out, but she says things like, while you're here, or, as long as you're here, or, if you were really living here I'd get you to … This usually comes after Grandpa and the kids have gone back to their place up the hill. No TV here. The nights tick by until it's late enough to go to sleep. Matt suggested a card game once, and she played, to please him, though her thoughts were somewhere else. She always goes outside to check on her goats before bed; this is his chance to use the computer if he wants, but that stupid dial-up sound! Grandpa's dog Shep may bark at something. The goats maa. Otherwise it's quiet, quiet. If he isn't in his room by the time she returns from the barn, he hears that exaggerated sigh, the stomping around from kitchen to living room, apparently look-ing for something she has misplaced, though he suspects it is her way of marking territory.

Matt's sense is that she wants him to move if Greg comes back. From overheard phone conversations, he knows they're going to try to get back together. Grandpa has suggested that Matt stay with him and the kids. You come over to us next week, Mattie. I could use your help getting the kids to school. He wants to give Annette and Greg a chance, even though he's not real sure about Greg himself. It's funny, Matt thinks, that people say one thing around the table and underneath is the conversation they're really having. Like last night. One thing Matt especially likes is the family suppers. Even when he was a kid they didn't happen every night like they do here; Grandpa cooks sometimes, but Annette most often, something good, like a roast chicken or lasagna, or enchiladas. Always salad, always something for dessert, cookies or ice cream, or a crisp from the apples that grow on the trees. Eve has started to bake, so they're getting cupcakes now, thick icing on top, usually pink. Matt feels like he's gained a few pounds. He has definitely gained some colour, except for his bleached hands.

There's the rush of getting things off the stove once Grandpa and the kids come in, but then everybody sits down, and Grandpa says that they will have a minute of silent thanks. And it is just a minute, more like thirty seconds, and then the food gets heaped onto everyone's plate and Aidan or Eve fills everyone's glass with water—good well water—and then they start eating and talking, and after the first night, Matt's has not been the main story; a lot is going on with Annette, with Aidan and Eve; and with Grandpa, you never know. One night he talked about his suspicion that anarchy was behind the fires burning up the state. State can't pay to fight them; perfect opportunity for some underground terrorist. More often he says something about the research he's been doing at the town library, having to do with medical treatment for babies with heart defects. It's because everyone in the family is worried that Elfie's baby will be born with a hole in its heart. That's the on-the-surface conversation, but underneath are the references that have put a lot of questions into Matt's mind. Stuff like, too bad your genes don't matter. Annette throws these things out and Grandpa shrugs, glances at Eve or Aidan, or Matt, who looks away. Whatever is going on, they don't want the kids to know and maybe they don't want him to know either. But he wants to be fully aware of everything. Their vagueness scares him, recalls the moment he hung above a river in Washington State. Just hung there with the toes of his shoes stabbing the fast running water. He wants to be present, in the know; he doesn't want to risk another several-day gap.

October

Elfie has been sending websites, pictures. Oh baby, Shinny wants to tell her youngest; just stop. It's too late. You'll never find him. But Elfie won't give up. In case she is his only child, her father will be glad to hear that he has a grandson, and she wants her son to meet his grandfather, too. Shinny continues to investigate websites, pictures of balding men playing piano for chamber music groups in major cities, jazz pianists, music teachers. Under the link to music, 1980, Vancouver, she discovers that the first jazz station went on air that year, that "O Canada" became the official national anthem.

Would she even recognize him were Elfie to find a picture of the right man? Could they computer enhance him like the police do to update the files of missing children? She remembers hip bones knocking; long fingers like rivers on her back, flowing down, catching fire rapids. Disturbing, arousing. That old memory. Was it him?

Elfie may be running out of possibilities as her pregnancy advances and the new mystery takes shape. Who will this child be? The brilliant boy of two brilliant parents? Someone sickly? Someone with less than a fifty percent chance of surviving his first year? These are just three of the possibilities, and the last ultrasound proved to be no more definitive than the first two. For now, his heart is still beating its unique rhythm. Abortion is no longer an option.

No pictures, no websites from Elfie today. No emails except for one in pink, from the dating website, reminding her that she hasn't visited in months, that several men have included her on their list of favourites. She clicks into the site's account menu and hits delete. Are you sure you want to permanently delete this site, the computer asks. She moves the cursor to yes and presses the mouse so hard she'd have killed it were it an actual and not a plastic rodent.

Dear Kate, she writes. *Have you been on vacation? I was wondering if you dried any of your herbs. You should be sure to get them in before the rain starts. It's been a great year for herbs but the rain will come. We all know that. Anyway, just thought I'd drop a little note. Be sure to say hi to Mattie if you hear from him. Tell him his Grandma misses him.*

Shinny stands at the balcony door watching the joggers in shorts and t-shirts, as if the seasons never change for them; the dog walkers, the grey of morning—because it's that time of year, morning low cloud that might burn or blow off, or not. The gulls scream, here we are, it's another day! Traffic shushes down Pacific Boulevard. Spiderwebs are forming in every corner, a perfect one on the window frame; one spider dropped silk around a fly, bound it, strand by strand over days. Amazing patience, spiders.

It's a day with no shape, but she can't stay inside and stew. The clock on the stove says 10:12, same on the microwave. The clock radio on her bedside table slightly ahead, 10:15. Once she has straightened the paisley-patterned duvet on her double bed and smoothed the pillows, dawdled over the pictures she has arranged on the dresser, of her parents, her grandparents, her girls when they were small, all of them in blue, at Stanley Park; baby pictures of Mattie and Mariah, the 8x10 of her and Glen, on the porch of his farmhouse—a picture Annette snapped and then enlarged and framed for a gift—after running a dust cloth over them and rounding up the few clothes that need laundering, not enough for a load, she considers the living room, the kitchen. Rinses her teacup, collects the remote controls and lines them up on the coffee table. There's no point in vacuuming the handkerchief square of carpet; she did that yesterday. This apartment is cleaner than any place she has lived, for what is there to do inside but rearrange keepsakes like the Mattie and Mariah's plaster handprints, from kindergarten, the large pine cones she gathered in California, the ceramic tomatoes she loves, actually antique salt and pepper shakers that belonged to Glen's grandmother and which Shinny hid away before Glen's son Evan and his wife could claim them. Some people in this

over-fifty-five building stay inside most of the day, watching TV, working on crossword puzzles. Not her, not yet. She eats a banana, showers,
dresses in her usual jeans and blue fleece jacket. In the mirror it doesn't
seem to be herself that she sees, yet these are her brown eyes behind the
turquoise-framed glasses, and her teeth, which used to be whiter. If she
doesn't remind herself of details like this, she isn't self-conscious about
smiling. Would a computer enhancement have predicted this image? She
has to get out of here, out of these self-discouraging thoughts. No one in
the hallway when she peeps through the spyhole; no one in the stairwell.
But when she steps outside she is surprised by the bottle man crouched
beside his cart.

"Hello! How are you today?"

The big beseeching eyes, wet, but maybe from the cold today because
leaves and scraps of paper are whipping across the bricks. It's as if he hasn't
heard her, he doesn't answer. "Well have a good day", she says, stepping
around him, into wind that's making meringue of the usually tranquil
False Creek. You just never know; he could be angry at the lack of bottles
beside the fence that shelters the garbage bin, yet, like migrating birds
whose habitat has been paved over, an inner program prompts him to
return. He could be deaf, or electing which voices to listen to.

She's across the striped pedestrian walkway and into the park before
she can complete the thought. A fast walker as she had to be for most of
her life, there's no reason to break the habit. Tired asters, dusty purple.
The Japanese maples turning, and a tulip tree whose heart catches fire, like
a flame about to consume the whole tree. She takes the long way round to
the grocery, where she tosses basics into her basket, basics for one: half a
dozen eggs, lettuce, a small head of broccoli, a single chicken breast, and,
on impulse, a bar of Belgian chocolate. Before she returns to her building
she stops at the Roundhouse to pick up a Community Centre Program
Guide and the *Georgia Straight*, a weekly entertainment newspaper. She
should do something that will occupy her, something that will take her
out of her thoughts and the fruitless search for her old lover, her grandson,
the risky terrain she would step onto were she to offer to testify on Sayed's
behalf, be a character witness for him. Sima and Tahir undoubtedly will
do so, of course, but what does Shinny, a part-time postal clerk, know of
Sayed? For now he is being investigated because he's suspected of being

someone other than who he says he is. A search of his condo turned up a couple of sets of false identity: passports, birth certificates, SINs, B.C. driver's licences. Sima says that she doesn't understand; Tahir says nothing.

Knitting for Beginners; Drawing on Life; Keeping a Visual Journal; Manology: Exploring 21st-century Masculinity; Women to Women; Gentle Yoga, Gentle Pilates, Gentle Racket sports, all the gentleness aimed at people with fragile bodies, people her age. The *Georgia Straight* is thick with ads for similar classes, for movies, plays, restaurants, concerts. Full colour large and small enticements to escort services, images of big breasted girls, muscled men, cram the back pages. And set off to the side, a section for people who want to follow up on the currents that pass between strangers in public places:

Starbucks, Robson Street. You were daydreaming until I ran into you, literally, and spilled a little coffee. I apologized and you assured me it was all right, and then we just smiled at each other. Why didn't I get your number? Buzz cut, a single gold earring. Brown eyes. Reply to Box number.

It gives her an idea. Sure, a long shot. A long shot, going to the moon, winning the lottery.

The ad appears in the following week's edition, which she grabs as soon as she sees a stack of them delivered to the box outside Davie News. There hasn't been a customer in ten minutes. Tahir is standing at the counter where his father often sits, but Tahir is going over records on his laptop instead of watching TV. CSIS has subpoenaed the store's accounts.

"But it should be okay, right, if they don't have anything to hide?" Shinny asked. Sima's response, another wounded smile, expressing knowledge Shinny is not privy to. Does Sima think her naive? Is she right to think so? All Shinny can do is offer to work more, to help them make it easier on themselves, which is why she is here today.

I first saw you at the Sea Festival in 1980. I was dressed in white. I last saw you sleeping. There was a grand piano in the room. Is your hair still red? I would like to talk…. Box number.

Will he read it? Will he remember her white hair, her white clothes? Is he even in Vancouver? She's had no luck with anything else. Elfie is either no longer mad at her, or is suspending judgment until the baby is born. She is thinking positive, she says, not even considering that her Johann will be born with a broken heart. Not a baby so well-loved. A broken heart. Meanwhile she continues to practise yogic breathing and meditation, plays her violin everyday, gives some classes. Brendan is thick into his work at the music school and nearing completion of his commission, which he has dedicated to Johann. Elfie says that everyone will think he's referring to Johann Sebastian Bach because Brendan used to play Bach's cello suites, was known for playing them in his solo recitals—there is even a CD of him doing so—until they know that he composed the piece for his son.

Although Shinny can cut through the Roundhouse courtyard for the fastest route home, she chooses the seawall this evening because she can smell the turning of the weather. The light is going already at 6:00. There are more fallen, brown leaves crunched up against the path edges, mixed with peninsulas of cigarette butts stretching out from some benches. Soon this walkway will be strewn with leaves and she'll have to endure the obnoxious leaf blowers city workers use to force them into piles that can be scooped up by equally noisy machines.

"Greetings. Good you arrive here where light be under land." Such cheery, positive, welcoming thoughts. "Come to time where people talk different but good together."

So optimistic. *Come to time when people talk different, but good together.* Tell that to Sayed, Tahir. When people talk different these days, other people think they are plotting a terrorist act. The thing is, what if they were, or had been?

Will anyone answer her ad? Maybe an impostor. Did he have a distinguishing mark that could be her trick question? But what would be in it for an impostor? A red haired impostor.

Advice everywhere you look. *Be bold, free, truthful* ; the graffiti she saw the day her worries about Tahir began to escalate. Though faded, it's amazing that the words are here at all. As if a city worker recognized the importance of the advice and decided against scrubbing them off.

To KEEP HERSELF BUSY, and to get rid of the cobwebs that always form in the fall, Lawreen has set herself up to wash the windows she can reach, on the lower level; Ken can get the ones on the second floor, or they can hire a professional. Housework frees her mind, almost a meditation, and when she finishes whatever chore she set for herself, she feels as if she has solved something, for a few minutes at least. It's a clear, sunny day, perfect for outside work.

She has her pail of water and vinegar and a stack of newspapers, which she is tearing into manageable pieces, when she is distracted by the classified pages in the *Georgia Straight*. Crazy. At least four pages, some ads in full colour, with sexy pictures of so-called "escorts". The photos remind her of the worries she had about Mariah appearing in porn films, a concern that spurred her trip to California. Three months ago already? She stayed in Mariah's apartment and found not a shred of evidence that her daughter had fallen into a sleazy L.A. scene. Just a young girl living the life, a closet full of beautiful clothes, a red convertible, friends, friends, friends. The bits of luxury she shared with her mother, brunch on the terrace of a girlfriend's parents' house, which overlooked the city, impressive despite the wide ribbon of smog that draped it; the outfits mother and daughter wore in Mariah's convertible, large sunglasses and scarves, like in classic movies with Ava Gardner or Marilyn Monroe. Drinks at the Polo Lounge of the Beverly Hills Hotel, Mariah's treat, because she had landed another part that morning. Another small part, but a speaking role, in a pilot based on the lives of girls who come to L.A. and end up swimming with the sharks, as the promoters, agents, wheeler-dealers are called. Deservedly so, too, Paul explained, that night. That one memorable night. Mariah had worried about her. Cute.

"Will you be okay, Mom? I mean I hate to leave you, since you came all the way down here, but it just wouldn't be safe for me to drive back tonight, you know?"

"Honey, I told you it would be okay. I'm going to see Paula for dinner. Drive safely. I'll see you tomorrow."

Mariah wore jeans that accentuated her curves but didn't advertise them in neon. She had fixed her hair in a top knot from which strands of various blonde shades fell around her cheeks and her forehead. Makeup, but that also understated. Ken would approve, for he didn't want Mariah to go totally Hollywood when she left Vancouver: don't turn into someone we won't recognize, honey. Oh, Daddy, she said, hugging him. You'll always recognize me. I'm your little girl! Lawreen had watched their goodbye hug with a mixture of sadness and impatience; sad because

Mariah was leaving, impatient because she was driving Mari to the airport and it was time to go. Much as she would miss their daughter, it was the right move for her to make. The visit in June proved it, for while not the big fish she had been in Vancouver, Mariah had won roles in important shows. That indie film Lawreen had worried about. Oh, that! Mariah said, dismissing it. I don't know if you'll ever see it, Mom, but I met some good people. Good meaning influential.

Paul agreed, when Lawreen repeated the director's name.

"Yeah, he's an up and comer. No Tarantino, but I doubt he's into porn. What's porn anyway these days, you know? You can see anything you want on TV. Even in prime time. I don't know how those old hack porn producers survive. Jesus, with the internet, everybody in business for themselves. Nope, porn has become mainstream. Just like celebrity. With YouTube and reality shows, everybody can be famous."

So that was that. Her excuse for contacting Paul in the first place. She had emailed him about the quick trip she planned to make to L.A., to check in with Mariah. Trying for a breezy tone, as if she did this every weekend, she said that maybe she would give him a call. Sure, he emailed back. We'll have a drink. She described the date to Mariah as a visit with an old friend, somebody she met on set years ago. Not as good an actress as her daughter, Lawreen turned on the blender to cover her tone of voice. Shouted, "Didn't you meet her? Paula? We kind of hit it off when you were on the set of Cuties, and we've kept in touch by email. Such a long time ago, no wonder you don't remember."

"Mom, I can't hear you!"

"Never mind. Do you have everything you need?"

She has finished the windows that she can reach. Now she needs a ladder, and more newspaper, and she wants to refresh her water/vinegar mixture. The squares of *Georgia Straight* flutter in the breeze she creates entering the kitchen. The girls in their push-up bras, their thongs. If there are this many ads for escorts, there must be that many potential customers: lonely, love- or at least sex-starved people. That awful man who went into a gym in Pennsylvania and shot several women as revenge for all the rejections he had experienced. Sick. The gym Lawreen goes to is upgrading security, and maybe that's a good thing. Everything is so unpredictable, scary. She doesn't like to think about it because the anxiety spirals up to the point where she wants to go to the drawer that secrets her blue medicine bottle. She resists for as long as possible because she fears addiction, but some days she needs a vacation. Most often when she's home alone with her thoughts. Work keeps her occupied, routine as it is, and she tries to keep her feelings under control when Ken is home. It's just times like now when the windows seem too big a job, she wipes and wipes but there's always a streak: Mariah will be rejected; Mattie? She doesn't know what to think about Mattie, but she considers that her mother may be right, that he has joined up and doesn't want anyone to know, that he was one of the soldiers patrolling the election stations in Afghanistan, trying to make it safe for people to vote; that Paul was just using her for sex, that she'll never see him again; that Mom has contracted some disease that she won't tell anybody about because she doesn't want Elfie to worry; that Elfie's baby will be born, only to die minutes later, plunging the whole family into grief. She wants to hear her mother say that everything will be all right, that Lawreen shouldn't worry. Has enough time gone by? Would it mean surrender if she called Mom as if nothing happened? One thing she has to know, was Larry Blake really her father? What if he wasn't?

Here it goes, breath coming in shorter puffs, shoulders rising and tensing, to prepare for attack. But awareness doesn't mean that she can stop it. Her mind flies to vivid worst case scenes: Mariah's body stuffed into a dumpster like that bikini model strangled late in the summer, right in L.A.; Mattie coming home in a body bag, when they didn't even know for sure he was over there. Ken finding out about her one-night affair with Paul, weeping, because Ken would never hit her, but he could divorce her and, being the careful accountant he is, what would she be left with? What if she had to move in with Mom, into that tiny apartment? She could live with Annette, but she hates farms; she doesn't belong there. She'd have to cash in her RRSPs and live in some kind of basement suite.

This can't go on. Just one, maybe a half. Yes, a half. She doesn't even have to go upstairs because a spare bottle rests in a drawer in the dining room. There, tucked in among her linen tablecloths and napkins, are the arms that will hold her and keep her safe from these spears aimed at her from all directions. The calming effect is immediate. Just knowing there is this chemical embrace to fall into allows her to breathe, check the phone for messages. Think of going to the computer when she finds no messages on the phone, but resist doing it. To return to the kitchen and methodically tear the paper into more squares, to fill her small red bucket with warm water, to add white vinegar from a large plastic container. Gradually, her thoughts become pleasingly slower, so that when Ken comes home from the dump and starts pulling things out of the fridge to make dinner, she suggests they order in, her treat.

"I guess you needed some time alone," Ken says. "You're looking very relaxed, honey. What do you want? Pizza? Chinese?"

She's crumpling the unused newspaper into balls; her hands are black from the newsprint. "You decide," she says. "I need a bath."

Finally Annette came right out and said that she'd like to have the house to herself; he would have to stay at Grandpa's. Matt said sure, he and Grandpa had already talked about it, but he would still help wash up if she wanted, and Annette said, we'll see. Annette had a determined and guilty look in her eyes, like a health food fanatic at a McDonald's take-out window.

Grandpa offered to fix him a bed in Aidan's room, but Matt doesn't want to invade Aidan's space; he saw the "dude" look in Aidan's eyes when his dad suggested the arrangement, as if he were saying, what's up Dad, isn't it my room? Matt jumped right in.

"Hey, you've got this great pullout bed right here, Grandpa. I'll be fine."

"Being out here in the traffic wouldn't bug you?"

"Not much traffic, Grandpa."

Which is true. The kids have their own rooms and Aidan spends most of his time in his. Eve hangs around, but Matt doesn't mind. He doesn't get too involved in her pretend games but lets her chatter, helps her work through recipes for her cakes. Makes sure she doesn't burn herself on the electric stove.

The kids leave early on the school bus, and if the weather's bad, or they're running late, Matt drives them up to the road to meet it. After they're gone, he puts the cereal away, cleans up. It occurs to him that he's cleaning more here than he's ever cleaned in his life, but that's okay. There's a lot to do. He didn't mean to get started on the fridge, but Eve wanted to make chocolate frosting for her cupcakes and Grandpa said he was pretty sure he had some chocolate back in there somewhere. Matt had to tunnel through rotting vegetables and stuff that was actually growing, that looked like undersea plants. Never did find the chocolate, but he threw out anything he didn't recognize, scrubbed the shelves. His Mom would be proud to know she had influenced this in him. Both parents are neat freaks. Maybe he could get a job as a school janitor. Be the quiet but friendly fellow the kids are glad to see when September starts. It's a thought. He'd need to be a citizen or get a green card; intriguing to think he could fake one of those—maybe he could. But no; he's given up that stuff. Still, just one more time and he could legally work here.

Half of the upstairs of the hexagonal house is more or less one open room, and this is where Matt sleeps; the kids' bedrooms and the bathroom take up the other half. Matt's first sight of the day is the T in the bar of the screen where it meets the frame of the slider, which he keeps open at night because he likes the smell of the woods. The slider faces west, so it's not the sun that wakens him but a greyness in his dreams that morphs into the morning sky, with the bars of the trees separating it into strips. It's been okay so far. Only that one episode last week, when he found himself by the dried-up stream under the willow tree. He couldn't have been there long because it was still light; he could smell Annette's supper. If a day had passed, someone would have come looking for him. He's wearing an old watch Grandpa gave him, now that he doesn't have a cell phone to tell the time; Matt frequently looks through the scratched glass at the old-fashioned dial in case he has another episode and needs to know how long he was out of it.

It's warm, though the fog hasn't burned away yet. Every morning starts with this haze. Grandpa says that it's worse than ever this year on account of the fires that are torching the state. He so often talks about the fires that Matthew pictures the shape of California systematically blackened, from the Mexican border on up. But it couldn't be that bad. What about Mariah? Somebody would have told them if Mariah were threatened. Grandpa is sitting out on the cement deck outside his downstairs room, on an overstuffed chair that used to be brown and still is brown under the cushion, though it's bleached to a sandy colour on top. He's drinking coffee and waiting for the sound of Greg's truck.

"Morning, Matthew," he says. "You get yourself some coffee?"

"Yeah, I did Grandpa. I got some right here. Nice day."

"Let's hope it stays that way."

Matt knows that he's talking about Annette and Greg, that he's worried. I just want her to be happy is all, he keeps saying. Greg can be an asshole, but hey, a deathwatch can change people.

"Yeah, it's a big day, I guess. Everybody's having big days lately, eh? I mean, Aunt Elfie, her big day is coming up."

This is Grandpa's chance to fill in the blanks Matt has noticed in conversation about Elfie and the damaged baby everyone is worried about, but Grandpa doesn't bite.

"She's got a bit of time to go, but it's going to be a big day for sure and we got to hope it's going to be not only big, but good. Listen to that. You hear a truck coming down from the road?"

"I think so."

"We just gotta leave them be, you know. 'Til they come over, or she does. We gotta give them their space."

"I know that, Grandpa. I will."

Grandpa takes another swallow of his coffee, holds the mug close to his beard, listens, as if he could eavesdrop from way up here. He's a nice guy; if Matt can talk to anyone it should be Grandpa, with his laid-back folksy style. An accepting kind of guy.

"Grandpa?"

"Yes, son?"

"Did you ever have a blackout?"

He chuckles. "Oh yeah, I did have myself a couple of those back in the bad old days. Everything you hear about the '60s? Well, it's true, Matt. If you remember, you weren't there. And I was there. Why do you ask?"

"Oh, no reason. Just curious. Something I read, and …"

"I think that's gotta be him. I heard a door slam. Did you? Your hearing's got to be better than mine."

Matt was going to talk about the time he woke up on the bench. He'd had a couple of beers, but not enough to black out. He wouldn't mention the other times. The Oregon episode. But as it turns out, nice though Grandpa is, his mind is down there at Annette's place. He's a good guy, Grandpa is. He just wants Annette to be happy.

"I have to pee. Do you need anything while I'm up there?"

"Nothing I can think of, son."

Aidan's computer is better than Annette's, but the dial-up is just as slow. Maybe he should start going into town and using an internet café, if there is one. There's got to be one. But here he is logged on, connected, if slowly, to Google. There's an email from Gran to Kate. It's been weeks since Kate wrote to Gran. Sweet Kate, who got him through the border. But he was going to quit this stuff. But if he just keeps it simple …

It's just as well Mattie isn't talking to his mother, Annette thinks; her spinniness might scare him. Lawreen has been thinking about moving to California. Not to northern California, but to L.A., to be nearer Mariah. "What does Ken think?" Annette asked. "Oh I haven't talked about it with him. It's just a thought."

A crazy thought, in Annette's opinion. But she doesn't say that to Lawreen, and she keeps her promise to Matt by refraining to mention that he is living with Dad. Lawreen chatters on. They have been talking to each other more often, the sisters, since they found out about their Mom, and they haven't been talking to their mother at all. Annette had only that one conversation, more a screaming match than a conversation.

"It was like that then. People believed in free love. What about your dad?"

"Dad didn't have any kids. Not like that. Not with someone he never saw again."

"We wouldn't know, though, would we? That's how it is for men."

"If he did know, he wouldn't have lied about it."

"Of course not. He can do no wrong. Not in your eyes anyway."

Annette continues the argument in her head. Shinny had the perfect chance to reveal her past when she visited the farm in June. Okay, maybe Elfie was not yet aware that her baby had a hole in its heart, but she was pregnant with a child carrying the genes of his mysterious grandfather. The truth means that Annette is the only one of Shinny's three daughters who grew up knowing her actual father, a fact that invites smugness, but it wasn't her who created the situation; it's not her who should take it on, suffer the guilt.

Elfie should have started all over, but no. She's going ahead with the pregnancy and she will not stop looking until she finds her father. Good luck. She has almost nothing to go on. What if he was not the tall pianist their mother remembers, but a freak, a psychopath? Desire can fuzz a person's view. Annette has been trying to keep it in check, to look at Greg for the person he is and not the man whose arms she snuggled into most nights for nearly twelve years. She hasn't had sex in months, but he has. Can she put the cheesemaker's sister out of her head, those images that tortured her through the summer?

Everything is tentative, temporary. For now Greg is sleeping in the study, helping as he always did. They're taking it slow. Matt didn't like being turfed out. After nearly a month sharing space, Annette had learned to read the signals he must think so well hidden.

"Matt, we always knew this wasn't a long-term deal, right?"

"Yeah, I know, and Grandpa thinks I should move over there. So I will. You won't need me anyway if Greg's coming back."

"Oh I'll need you. We all need you. You know how much there is to do around here, but you're more of a natural with the kids. Eve especially. She's crazy about you."

"Sure. Should I go right now?"

"Anytime you're ready."

Mattie's hair has grown out since he arrived. He looks better, even handsome. He's let his beard grow, too, but it's wispy. He still doesn't like to get too close to the goats, but he took over most of the house duties. She misses that, but she can't exactly invite him over to sweep and scrub and sterilize her milking equipment now that she has more or less kicked him out. To know he was lying in the next room while she and Greg tried to feel their way back to one another, it would never have worked. Now they can take their time. She tosses in their couples king-sized bed; Greg spills over the edges of the single in the computer room. The house beats with the tempo of the blood pumping through her heart. She has to make the first move, if there's a move to be made, and it can't just be about needing him to relieve the ache between her legs, the sensation that moves from chronic to acute as she lies listening to him clear his throat, sigh, bump into the wall beside the bed; as if she needed any reminders that he was there.

She rises earlier than usual to give herself time to wash her face and comb her hair. When she returns to the house with the first milk, there's coffee Greg has made for himself and a thermos of tea for her. He may be watching from the deck, his cheeks scraggly as Matthew's. He's letting his beard grow, too. Must be something about the country, all the fur on the animals, that inspires them. But it's good; he no longer resembles a greaser going to court. He's settling in.

Tonight, after supper, after Dad and the kids and Mattie leave, Greg puts a CD on their portable player. Rufus Wainwright covering The Beatles. One of Annette's favourites.

"Go ahead, sit down, put your feet up. I'll finish this off," he tells her.

Annette is barefoot, in loose cotton pants of a Guatemalan woven fabric, a blue and black plaid that she concentrates on, trying to imagine small brown women working at their looms. She has been keeping her feet clean, the edges of her heels scraped of dry skin so that they are softer, less like hooves. Crazy. Almost twelve years together, only six months apart— longer if you count his mental absence. He knows he has to work for forgiveness, and he has been working, and he hasn't been smoking so she has given it up too. If they're going to reunite they must come out from the screen weed erects between people. The smell of bleach is clouding the mood with reminders that she has to be up in eight hours to milk and feed. She should go to bed and let him tinker with whatever part it is he's working on, which he brought into the house but thoughtfully set on old feed sacks, so that the engine grease won't stain the wood planks. He was not so thoughtful before. Lovers take so much for granted. Kiss my neck, lick my eyelids, run your hand over the hills and dips of my body, kill me with orgasms and you can walk all over me. Is that it? Or that sleeping together all night, united in flesh and even in some dreams, engenders such familiarity that one never considers that the other might not think the same, act the same; that the partner might be a discrete human being.

Annette likes the respect he has shown. She doesn't want to give that up. Rufus sings, "Words are flowing out like endless rain into a paper cup ..." The pulse of the house deepens as Greg turns off the overhead kitchen lamp and lights a stick of incense to counter the bleach smell. As if they want to move towards one another but their boots are stuck in mud, the picking up of one foot, then the other, makes such a sloshing, sucking sound, each step broadcasts their slow progress.

HILDA WISHES SHE COULD play "Autumn in New York", because it is autumn in New York. Elfie agrees that it is a great song, but Hilda is not ready yet. She has moved on to "Go Tell Aunt Rhody" and she has played it without a mistake, hitting every note and handling the bow more sensitively, so that too much pressure does not release the shuddering squeaks she used to produce. Elfie resumed teaching because they can use the money and Elfie can use the distraction. She has given up auditions instead, and continues with only a few students: Hilda, of course, and Brian; River and two young people from the neighbourhood.

Hilda stands five feet in her sandals, her ankles swell and redden when she walks too far, but this doesn't stop her from trundling around the city, just as her lengthy learning process hasn't stopped her from persisting with her music lessons. Her goal is to play Bach someday, and the three minuets in Book 1 are within reach, but her short hair, tight black and white whorls, may be completely snowy by the time Hilda gets to the minuets. Her fingers strain to arch over the fingerboard of her instrument; she's an adult, she should be playing a full-sized instrument, but since everything about Hilda is sawn off, the violin seems too large for her. Elfie watches the large blue stone of her ring, a star sapphire, rise and fall as Hilda plays: Go Tell Aunt Rhody, Go and tell her now, Go tell Aunt Rhody, the old grey goose is dead.

Hilda brought chocolate rogelach today and she expects Elfie to invite her for tea. The post-lesson tea has become their ritual since Hilda arrived one day when Elfie couldn't hide her blotchy face, the reddened eyes. She had resumed lessons Week 24, when she had made the decision. There could be no reversal now, Dr. Radan cautioned her. Are you sure? I'm sure.

"What's wrong, dear? Not to pry, but you look sad. Did you get bad news?"

"Oh, sort of, Hilda. Don't worry. Have you been practising since I last saw you? Shall we start with some scales?"

And so they proceeded, but Hilda reminded Elfie that their habit was to finish the lesson with a song. Something beautiful to inspire me, is how she put it. That day Elfie couldn't concentrate. With the first notes of the partita that had become her theme, her eyes began to sting; she sniffed. Hilda saw the distress, wanted to help, if not push herself on her teacher.

"Not to be so forward, darling, but I think I should make us some tea."

Elfie spilled all. I don't know what to do, Hilda. I can barely think, she admitted. He that can't endure the bad, will not live to see the good, Hilda said, quoting someone Elfie doesn't know. Hilda adores her and believes that Johann is going to be fine. With a name like that, darling? She's glad that Elfie didn't go through with an abortion. She claims that her sixth sense is telling her that the baby will be beautiful, perfect. As for Elfie's mysterious father, Hilda is thrilled by the story. What if he's right here in New York, darling?

But what to look for? Pictures? Names? You'll know, dear. You'll recognize your father. When you see his face, you'll know in your heart it is him. Elfie doesn't share Hilda's confidence; doubts bore through her like the tunnels beneath the city where all the trains rattle along in the dark.

Today Hilda is thinking of the rogelach, the talk they will have instead of Aunt Rhody, and after playing the bridge almost perfectly once, she stumbles again. Stout people don't wrinkle quickly as they age. Hilda's oily tan skin is smooth, except for the bristles at the corners of her mouth.

"Concentrate on your scales and Rhody, and next week we'll move on to "Come Little Children", okay?"

"I will practise morning and night. Next week I will give you a perfect Aunt Rhody. Now you put your feet up and let me make the tea. Maybe I should turn on the fan, darling? You're all flushed."

"Thank you. I'm okay. It's just my skin type."

Hilda has started for the kitchen, her sandals pointed to the sides. She waddles back with the rogelach on a plate; next time with two white mugs, the tabs of the tea bags hanging over the rims; a third time with a carton of milk and a jar of sugar.

"They say a hot cup of tea cools you down. I don't get it, but they're experts on everything, whoever "they" are. You can't argue with genius. You know, darling, I heard of someone in a position such as you find yourself in. She found out the truth with DNA. Something, what they can do with the DNA."

"I know, but I can't do it, Hilda, until I at least have someone I think could be a candidate."

"It will happen, it will happen. Never lose your faith. I have an old friend, did I tell you? Used to work at the 42nd Street library."

"Yes you told me."

"She knows how to find everything and she's going to help, so don't you worry. Now tell me about the baby. Still kicking?"

He is kicking, and this is a good sign. All normal babies move about in the womb. There are times at night when they lie on the bed together, Elfie with her legs spread because a rash has developed on her thighs, and Brendan resting his hand on the hill of her swollen uterus; he has tried tapping a finger, to see if Johann will reply, if he understands. According to the website Elfie follows on fetal development, Johann can hear. Still, it's expecting too much that he would respond in kind to the rhythm his father is fingering layers above him. Now that they've made the decision to go ahead, Brendan occasionally lets himself enjoy the wonder of the pregnancy, no doubt worrying, but what new parents don't worry, about health, about money, the state of the world their child will be coming into? They have to be careful, Elfie especially, about contracting the H1N1 virus; they have to avoid the large and sometimes violent rallies where people argue the pros and cons of health care reform. Obama offered hope, but events have dragged him down. He's sending more troops into Afghanistan; he hasn't been able to put the millions of unemployed back to work; bank executives are still rewarding themselves with obscene amounts of money.

Mostly Brendan is preoccupied. He has been invited to join a quartet; he is the featured soloist at the faculty concert next month. And he steals whatever spare hours he can manage to refine his symphonic poem. He listens to drafts on his iPod, he changes the notation on the score sheet, tries rhythms on the walls of the shower, on the table while they're having dinner. Makes odd sounds, not singing, but sounds that simulate the voices of the instruments he's writing for. Ping has been clamouring for a look, a listen. Trust me, Brendan tells him—but he doesn't trust himself.

Although he thinks Elfie's search for her father ridiculous, he doesn't ask about it anymore. As far as he's concerned, there is nothing to do but wait for the birth, hope for the best. Yet the news that her mother delivered that August morning has opened up the potential for rebirth, too. Elfie's sense of self expands. Always the odd one in the family, the daughter that people looked at curiously, not just for her colouring and her tall slim build—in those qualities she is not so different from Lawreen; through her life it was as if she and Lawreen shared a heritage, not she and Annette, at least physically. So talented, people would say, now where does that come from? When Elfie was little Mom listened to music only on the radio, the Golden Oldies station, and Smokey prided himself on being a blues man, had a collection that included some classics, but not the classics Elfie discovered when she started playing the violin. Late, compared to most of her musician friends, whose parents enrolled them in classes when they were as young as four. But it came to her easily, the music, and she never hated practising. Mom would hush her, because they lived in that co-op apartment. Elfie, that's great, honey, but we don't want to keep people awake. The music is enough. The security she feels with the fiddle in one hand, the bow in the other, the coming together of instinct, note, hearing it a split second before the bow contacts the string, settling into a phrase she knows, like a path she has walked hundreds of times; yet technique demands attentiveness, even after years. It isn't automatic. She doesn't need to perform like Brendan, she doesn't have to compose like him or be the best in the world; she doesn't crave recognition, though she had some back then, in university. The scholarships, the invitations to join trios and quartets. Brendan.

People call it a gift; such a cliché, that phrase, but it is a gift, and if what her mother thinks is true, then this is a gift from her father. It's not so strange that she can identify pitch, hear the music as she sees it on the page, but natural, how it must have been for him. Her ear for music, as it is called, has personified her. But will her musical voice change, as her knowledge of herself has changed? The history she thought true? Brendan thinks she's making too much of it. If she were writing, yes, she could be influenced, but as a player, no. Elfie disagrees; everything will be transformed in some way.

"I'll just clear these things away, you lie down now. Don't you worry about me."

"Rest won't help, Hilda. It's better to be active. I'm still going to yoga."

Brendan comes in whistling "Finlandia"—"Finlandia"? —kisses her, nods to Hilda and turns to the computer to find a version of the piece, the beautiful theme introduced by the wind section and then taken up by the whole orchestra. Another patriotic phase? Like when he was listening to Smetana, in the spring? Hilda thinks him a genius and quietly gathers her things, hugs her teacher and whispers goodbye, so not to disturb him.

HE MUST BE THERE. The email has just popped into her box. It's her chance. She hits the reply arrow.

Mattie? Don't turn me off. I NEED TO TALK TO YOU AND YOU MUST BE THERE. WHERE IS THERE? I just got your mail. You must be siting at a computer somewhere and I HAVE TO TALK TO YOU. There are things happening that you should know about. My sister Elfie's baby is in trouble and my mother shocked us all by telling us that John, my step-dad, is not Elfie's father. Now I'm not even sure about MY OWN FATHER. IT'S A BIG MESS. It makes me realize we should always tell the truth because if Elfie knew who her real father was she'd know what to do about the baby. DID YOUR GRANDMA PUT YOUUP TO THIS DISAPPEARING ACT?? Did she tell yoou that when I got pregnant I thoought of terminating the pregnancy?THING IS, MATT, THAT'S NOT WHAT'S IMPORTANT. WHAT'S IMPORTANT IS THAT I DIDN'T!! So you were wanted, whatever she told you, and you're wanted now.If I knew where you AREwere there's one quesiton answered.COULD YOU JUST ANSWERTHAT ONE QUES-TION SO I CAN MARK IT OFF MY LIST????There's just so uch we don't know, we can't knowthat what we can know w'eve got to know.Like if wec had insurance for everythig maybe it woauld be better, maybe we wouldn't get thin in our feelings, shaved into a thin slice that could blow way in the wind.At my work they call it risk assessment.Oh Mattie I hope you're not at war, but for god's sake answawer me.. TELL ME ARE WHERE YOU ??!!

November

YA! Annette wants to scream. From developing peace to THIS! Greg, Eve and Aidan, Matt. All of them expecting her to figure out how they're going to deal with a bedridden old man; what's expected of Greg, if she wants him to stay. The reconciliation has been going well, but she wanted to take it slow. She didn't want to be pushed into making a commitment. All four of them are lined up on a bench, some big family joke, Matt and Greg even posed the same way, hunched over, elbows on knees, while the two kids are slumped, chins on their chests. Above them signs that say no smoking, arrows that point people to radiology, to outpatient care, to the cafeteria, to admissions.

In the ambulance, Dad made her promise, no nursing home. If I make it, Nettie, don't dump me in one of those old folks' homes. Oh, Dad, you're not dying. You're just hurt.

A broken hip, as it turned out, so Dad is going to have to live with her, if she's going to care for him the way he needs to be cared for. How that will affect the reforging of her bond with Greg, she doesn't know. Because Greg will have to stay with the kids, unless Matt sticks around indefinitely. The sight of her dad lying there, his eyes dark beer with a skim of foam, scared, obviously; amazingly, the first time in hospital since birth, facing surgery to repair his broken hip. Pain. A lot of pain and fear. Then grateful spaciness, once the morphine kicked in. Eve and Aidan were allowed to see him before the nurse rolled him into surgery.

With his whole family there to witness, Dad pleaded with her. "Promise, Nettie? No old folks' home? It'd kill me."

"Aw, Dad. We'd never put you in a nursing home. You know that. We WILL figure something out."

What, though? Greg and the kids think she's pacing because she's worried about her father surviving the surgery, but she isn't worried about that. The doctors declared such hip repair standard procedure, that Dad's vital signs are good, considering his weight; that he must have good genes. Which makes her feel special but also sad, because Elfie doesn't know what genes she inherited. No, it's not the surgery but the aftermath that concerns Annette. They won't keep him here long and he won't want to stay. So what? She keeps thinking, and all of them including Dad have said, at least once, that he shouldn't have tried to go back up the slope by himself. Why do people hang onto things they can't change? Why do you, she asks herself. He did attempt the slope by himself and the scene flickers in her head like a film stuck on pause: Matt vaulting the stairs onto the deck, it's Grandpa, come on! Greg out the door before her, up the path alongside the pasture, the beam of Dad's flashlight poking through the fence. Dad breathing hard, grunting, sighing with pain. Sweating. In shock, Aidan said. Aidan! Who had taken a first aid course at Scouts. A twelve-year-old telling them what should be obvious. Greg and Eve stepping past him, Greg to phone for an ambulance, Eve to get blankets, while Annette sat on the ground with Dad's head in her lap. Crying, soothing his forehead, frightened by his shallow and punchy breath.

"Oh, Dad. You shouldn't have gone by yourself." A stupid thing to say when what she really meant was you shouldn't have fallen, you shouldn't be hurt; that things should be as they were. Now what?

The ambulance attendants had to park at the edge of the pasture and use headlamps to guide their feet as they carried the stretcher. This was more a job for search and rescue, one of them complained. The goats freaking out, thundering up and down the hill, bleating, some of them, standing watching from the fence line so that their hay-breath animal smell became part of the scene. She rode with Dad in the back of the ambulance into Santa Rosa, and what that was going to cost she hated to think. But there was no choice; it wouldn't have been safe to move him themselves. Money is just money. They'll figure it out somehow.

"Net? Eve is hungry." Annette gives her a twenty and suggests that Matt take her and Aidan somewhere for breakfast and then just go on home. There's nothing they can do here. "Okay, Matt?" He nods, biting his lip. Shifts his head toward the hallway, and Eve and Aidan get up and shuffle after him. Matt's quietness is now clearly dejection. Nobody is interested in protecting him and his secret anymore. It's stupid in the light of things. Before she climbed into the back of the ambulance, Annette asked him to call Shinny. "I can't," he said. "You know."

"Whatever's up with you, Matt, it's over as of now if you want to stick around. We need you."

He nodded. Maybe he called and that is why he is dejected, or maybe it is because he is sad about his Grandpa. If Mom does not know yet, she will learn the news after the operation. Annette will call herself. Two months without speaking to each other. She hasn't forgiven her mother, they will talk about the big lie again, but she needs Mom now. Stupid elevator dings, intercom voices. Reminds her of the hospital shows she used to watch on TV when she was a kid. She didn't sleep last night, only dozed on a chair in Dad's room, waking when he moaned, when nurses came in to check him. She needs a shower, some clean clothes. ANSWERS!

Greg comes over and steers her to a window, puts his arm around her. It's only the parking lot they're looking at, but still it's outside. How long has it been since she spent so much time in a building?

"Smokin' John's a tough customer, babe. He's gonna come right through this operation and then he's gonna to have to take awhile to recuperate, and then he's gonna be your old daddy again. Don't you worry."

"I bet it reminds you of Delores, all this, right?"

She feels him slump a little, suck in some breath.

"I guess it does. But mama was ready to die. Nobody dies of a broken hip."

"Life is going to be different, though. What are we going to do? How are we going to take care of him?"

"We're gonna figure somethin' out, babe."

"Meantime, somebody has to get back to the goats. It's way past time."

"I'm on it. Gimme a call when he's out of surgery. You sure you're going to be okay here?"

"I'll be okay as long as I know you're taking care of the farm."

This is it. Without dad to help, she needs Greg. This will skew her decision about the future. She will be pushed by circumstance. Hours seem to pass before the nurse comes by to tell Annette that her dad has been moved to the post-op recovery room, that she can see him if she wants, but only for a minute. She doesn't look like nurses Annette remembers. She isn't wearing a white uniform and a little hat, but shirt and pants in blue. Annette follows her down the hall, into a darkened space, past the white divider screens into where Dad abides in a warren of tubes and wires and monitors, his bad leg half exposed, the sole of his bare foot yellow as feed corn. She leans over and kisses his cheek and his eyes open a little; though he can't have lost any weight overnight, he seems smaller.

"Okay, Dad? They say you're going to be fine. Do you feel fine?"

"Some pretty good shit they give you, Nettie. 'Magine what they'd get for it on the street?"

"It must be good if you can joke. Just don't worry about anything, ok? We'll talk after you've had a good long rest."

"I will, sweetheart. Rest good knowin' my big girl's gonna look after me. 'Member I don't want to be one of those dudes tied into a wheelychair waiting for porridge time."

"I know, Daddy. I know."

His hand is damp, the palm soft between the callouses, the nail beds flat and the nails trimmed. She pictures him in his downstairs room, in the overstuffed brown chair he likes, trimming his nails with clippers, but not his toenails, which he probably can't reach, because his are overlong, the same old corn shade as the calluses. Why should that observation cause such immediate wilting inside her chest?

EVE AND AIDAN HAVE been fighting since they got home from school. Aidan thinks Eve stole his iPod, but Eve has an iPod of her own. I wouldn't touch any of your smelly stuff, she yelled. Aidan stomped into her room and started throwing things around; Eve jumped on him. Mattie told them to cool it but they didn't hear him or didn't want to listen, and he's too wrecked to care. He tries one more time, shouting, "Cool it!" His voice an axe that splits them; they stop. "I'm going outside and when

I come back we're gonna fix this place up for Grandpa, for your dad."
They're hollering at each other again before he gets the door open.

Big, old, hairy Shep sidles up, his matted tail wagging, but not in
the usual perky, happy way. "Come on, boy," Matt urges. Since Eve first
dragged him up to the highest point of the property soon after he arrived,
it has become progressively easier to hike to the mossy clearing that has
become his refuge. Shep is used to Matt's routine, but instead of bound-
ing ahead as usual, he trudges behind. The goats line the fence to watch
the young man and the dog pass, then scamper off to their rock cliff, their
snags and stumps on the other side of the pasture.

Matt doesn't see the lichen-covered boulders tumbled alongside the
trail, the new green cones dropped from firs onto the brown earth path,
the smaller seed cones of the redwoods. His mind is filled with Annette's
face, her hair wavy as the lines in cartoon hair, her dark eyes smudged
beneath with the purple of exhaustion; the white-veined wrinkles she got
from squinting all summer.

"I indulged you, Matthew, because you're family and you're on some
kind of thing. A retreat or something. Trying to find yourself, Dad says.
But it's got to be over now. We're going to need a lot of help to get through
this, Mattie."

She assumed that her nephew would join right in, but Matt has been
thinking about leaving. With Greg back, the balance has shifted. Instead
of Grandpa sitting at the head of the table, Greg takes that spot, and they
don't always eat together like they used to. Whether this was Grandpa's
idea or Annette's, Matt doesn't know. Greg says things in such a way that
Annette and Grandpa understand, but not him; in-jokes, secrets, keeping
Matt out. At least Greg's beard is growing in; without it his chin looked
too shiny, his lips too thin. When he first returned to the farm, his hair
was short, too. If it weren't for how Greg dressed, in the standard jeans and
t-shirt, with a plaid shirt thrown over or not, depending on the temperature, you could have mistaken him for the men in suits and ties who used
to ring the Websters' doorbell on Sundays, smiling, smug. And how are
you Matthew, Greg would say, when they did eat together; what did you
get up to today? Like he suspected Matt got up to something. As if, Matt
thinks. What was there to get up to unless Grandpa loaned him the truck
and he drove into Sebastopol or Santa Rosa. Nothing to get up to here.

He could split right now. Send Shep back, keep hiking through bush 'til he reaches the road, thumb his way to the coast and head south. He hasn't seen Mariah yet. Oh, man. He's got himself mixed right into life here, despite intending to keep his distance, hide out a bit and move on once he felt sure of himself. Which he is now. Except for one ten-minute episode that ended under the willow tree, he's been fine. It's over. They have no doubts about who he is; he has regained Mattie Webster, the easygoing, helpful, quiet young man they expected him to grow into. If a little lost, not so unusual for his age. Grandpa and Annette have been glad that he doesn't spend so much time in front of the computer. He tried a beard, shaved it off, and when he did he noticed that the rest of his face was tan. His legs and his arms have developed muscle, and while the goats still scare him, he's great with the human kids, especially Eve.

The moss he's sitting on scratches through his jeans. It's yellow and brittle and doesn't look like moss should look. Though the sky is cloudy it hasn't rained much all month. He grabs twigs and forms a T shape.

This crisis would never have happened if he'd gone to dinner with Grandpa and the kids, but on top of not wanting to hang out with Greg if he didn't have to, he wanted some time alone with Aidan's computer. Since Aidan has been taking his laptop to school, Matt can't use it when he wants, and he can't default to Annette's workhorse oldie unless he wants Greg looking over his shoulder. When he sat down on Aidan's bed and logged in that night, the clicks and hums of the dial-up connection establishing made him mentally salivate as he would physically salivate sitting down at the table. He's been thinking of getting a laptop of his own, but for ordinary use. He won't get back into the identity business; the only thing he's kept up is Kate, because Kate connects him to Gran.

He's working out a way to confront Gran about something Kate wouldn't know about, though. So that's what they've been so hush-hush about here? Elfie's dad. Is Matt just supposed to pretend that he doesn't know anything about it? After that crazy email from Mom? What's wrong with her? The good thing about making stuff up is that it is often kinder; the truth is harsh. Why did she have to say anything? Every once in awhile he dreams that he's being sucked up by a giant vacuum cleaner. Which is stupid, since he is not even sure how abortions happen, and she decided against it anyway. He's here. Alive. A big hawk dives in front of him, so close that he covers his head and doesn't see what it snatches from the brush, a snake, or a mouse. Shep struggles up—his hips almost as bad as Grandpa's—barks at the bird and tries to chase it, but the hawk is soaring away. If I could do that, oh man, Matt thinks. But he can't; he either splits or stays and lets himself become part of this weird family. If he splits, should he go back to Canada? Is nine months enough for everything to have blown over? Has Berk given up? Questions he can't answer. "What should I do?" he hollers at the sky. Too bad it's overcast. His first trip up here was a hot, sunny August day when colours jumped out, the barn with its fading red paint against the yellow-brown dirt of the clearing below, the green metal roof of Annette's house; Grandpa's six-sided, shake-covered house, mushrooming up from the woods on the side of the hill.

Shep noses the air, barks and starts gimping down the trail, then hobbles back up, happy, leading Eve, who is tall for nine, though her dirty face is small.

"Why are you up here, Mattie?"

"Just takin' a break, Eve. Is he still bugging you?"

"No, he's sleeping."

Has he been up here on this hill long enough for them to finish their fight and for Aidan to flake out? It's been grey all day, but yeah, it's darker grey now. Shep, who has been circling, looking for the right spot, finally slumps down between them. Eve sits and hugs her knees into herself. Matt can see goose bumps on her arms.

"You should have put a hoodie on, Eve, and tied your shoes. You'll fall like Grandpa. I mean, your dad."

She starts crying. He isn't sure that it's crying at first because she sniffs the way people do when they're outside and their nose runs. "I'm not tryin' to boss you, Eve, but you know, we all have to take care of ourselves 'til he's better. All the time, really."

And then there's no mistake, she's full out sobbing, actually wailing, and he doesn't have any choice but to step over the dog and put his arm around her. Despite her size, she's little inside, and she's afraid her Dad is going to die.

"Aidan says he was too old when he had us. We don't know where Mom is. We'd be orphans if he died."

"He's not going to die, Eve, not yet. Not from this. It's like breaking your leg, except it's a hip. He just seems weird because of the drugs they give him for pain. He's gonna be fine. Anyway, you wouldn't be orphans, you've got your sister and brother. You've got all of us."

All of us; it came out automatically. Eve doesn't have Kleenex and he doesn't, so he takes off his hoodie and lets her use the sleeve to wipe her face. Her heat is enough for him anyway. Her hair stinks; she needs to wash it and take a bath so that she smells like a girl more than a goat. Or the dog, because the goats aren't too bad, just a hay smell, unless they've been out in the rain.

"Hey, come on. I don't blame you for being worried. But he's going to be okay. He said so and Annette said so. You know what I picked up for dinner? KD. In Canada I used to eat it all the time. A frozen apple pie, too, and ice cream. Let's go down and make it, and then we ought to wake Aidan. I tell you it's going to be okay. A lot of people care about you. Your Mom might even show up someday and you guys will all be together again. You can't, like, give up. Come on. We don't want to be going down the path in the dark. That's how Grandpa got in trouble, right? Come on, let's just go."

He takes her hand and they walk together until the path is too narrow, and then Matt lets Eve walk ahead. Always shorter returning from some-where. Would it be that way if he went back to Canada? But then there's all he'd have to deal with there. His wacky Mom, and Gran. Gran?

When the house is in sight, Eve runs ahead, turns and waits for Matt to catch up so that they can enter together.

"Hey, why don't you go take a shower and change clothes before Aid wakes up. I'll get our dinner started here, then, after we're all full, we can start the overhaul. We want it good when Grandpa gets back, right? I mean, your dad."

"Okay. I need some clean stuff."

I'll go down and look in the dryer, okay? I'll bring up anything I find and put it on your bed."

She smiles at him, a nine-year-old girl with a streaked face and tangled hair and gratitude rising out of her eyes like steam from tea. Crazy. He's made her feel better. Shit, he doesn't want to get too wound in here. But he can't desert the kids. Aidan was right: Grandpa was too old to be having kids, especially with a wife young enough to run off and look for someone better, if that's what she did. No one really talks about her. Oona. Aidan can barely remember her, Eve not at all. A phantom mother. Phantom mothers, wacko mothers, lying mothers. Matt asks himself, how can I split before I know if everything's going to be all right?

Passing through Grandpa's room on his way to the laundry machines, he sees that if Grandpa did die—he won't, not from this, Matt wasn't lying to Eve—but say he did, people would find his chair-side table piled with all kinds of paper, a book, Edgar Cayce, *The Sleeping Prophet*, some old copies of the *Santa Rosa Press Democrat* scattered around the floor, cups of half finished coffee, glasses with water gone bubbly; another book, a fat one, the *I Ching*. Pictures of everybody, some on the walls, some propped on the dresser. Here's Oona, it's got to be Oona, with a baby. Must be Eve, with the dark hair. You can't tell that Oona is spacey from this photo; she's looking at her baby, her head bowed, so you can't see much of her face, just the top of her head and the corner of her mouth, which is not turned up in a smile. School pictures of Eve and Aidan. A snapshot with curling edges tucked into the frame of the biggest one, which shows Grandpa as a mid-aged man, wearing overalls and a straw hat and holding a pitchfork. Goats in the background. Must be here, this goat ranch. A black and white picture, framed. The curling-edged one tucked into it is of Grandma and her three daughters. Must be about the time Matt was born, he thinks, because his Mom is pregnant and Elfie is about the same age Eve is now, but smaller than Eve, skinnier, lighter haired; Annette is wearing a lumberman's shirt and her hair fans out like Grandma's, and she's frowning at the camera. Woo, if you could really time travel. This is what he was born into. There's even a picture of him, a studio portrait in a cardboard folder, of Mom, Dad, him and Mariah, when Mariah was about one.

He sits down and breathes in Grandpa's old man essence. Everything has got so complicated.

"Matt?" As if she's read his thoughts, Eve calls to him from the top of the stairs. He doesn't want her coming down and seeing so much stuff of her dad's and getting sad again.

"I'll be right up, Eve. Just wait a sec. I've got your clothes right here."

He hasn't made it to the laundry machines, but he's sure he will find the dryer full of fresh, if wrinkled, clothes that belong to Eve.

IT's TERRIBLE TIMING; ALL of a sudden everyone's focus is split. A selfish thought, but if there was ever a justification for selfishness ... Elfie wants the family's energy directed at her and Johann, a gathering of light that will shine good fortune upon them. Not that she wasn't concerned about the man she had thought her father all these years, surprised to hear that Mattie ended up there. Matt the country type? She wouldn't have thought so, but what does she know about any of them, really? What can anyone know about another human being, ever?

"Oh, come on, Elfriede. It's just your hormones."

"No, I mean really, Bren. What CAN any of us know? I had no doubts about who I was, just accepted it, never considered I might have another set of genes making me who I am. Like people who were given false birth-dates. All their lives they've been operating as if they were Libras and they find out they were born in January, not October."

"The stars impel, they don't compel."

"Okay, so you read the Shakespeare quote on my astrology book. You know what I mean."

Brendan has had a breakthrough. While he thought the looseness, the opportunities for improvisation were foiling him, the real challenge was determining the correct proportions and overall shape of the piece. He went back to his central image; he lost himself in it for hours. Not much time to revise. But that was last month. Now he's writing out the separate parts for each musician, a tedious but manageable task, and the computer makes it easier to properly place the little black dots that convey so much. He copies from notes he made on paper score sheets through the process. He can be home more, and he has been home more, but not tonight. To-night he is the featured performer at the monthly faculty concert.

"I wish I could be there, but everybody thinks it a bad idea."

"On the way back I'll pick up some ice cream. Do you want anything else?"

"Just you. Break a leg."

Elfie can never get comfortable, never quite sleep, which means that she is often tired, and tired of being tired. Not to mention the worry that has deepened the grooves in her forehead. As for her mysterious father, the story has become embarrassing. She told everyone that she would look until she found him, but now, mortified to have begun the search with such blind zeal, she has given up. Needle in a haystack doesn't begin to describe the challenge, because that analogy refers to someone who would actually know what they were looking for, the elusive needle. Her story will not be the stuff of legend, no tragedy of Oedipus. Or the sweet tale that wound through the music of Vivaldi on the CD Mom gave her so long ago: the orphans, one of Vivaldi's pupils, whose father turns out to be a prince. Depressing, but she's not going to cry tonight. Tears have welled so often lately; she has explained to Brendan that her levels of estrogen and progesterone are at their highest, that she'll cry about anything, and it's generally so, yet a deep existential ache comes from realizing that she may never know her true origins. How could her mother have thought she wouldn't care? That it would not matter?

Six-thirty in New York. Mid-afternoon on the West Coast. She feels like calling, but for what? Her mother may not even be in Vancouver, because last time they talked, when she phoned with the news from California, Mom said she might fly down there to help with John. Her voice broke. She apologized. Elfie's first, genuine reaction was sympathy, but she didn't know what to say. She promised she would call him herself. So awkward. Dad, but not Dad. She can't say Dad anymore. John?

"So Mattie, is he going to stay there?"

"I don't know. I don't think he knows. Lawreen didn't say and I haven't been able to reach him directly. Hold on a minute, Elfie; I have to get a Kleenex."

If her mother feels so bad about Smokey/John, why did she step out on him? Why didn't she agree to move to California way back then?

"I'll keep you posted. And then, almost as an afterthought. Everything's okay with you? You're feeling good? No more news about the baby?"

"Oh, don't worry about me. Not today."

Elfie wishes she would have genuinely felt the generosity she expressed, instead of thinking that now she would have to compete for the family's sympathy. But would it have been any better if he had broken his hip last year, before she got pregnant, before she knew that he was not her real father? Not for him, of course, but her feelings would have been less muddy.

Johann is aiming his little foot directly at her bladder. She needs to pee again, and then to lie down. The window beside the bed is open because it was one of those unexpected Indian summer afternoons, but the temperature drops fast when the sun sets, which it did more than an hour ago. Dying leaf smells from the park across the street dominate the usual city stench of car exhaust and garbage; for a minute she imagines being back in Vancouver in the fall, the morning fogs, the spiderwebs everywhere. Erasers freshly pink, bright yellow pencils newly sharpened, the pencil cases Mom bought for her every year, even in university, though she claimed she did it for a joke then.

Despite the fine weather, Hilda has told Elfie that she shouldn't be going out; not unless it's absolutely necessary, she scolded, when she saw Elfie testing the ripeness of tomatoes at the greengrocers on First Avenue. Let me do your shopping. And please, darling, don't even think of sitting in a concert hall. Hand sanitizing solution is stacked in storefront displays. Signs on the subway platforms urge people to practise hygiene. The mayor is predicting hundreds of deaths before Christmas. It's as if bad timing is the theme of the season. Swine flu on top everything else.

Enough of the crisis mode! She rolls up from the bed again to turn on the Partita 1 in B minor, the piece that has been the sound track to the pregnancy, that she will ask Brendan to play in the delivery room, and returns to the bed to practise breathing. Johann's flutters quiet with the music and the breathing. She doesn't worry as she first did when he doesn't move for a few hours. Fetuses have to sleep, too. The radiators tick and gurgle, doing whatever they do to create heat, and she's feeling peaceful—unusually peaceful—on the edge of sleep when Brendan's key turns in the lock, the first key and the second key.

"Hey, I got Chunky Monkey? You up for it?"

He smells of cold air and decaying leaves, of the shampoo he uses, and leather.

"Come here," she beckons, wanting him more than the ice cream.

"I have to wash first. Lots of flu germs out there. I'll be right back."

She rakes her hair with her fingers and slips off her stretchy-front pants, scoots up to light the candle on the bedside table. Brendan returns with two bowls of ice cream, which changes her plans, so that the flicker of passion sputters with the clicks of spoons hitting china.

The sarabande movement of the B minor partita begins, and Brendan picks up on the stately dance rhythm, first beating time on his bowl, then putting the spoon down, taking her bowl from her, lifting her arms, leading her out of bed.

"Hey, I'll get cold."

Her floppy, chocolate spotted t-shirt rides above her belly, which curves from her pubic triangle to just under her breasts. She might be wearing a ball gown, though, the way Brendan bows formally, then takes her into his arms to dip across the creaky plank floor, to the center of the flat, then back towards the bed. This mood, the playfulness that surfaced more often before the trials of the last six months. He must have shown his composition to someone. They must have liked it.

"You tried out "At/Pac"? You showed Ping the new piece?"

"Maybe," he says. Coy. How much he revealed and to whom hardly matters. He pins her to the bed and kisses her and in that way lets her know that it's going to be all right. Maybe brilliant.

SHINNY HAS WORKED EVERY day this week, leaving Tahir the hours he needs to go over his books with the police auditor, the forensics auditor. The MoneyGrams to Afghanistan. How will the police interpret those? She worries for Tahir's family, but also for herself. Who will hire a woman her age if she loses this job? Or she could die of swine flu. A sign in the lobby of her building advertises a clinic for vaccines, though they say, the experts, that people her age may be immune and should let young people, pregnant women go to the front of the line for the vaccine. The poor family of the boy who died so suddenly, Evan Frustaglio, whose name has entered the litany she recites when she can't sleep, when she has time to pass, such as now. She taps the rain that has gathered on her umbrella onto the carpet in the lobby of the building to the rhythm of the syllables: Mikael Samuelsson, Christian Ehrhoff, Guillaume Desbiens. The best names are foreign, and the Swedish ones not as rhythmic as the Russian. They don't have Russians on her team, as far as she knows, but the season has started and there are visiting teams. Alexander Ovechkin, Sergei Fedorov. Oleg Saprykin join Manmohan Singh, Michael Ignatieff. Though she doesn't have to worry about Mattie now that she knows where he is, the names of dead Canadians continue to knell. Jonathan Couturier, Justin Garrett Marshall, Steven Boyes. And there's Kev, Kate's friend, though she has not heard that he died. No wonder he never found Mattie. Mattie is not patrolling those dusty roads, riding past the randomly planted IEDs that have exploded so many soldiers.

Dark when she steps into her apartment, but the lights of the city burning from various buildings, from separate rooms and offices and shops and stairwells, illumine her few steps to the kitchen, where she switches on the fixture over the stove. She could do it without the lights, the route is so familiar. Habits, too: hang the coat over the shower rod to dry; drop the umbrella into the tub. Flick on the lamp by the couch, return to the kitchenette to open the fridge. She's back to eating eggs too many nights of the week, but she has been too lazy to shop. Press the power button on the remote that controls the TV. Turn on the computer. Stand at the balcony door while her personal settings load, including her email account. The park is being transformed into a site for the Winter Olympics. Fences surround the playing field.

The dating site persists in contacting her. Did you find someone? Let us know. We love stories with happy endings. No more replies to queries she sent out regarding the identity of Elfie's father. No more Mattie, for while she knows where he is, she doesn't know why he went there or how long he's staying. Like the rest of the family, he has pushed her not away, exactly, but off. Maybe even decided that she is expendable, which reminds her that her presence in the lives of her children is temporary, a thought she is not yet willing to embrace, though its arms await her.

Two lines in bold. New mail! And one is from Kate.

Dear Mrs. Shinnan, Sorry I haven't written. Yeah I did put the herbs in the paper bags and hung them from the ceiling, to dry. Maybe I'll send you some? You'll have to give me your real address, then you can see how I did. Yeah, Mattie. Well I guess I won't seem him forawhile and neither will you if he's in California.. You think he likes it there? At least you know he's not in the army, but I guess he could go when he comes back if he's got nothing better to do. I guess you've decided it would be ok Or what? I can kind of feel for my old friend Mattie because I'm kinda in a spot like that myself I mean not in California but confused, you know? Here I am, same age as him and I don't know what I'm going to do with mself. You might say well you seem to like gardening, and that's because we talk about it in email, but you know I live in an apartment and I don't like gardening that much. You said you think he's mad at you About what?Maybe he's just thinking things over. People my age don't say everything on theirmind especially the quiet ones like mattie. Well maybe he's being some kind of male nurse or something. You say he's taking care of his grandpa, right? well I guess it takes a while to figure things out. I don't know. But I don't mean to sound ll depressed I'm not that depressed. Well now maybe its you who's going to have to tell me about mattie, what he's up to. Tell him I said hi. He does't answer my emails.

Yrs truly,

Kate Babcock

The other email is from a production company, a reminder that the new series, *Lost Again*, premieres at 9PM Pacific, October 30th, starring a list of names Shinny hasn't heard of, names that are unlikely to become part of her litany, except for one near the end: Mariah Webster.

Nothing from Annette, and she hesitates to call because they're all so busy down there. John will be released from rehab soon. Greg and Mattie will take turns driving him into Santa Rosa for physiotherapy. Considering what it will take to heave him into the truck, it would be easier to leave him in rehab, but Annette promised him she wouldn't do that.

"You're good, Nettie," Shinny told her.

"What choice do I have, Mom? I promised."

The phone rings before she can go back to Kate's letter. It's Lawreen, who has been speaking to her again, who seems to have forgotten she was angry, who was not surprised to hear that Mattie is in California because Mattie has written to her now and then. Why didn't you tell me, Shinny demanded. I thought he joined the army. I've been worried every time I hear another soldier died! Didn't I tell you? Lawreen sounded genuinely confused, as if she had completely forgotten the conversation they had months before, her every word warped by the sarcasm that was her response to Shinny's confession about Elfie's actual father.

"Mom did you get the email about the series? Do you want to come over? We're going to have a little premiere party. Just tapas. Wine. A few people. Dessert. I might ask my boss, oh and someone who used to work here. A cameraman. But he might not be in town. Anyway, sushi."

"Slow down, Lawrie. Sure I'll come. Tell me what to bring."

"Oh just nothing, or wine. Come early so we can get the talking out of the way before the show starts."

"Too bad Mariah can't be with us. But it's good, too, that she's too busy to come. Did you tell Annette? They can have a premiere party at her house, too."

"Well they could if they had a TV."

"So you've been talking to him?"

"Talking is stretching it. He said he was sorry; he said he needed time to think. He didn't tell me much more than that. But you know Mattie. He plays his hand close to his chest."

They're on the cliché highway again. It's time to hang up. "Okay then, Lawrie. This will be fun. Like the old days."

They used to gather in front of the TV whenever Mariah was featured in a show, which meant every week the season she starred in Cuties. Shinny would drive over to Ken and Lawreen's house, and if Elfie or Annette were home, they would come too. Lawreen or Ken would cook, and Shinny would bring dessert. Mattie would sit next to her on the floor by her chair. She misses her grandson. While she is grateful that he's safe, knowing where he is doesn't fill the space created by his absence.

She has several email addresses for him and in the To: line, she enters them all.

Dear Mattie. I'm so glad to know that you're safe. I know you're big enough to look after yourself. You're independent now, but we didn't hear for so long, I was worried. I also miss you, but I think it's great that you're helping out down there. I know that Nettie appreciates it and your grandpa, not to mention the kids. They're pretty nice kids, I think. I want to come down and help too but then I might have to go to New York. I wish I could split myself in half and be two places at once. By the way, I had another note from Kate today. She's sounding kind of lost and I think she'd like to hear from you too. We've become pretty good pals. I hope I meet her someday. She sounds like a nice girl, and I think she really likes you.

Let me know how it's going down there, ok? Or maybe you'll be there when I call. I've been talking to John, your grandpa, every few days. To me he sounds tired. Anyway, Matt. I just wanted to let you know that I miss you, and that I'm not mad about anything. I just want to see you again. Are you coming back?

Love and hugs,

Grandma

Within seconds of sending, her inbox fills with delivery notifications: delivery has failed. She satisfies the urge to communicate by typing Kate's name into the To: line.

Dear Kate. It is so good to hear from you. Yes we do get in those times of life when we're too busy to write. But I'm glad to know about your herbs and that everything worked out. Have you thought about horticulture courses? I guess that wouldn't work for you if you don't like gardening that much. Maybe cooking? A cooking school? I guess we old folks suggest school to people your age because when you get older you understand how much there is to learn. School gives you ideas, such as, if you take a science course you might find out you're good at it and maybe you go on to be a teacher. Or maybe you try everything and find nothing you like in school so you go through different jobs; or maybe you get married and have kids while you're young and devote the rest of your life to them. It's not as boring as maybe it sounds to you right now. You might have to get a job to help out with the family finances, and it doesn't really matter what it is as long as you can manage time with the family and earn enough that it's worthwhile. You might even find that you like it. Then all of a sudden the kids are grown up and through them you've learned something else that you like, maybe, soccer or something. Or French. And pretty soon you're a fan. And then maybe you join a team. Or travel to France. Well, the thing is, Kate, I'm rambling here, and all I really want to tell you is something you might know already, that life is full of things to discover. I've got to go now because all of a sudden it's got stormy and maybe the power will go out. But I'll write again, and you write to me, anytime, ok?

The gulls are screaming, as if sounding an alarm. When she tries to open the door to the balcony, to rescue the sweater she left out to dry out this morning, the wind pushes back with such force it's actually frightening. She hasn't been paying any attention to the news. The announcers have blathered on about this and that, breaking the quiet, but now she turns to the weather channel, where the red screen is a sign that there is a weather emergency. Maybe another windstorm, like the one that tore through the city a few years ago and blasted entire sections of forest in Stanley Park. Thousands of trees down.

This is a warning that significant rainfall is expected or occurring in these regions. Monitor weather conditions. Listen for updated statements.

The gulls might have been saying the same thing, for the rain intensifies, not the gradual patter that builds into a steady drumming that can be overwhelmed by cars splashing through puddles, but suddenly, violently, as if someone has unzipped the sky and it has dropped the accumulation of centuries—water sucked up and stored from the time when Vancouver was still a rainforest with trees whose trunks were broader than city buses; when the Chief wrote those words she reads on her seawall walks, *Welcome to the land of light; here you live like chief. World like in palm of your hand.*

It is loud enough to absorb the usual sounds of traffic and the inner workings of the building. She turns the TV off. From where she sits she can't distinguish drops or slanting silver dashes; the rain falls in whole sheer sheets through which the lights in the buildings across False Creek glow like underwater phosphorescence in the summer, except more yellow than green. Here, on the top floor, she hears the rain at its loudest, almost as if it will break through the roof and wash through all the apartments on the ninth floor, float the residents up and out into the hallways. She pictures herself bobbing in the stairwells with neighbours she normally does not see, the East Indian woman who treats floor nine like an extension of her own apartment, walking the halls barefoot. The former British army officer who gets many papers delivered to her and obviously sleeps late, because the papers remain on her doorstep through the morning. Shinny turns off the lamp and watches the rain scallop down the window, the door. Frightening but fascinating. While it is too heavy to last, a cell or a squall, it isn't letting up yet. Significant rainfall has occurred and/or is occurring. No prediction as to how long it will last. All these weather extremes. Wildfires destroying sections of California bigger than some European countries. Tornadoes whirling down from the sky in places where they are rarely seen.

Glen would have something to say about this. "Wouldn't you?" she says aloud.

Some people believe you can talk to the dead. Irene once announced that she talks to her late husband all the time. Shinny doesn't know what she means by that. Is it actual conversing, or imagination? She used to talk to her mother, but it was one-sided. Does Irene's husband really talk back? Glen doesn't, or if he does, she can't hear him answer: Yes, I have plenty to say; the climate is changing just as predicted. If not for missing you, I would be relieved to be gone. The cadence of his speech used to remind her of a fisher spinning out a line, then carefully reeling it in. You'd see that he was getting at something, in his own way, slowly, then you'd see what. Rain loud as thunder. It may even be thunder; the rain is so loud she cannot distinguish. If he were here, he would have his arm around her. She would feel that bony part in his shoulder and scoot around to reach the soft part, a little lower. His free hand would rest on her knee and doodle, half-consciously. They never got this kind of rain in Washington, not in the valley where Glen lived, which was just on the edge of the dry zone. It rained, sure, and Glen was always glad for it because he didn't like to irrigate any more than he had to. A natural conserver, Glen. One August when there had been no rain for two months and the grass outside the house was yellow as straw, only the leaves on her flowers green because she watered them sparingly; that one August afternoon when clouds dark as eggplant lowered over Mount Hood and Mount Adams, Glen led her out to the front steps and they stood together, waiting, smelling it first before the first big drops splatted explosions in the powdery dirt. There, said Glen. That's what we have been hoping for. They retired to the old sofa he kept on the porch and watched it come down, nothing like tonight in Vancouver, but gently, steadily, all the rest of that day.

PAUL WAS SHOOTING LATE and couldn't make the party. The next day he was gone. They managed one lunch, and though he kissed her, quickly, yes, but on the lips both when they met and when they said goodbye, and smiled as if everything was fine, he didn't suggest that they go to his room. Oh that dirty feeling of rejection; the sense that you've done something wrong. If she had a tail, it would have been between her legs.

"Have a nice time last night, honey?" Ken called, over the clatter of his little train chugging along its little track.

"Yeah, but it was a late night."

Why couldn't she be one of those women who could kiss, even fuck, and walk away? Like her Mom, who continues to insist that it was only that once, that she didn't lie about Larry Blake. But how can you know for sure?

Just a bit of a midlife crisis, Lawreen tells herself. She loves Ken, and Paul hasn't been mean. He keeps in touch, and Mariah's show was no big deal, especially not for someone like Paul. Mari was on screen for such a short time, not like when she starred. Even then it would have been routine for Paul. He might have looked at it critically, said something about the lighting or the camera angles. She should have realized that watching Mariah on a TV show would have been what Mom used to call a busman's holiday for Paul. Mom made a fuss, of course, although she thought that her granddaughter should wear more clothes if she was going to be on national TV.

"International TV," Lawreen corrected.

"Oh, they all dress like that," said Ken, the eternal peacemaker.

At that point she had not taken another Ativan since she woke up, and that was the low dose, half a pill. While Mom and Ken debated the changing styles, she slipped upstairs to the drawer where she kept her main bottle hidden and shook out a whole pill. It would take a while, but they would notice her getting drowsy; Mom would thank her for everything, say goodbye. Lawreen would be sleeping when Ken came up to their room. She would go to work the next morning, and did.

The days have been turning, yet it's slack. No wind puffing her sails. Now that they know where Matthew is, maybe Matthew will come home and she can help him get his life on track; maybe she'll go to New York with Mom when Elfie's baby is born. Maybe ... She started too early, packed everything into twenty-five years—marriage, motherhood, work. Retirement in sight and she hasn't hit forty-five. Nobody seems to want her, to need her. Oh, they would say they do, if she asked, but, really, would her children miss her? Her boss? Would Ken? He'd go through the motions, the weeping, the funeral, then add another section to his train tracks, paint up more fields of flax and canola, build another grain elevator, secretly happy, self-sufficient.

It's only 7:30. Raining outside, and cold, with that wind that cuts up at the intersections. She doesn't want to go running. Vancouver is not as safe as it used to be. Even here on the West Side. In September, charged with possibilities, she considered signing up for a course: yoga or tai chi, or pottery or something. A girl at work pots in her spare time and makes the cutest gifts for people. She could redecorate, but the house is fine; she doesn't feel like redecorating. She could plan a vacation; they could use a winter vacation. Mexico. Except on their last visit she drank a margarita with impure ice and got stomach-wrenching sick. What if that happened again? What if it got worse? She'd never felt so sick. And the parasite isn't necessarily out of her system. She imagines it making a home in her intestines, reproducing, thousands of parasites not content to stay in her intestines, but migrate to her brain. It could be why she has such anxious thoughts. She hasn't recalled that trip to Mexico for some time. Maybe it's a parasite making her worried.

Ken should be home by now. She peers through window at the blowy night, steady rain. A car moving down the street, parking lights only. She lets the curtain fall. Who would be fool enough to drive without their lights on a night like this? Someone who doesn't want to be seen. But who? Some anonymous thug, a gang member? The East Indian family that moved in down the block? Are they really a family, or are they gang members? Is she going to have to worry about drive-by shootings? Gang wars? There have been more murders in the city this year than ever. If she didn't know from the headlines in the commuter newspapers that litter downtown streets, her mother would have told her. Be careful, Lawrie. It's not the same place you grew up. More murders … Or maybe it's Mom doing this to her; so many, a lifetime of "be carefuls" have made a nervous wreck of her. She sneaks another look, from the dining room window this time. It's darker in the dining room. He's still there. The car, idling in the middle of the block. A black car with the suddenly heavier rain bouncing off its hood. Why would any honest person want to be out, just sitting there, on such a night?

She checks the back door lock, the front door lock, the locks on the windows and on the slider to the patio. Runs upstairs with her cell phone. Punches in the number of Ken's cell.

"Where are you so late?"

"I'm on my way. Turning onto 16th and Dunbar as we speak. It's coming down hard out here. I can barely see out the windshield. Are you okay?"

"There's somebody outside the house. A car with its lights off, just idling there, Ken, practically right in front of our house."

"It's probably nothing. I'll check it out. See you in a minute."

"Okay, but be careful, will you?"

"'Course I will be. Settle down, ok?"

Easy for him to say, settle down. She would run a bath, but it's better to wait until Ken is here and has checked out the car. When did she take the last Ativan? It must be time for another. Anyway, it will be better when

Ken comes in; he won't worry if she's on her way to calm land. Her ticket to calm land. The blue plastic bottle that rests in between panties and bras in her top drawer. Here. Except, where is it? She feels around, patting to discover the shape, the feel of something firm among these lightweight underthings. Pat, pat, pat, silk, lace, cotton. Where the hell is it! The panties fly, the bras. The lavender sachet Mattie gave her so long ago, and which she has kept for sentimental reasons only, because the smell is gone. Who could have taken her pill bottle? Has the guy outside already been here? A druggie, looking for whatever he can find?

Finally! Caught in the cup of her black underwire. No wonder! She twists off the cap and pinches out a tablet, slips it onto her tongue and closes her eyes, counts. Ken finds her standing there amid the chaos of her upended underwear drawer when he comes in.

"Lawrie?"

She jumps and the opened pill bottle sprays tablets around the room.

"You just about scared the life out of me! Why didn't you say you were home?"

"What are those pills? What are you doing?"

"Just vitamins. Well, calcium supplements. You scared me!"

She's on her knees, picking them up, the little white pills that look like a house with a peaked roof, a perfect little house where everything is peaceful inside. She doesn't want to lose any. Ken bends to help.

"Thanks but you're wet. I'll do it."

Rain on wool. He smells like beer, too.

"Lawreen these don't look like vitamins."

"They're not exactly vitamins. They're supplements, like I said. Calcium. Women my age need that."

Soon, soon she can relax; General Ativan will stand guard. She gathers the underwear, piles it on top of the dresser. Ken hasn't moved. In his damp jacket, stocking feet, arms at his sides, he looks lost. Ken has left life's messy bits to her to work out; she can almost count on the fact that if she reassures him, he will accept what she says, go downstairs, remove his jacket, fix himself a drink, turn on the TV.

"The drawer was stuck. I had to pull these things out to get it open. Did you see that car I mentioned? Is it still out there? I think we're going to have to watch for stuff with those new people."

"You mean the taxi?"

"I didn't see a taxi. It was a black car, lights off, except for the parking lights. It just kind of hovered there."

"I didn't see anything but a taxi. I guess you didn't see the sign."

"I'm going to take a bath, ok?"

She thinks she has them all, but she can check later. She starts bustling, pill bottle in pocket, nightgown from closet.

"Sorry I worried you. They should light up the signs, like the yellow cabs do." She kisses his cool cheek as she brushes past.

Since he has been looking after the kids and staying in Grandpa's room while Grandpa was in the hospital, and then the rehabilitation place he called a nursing home, Matt feels that he's entitled to keep using Grandpa's room. He respectfully stacked Grandpa's books and newspapers, washed the sheets and wiped down shelves, swept the floor, so it will be nice, welcoming, when Grandpa comes back. But for now Grandpa needs Annette's big bed, which means Annette has to sleep in the computer room, which means that Greg has moved up here to Grandpa's house. Hope you don't mind, Matt, Greg said, automatically assuming that Matt would revert to the pull-out couch. Now Grandpa's room is strewn with Greg's bits Annette with Grandpa; he helps with the goats. Matt has become a full-time kid sitter; he launders their clothes, shops for them, picks them up and drops them off at friends' houses, at games, parties.

It's not a life he ever imagined for himself, but it's also true that he had no clear picture of his future; that's why he got out of Canada before someone else, maybe someone wearing a uniform, filled in the picture for him. All that seems far away. Berk. Their scam. Matt has another computer now. Had to. Aidan became possessive. But he's keeping it straight. He looks at Canadian online news. He has Googled Berk, but nothing came up. This is good. Wherever he is, he hasn't been caught; looks like they've both gotten away with it. Skated away with the money, unless Berk found another nerd to do the identity putting together stuff Matt used to do, and he hasn't skated anywhere.

When he talked to her on the phone right after Grandpa's fall, Mom was relieved, then mad, just as he thought, spun out. Jittery.

"God, Mattie!"

"But I wrote, Mom. I tried not to worry you."

"Well you could have been more informative."

That was it. He's had one or two emails since, both one-liners, the last to let him know that he could stream Mariah's new show. But streaming with dial-up? He waited until he could get to the wireless café in Santa Rosa to watch his beautiful sister slide down some muddy hillside for less than two minutes before she fell unconscious, her shirt hiked up so you could see she wasn't wearing a bra. That was it. A start, Mom said. It takes a while to establish yourself in Hollywood.

Eventually he should be able to slip back into the country, see his Mom and Dad, Gran, who keeps writing to Kate, who writes back. Kev is going to write to Gran after he recovers from a minor injury he suffered in the explosion of an IED. Minor for Kev, but another guy lost his legs. Now that it's easier to surf, Matt has been checking out the Forces site again. He needs specifics for Kev. That's part of it. Kate and Kev will feed his craving, like nicotine gum for addicted smokers, but he won't make up anyone new. He has no reason to hide anything anymore. His laptop is clean. Only him, with a Hotmail address, almost no mail. Until today. Oh no! How did he do it? Did he call Mom?

Hey, rat. We got things to talk about. I want to know where the stuff is. You know who.

Berk. Fuck! And he thinks Matt has their raw materials? The identity pieces? He's going to have to ditch this email address, too, but before he does he writes his Mom. *Mom? Hey, did I mention not to give my email address out? It's just that I've been wanting to start over, ok? In fact I think I'm just going to ditch computers altogether until I get settled, so don't be surprised if you don't hear from me for a while.*

Did she tell Berk where he was? Shit. Stupid Berk thinks he's been carrying all those discs around?

He claws dry clothes out of the dryer and, with no clear surface to put them on, drops them on the floor so that he can replace them with the damp ones sitting in the washer from last night, then put the dirty ones in the washer, take the clean ones up. But he picks up the wrong load, the ones he just took out of the dryer, and they're already wet with the water pouring into the machine when he notices the dirty ones he just brought down. How do they do it! How do people, mostly women, do stuff like this all day, just part of their routine? He's sick of it. Ready to leave, but if he leaves right now, when they need him, they'll hate him. He can't pretend he has an appointment somewhere, somewhere to be by a certain time, because everyone knows he has nowhere to go. But if Mom told Berk he's in California, how long will it be before Berk shows up?

What he is feeling is homesickness, he thinks, which is funny consider-ing that he doesn't have a home. Oh, there's a room at Mom and Dad's, he could go there and, as usual, Mom would barely notice him. It could be okay to hang out with Dad, work his train set with him. Unless Berk is watching the house. Maybe Dad would help him look through the college catalogues to find a program he'd be good at. In the office of that counsel-lor he went to, they gave him a form to fill out, to determine his strengths. He scored high on computer skills, but who wouldn't? And persuasion. What was that supposed to mean, that he should work at Future Shop selling laptops? Dad's never been too involved. Whatever you think, son, is the sort of reply he gets when he asks Dad's advice. He's trying to be nice, but it isn't that nice to blow off your son with "whatever you think". How helpful is that?

Greg pushes in from the deck. "Hey Matt, could you stop the washer 'til I shower?"

Matt is tempted to say, fuck you; instead he concentrates on the han-dle of an old mower, which makes a clear T against the dun light falling through the open door. Shrugs, "I guess." Pushes the starter knob in. Greg yells from Grandpa's bedroom.

"Elfie called. So far so good with the kid. Just a drag Shinny can't find the one-night stand man."

"Oh yeah," says Matt, not liking the picture. The one-night stand man. Jesus, Gran. He doesn't like Greg thinking about Gran the way he obvi-ously is, but if it's true ...

Greg walks naked into the laundry room, stands at the shower stall, turns on the water.

"Shinny. What a kick in the pants. A red-headed piano player. 'Course she was a hippie."

Upstairs Matt loads cereal bowls and coffee cups into the sink, wipes toast crumbs. A musician, like one of those full-of-themselves rock stars. Red hair, probably long. The kids aren't much use. Not that he was at their age, but here it's different. They shouldn't be thinking he's the house-keeper or something. Even if he's staying here for free. He offered to pay and Annette just looked at him. Are you outta your mind, Matt? You're FAMILY! Family, yeah, but not so much that they let him in on the news, which is doing weird things to his head, or his stomach. How come she didn't tell him? Those trips they took together, camping; they used to lie awake and tell each other stories. It was the perfect time. She must have been embarrassed. How come he had to hear it from stupid Greg, wacko Mom? Maybe he should just keep going. Mom wouldn't miss him; he's out of her life now. He can stay out. Seems like he's always got his hands in hot water, and then everything's done in the kitchen, then the kids come home from school wanting some kind of snack before dinner, and it starts all over. He's getting to sound like his mom. Okay, but don't forget to clean up after yourself. Who doesn't have a dishwasher? More to the point, what is he DOING here?

Screw the laundry, the dishes, the whole place. He's got to get out of here, but it's drizzly, the sky low. If he hikes up the hill, he won't see anything. And it's cold. He left Vancouver in summer, without any heavy clothes. Not that he had many clothes to bring. He could use something of Grandpa's, though all the jackets are more than twice his size and they all smell funky, too. Separate a person from his clothes, his things, and those things lose their personality in general shabbiness. Everything here needs a reno, but it's not going to be him that does it.

Family? He felt secure here, but he sees that they don't really consider him one of them; Greg's stature is higher, despite the way he betrayed Annette.

Clouds so thick, everything's still dark though it's got to be noon. He could go down there and tell them he's going into town, but he doesn't want to see any of them, Annette, Grandpa. Except it's Grandpa's truck and they always need something from town. The oh, could-you-pick-ups start as soon as he mentions that he's going into town early, he has some things to do. Annette doesn't even ask what he's got to do; what could he have to do in the little town where the kids go to school? Well, he's going further. He's going to get himself some rain gear and check out bus sched-ules. Yeah, I'll get that, he says. Yeah. It's easier to agree with everything. To just do it.

Grandpa's truck is as old as Matt himself, but Greg has kept it running. That's one thing, about the only thing, Greg's good at, as far as Mattie can see. He wishes that Annette hadn't taken him back; maybe she'll ditch him when Grandpa gets better. It was definitely easier here before Greg returned, but the weather was nicer too, and Grandpa wasn't confined to a reclining chair. A few months ago, everything was different. A year ago, another world. Except that other world persists in repeating on him, like something bad he ate. Fucking Berk might know where he is!

Once he gets through Sebastopol he can pick up speed; maybe he'll go all the way to San Francisco, somewhere other than dinky Santa Rosa. He misses Vancouver, the view of the harbour he had from his apartment, his late night walks through the Downtown Eastside. Scary sometimes, yeah, but not as boring as this. Gravenstein Elementary. A school named after an apple!

He misses Canada, too, but he can't put a finger on what. People are easy around here, it's not that. The American flag is on overkill; everybody hangs it, and there are signs about alerts of various levels, with various colours. If he weren't a total stranger, he could really get paranoid. But nobody pays him much attention in Santa Rosa, and even this is a good change from the ranch—that's what they call it anyway, the farm where they keep the goats. Once he gets a Gore-Tex parka he'll look like everyone else on the West Coast, not that he wants that so much, but only to wear something waterproof that isn't three sizes too big and doesn't smell like old man sweat.

YESTERDAY SAYED WAS TAKEN back into custody. That's how the news reporters put it. On top of money laundering charges, he has been accused of impersonation with intent to gain advantage.

"What did he do?" Shinny asked Tahir.

"He does nothing."

Conversation finished. As has been the case since the beginning of the drama, Shinny did not learn more until Sima arrived to relieve her brother-in-law. Thankfully, the allegations of terrorism have been dropped. That's not how Sima said it. She said, "They know he not making for bomb. But they not liking documents they find. Also they want to know where money is it coming in. They think drugs."

"Drugs?"

"Sayed is good man. He help his people."

Sima had her head covered, but whether for political or religious reasons, or because there has been a cold snap, Shinny doesn't know. Allegations of terrorism, another phrase from the news. For as much news as she watches, she should be able to understand more, but stories about alleged terrorists get dropped soon after they make it to the 6:00 broadcast. If they are eventually found innocent, she seldom hears about it. The Toronto 18. The London eight. All the people on the no-fly list. Until Sayed is cleared, if he is cleared, Tahir and his family and Shinny herself can only wait. The store remains open, customers ignorant of the wobbly foundation that underlies their opportunity to conveniently mail packages, buy stamps, pick up a pack of cigarettes, a lotto ticket, a MoneyGram. The biggest change for Shinny is Sayed's absence. No longer does he barrel into the store in his iridescent shirts, demanding to see Tahir, demanding something. First impressions penetrate, and in her view, Sayed is the arrogant bully she first saw storming out of his SUV the day of the accident nearly a year ago. But then, what does she know? He help his people, Sima said. Commendable, but you can't just do anything, no matter your motives. This is Canada, Shinny argues, in her mind. Come to think of it, Sayed's SUV must have been impounded too. In this potential crime situation, a police incident, all her language comes from the news, or the cop shows that dominate prime time.

She wants to show her concern, but what can she do? Last night, to keep herself busy, to keep her mind off what may happen this afternoon, she made cookies. She packed them into a tin and gave them to Tahir this morning. For your family, she said. He nodded his thanks for the small, possibly not even appropriate gesture. She could change her mind about being a character witness, but she doesn't know any more about Sayed than she ever did, only the memory of the accident, his temper, his audacity. If he has been Tahir's financier since the beginning, why did she not see him before that day? The one thing she could do to help would be to work the whole shift, to give Tahir some time off. But not today. Not today.

The man she is meeting has not given her his full name, but he asked if she would wear white, so that he could recognize her. Does that mean he is soft? Sentimental? Romantic? Or simply practical. White is what she was wearing the last time she saw him. One-thirty now. Too early to get dressed, but she can take another look at her wardrobe. November! A white sweater? She doesn't own a white coat. She'll have to take off her purple raincoat and wait in her white sweater. She has done what she can with her hair, which is shorter now, true, but still white, naturally white now. She took a bath, waxed the hair that wasn't growing where it does now when he explored her face with his fingertips years ago. She has also lathered herself with cream several times a day since she received his note. Never too late? A lie. Despite having piled enough grease on it to lubricate a moving van, there's little difference in her skin. And he hasn't seen her with glasses.

Of course he won't look the same either. He may be bald, because it seems that redheads often lose their hair early; fat, at least paunchy. Maybe even shrunken. But he's younger, she thinks, and people today are more conscious of fitness. Not that it matters; this is no tryst she's trying to set up, though he may think it is. And there is still the possibility that he's an impostor. She will ask a question only the true man would know the answer to: can you remember the first thing you said to me? If he says, the way you glow, you can only be the good fairy, he's the one. She winces thinking of it, so cheesy, as the kids say. If he remembers that phrase, and if everything else fits, he is definitely the one, and she will announce that he is not only a father, but about to be a grandfather.

Less than a month before Elfie delivers their grandchild. She hasn't told Elfie about this rendezvous, and although Annette is aware that she placed the ad and got a reply, she has promised not to say a word until Shinny knows for sure if the man who answered the ad is the right man. In their last two conversations, Elfie hasn't mentioned her lost father, just Brendan, herself, the baby, that woman Hilda, who seems to visit every day and do things for Elfie that Shinny herself would like to do. But Elfie doesn't want her mother there. Not now. Not until the baby is born.

"You know how small the apartment is, Mom, and there's really nothing you can do. When Johann comes I'll need your help. Hilda said that she'll help, too."

Shinny is not convinced that Elfie is not still mad at her, but she has exhausted the "sorrys". She won't call every day; it would drive Elfie crazy and it wouldn't accomplish anything. But if she gets news today that's important for Elfie to hear, then what? Just say, I've found your father? He wants to come meet you? Will he? She taps the space bar to wake up her computer. The weather icon shows grey clouds; grey as the actual sky over her shoulder. For once the image matches the reality. No news headlines since she checked half an hour ago. Nothing new in her mailbox. As has become her habit when she needs to talk to someone and there's no one to talk to, she types Kate Babcock's name in the To: space.

Dear Kate,

Long time no hear from. I hope that new computer isn't giving you any trouble. Like I was saying in my last email, I do think education is a good thing. Did you find a course you like? You could start with one. I'm not the big expert or anything; I never went to college. I'm more like a school of hard knox grad. But my youngest daughter has two degrees and she's married to a man who composes music in New York. Maybe Mattie told you? The education they have, it's like money that can never be stolen. My first two daughters didn't go. Well, I didn't have the money to help them out, but they didn't want to go either. Not when they could, ie, right after high school. Then the oldest got married and had a baby, that's your friend Matthew, and the next one moved to California and eventually became a goat farmer, like her dad. I think you should try somethgin. Maybe you won't like your first choice, but then you can try something else. Well, Kate, let me know what you do. I always enjoy hearing from you. We're pen pals now, for sure, even if we don't use pens!

SS

Still not even 2:00. False Creek is like a paper someone has pencilled on top of a ribbed surface. But the rain has ended for the day, according to the icon on her computer, according to the weather girl on the news at noon. She'll bring her umbrella all the same, to protect the scrapbook she has made, with pictures of Elfie. Just a few, but enough to show her progression from smooth-headed babyness to the latest, last Christmas, with Brendan. From the skinny little blonde who dressed exclusively in pink for several years, to the slim, pony-tailed teen in serious black for a violin recital, to the one of her smiling broadly as she accepted the plaque she won at the UBC competition; then a couple of beautiful smiling kids, Brendan and Elfie, on the Ligurian coast of Italy. Oh what that girl's father has missed, but Shinny can't blame him. It was her who thought one night enough; she had a tie to Smokey, she had her two girls.

Nothing more to do. She pulls the white sweater over her head, tugs up the khaki pants. Cleans the lenses of her glasses, fluffs her hair. Scrubs teeth with toothpaste that is supposed to whiten, brushes a salmon-coloured blush on her cheekbones, applies dark coral lipstick. Perfume? She doesn't have any. This is not a date, she reminds herself.

Imagination fills her mind with possibilities good and bad as she crosses Pacific Boulevard—what if a car streaked around the corner and struck her down before she could meet him? Turns the corner at Drake and Homer and walks through wooden tunnels alongside construction sites, past an anorexic young woman begging outside the Shoppers Drug Mart; stands back from the corner while she waits for the light to change, to avoid the splashes of speeding cars. A pink-cheeked veteran in a black beret holds his tray of poppies beneath a large umbrella.

The library was designed to resemble the Roman Colloseum. Shinny toured the building with Elfie when it opened in '95 and learned that in the original colloseum, half a million people and more than twice that many wild animals were slaughtered. The guide made a joke about murder mysteries on the shelves instead of actual murders, and Shinny laughed along with everyone else, but remembering those associations doesn't make it any easier for her to climb the south-facing steps, where people sit in fine weather, but which are empty today. Nolan Baumgartner, Sergei Shirokov, Hamid Karzai, Maxim Afinogenov. Clearly, at the end of the day. Brutal attack. In a surprising reversal. If she can't think of what to say to him, she'll drag up something from the collection at the bottom of her mind. Clearly … At the end of the day … Remember how we didn't want to get each other's names? We said names didn't matter, only presences. Do you still play the piano?

A siren snaps her attention to the street, then a horn blares notice to walkers and drivers, as if the siren isn't enough, that emergency vehicles are coming through. A fire truck first, stopping right here; right on the plaza. She instinctively flattens herself against the window of the florist's shop. Now an ambulance pulls up alongside the fire truck. Men and women in uniform jump out. A fire? Now? People are stopped, waiting. The library's automatic doors are open, and the ambulance attendants hurry after the firemen, carrying a stretcher right past her, right through the doors, into the concourse. So it's not a fire but someone having a heart attack? Or jumped through one of the high windows all the way from the sixth floor onto the paving stones of the concourse? She can't face that. And what if it's him? No. He might have a heart attack after she tells him, but not first, not now.

Your problem is that you don't look before leaping, Sharon. Her mother used to tell her that, but Shinny can't seem to brake a certain fateful energy that has always propelled her and does now, as she follows the emergency workers through the doors before the authorities decide to close them for some reason, possibly having to do with security. No one is looking at her, but only at the firemen rushing toward the library entrance, in the centre of the concourse. She stands near the tables alongside the coffee shop, watching the firemen like everyone else, but also scanning the tables, where action has stopped for a moment; people with cups in hands, newspapers lying unread. Is he here yet? Is that man sitting at the table by himself, could it be? No. He's dark, darker skinned than Brendan and with black hair, and he's too young. But he looks worried. Well no one knows what might be going on. A simple heart attack? A terrorist threat? No, people would be evacuated were it terrorism, wouldn't they? She slips onto the nearest chair at the nearest empty table, shrugs off her purple raincoat, fluffs her hair without thinking. Lays down the scrapbook. But she should buy something to justify occupying the table; she doesn't want to be shooed out. Leaves the coat, takes the scrapbook, orders a decaf at the counter inside. Make that a latte, she says, immediately regretting it, because she'll have to stand here while the barista makes it. Action has resumed, but tentatively, as if everyone in the concourse—which is just as busy as usual, patrons walking in and out of the library itself, the shops, the banks of doors at both ends—as if all have sensed the fragility of the hour; any abrupt movement could shatter the entire scene. Newcomers look around, sensing something different, something they have missed. Everyone is expectant, unless it is just her, waiting.

At the next table, an Asian woman, a teacher obviously, is working with a younger woman. Shinny catches a few of the phrases they're working on: mere beauty. Does it make beauty sound better? The young girl, pretty, her hair that bottomless enveloping black, looks puzzled. Shinny's view is hindered by a tall, hunched, toothless man wearing hip waders, who angles around the tables to the plastic garbage can and lifts the top, looking for bottles and cans he can turn in for the deposit money. He moves past, opening sight lines.

White letters on the glass wall opposite honour the donors who contributed to the Library Square Project: MacMillan Bloedel Limited, The Forest Rogers Family, Westcoast Energy Inc., Mary and Gordon Christopher. Sipping the latte, glancing through the *Metro* commuter paper, as if she needs to know the day's headlines again. Feeling the energy change as a quarter of an hour passes and no more emergency personnel arrive, nothing really changes. Is that the nature of terrorism? A permanent state of suspension? How long should she wait? Her cup is empty but she raises it to her lips, frowning, now and then; the lipstick must be gone. She reads the same front page story over and over again, turns to the back pages to gawk at the full-colour celebrity photos. The horoscopes. She reads all the horoscopes, wondering what might be influencing him today. Not that she has any idea when he was born, not that she puts any stock in astrology. But you never know.

Some action at last, which stops everyone again, those who remained to see what happened, those who have arrived since. The blue-shirted firefighters trot beside the stretcher the ambulance attendants roll out the wide library doors, past the security guards and through the concourse, heading for the exit just beyond where Shinny sits. The person on the stretcher is wholly covered, as far as she can see. The big men walking at the head of the stretcher block the face, but if that's covered too, the person is dead. They're gone before she can stand to get a better look. Out the doors, down the ramp, out to the ambulance whose lights begin to flash, red, red, red, whose sirens wail like those women in their hijabs kneeling in the rock-strewn dust on the evening news, when a child has been struck by a bomb, by mortar fire, rockets.

She is still standing, as are some of the other coffee drinkers in the concourse, when a man walks through the doors. Frowning, hurrying. A tall man, on the thin side. A green rain parka, jeans, running shoes. A brown tweed snap-brim hat covering white hair that wisps over his ears. Glasses with rectangular metal frames. He's looking around. But he isn't wearing a blue jacket, like he said he would. There's no way he has red hair, or even the complexion common to redheads. She feels like a contestant on a game show. Stands. Smiles. Because the way he's looking around, there's a good chance this is him.

He sees her. But what does he see? Is that disappointment on his face, or is he frowning because he has to work through a maze of tables to reach her? He is definitely coming her way. If he says the words he said that night, if he says them now. But no.

"Are you?"

"The woman who said she'd meet you here?"

"SS at Hotmail?"

"Yes. I'm SS."

No magic words. But he's the person who answered her ad, and through the smokey tint of his lenses she sees that his eyes could be green. His frowning face is textured with acne scars she does not recall. Of course it was dark.

"I bet you wondered if I was going to show up. Everything is jammed out there: fire truck, ambulances. What's going on? I should have walked. I often walk down here."

"So you're still …?"

"In the West End? You know, I never actually lived in the West End, but I moved back to Vancouver a couple of years ago, just when the Coal Harbour development was opening up. I like to run. Stanley Park is just next door."

He's glancing around. There's so much to ask. To tell. If he never lived in the West End, what was he doing in that apartment?

"Someone died."

"I'm sorry."

"It's nobody I know. Here, just today. Now. That's why there was a traffic jam. Someone died, I think. Right in the library. They rolled the stretcher out just before you came in. The person's face was covered; that would mean he was dead, I think? Or she?"

"Jesus! Sorry. That's not the first thing I expected to hear. I need a coffee. Can I get you anything?"

She looks at her empty cup. Thinks of the extra minutes it takes for the barista to produce a latte. "A decaf latte, please." Not wanting to assume anything, she reaches in her purse for change, but he's off and she has time to settle, to assess. It seems to be him. But he never lived in the West End? More questions. He's the height she remembers, but was his hair ever red? How has that image persisted? What memory fueled it? His voice seems familiar, but circumstances are different. He was talking quietly that night, softly, seductively. She thought he was younger but he could not be much younger; his shoulders have begun to curve forward slightly, his hair is as white as hers, what she can see of it, and his forehead is lined. Elfie developed wrinkles on her forehead early, a scrim of lines that deepens as the years pass. Shinny's stomach growls. She should have asked for a muffin. She should bought one herself. But she has been distracted. Her meetings with significant men have happened at times of crisis: Smokey at Stanley Park because she was searching for Lawreen, who had wandered away. Glen when she had contracted poison oak. Now this man, whose name she still does not know, on the day of a death in the library.

"Here we are," he says, putting their cups on the small table, which wobbles. "Oops. Careful!"

If he were not wearing glasses that darken in the light, if there were not just enough daylight coming through the skylights above the concourse to set them darkening, she would be able to determine whether or not his eyes are the green she remembers. They sip from their cups. What now? He must be thinking the same thing, because he shakes his head and lifts eyebrows from which white hairs shoot.

"Do you think we're the right people? Do I look anything like you remember?"

"Sort of. It was short."

What is he thinking, that two other people had a similar encounter, the same night? Is that possible?

"What about me?"

"Sort of, too. It was summer then. The Sea Festival. I don't think they have those anymore. When I first saw you? On the seawall, you looked like a fairy, not in the way they used to mean it then, but a fairy tale sort of fairy. You kind of glowed."

It's him. She swallows coffee to stop the stinging in her nose and at the corners of her eyes.

"I was sorry to see you gone the next morning, and I had no idea where to find you. Remember how we didn't want to get each other's names?"

"We said names didn't matter, only presences. We were smoking pot, though. Did we mean it?"

"We meant it at the time. I did anyway. I was escaping that night."

"I wanted to see you again. I should have advertised, like you did."

"People contact each other all the time."

"You can do that now. You can find people on Facebook, you can Google them. But you have to know their name. I didn't know your name."

"And I didn't know yours. I still don't. The SS? It stands for Sharon Shinnan. Most people call me Shinny."

He extends his hand, oddly formal.

"Shinny. I'm James Dekker and that's what people call me. James."

"If you never actually lived in the West End, what were you doing …"

"In that apartment?"

He laughs, a nervous laugh; strange for a tall man, that he might lack confidence.

"I was out here applying for a job. It was a friend's place."

"So that piano wasn't yours, then. It's the first thing I saw when I woke up, the lid of that piano, and it's what I've remembered. I always thought you were a piano player."

"Oh, the piano. I play, but I wouldn't call myself a piano player, not in the professional sense."

He is not what she thought, not what she told Elfie. The image Elfie adopted when she heard the story of her conception is just as false as the sense of self she had when she grew up thinking that John was her father.

"Sorry to disappoint you."

He empties his cup. Sets it down. Are we done, he may be asking. Can I be excused? It's apparent that he shaved for this rendezvous, and with those pockmarks it must have taken time; if she were to put her cheek against his, she would probably smell aftershave. She imagines him in his apartment in Coal Harbour, preparing. What did he expect?

"It's not that I'm looking for a piano player. And, you know, just to be straight from the beginning, I didn't place that ad because I'm looking for, well, you know, romance."

Does he look relieved? She can't tell, and if he does, he won't be relieved for long.

"That's fine. You were curious. A lot of people are looking into their past. You can find people, old lovers, high school friends. You don't have to apologize. I was curious, too; that's why I answered your ad."

A dark-haired woman with vermillion lipstick approaches the empty table next to them, sets down her coffee, opens what looks like a textbook. Almost immediately another, older woman joins her: *Hola! Como esta?*

"Well it's more than curiosity, really. That night?"

"*Es-TA,*" the first woman says, loudly, emphasizing the last syllable. "You put accent on the end, *Es-TA? Entiende?*"

"Pretty noisy here. There's a pub next door. This time of day it ought to be quiet."

She slips her purple raincoat back on, walks alongside him. Neither tries speaking. It's just outside the concourse doors, Library Square Public House, and it is quiet. Just a few patrons here, around 4:00, but it will fill as people get off work and stop for a quick one, and there's a game tonight. If she's going to say it today, now's the time, before the big screens mounted around the room display the dazzling ice of a hockey arena instead of men in black t-shirts, some wearing sunglasses, who stare down at a pile of plastic chips on a poker table while the screen displays the hand they were dealt. But he speaks first.

"You don't look exactly like what I remember. You had big hair then, but you haven't put on any weight. You were small, like now."

"Except my hands. I have unnaturally large hands for my size."

She holds them out and he puts his right hand next to her right hand, which shows that hers are not as big as she thinks, not compared to his. Certainly his fingers are an inch longer, and freckled. The freckles. White-blonde hairs fringe the joints. Who cares, hands, fingers?! She must say what she came here to say.

"Not that big. But what I was going to say is that while you're obviously older and the big hair is gone, you seem the same. I remembered you. I know we said we were going to keep it casual, but I regretted that. Like I said, I would have called but you didn't leave me your number."

"I was in a relationship. A man I'd been with for years. Father of my second daughter. He wanted to keep it open; he travelled a lot, but I was never comfortable with that arrangement. It was sort of an I'll show him impulse. I remembered the silliest things. The piano lid. Your green eyes. They are green, aren't they?"

He pushes his glasses down his nose and she sees that yes, they are green; a sort of olive green with a blue rim around them. Not the shade she remembers, but green. Like Elfie's.

"Images, really. The arrow pointing up in the elevator."

"You were very—enthusiastic. I never forgot you."

Oh. Of the details she has retrieved, she has avoided the actual sex. Enthusiastic? Smokey had been gone for months. She missed sex, she missed touching, skin against skin; the tentativeness with a new person, assessing the taste, the feel of lips, tongues. Everything about him—James—leaner, firmer, drier, compared to John, or Smokey at that time, who was already what he called healthily portly and who sweated easily, whose full mouth yielded like marshmallows when they kissed. How could she not compare them? For someone who must have seemed like a loose woman, given that her two daughters had two different fathers, James was the third man she had slept with. Though she didn't sleep long. Enthusiastic? She can't think these thoughts now or they will undermine her purpose.

"The reason I placed the ad? I came away with a souvenir."

"You took something, from that apartment? I never heard that something was missing."

"Nothing like that."

"You couldn't have caught anything from me, as far as I know. I didn't have anything. I wasn't the sort of guy who played around much. I'd been in one relationship for years; did I tell you that? No, probably not. We were trying to keep it light. Magical. We were young; I guess that was it."

"Not that young."

"True. But listen, if an impulsive one-night stand was out of character for you, it wasn't exactly my style either. That's why I remember it."

He seems like a very nice man. He's not pushy or showy, at least so far; he isn't monopolizing the conversation. Elfie would like him, she thinks. Would he like Elfie? She understands why people take a big breath before doing something difficult; you have to summon all your energy—you have to be prepared for the worst.

"The thing is, James, I got pregnant. You're the father of a girl you've never met and you're about to be a grandfather."

There. It's out, and the room isn't crashing down, and the music on the speakers hasn't stopped or changed. It's like dropping a bomb that doesn't detonate. The bartender is still puttering behind the bar, the waitress, shuttling back and forth. Shinny registers the motion but the sound she hears comes from inside her, gong, gong. "A Day in the Life", by The Beatles, the sound at the end that rises and rises. She widens her eyes, takes another deep breath. He's speechless. Clearly, at the end of the day, this reversal of events has taken his words from him. He takes off his hat and scratches the sparse hairs on the top like a character in a cartoon who has just received puzzling news. The bald part of his head is shaped like False Creek. His eyes really are Elfie's, and the lean body type. Now he looks down, reading the tabletop. That's something Elfie does, too. Avoids confrontations. She ran into the bathroom of her New York apartment and stayed there for hours.

"I guess it would be insulting to ask if you're sure."

"That my daughter is yours? I just said I didn't do that sort of thing. You have no idea the trouble I've gone through to find you. God!"

"I know, I'm sorry. I didn't know what else to say. I think we're beyond coffee. You?"

He could have signalled the waiter, but he chooses to go over to the bar. Long legs, a brown sweater over a plaid shirt. An ordinary man. She can't imagine what's going through his head. He hasn't said that's wonderful; he hasn't accused her of wanting his money. If he has any money. Nothing about him screams wealth. He returns with a double whiskey for himself and a glass of wine for Shinny. If he had waited for an answer she would have asked for whiskey, too, but the drinks are beside the point. The last few minutes have elapsed in a new language; the vocabulary is unfamiliar to her. She has no confidence that she is actually communicating. But the scrapbook is open now so that he has something to look at when he lowers his eyes to the table. It seems they should be toasting this news, their reunion. But he sips before she can suggest it; he sips and looks at the pictures, each page drawing him deeper into Elfie's life. Shinny senses him teetering; it has to be some kind of joke. He's going to finish his whiskey and leave this crazy woman.

"I tried to find you before, when I knew. I thought I should tell you. I actually waited outside that apartment building for hours one day."

"I was living in Toronto, out here for a job interview. It was a recession back then, too, remember that? The mining industry shot to hell. I was a surveyor. I didn't get the job so I went back to Toronto. But she's a musician? And you thought that talent came from me?"

"Nobody in my family is a musician. My grandfather loved music, but not like Elfie. That's her name, after my mother, Elfriede Shinnan Singh-Gill.

The Singh-Gill is from her husband, Brendan. He's a musician, too. And a composer. Look. That's when they were in Italy. They got married there. Elfie's pregnant now. That's what started all this."

She likes the way he frowns; he seems like a man who is sure of what counts, but out of his depth now, and he isn't trying to hide it.

Another deep breath. A sip of wine, and she remembers to wipe her mouth with her hand, because Lawreen has told her that whenever she drinks wine she ends up with a red ring around her mouth.

"She didn't know about you until a couple of months ago. She thought that John, her sister's father, the man I was living with, was her father, too. He's the only one I told and he kept my secret. All through Elfie's life I debated telling her, then didn't. I thought I'd die and she would never know and what difference would it make? But the baby has a heart defect, and we need to know your family medical history. A hole, they call it. The doctor gave her the choice of aborting. In the beginning they thought she might spontaneously abort, but it didn't happen and it's too late now. The baby is due in a few weeks. Elfie is ready to take the chance, but she'll feel better knowing it isn't hereditary."

She has talked straight at him; there's so much to say. He has nodded half-consciously now and then, as if to confirm he's listening. The lenses of his glasses are fully clear now and she can see the expression in his eyes change from attentive to apprehensive.

"A father and a grandfather in one day? I'm going to have a grand-child?"

"Grandson."

"Grandson! But he may not survive?"

"We've all been living with that possibility."

This time he does not go over to the bar, but waves to the barmaid. Shinny hasn't finished her glass, but the wine has loosened her. It's happened: she has found him, she has told him. Not the end of the story but a break in acts, an intermission, and she's exhausted. She imagines the leaf shapes pressed into the Homer Street sidewalk, the lobby of her building, her apartment and the warmth it provides on days like this. Almost dark already. Nearly 5:00? People are coming into the bar. The pre-game show has begun. The genial Jim Hughson and his cuddly sidekick are assessing the team's chances of winning tonight. If she goes right home, she can spend the next few hours with them.

James sips his whiskey and turns the few pages of the scrapbook she put together.

"Am I going to meet her?"

"You want to?"

"I want to tell her myself that as far as I know, there's nothing to worry about. But first I have to check with my sister. She looks a little like my sister. The nose; it's a good straight nose, and her smile. Is she shy? Or was she? She's young here. She must be a good violinist, too."

It's the award picture. Shinny in the audience with Mattie because Lawreen was off somewhere with Mariah, and Ken had to work. Annette and John were in California. How nice it would have been to have James sitting next to her, handing her his handkerchief to blot her tears of pride. If he carries a handkerchief. Maybe nobody carries handkerchiefs anymore.

"You have a sister? Other children?"

"I have a sister; no children. My wife had a miscarriage. After that she couldn't conceive."

"A wife then."

"A late wife."

"Oh," says Shinny, thinking of all that has happened to him, to her since that night. Both of them widowed.

"I just wish I'd known."

"I tried."

"I know."

FOR ECONOMY'S SAKE, ANNETTE is breeding three does at a time this season, and only six in total, meaning that she can get by with two visiting bucks and determine if either one has fathered better goats than the other, better meaning beauties with good temperaments and well-formed udders. Through the summer and early fall she visited several herds and checked out the bucks the owners had cleaned up for the occasion of her inspection. She read their breeding histories and, by chatting with their owners over coffee, got a sense of how they had been cared for. Five farm visits, two bucks, both Lamanchas, one with a hide uniquely spotted, like a pinto pony. She would not have chosen him on that basis alone, but since his owner had records of the impressive milkers he sired, he was a good bet in that department too. Maybe she'll get pinto kids from one of the girls she has chosen to breed him to.

Pancho Villa is the first to visit, and though he and each of the three does in heat spend only an hour together in the breeding stall, it turns into a full day, and a social one. The visiting owner expects coffee at least. Also part of the tradition is for the host to offer a sample of the farm's chevre, so Annette puts a round of Josie's camembert and some apples and pears on a plate with the loaf of the whole-grain bread Eve helped her bake last night. Eve made brownies, too. The socializing is a useful way of sharing shop talk, and Dad enjoys the break in his sedentary routine. Seven weeks home and he can sit in the recliner Greg picked up at a second-hand store in Santa Rosa. Still, Matt shouldn't have left without saying anything. Without him here to help, there's more for everyone to do and Annette is still mad about it, considering how she welcomed him, the free ride he had during his stay.

While Pancho takes a break between Loretta and Kathleen, Greg monitors the barn, in case there's any trouble. During the business itself, Annette kept her eyes from his, imagining the frustration he must have been feeling as Loretta's back arched. There's nothing romantic about goat fucking. It's all business. The buck gets it in as often as he gets erect, which is often, and fast, until he is taken away. Yet the raw sex used to turn them on. Now, just as they were moving closer to one another, everything changed. With her in the computer room, Dad in her bed and Greg in Dad's bed, they won't be completing the journey towards each other this breeding season. Which is too bad, Annette thinks; or maybe not. When they are free to consider each other, it won't be the spur of the moment jumping into the sack it might have been with all these hormones in the atmosphere and the house to themselves.

Eve has the sniffles, which is why she is home from school today, snuggling next to her dad while he jaws about land use changes in the county with Pancho's owner, a former school teacher from the Bay Area, who started his goat herd a decade ago, when the cutbacks in school budgets meant teacher layoffs. Annette hopes that Eve's trouble is not the beginning of swine flu, which is particularly hard on children her age. A boy in Canada died of it, almost instantly according to her Mom. That news before the bigger news for the family, that she found Elfie's father.

That she thought she may have found him slipped out when Annette asked if her if she'd had any luck with the search. Maybe, Shinny said a couple of weeks ago, and Annette dragged the rest of the story out of her, the ad in the Georgia Straight, the reply, their intended meeting.

"But please don't say anything to Elfie," she begged. "I wouldn't want to disappoint her. Okay? Promise?"

"What are you promising? What's the news?" Dad asked, looking for any diversion from the prison of his slow-healing hip.

"Mom thinks she's found him."

"Don't tell me that, daughter."

"You mean you're jealous? You still have a thing for Mom?"

He laughed it off.

"Don't listen to me. Don't you know I'm half the time outta my right mind? This is news, that's for sure. Hard to believe, though. I just hope she doesn't get mixed up with a crank."

She saw the usual pain, him reaching for his Percocet. After Greg and the kids went up the hill, she helped him settle in bed and he never said another word about Mom or her former lover, Elfie's father. Aside from the grunts and groans he couldn't help making as he shifted from his wheelchair, he was quiet, thanked her. The look on his face when she rose from kissing him goodnight, what was that? Apology, regret? Just plain sadness that softened his eyes? Such an easygoing fellow, Dad, but with Mattie gone, he was alone with two kids, little chance that would change. He'd cleaned himself up for Mom's visit in the summer. Would he rather Mom had not found Elfie's dad? Was he feeling threatened by someone else on the scene? He wouldn't lose Elfie, nor Mom, though it is true that Elfie doesn't call as much as you'd think considering his condition, and that, until now, he is the only dad she has known.

Pinto Pancho serviced all three does and his owner led him into his trailer smelling gamey and rank with urine and semen. A sloppy, smelly business. Greg is at Dad's, showering, and Annette has a roast in the oven. When she comes back inside to check it, Dad has gotten himself to standing by himself and is leaning on the aluminum rails of his walker.

"Net, I gotta get back to my own place."

"Are you kidding?"

It would be great to have her house back, but she's locked into her sense of responsibility and her overwhelming practicality. Would it really be easier for her with him up there?

"The kids need to be back to something like normal. I'll be just up the hill. We always ate together; now the kids can bring me something when they come back, or they can learn to cook. Eve made that cake for Matt. She can do it. I'll be right there."

"Dad, she's barely ten. If Matt hadn't skipped out it would be different."

Yet there is no reason he shouldn't move, if he wants to. The doctors have told him to add activity as he feels ready, and carefully; it's better for him to move than keep himself frozen in the recliner. He has the walker, he has crutches, a cane. But the kids are not so confident when he makes his announcement. Aidan locks eyes with Annette, Eve puts a finger in her mouth.

"Aidan, Eve, sweetheart. I'm movin' back home, kids. It's gonna be you and me again, like it used to be. And I'm gonna need your help. Can't expect your big sister to be running up and down that hill all the time."

Greg has just come in, smelling of soap, the skin exposed above his beard is red with the cold of the early night.

"You sure, John? You all ready for it?"

"With a little help, damn right I am. You two are right down here. But I'm going to be in charge of these rascals again. And we're gonna start right after supper with homework. Aidan? What you got tonight? Arithmetic?"

"You mean math, Dad?"

"Okay, math. After we're finished here, I'm gonna have a look. You have your papers with you?"

"They're home. You know."

"I do know. That's just what I mean."

Annette lifts the bowl of mashed potatoes and stands to spoon some onto Dad's plate. Greg passes the gravy over and Annette follows his hand as he draws it back to his place. Her chin slides an arc across her chest to peek at his reaction to the news; Greg, who has begun to resemble the man she fell in love with, the way his shoulders brushed the door frame when he came back from the kitchen with a home brew and a pitcher of water. Hairy again but white strands soften the dark waves around his temples, and his chin looks like the aging Shep's. Greg swallows a third of his beer, sets the mug down. Nods at the table. Glances up at her, a quick silvery blue flash before he returns his gaze to the table.

December

No sleep, no dreams. He's nervous about even shutting his eyes, though it's late, past midnight. This is Hollywood, but the bus station on Cahuenga is hardly glamorous. Cahuenga. How do you say it? Only one wicket open, plastic seats bolted to metal rods, old-fashioned candy machines with glass bubbles full of some kind of red and green and yellow beans that could be jelly beans or could be some kind of rasta drug. He watched while a kid, maybe three or four, dressed in white but dirty, barefoot despite the time of year, dropped in a coin and the beans spilled all over the floor. Then the kid picked them up and shoved them into his mouth.

Mariah hasn't answered his calls. She may be out of town. She'd at least answer, wouldn't she? Not that they were ever that close, her being gone so much. Not like Eve and Aidan will be as they grow up. Those two spend most of the day together, often torturing each other, Eve as hard on Aidan as he is on her; but they move together when something comes up.

Matt retains an image of Eve on top of the hill, kneeling on one knee, the other bent, her chin resting on it, making a human swastika. How she wouldn't look at him when she asked if her dad would die. How he felt for her, really felt for her, and now regrets just having walked out on her, on all of them. But shit, he came down here to get his head together not to adopt a whole family. And he can't explain to them that Berk might know where he is, that Berk thinks that he's still in business. If Matt were to write and tell him that he dumped all the discs, everything, into the North

Saskatchewan, Berk might be even more determined to get him. He sure can't tell Eve what he was up to before, so he had to get out of there, and he couldn't tell them where he was going, so he walked up the drive, out to the road, and hitched into Santa Rosa. To the hippie-ish couple who picked him up he explained nothing. You can be quiet. People accept that.

He's still got money, he could have gone to a hotel; he doesn't need to stay with Mariah. Maybe that's what she was worried about, that he'd cramp her style. Last night he stayed in a motel just down the street. Hollywood Boulevard, but it was creepy. Expensive, because of the location, but the carpets were dirty, the blankets smelled. The clerk didn't even look him the eye. What went on here? Drug deals? Sex for money? It had taken all day for him to bus down to L.A. from San Francisco. Most of it pissing rain.

He will miss Eve. Eve liked him, didn't pester too much. She seemed happy to be alongside him, to help with the dishes or fold the laundry, and she was just ten. It was good he stayed for her birthday. She insisted that he sit next to her, too, while she opened presents and blew out the candles on the cake she had made for herself. Was it okay, that brief note he left? He hopes that Greg saw the note before the kids got home. He did leave Eve a private note, in which he said he was sorry. He pinned it to the purple t-shirt of his she liked, with $20, and said he'd keep in touch and come back to visit sometime. Still, he thinks she'll be sad. There's the Mexican family taking up the row of seats against the window, a couple of decrepit looking old people and him. The man behind the counter. Only one more bus scheduled to leave before the station closes, and that's the one he bought a ticket for, to Seattle. It'll take him over a day to get there, but that's okay. Lots of time to think. Make plans.

Of the various portions of the Canadian Forces site he has memorized, one in particular flashes through his mind: *Potential CF members are subjected to an enhanced check to confirm your reliability and trustworthiness in the performance of your duties and in the protection of the assets and interests of the Canadian Forces and its personnel. This check will only be conducted with your consent. Should you withhold your consent or not authorize the necessary checks, your application will not be considered further.*

He has decided that once he crosses back into Canada, he'll enlist. And he can't refuse the reliability check, or there's no way he'll get in. Will he pass it? He doesn't have a record. If the police are after him, he'll be stopped at the border; he won't be able to enlist because he'll be in jail. As far as he knows, the only one pursuing him is Berk, and Berk won't be able to get to him in the army.

The bus pulls in late; the Mexican family stands, but people have to get off the bus before it continues on. There's still some time to wait. Almost midnight. He could try Mariah again, he could say he was passing through. Before he can let himself think of it for long he presses in her number, listens to three rings, listens to the voice message: "So sorry I missed you! Please do call again!"

The baby in its mother's arms has started to cry. Oh, man. A fat man and wife, fat but young; he's got tattoos on his bare arms, a black muscle shirt; she's wearing a tank top under a nylon jacket and jeans, and her hair is streaked with yellow. One fat kid, another skinny kid—the one that picked the candy up off the filthy floor and ate it, and his parents didn't stop him—and the baby. A bald guy, who smells of liquor; the gaunt white-haired couple, both of them straight faced. And him, who doesn't have to do this. Who has the money to fly. But where? Direct to Vancouver? He wouldn't have any time to think about anything. And so he boards the Greyhound, takes a seat in the middle, hopes no crazies board and cut off his head the way that crazy man cut off the head of a kid riding to Winnipeg last year. Freaky. Hopes the family sits way front or way back and gets his wish as they struggle to the back with their kids and their bags, and the bathroom door opens, letting the stench of urine escape.

Fight fear, fight distress, fight chaos. Maybe you can fight them, but can you ever win those battles?

ELFIE EXAMINES THE DOCTOR'S face for concern and finds only the usual concentration.

"So far so good?"

"We'll remain optimistic but vigilant," says her obstetrician, professionally friendly. Cool. Cautious. Doctors have to be cautious; there's the malpractice issue hanging over the medical profession, but it is also true that Dr. Radan cannot promise Elfie that everything will be all right. Nobody can promise that everything will be all right because nobody knows.

"So far so good, but we are not going to let your due date pass by. If purposeful contractions do not begin before next week, we will induce. We want to give this little gentleman his best chance."

"At least we know it's not hereditary. So it might be all right. It might be."

Brendan is sitting in the corner, out of the way of the fetal heart monitor machines, the examining table, the doctor's desk.

"It won't be long now," the doctor says, extending her hand. Brendan's hair is longer than usual and curls over the neckline of his white sweater. In a different setting he might be mistaken for an Indian mystic, Elfie thinks as he puts his arm around her to help her sit, then slide off the examining table.

"So, one way or another, we'll see you soon."

Elfie is smiling, a little giddy, because what the doctor is saying is that one way or another she will have Johann in her arms by next week. He has grown to term, the murmur is no more pronounced, though his heart has grown in size. A pediatric cardiology team is on standby. She has had her days of depression, but not today. While she's grainy from having slept so little last night, and Johann is pressing on the nerves that cause tweaks in her back, she's ready. More ready than Brendan, whose exam schedule has unfortunately coincided with the due date. He's given notice to his students and made arrangements with the administration. Only once has he mentioned that the New York Rangers are playing host to the Vancouver Canucks next week, a game he hoped to see in person at Madison Square Garden. He calls for a cab because it's snowing, a wet snow. It's raw out there and Elfie has nothing big enough to completely cover her. They have been cabbing it to the clinic the last month because Brendan doesn't want her falling; he doesn't want her to get cold. At home he urges her to lean on him, though they barely fit in the narrow stairwell.

"Bren, I'm not crippled, I can still walk up stairs."

"Will you be okay if I go into the office for a few hours? Can you get Hilda to come over?"

"There's nothing you can do, nothing I can do. Nothing Hilda could do, or anyone. It's a waiting game. Out of our control. I'm fine, honey. Really. I'm fine."

"I can pick up something on the way back. Chinese?"

"We'll be doing that when Johann is here. I'm fine, really. I'll make something simple. Pasta."

They haven't had sex since the night of the sarabande. He fears disturbing the baby or hurting her. She has said "I'm fine" so often she feels she might as well have it tattooed on her forehead.

"Okay," he says, not having taken off his coat or even his boots, which are dripping onto the floor. "You know where to get me if you want me."

The radiators tick, honking comes from far away. Almost dark at 4:00, but then today it has been dark all day. In her inbox, a message from James Dekker. Dad.

Dear Elfie,

Just wanted to say that I'm thinking of you and your baby. When the time is right I want to visit you in New York. I used to go New York on business. Last time a couple of years ago. We might even have passed each other on the street, although I didn't get to the East Village often. To a restaurant once. I'm sorry to disappoint you about my career. Traits are not necessarily genetic. Your musical gifts are your own, and with your husband having the same, there's a good chance that your son will inherit at least a love of music. That's something I've always had myself, though with so much travel I had to give up playing the piano. I have a feeling that the baby will be healthy, but I know you're worried. We all are. My hunches are pretty good. When I saw that notice your mother placed in the paper, I knew it was her. I didn't hesitate to answer straight away. I look forward to meeting you when the time is right, Elfie. Until then, all the best.

James (Seems presumptuous to call myself "Dad")

This pregnancy has resulted in a father as well as a son. Would Mom ever have told her? She says she doesn't know, that every time she thought of telling her, something came up. Elfie wonders if there are any more secrets, because once someone has been found out, it's hard to take them at face value; you wonder about what lies behind the face.

"Well think of it," Annette said, when they last talked. "Are there things in your life that you're not telling anyone? Stuff that would make people think you're different than you seem?"

"What are you trying to say, Annette? Is there something you're hiding?"

Annette laughed. "Me? As if."

She and Annette have talked several times these last two weeks. News about John, speculation about Mattie, who just disappeared, Annette said. Left a note and walked out somehow, but the discovery of James Dekker immediately displaced that news. Odd that she should feel closer to Annette now that they both have fathers, their own separate fathers. Lawreen does not, and they don't want to rub it in, but could that be what pushed her over the edge? Lawreen has been in hospital. Just a rest, Ken assured them all, via email. A few days; no, she doesn't want to see anyone. She isn't taking any calls, but she'll be all right. It's hormonal.

Elfie stands, stretches. Johann performs the flutter kick that always sends her to the bathroom. Brendan thinks that they should install a zip-line, she's back and forth so much. But the exercise is important, the only exercise she's getting with the weather so miserable and the threat of swine flu. The news still full of election analysis. Bloomberg re-elected, no surprise, but in Boston, a right-wing Republican got Ted Kennedy's old seat. People blame Obama. She hears the talk, sees the headlines when Brendan brings home a paper, but it all seems very distant.

Back at the computer she hits reply.

Dear James. Thank you for your note. We're just back from the doctor and so far so good is what she says. We'll post a picture of Johann as soon as we can. It will be sometime between now and next week because the doctor isn't going to let me go past my due date. I look forward to meeting you, too. Elfie

She wants to say Love, Elfie but she doesn't love him yet, just the idea of him, even if he was a surveyor rather than a musician. He sounds nice; Mom says he is kind, and that Elfie obviously gets her build and colouring from him. She has an aunt, Colleen Dekker-MacLeod, and cousins to meet. No more siblings, which means she is his only child. This has all happened so fast; Mom didn't want to get her too excited, but she wanted to reassure her about the heart defect. No pictures yet. He's seen pictures of her and said he was sorry to miss her growing up, that it was all just a big misunderstanding. That she shouldn't blame her mom because anonymity was just as much his idea as hers; but he also said that back then he wanted to see Mom again, that he regretted not getting her name. She showed Brendan this email, the first, and he said, "How can people do that? I mean maybe sleazy people, but grown-ups?"

"Didn't I say?" Hilda relished all the detail as Elfie could give.

"Conversation? So it was fireworks, dear? It was summer? How old was she, did you say? Do you have a picture?"

And before she left, with a hug and a promise to return the next day: "Don't sell the sun to buy a candle." She often speaks in proverbs, but Elfie doesn't get this one and Hilda didn't explain.

WEEKS AGO SHINNY TOLD Tahir that she might have to leave town suddenly. Tahir knows that her daughter is pregnant. She reminded him again yesterday that the time is near. He nodded forbearingly and turned his small head to the side, as if there might be a teleprompter out the window that could script his response.

"Hard to say, I mean explain this. Actually, not I want to do, but my friend Sayed, his trouble? They put freeze on funds. On his money. Now we have to be careful, to keep store. Maybe, when you come back from your daughter, you lay off 'til all is settled."

He pressed a key that opened the cash door, closed it again, and glanced towards the door, hoping for a customer to relieve his discomfort.

"That bad is it? Well, I'm sorry, Tahir. But I understand."

"Not like firing. You do good job here."

"I understand," she repeated, and she does understand, and right now the job is the last thing on her mind. "Don't worry about me," she assured him. "I should probably retire anyway."

Out on bail, Sayed came in the day before, with a younger man who waited by the door, as if a bodyguard. Familiar somehow. A face baby-smooth, almost two-dimensional. Sunglasses, despite the clouds. She had thought Sayed would have lost girth, but he actually puffed up in jail. Plumper cheeks, more of a belly. Maybe he's one of those people who eat in times of stress. When he saw that Tahir was away from the store, he stepped behind the sundries counter and opened the cash drawer; having learned his role here, Shinny could hardly protest. He lifted the coin compartment, snatched a paper from beneath, slammed the drawer closed. When a girl who had pushed past the bodyguard placed a can of Coke on the counter, he didn't notice.

"Sir?" the girl said. Sayed squinted over the top of whatever he was reading. "The Coke please?"

Sayed pointed to Shinny, who joined him behind the counter to take the girl's five-dollar bill and return change. The girl thanked her, with a lift of her perfectly waxed eyebrows and an impatient glance at Sayed.

What will happen now? Tahir suggested that she should work until she goes to New York. But when will that be?

She has a last-minute flights site bookmarked on her browser. She doesn't even need a ride to the airport but can hop on the new transit line, kitty corner from her building, and ride all the way out. No more cabs, no more leaning on Lawreen and Ken for a favour. And that's good, because Ken has enough to do with poor Lawrie out of commission. But better now, thank God, after withdrawing from that awful drug. The doctor prescribed rest, a mild anti-depressant. Sent Lawrie to a counsellor she appears to trust.

"Oh Ken, I'm so sorry," Shinny said, when he called to tell her that Lawreen had been admitted to hospital. "I'll go right over." But no, Lawreen was ashamed. She refused to see anyone, especially her mother, and she would have preferred that no one knew.

Even now she explains her drug dependence as hormonal imbalance, and keeps her distance, though she did agree to let her mother visit today, does accept the hug, loose in Shinny's arms. Shinny is not what she used to be for them, the girls; it's an alarm that keeps ringing as if she has repeatedly hit the snooze instead of the off button.

Lawrie has been tucked into Ken's recliner in the TV room, which she returns to, a nest of white blankets, after opening the door for her mother.

"It's been such a crazy year. I should have noticed you weren't yourself. We make excuses, you know? We were worried about Mattie, then Elfie. I know you've been missing Mariah. Have you talked to her?"

"Oh, don't say anything to her, Mother. I'm okay. She's in love. She's happy."

"You sure? You feel better?"

"I just need a little rest and the counsellor I talked to in the hospital helped. She's dealt with other women who have acute hormonal imbalance. I'm on a program now. It's just going to take awhile."

Ken's plywood landscape and the tracks that circle it take up half the space in this room. Shinny regards the miniature prairie fields, the grain silos, imagines the lonely sound of the train whistle. The TV is on but the sound is muted and the low sun beams through the window, illumining the tiny golden hairs on Lawreen's chin. Without makeup, without the severely styled hair, she looks both older and younger. Shinny wants to hug her again, to smell the flower breath that comes from the chamomile tea Lawrie has been drinking, that reminds Shinny of summer in Meadowvale, the chamomile that grew in dry patches around her mother's house, where she and Lawreen lived until John—Smokey—entered their lives and they moved into the city and Annette and later Elfie came along. But something on TV catches Lawrie's attention and she turns the volume up.

"Do you mind?" she asks.

Shinny goes to the kitchen to prepare the fruit she brought. Lawreen is off sugar, but pineapple, papaya, strawberries please the eye and the palate and show that her mother wants to spoil her.

"I'm really not hungry," she protests when her mother brings in the tray, but when Shinny returns with fresh tea, a wedge of white plate has appeared between the slices of papaya and Lawrie continues to nibble while they watch singers, black and white, man and woman, even the blind man with the terrific voice—all Oprah's friends, apparently—celebrate the coming holidays with their songs. By the time Shinny leaves, the plate of fruit is almost empty.

At home she dials Elfie's number, which she has been trying not to do every day, but the time is getting close.

"Tell Brendan to call as soon as you go into labour. I could be there in hours, you know."

"I know, Mom, but I think it's best for you to wait until we know what's happening, then you can tell my dad and everybody, and we'll set a date for you to come, okay? How's Lawreen?"

Shinny suspects that Elfie wants to keep her distance. Otherwise, why wouldn't she want her there? Why wouldn't any girl want her mother present for the birth of her first child? Or could she be more frightened than she sounds? But if Johann is born disabled, she'll need even more help.

It's 6:00, news time. She turns the TV on out of habit. The park across is dreary; yellow reflections of lights wobble on the large puddles that have formed in tracks left by the machines that are transforming the playing field to a celebration site for the Winter Olympics.

The phone rings and she jumps. Elfie changed her mind? No, it's James, wanting to know if there's news.

"I promise I'll call."

"Are you busy? We could see a movie, pass the time."

"Oh I couldn't leave. I'm waiting for Elfie's call. I wouldn't be able to pay any attention to a movie. But thanks."

She should ask him over to watch a DVD if it's a movie he wants. He's a gentle man, an unmarried man. And he is enjoying this unexpected turn in his life. Shinny thinks of Glen and a new tab opens in her mind. Glen's image: dear, sweet. She thought he would be her last lover; but James, is he interested? Beyond friendship and their unique bond? Is she? Should she be? At least James is a flesh and blood possibility and not an awkward website photo. To start all over, to patiently build the familiarity that takes years to establish. To brush edges, gradually relinquish yourself, sink into the other. Her heart is not leaping at the prospect. Yet his may be. In fact, when someone raps on the door, she almost thinks he has read her mind and hurried over to explore possibilities, but it can't be. He's still on the phone.

"James, I have to go. Someone's knocking. But don't worry. I'll call you as soon as I know."

"We could just fly out. I'd give you my points."

"Tempting idea, but Elfie wants me to wait. Anyway, there's someone at the door."

"I'll call you back."

HE KNOCKS AGAIN. SHE'S looking at him through the peephole, she must be, and so he smiles.

A soldier stands in the hall outside her door. A soldier in desert dress, the sandy beige camouflage outfit that resembles a printout from the computer. Shinny can't get her breath. The short hair, the ears a little pink where the ceiling lights hit them. The slight overbite. The smile spreads and the soldier says, "Hi, Grandma!"

The door opens and Gran has her arms around him before he can say anything more. He's in uniform, not a real uniform but one he picked up at a paintball supply store, until he gets his own. Maybe that's why she's crying. She told Kate that she thought he joined up months ago, but she knows now that he's been in California, so why the tears?

Face against the fresh, starched-feeling material, remembering when she was taller and lay her head down on his, the sweat that used to rime his scalp, beneath his hair. Now it's his head resting on hers, strong arms hugging her, hands warm against her back. She should stop crying, and she must not pepper him with questions, because Lawreen always hated it when she did that. They can't just stand here in the dim hallway, and he must be hungry. Boys are always hungry, though he isn't a boy anymore, she has to admit, and the uniform. "Oh God, war? Mattie?" The tears continue.

"What kind of greeting is this, Gran? I'm here, I'm okay."

"But you never wrote. Is this a leave? Come in, come in! I'll make some tea, or you'd probably rather have a beer. I have some beer. Why didn't your Mom tell me you're back?"

"Well because she doesn't know yet, Gran. I came here first."

"She'll be happy to see you, honey. She's been a little sick."

"Aw, Mattie," she says, and hugs him again. "Are you hungry?"

He has a lot to tell, but it's good to be back in Canada, at Gran's. He'll take her out for dinner, that's what he'll do, and he'll tell her about his trip. How he had to leave Annette's because … what should he say? Could he, should he tell her how he really felt? It was not just that he felt out of place on the farm; he wanted to come back. Once he got to the border, no questions, no suspicion; when the customs officer asked him if he had anything to declare, he said no, only gratitude for being back home, and the first thing he did the next morning was to take his application to a recruiting office. It seemed okay with the Forces that he'd done some consulting and worked for his aunt since he dropped out of college. All true, if not the whole truth. They didn't seem to want to check, and Matt has decided that it's right to fight for Canada, even if Afghanistan isn't Canada; he'd be fighting for something and getting trained for a career. Anyway, Canada is not going to fight in Afghanistan much longer. Grandma brings the beer, goes back to her tiny kitchen to cut cheese and dig crackers out of a box. Returns with that, talking all the while, about Elfie, whose baby is going to be born sometime soon, the baby, whose heart is still a question, though it's working for now.

"How long can you stay, honey? Because when we get the news, I might be going out there, and her dad … Mattie, I don't know what you heard from your aunt and your grandpa. There's something I ought to tell you."

Their talk is the duet, her thoughts the many-voiced choir behind. If he is on his way to training camp, why is he in uniform? The bass notes of war sound in her heart. The soldiers who died there, the names in her litany, Andrew Richard Nuttall the most recent. An image of the pink-cheeked veteran selling poppies. Kev, whom she has not heard from in a good month. Longer. Mattie is talking about training, intelligence, his skill with computers, something he emphasized on his application form. About serving his country. Has he been paying attention? Tahir, Sima, Sayed, old Hassan … the relatives she hasn't met, the people walking the streets of Vancouver who have sought refuge. Mattie doesn't have to go over there to do something good for the world, the people in the world who need defending. He can do it here. There's so much to say. He has been away for so long, and he has matured. Without being asked, he left his boots in the hallway and props his feet on the table, the black socks that look out of place with the camouflage, but then the enemy wouldn't see socks, she realizes; it wouldn't matter. Big, of course! His size is enhanced by the confidence the uniform gives him. As if he is somebody now, swelled to fit the outlines of his new self. Okay, she can see it, and yet … Where did he get that phrase, undermine our values? Who taught him that? What values is he talking about?

Oh, but here's the phone. Elfie? Already? Little more than an hour after they talked? She watches Matt drain his beer and take it to the kitchen counter. It's a market research firm. A worthy subject. Environmental habits of Canadians, but the timing!! She waves to Matt to help himself to another, but he shakes his head. She hates to be rude but the caller won't give her a chance to break in and say that it's a bad time, she can't participate now. So she just hangs up. She has to tell him. Or does he know already? There was so much going on down there in California, and then he left. Maybe he doesn't know. Does he know?

"Mattie," she begins, but he excuses himself to go to the bathroom.

"Just a sec, Gran. I'll be right back."

Standing at the toilet forces him to face the large mirror that takes up half the wall in the bathroom, like the mirror on the wall in the living room. Plenty of places to look at yourself here, but he did that in the hotel after he bought the clothes from the paintball store. Now it seems cheesy, wearing a uniform before he is entitled to wear it. He intends to change before moving on to his parents' house. But first he has to skate by Gran because he doesn't want to hear what she has to say. Maybe she found him. The man she screwed just once, which was enough to make Elfie. The thought of Grandma having sex makes his face hot. He splashes cold water on it before opening the door, where she is standing, waiting.

How she will say this to Matt? He isn't a child. Will he understand? Would it be asking too much of him to picture his grandmother as a girl? How do you describe need, that kind of need, to your grandson? But when he comes out he seems to be in a hurry. He stuffs his foot into a boot and bends down to tie it. A black boot. A combat boot?

"Matt? Before you go …"

She says it again. Something she wants to tell him.

"Yeah, well don't worry about me, Gran. I'm here for a week, then I'm going east for training. But I'll be back again before they ship me any-where. You gotta be with Elfie. I understand."

"But, Mattie, there's something … Do you think it will be Afghani-stan?"

"It's okay, Gran. I have to get trained first."

"You should meet my boss, his family. They come from Afghanistan. I know where their village is, too, I saw it on a map. I used to do that, honey, when I thought you were over there? I looked at maps on Google. Now you might really be over there, but I hope not."

She wants to tell him about James and she doesn't want to tell him.

"The Prime Minister keeps saying we're getting out of there."

He wants her to tell him the truth and he doesn't want her to.

"Not for a while though, Gran. Canadian Forces go where they're needed. There's a lot of trouble in the world. You see that ad on TV? Fight fear, fight distress, fight chaos."

Then it hits her, the bodyguard. Could he have been Matt's old friend, who visited she and Glen in California? That face, distinctively flat, soft looking, as though there's no bone structure supporting it, which of course there has to be or it wouldn't be a face. It's the small nose, as if someone had pinched up a bit of skin. But still.

"Remember that boy that came with you to the farm one time?"

"Yeah, why?"

"There was a young man in the store, with one of my boss's friends, that reminded me of him. That smooth face of his. You know what I mean?"

"Yeah, but I doubt it was him. You just told me they're Afghans. He's Turkish, Gran, why would he be hanging out with a bunch of Afghans? Anyway, he lives in Alberta."

"You're probably right. I didn't get a good look at him. He was wearing a cap and sunglasses and he stayed by the door."

She accepts that, but how does he know where Berk is? Berk, again!

"I don't think I've ever had an actual conversation with a soldier, Mattie, except for a kid who wrote to me a couple of times while you were away. I haven't heard from him for a while, and I hope that doesn't mean the worst. He's a friend of Kate's. Have you seen Kate yet, Mattie? I think she has a crush on you. Oh, Mattie."

She hugs him for the third time and he notices how small she is. He tries to picture her young, drunk or stoned. Those pictures of her when Elfie was a baby. She looked a little crazy with that wild hair. He supposes that she was crazy. It's hard to think of your grandma as a girl. She is who she is to him now. Bony, white hair, glasses, through which she is sort of pleading with him. He has changed his mind about taking her to dinner. It could just be too awkward. And Berk!

She hugs him again and thanks fortune, God, whatever is responsible for him being here, home, after such a long journey.

The elevator doors snap open and he turns to wave at Gran, then steps in and lets himself be whirred down, distracted, wondering if Berk will, like some evil villain in a graphic novel, rise from a pool of black inked white to show the gleam of possibility, of things that never end.

A New Year

January

"Eat, little baby boy, eat," Elfie whispers to her son. The draft forcing through faults in the old window chills her bare shoulders, but Johann is nestled in blankets beside her, his little head against the sheet, his bud mouth furled around her nipple. She taps his cheek to keep him sucking, for he must gain two more pounds before the doctor will proceed with surgery, which Elfie wants and doesn't want. To relinquish this warm bundle to the care of the surgical staff, to think of his bird's chest opened, steel instruments piercing his fluttery heart. That as much as the draft causes her shivers.

A key in the lock. Brendan is home, and from the look on his face, he's still listening to the section the orchestra was going over tonight to try out the soloists Ping, in co-operation with the conductor, has chosen to present "At/Pac" at the Young Composers Festival in May. The triangles, ehru, all the tinkling bells, the xylophone. Ping's trickle of violin that begins the flow towards confluence. James follows him into the room and waves to Elfie, puts a finger to his lips and nods to signal that he knows they must be quiet, though Elfie does not want Johann sound sensitized.

"It's all right. Come in. How was it?"

"Wonderful! He's a genius!"

He and Brendan are the same height, but James's colouring is shades lighter. He wears glasses, the lobes of his nose are traced with purple veins, the tips of his ears are red. She visually devours her father when they are in the same room. What colour was his hair when he was younger, could he send pictures? And what else? Does he have hay fever? Is he prone to daydreaming? He must have been good at math, or was he? What does connect them, demonstrate their genetic link, the traits that tie them as father and daughter?

While Brendan goes to the kitchen to open the wine James bought, James steps towards her, clenched hands belying his smile; he's happy to be here despite his discomfort. Maybe he is as desperate as she is to find something to hold onto so that they can confidently start to hand themselves over to that place where they settle in and say, I know! And laugh, because it's clear they do know what it's like, that daydreaming tendency, the ease of calculating numbers in their heads, whatever it will turn out to be that connects them. Though it is not his fault she grew up without him, he has taken responsibility. Written a cheque, promised more. Filled the fridge with expensive food. Started a bank account for Johann.

Elfie turns back a corner of the blanket to give her father another glimpse of his grandson. Johann has the rosy pecan skin that blends genes from both parents, and not a shadow of blue despite the hole in his little heart that murmurs, I'm here; be careful. Things can change in a minute, Elfie knows, but darkness finds no place in her imagination tonight as she watches her father breathe on his hands, to warm them, before lifting his grandson out of her arms into his own.

ON TUESDAY MORNINGS GREG drives the kids to school and Dad further, into Santa Rosa, for his therapy. Annette is cleaning out the barn, enjoying the scrape of rake tines on the cement floor, the funky, familiar smells of goat piss and grain, the thick damp rectangle of sky beyond the open barn door. Marie watches from a kidding stall, inside today not so much because she is ready to kid, but because temperamental Cleopatra nipped her and Annette wants to give the wound some time to heal before releasing Marie back into the herd. Poor dear Marie, at once the most reliable milker, and yet also the one most prone to injury and foot problems. She ma-aas, as if in agreement, bites up another wad of hay, and her jaw moves from side to side as she chews.

Greg is on the weed again, having started with Dad when he was withdrawing from the Percocet. While it made some kind of sense at the start, it's dangerous for Dad to smoke; he should have his wits about him, given his shaky state. He can walk with the help of a cane, but not far, and only the outside ramp Greg installed makes it possible for Dad to get from downstairs up, to use the kitchen and see what the kids are up to in the rooms he had been unable to visit since his accident. Greg is over there often, which is good in that he provides company and services that Annette would otherwise have to cram into her day. But with the smoking, with his hair and beard grown back, he may be simply an older version of the man she first met at Dad's. Can she trust him to keep his hands off the physiotherapists, the waitresses, whatever other young women may be mesmerized by his light blue eyes, turned on by his drawling speech, as she was? Do people really change? Can they?

TIME TO GO BACK to work. For one thing, there's a wedding to prepare and it has to be perfect. As soon as Mari told her the news, Lawreen called all the choicest venues to determine their earliest available date. She has assembled a selection of beautiful settings to offer Mariah and Jason. Jason. Lawreen will have a son-in-law, which makes her feel old. But she is old. Older.

Her company is one of those that pledged to have their employees work at home during the Winter Olympics rush downtown. She won't have to leave the house for another month; she can ease back in. Are you sure, her boss asked. Are you ready? Oh yes, she insisted. It was just one of those hormonal things, you know, she smiled, shrugging. Her boss is younger by five years, a UBC Commerce grad who wears stiletto heels to work and never seems to have to take them off to relieve her feet.

Are you sure? Ken asked. Lawreen reminded him that the wedding would be expensive, because she wants Mari's wedding to be perfect. Even though Mariah has plenty of money herself, and Jason is a millionaire at least, it's the parents' traditional role. And hasn't she always given her daughter the best? From the beginning of that beautiful child's life? Still, she had to bite her tongue when Mariah announced that she would be leaving show business, that she was finished with the movies. She won't need to work, true; Jason's software company brings in enough to support them in high style. But won't you miss it, Mari? The fun? Not really, Mom. I want a life like yours: a nice house, kids. Jase doesn't care. I can work if I want, but I started so young, Mom. I've had enough of it.

What could Lawreen say? It's Mari's life. But she wonders, Lawreen does, is this just it then? The end of the dream? What was the dream? In her attempts to visualize its disintegration, Lawreen has found it hard to hold in her imagination. Bits keep sloughing off like the sand castles she used to make at the beach in White Rock when she was little, before her sisters were born. There was never enough water to keep the sand moist; she had to make endless trips to the tide line and wait for a wave to slip up from the ocean into her plastic bucket, for more.

WEEK THREE HE WANTED to quit. Sick of the harassing, the fuckin' this, fuckin' that, sounded like a bunch of gangstas. Whoa, what did I get myself into? Push-ups, sit-ups, crawling over obstacles. Eat with guys, sleep with guys, shower with guys. No privacy, no rest, no respect. This isn't him, he thinks, yet it's him now. No need to make up this identity and step into it, like a shadow on the snow. He could run away from that shadow, he knows how to escape, he has toyed with the idea; some recruits have left, or failed and had to be recoursed. The commanders make them renew their commitments pretty much daily; they present it as a matter of honour, of pride to stay. The officer who delivers the speech reminds Matt of the face on the Forces website. The best face. Maybe he should have left the first time he got the urge, because today it has to be thirty below with the wind chill and they're supposed to crawl through the snow with their rifles, stop to shoot, crawl. The sun glares off the ice crust, his eyes sting. His balls are numb. He's not crawling fast enough. The sergeant yells; you gotta get outta dere; you going to be killed. With a thick Québécois accent. So many Frenchies here; well, they're in Quebec, which is why it is so fucking frigid. Once, after some guy forgot to close his pockets and lost a magazine, they had to search the range for three hours. Then it turns out the guy never had it to begin with. Nevertheless, the sergeant made them do twenty-five push-ups right in the snow, as if they were all as dumb as the guy who forgot to bring an essential part of his kit.

Matt is not naturally a hard guy like some of those who took to bayonet training so easily, who grunted and yelled like soldiers in an old war movie. But he is harder than he was. If he ever runs into Berk again and Berk is stupid enough to try anything, he will be surprised at the response he gets from his former partner. But Berk, everyone, so far away. He gets little time to even think of them. The rare moments for personal time on a computer there's always an email from Gran. *Dear Mattie*, she starts. Mattie, he thinks, who was that?

THIS TIME LAST YEAR Shinny looked out on a snow-covered park; now when there should be snow, for the Olympics, it's warmer and wetter than usual. But that does not discourage organizers from setting up tents and giant screens for those who couldn't afford tickets to the actual events. Shinny is going to miss everything. She will be staying in New York for a month to be with Elfie for Johann's surgery. Now that she will not be deserting Tahir and risking her job, she is free to leave Vancouver, and she can live on the government pension without having to withdraw too much at this bad time for the funds remaining in her investments.

Accustomed to doing things by herself, the wheels on her suitcase make it even easier to be independent. What a jet-setter. Her third trip to New York in six months, and while it is a kind of end to the issue that started when she told Elfie the truth about her father, it is also the beginning of her life as Johann's grandmother, if the surgery is successful. The pediatric heart surgeons expect success, declare it a routine procedure with anomalous hearts. Routine/anomalous. Like standard deviation, the words seem to cancel each other out.

The morning is still dark when the plane takes off. From her window seat Shinny watches streaks like stretch marks on a pregnant woman's belly striate the sky with lavender, then pink, then orange-gold, until the clouds clumped beneath turn brilliant as the sun that finally rises above them and remains in that position, resting above the cloud layer, as if stalled for her appreciation, a good quarter of the way across the continent.

about the type

This book is set in Adobe Garamond Pro, a typeface belonging to group of old-style serif typefaces named after the punch-cutter Claude Garamont (c. 1480–1561).

Garamond's letterforms convey a sense of fluidity and consistency. Some unique characteristics in his letters are the small bowl of the a and the small eye of the e. Long extenders and top serifs have a downward slope.

Garamond is considered to be among the most legible and readable serif typefaces for use in print (offline) applications. It has also been noted to be one of the most eco-friendly major fonts when it comes to ink usage.

www.ingramcontent.com/pod-product-compliance
Lightning Source LLC
Chambersburg PA
CBHW060348030726
47497CB00003B/640